Praise for Maxim Jakubowski

"Written by a giant of the genre…highly recommended."

—**Lee Child**, author of the Jack Reacher novels

"I have been a fan of Maxim Jakubowski for years. There just is no finer mystery writer and editor anywhere. Find a comfortable chair and a strong drink and prepare to be enthralled."

—**Alexander Algren**, author of *Out in a Flash: Murder Mystery Flash Fiction*

"A stunning collection, simply the best short mystery and crime fiction of the year and a real treat for crime-fiction fans. I highly recommend!"

—**Leonard Carpenter**, author of the Conan the Barbarian books and *Lusitania Lost*

"Maxim Jakubowski is deeply experienced in the field… Sometimes a brief zap of great writing is just what you're in the mood for or have time for. That's when anthologies like his are ideal… intellectually outstanding."

—*New York Journal of Books*

T0150863

THE BOOK OF EXTRAORDINARY FEMME FATALE STORIES

Cover Design: Megan Werner
Cover Photo: Esteban Martinena / stock.adobe.com
Art Direction: Elina Diaz
Layout & Design: Megan Werner

For permission requests, please contact the publisher at:
Mango Publishing Group
2850 S Douglas Road, 4th Floor
Coral Gables, FL 33134 USA
info@mango.bz

For special orders, quantity sales, course adoptions and corporate sales, please email the publisher at sales@mango.bz. For trade and wholesale sales, please contact Ingram Publisher Services at customer.service@ingramcontent.com or +1.800.509.4887.

The Book of Extraordinary Femme Fatale Stories: The Best New Original Stories of the Genre Featuring Female Villains, Detectives, and Other Mysterious Women

Library of Congress Cataloging-in-Publication number: 2022935523
ISBN: (p) 978-1-64250-873-4 (e) 978-1-64250-874-1
BISAC category code FIC022050, FICTION / Mystery & Detective / Collections & Anthologies

Printed in the United States of America

THE BOOK OF EXTRAORDINARY FEMME FATALE STORIES

The Best New Original Stories
of the Genre Featuring Female Villains,
Detectives, and Other Mysterious Women

Edited by Maxim Jakubowski

CORAL GABLES

Table of Contents

Introduction

Maxim Jakubowski

Welcome to the sixth volume in our crime and mystery anthology series from Mango Publishing. We've surveyed Historical Crime, Private Eyes and Amateur Sleuths, Impossible Crimes, and twice visited the fascinating Victorian world of the immortal Sherlock Holmes.

So where could we go next?

Well, inspiration could be said to have been sparked by the enigmatic figure of one of the sleuth of Baker Street's most ambiguous opponents, the beautiful but treacherous Irene Adler. To her charms, he was far from indifferent both on the page and on some occasions the screen (and even more recently in a graphic novel scripted by one of our regulars, Lavie Tidhar).

With apologies to the other sinister female figures of the penny dreadfuls, Irene Adler must surely qualify as the first femme fatale of mystery fiction. She is maddeningly attractive; she is dangerous; she is eminently untrustworthy; she is a master of disguises and never allows her feelings to put the brake on her misdeeds. Her heart traverses that murky zone that lies between good and evil. No wonder she stirred more than just Sherlock's grey cells!

The image of the seductive but dangerous woman quickly became a steadfast tradition in crime and mystery literature thereafter, with many a murderess, poisoner, traitor, spy, and imposter turning out to be a female of the species, much to the delight of the readers. And then, of course, she was all over our screens, navigating the world of noir with slinky elegance and dragging many a man to a fate worse than death. Indeed, the femme fatale is the sheer epitome of hardboiled tales, the moll, the broad, the beauty whose features hypnotize you and prevents the captive male from recognizing her true nature.

And, however bad they are, they attract us, fascinate us, deceive us with gusto and draw the reader into the spider's web of his own fate.

She is the Bride in Cornell Woolrich's *The Bride Wore Black*, Matty Tyler in *Body Heat*, Amy Dunne in Gillian Flynn's *Gone Girl* (and portrayed so well by Rosamund Pike in the film), the Girl in Marc Behm's *The Eye of the Beholder* (and Isabelle Adjani in the film adaptation of the novel), she is Cora in *The Postman Always Rings Twice*, she is both Judy and Madeleine as portrayed by Kim Novak in Hitchcock's *Vertigo*. She is everywhere. She manages to combine drop dead beauty with intelligence. From Barbara Stanwyck and Marlene Dietrich to Jodie Comer as Villanelle, Lisbeth Salander—the girl with the dragon tattoo—Mata Hari—whose real-life exploits took on an almost fictional nature—and every black and white exotic dancer from Frank Miller's *Sin City*. Her face and aura are universal.

She attracts and she repels, a vision of another world that stands in parallel to ours and draws us towards it when night falls.

Once I announced the chosen theme for this volume, I have never had so many submissions from writers, proof of the terrible fascination we all have to femmes fatales and dangerous women.

So, plunge fearlessly into these pages for a delightful menu of villainy and seduction and relish the badness…

Hava

By Lavie Tidhar

Hava washed the dishes. The water was hot, scolding the way a mother scolds. She scrubbed and scrubbed the plate, the tips of her fingers white where they pressed against the china, the palm flesh red. Her wedding ring was in the soap dish on the counter. She'd picked the kids up from school earlier. Now the boy was outside, and the girl was watching television, *Krovim Krovim* maybe, judging by the laughter track. It was hot outside, but the apartment felt cool. Hava scrubbed, rinsed, put the plate onto the drying board and picked a coffee cup. Nobody called on the phone. The birds whistled outside the window. Cars went past on the road below. She could hear the boys kicking the football outside, *whack, whack* against the wall. She wondered if there was anything in the newspapers. Ehud was away again. He was always away. The kids saw him more on the television than at home. He was always interviewing someone important. He was always on the television. Well, he did what he had to. He worked. She remembered how handsome he was when they met. He had seemed so sophisticated. And he was besotted with her. She looked good, too. She always wore sunglasses. And she'd smiled a lot. Her mother always told her to smile. She scrubbed the coffee cup. When did she get up that morning? Six thirty, maybe? Made breakfast for the kids, took them to school, then drove to work. It felt good to be at work. She liked working. She liked the hush of the bank, the air conditioning, the crisp suit she wore. She liked to dress nice. Money had a whisper to it, an air that was like—she tried to think of what she meant. Like when you were a kid in the library, maybe, that hush of books, the soft tread of the librarian, that book smell. Money wasn't like that, it smelled different and the hush of it was of a different pitch. Maybe like when you put a seashell to your ear, like the boy liked to do, and then hear the faint cry of the ocean far away. Like waves trapped in a seashell. That's what it was like. She liked it. She liked the tread of her heels on the hard floor of the bank. The spray of perfume she always put on before leaving the apartment. The perfume lingered, followed her. It made an impression. You had to look and smell right. To give the right impression. She loved crossing the lobby and going behind the glass window, the safety of it, her and the world separated by glass. She liked counting out the money and filling the forms, the filing especially. She liked the whisper of the pen across the paper. When she was at the bank, she wasn't anyone's mother, she wasn't anyone's wife. She was in a world apart, a world that was made for her, where she mattered in a different way. She even liked the customers. Every customer had a story and a face to go with that story. You could learn so much about a person by the numbers in a column, their incomings and outgoings, their profits and losses.

Take Mela Malevsky, for instance. When she first saw Mela across her desk, when the older woman sat down and folded her hands over her handbag in her lap and looked at Hava and smiled, you could see in her eyes and in every line etched in her face that she'd lived. Mela spoke English with an accent. She didn't speak much Hebrew but that was fine with Hava. Mela was visiting from New York, and she wanted to put money into her new account. She was thinking of investing, she told Hava. She wasn't shy about it, but she still seemed a little unsure. She wanted to put back into the country. Into Israel. She was planning to visit often. Her husband was a dealer in pearls. She had three children, three grandchildren too. She showed Hava their pictures, smiling proudly but a little self-consciously. She was such a nice woman, they had really connected that first time, and Hava helped her with the transaction. Then, with a little regret, she said goodbye to the client as she left.

She washed the coffee cup and put it on the drying board. The *Whack! Whack!* of the football outside. Kids shouting. A car honked in the distance. The girl laughed in front of the television. Hava picked up another plate to clean.

She'd got used to seeing Mela when she came to visit. She always stopped at the bank. She kept quite a lot of money there really. They always talked, learned more about each other. Mela was very impressed that Hava's husband was so famous, a journalist, on the television. And Hava just felt a connection with the older woman. Something she couldn't quite articulate. She didn't have many friends. Family friends, yes, couple friends or her husband's friends. But not so much just for her. Eventually she suggested going for a coffee and, why not? Her life didn't revolve around the bank. She sat with Mela at a café, she was still working for the bank in Jerusalem then, and they had talked for hours, and laughed a lot. Mela never talked about the Holocaust, about what happened to her there.

She came to Israel two or three times a year, usually. Sometimes she brought little presents from New York. Small, but tasteful. A new perfume for Hava, one that smelled of America, not Israel. A scarf. Ehud was always taking off somewhere like New York or Paris, there was some talk of sending him to America, but he said it was punishment for being so opposed, publicly, to the idea of a peace accord with the Arabs. He just didn't believe in it. He was a good husband. A good father. A good man. She told herself that. He was a public man. She told Aviva that. Aviva always laughed. Aviva laughed a lot. She said, "All men are bastards, even my one and he's a poodle."

Aviva was her best friend. Why was she thinking about Aviva now? She scrubbed the plate, but it still wasn't clean. She put more soap on. Her hands were so raw, but she didn't even feel it. She kept scrubbing. Aviva said, "This friend of yours, she sounds nice."

For a long time Hava felt as though she and Aviva were like two children born together and separated by some malevolent force since childhood, yet somehow they found each other again. They had lived together in the same block of flats in Jerusalem. Hava worked in the bank and Ehud for the television and the kids were small and Aviva lived in the block with her own children and her own husband, and they started talking and then spending more time together. Aviva wasn't pretty, not like people said Hava was pretty, or at least glamorous, but there was something about her. Aviva was like a woman people don't notice but then can't not notice, once they'd realised. Once she'd let them. She could move so quietly through the world and yet upset it when she wanted to. She worked in a pharmacy she owned with her husband, but the business wasn't doing so well. She didn't like to talk about it, she said. Let's not talk about money. But Hava loved money, it was her job, the moving it and changing it and putting it here and putting it there. And Aviva always did talk about money, even as she protested, how the pharmacy wasn't doing well, how it was hard to pay the suppliers, how she would need to make a plan. They talked about investments, which was something Hava was really into now. The Tel Aviv Stock Exchange was exciting just then. People were talking about new technologies, telephones you could put in your car, computers you could have in your home.

She started putting some money into stocks. Only a little at first, then a little bit more. Taking a chance. Risking her money. It was so thrilling. In the mornings she'd make the kids breakfast and take her Valium and then take them to school and then go to work and then come home and pick them up from school and make dinner and help with their homework and clean and wash and give them their bath and make sure they brushed their teeth and said goodnight and kissed them to sleep and watched television with a glass of wine. Sometimes she'd even watch with Ehud, who liked to watch himself on TV. Hava said, "Maybe one day I'll be on TV." Ehud said, "What do you need that rubbish for? You're perfect just as you are."

But in between she'd play the stock exchange. She went up, she went down. She put a little bit more in. Then a little bit more again.

There was no harm.

Aviva and her husband had to sell the pharmacy. They weren't paying the suppliers. The suppliers all threatened to sue. Aviva did something, she was hazy on the details, but it made them stop. Some sort of arrangement. Hava didn't really press her. Aviva had a way of getting out of things. She got by. She was scrappy. She was stealing money from the suppliers, maybe. Borrowing, she said. When they found out, they wanted to call the police. So why didn't they? Hava said. Aviva said the suppliers were stealing money from the government. Everyone was taking so she was taking too, that was all. She said she told them it's better not to involve the police. They agreed, so it went away quietly, but Aviva and her husband still had to sell the pharmacy to pay back some of the money. Well, it was a minor thing. So, you borrowed some money. So what? She paid it back. Hava admired Aviva. She didn't let the world push her around. She played it at its own game. Hava wished she could be like that. They couldn't be more different, really. It was nice to meet up with Mela the next time she came to visit. She was thinking of investing quite a lot of money. Did Hava have any ideas? Hava admitted she'd been playing the stock exchange. Her own money, she said. She'd been doing very well. Very well. But she didn't push it. She watched Mela's bank balance grow with each visit.

She needed more soap. Which plate was she holding? The girl was watching television. The boy outside, the football going *Whack! Whack!* against the wall.

She'd lost her train of thought. Would Ehud call? Will he be home tonight? She rinsed the plate and put it away. Aviva hadn't called.

She thought: which of them had brought along the rolling pin?

She wished the radio was on. She should turn on the radio, listen to something nice. Arik Einstein, maybe. She used to like Arik Einstein. Well, everyone did. But she didn't anymore, not since the thing. But maybe there'd be something else on. She should turn on the radio and find out. But her hands were wet. She was always worried about touching anything electric with wet hands. She could turn off the tap and dry her hands but there were still dishes in the sink, there were always dishes. She didn't have big dreams. She scrubbed up well, like they said. She kept Ehud company when he went to functions. She knew people. For a moment she thought of the man she was seeing every now and then. He was a member of the Knesset, a politician. He had a family too. What they had worked for them both. She was sure Ehud had women on the side too. Why couldn't she have someone on the side? It wasn't complicated, she and the man. Just bodies, and a little affection. She saw him in Jerusalem when she could. Sometimes he saw her when he came to Tel Aviv. Hotel rooms, always. In between the kids and the job. When they could.

She scrubbed the cutlery. A fork. A knife. It had been Ehud's car. Their car. She liked to drive. She told Mela not to play the stock exchange. Keep your money in the bank, where it's safe. It was good advice. Mela listened to her.

Why was she thinking about Mela? She wished the kids would stop it with the ball already. Sometimes she wanted to scream. It was so hard being perfect. A perfect wife, a perfect mother. Always with the sunglasses on and the nice clothes and the trail of perfume. Someone who is seen. Aviva was the opposite of her. With that big hair and those big glasses with the thick lenses and a husband who wasn't on TV. Hava hadn't liked living in Jerusalem. She was from Tel Aviv, from the sun and the sea. Jerusalem was cold and so were the people. She was so glad to have met Aviva.

The teaspoon was smudged. Why wouldn't it come off? She rubbed and rubbed. She needed the Brillo pad. She reached under the sink. She was going to scrub it until it was clean. She couldn't stand mess. The tyres, they couldn't have kept the tyres. They were in the car. Hava was driving. She enjoyed driving. The sun had set and it was dark. Aviva and Mela were in the back seat together. Which one of them brought the rolling pin? She couldn't remember. It was a nice drive. Three friends together. Just to talk things over.

She should check her horoscope, Hava thought. Aviva got her into astrology. She was very interested in it, how the movement of the stars could influence your health, your wealth. At some point they both left the apartment block in Jerusalem. Aviva got a job at a warehouse, she was a manager, she was well liked there she said. Aviva was back in Tel Aviv. Mela came to visit twice a year, maybe three times. She said, "Hava, I think some of my money is missing."

Ehud's car. Why was it Ehud's car and not her car or the family car? Ehud's car. Just like she was Ehud's wife. Did she even love him? He thought she and Aviva were Lesbians for a while, that she was cheating on him with Aviva. Like women couldn't just be friends! He didn't like Aviva. He tried to forbid Hava from seeing her. Aviva, who was her best friend! Aviva said, Mela, we need to resolve this situation. The windows were open in the car. A warm breeze. Few lights. Hava had driven without purpose. She found herself going towards the sea. Tel Baruch, which was not a good area, it was a place for prostitutes, at night the sands were haunted with lonely women and desperate men, anyone from army generals to yeshiva boys went to them, it was the quiet of the place, the isolation and privacy. Why did she choose Tel Baruch? It was a terrible place.

That's not true. She'd told Mela they'd go to the Mandarin. It was a nice hotel. They'd have a drink, all together. Work things out. So why did she go past it? Why did she turn down the dirt road to the sea?

"My money," Mela said, "what happened to my money?"

Hava wanted to explain to her friend. It was just a mistake in the accounts. Was it worth making such a fuss about everything? It would cause everyone problems. Surely Mela could be made to understand? Hava tried to be reasonable. The radio was on. Arik Einstein singing "Drive Slowly." She loved his voice. "Come on Mela," she said, "we're all friends here."

"My money is missing," Mela said. "It was a lot of money."

It was what, fifty thousand dollars maybe? It was hardly a lot. Barely enough, even, Hava thought. She kept investing in the stocks, but the money just kept vanishing into that hole, and eventually she had to tell Ehud, and they had to sell the flat. But it was still not enough. She tried to explain to

Mela, "Mela, listen, everything can be resolved, the important thing is to
calm down—"

"Calm down?" Mela said. She was breathing hard. "Hava, how can I calm
down? I don't understand what happened, I trusted you—"

"Calm down!" Aviva said. Was it Aviva in the back seat that night? Was it
Hava who drove? Who brought the rolling pin? "Mela, it's not stealing, it's
borrowing, we can work it out—"

Arik Einstein on the radio and the dark sea nearby where furtive men
had hurried sex with women who took it for just a transaction, didn't Mela
understand? It was just ins and outs, just profits and loss, numbers in a column
that didn't mean anything. "Mela calm down—"

"Thieves, thieves!" Mela shouted. Why did she have to shout? Hava
hated shouting, everything in life had to be done quietly, you didn't want the
neighbours talking, you always—

The rolling pin smashed into Mela's head.

It was just to calm her down. It wasn't... It was just a tap. Mela? Why did
you have to check? Mela, why did you go behind my back? We don't want
to worry the bank, Mela. It was just a bit of money. You gave me power
of account, didn't you? And if you didn't, and Aviva wrote it instead, the
signature still looked like yours. Enough to borrow. That is all.

"Such a bitch!" Aviva said. She was breathing heavily. It was dark and quiet
outside. Tel Baruch, with not even a prostitute in sight. Hava stopped the car.
You had to do everything with purpose, this was always a rule with her. To
be methodical, neat. Her father was a trader, it was such an embarrassment
growing up. To be in trade. But she got out. She was a respectable woman,
a society woman. So what if she and Ehud had problems? Everyone had
problems. They had beautiful children. A lovely kitchen, with all the latest
accessories. She scrubbed and scrubbed, her hands raw in the water. "Quick,"
she said, "let's take her out."

They pulled Mela out of the car. Was she still breathing? There was blood
on the back seat. There was blood on the sand. Mela looked ridiculous
sprawled across the sand. The waves lapping gently against the shore in the
distance. That smell of the sea. The city seemed so far away. This was how it
had always been, will always be. Three humans alone against a vast darkness.
The stars were so cold in the skies overhead. She got into the car and started

the engine again. This is how it had to be. Who was driving? Was it her or was it Aviva? Who brought the rolling pin? She reversed.

Whack! Whack! went the football outside.

She stopped, shifted gear. Ehud's car. Drove it forward.

Whack! went the ball outside.

And again. And again.

The girl was watching TV. She could watch it for hours. And the boy, she worried about the boy, he wasn't always… He wasn't always present, she thought. Such a loving family. When her father died, how did she feel? She barely spoke to her mother. She stopped the car and stepped out.

"What now?" Aviva said.

"She had an accident," Hava said. "She was run over, maybe a truck hit her. What was she doing wandering out here on her own?"

She felt sad. She liked Mela. Mela never talked about the Holocaust, about what happened over there. That silence of a generation. It was only fifty thousand dollars, she wanted to tell her. What difference did it make? Mela's husband was rich. Not like Hava's, all Ehud wanted to do was talk about Arabs on TV. He loved the cameras. He loved the sound of his own voice. How much she hated him sometimes.

"There's blood on the tyres," Aviva said. "I know a place."

Hava hugged Aviva. "All this fuss," she said. They got back in the car. Mela didn't look like nothing, lying there on the sand. Hava could see the lights from the nearby airfield in the distance. Only a short drive and they were back on the road. This never happened. This never happened. "I know a place," Aviva said. Hava drove until they got there. They changed the tyres.

There were no more dishes in the sink. She stared at the suds of soap in the water. She shut the tap. "Mummy?" The girl said. "I'm bored."

"Go play with your brother outside."

Hava made herself a drink and took a Valium. She wondered if Ehud would be home. He did love her. Didn't he? Some prostitute found the body. At first, she thought it was another prostitute who was killed by her pimp. Then the police identified the body. They informed Mela's family. Her husband in New York, the kids. Hava felt sorry for them. It was in the papers, but it wasn't big news. A dead tourist. It looked like an accident. It was sad, but such things happened. It didn't even stay in the papers a week.

The kids weren't kicking the ball outside anymore. Hava waited for the phone to ring, for anyone to call, but no one did. She looked at the family photos on the stand. They were so happy together, smiling for the camera. She thought, she had such a good life.

***

Author's Note:

The body of Mela Malevsky was found in March 1985 on a dirt road in Tel Baruch, outside Tel Aviv. The police initially assumed she had been killed in a hit and run. Investigation eventually led them to her bank records, and to the woman who handled Malevsky's account, Hava Ya'ari, the wife of a well-known television presenter. Ya'ari was arrested some eight months later, along with her accomplice, Aviva Granot. The two women, formerly best friends, turned on each other in custody, with each blaming the other for Malevsky's death. The trial was widely covered in the media of the day.

Both women were eventually convicted for the murder.

How to Craft the Perfect Story

By SJI Holliday

The metal gate clanged shut behind them as they left the echoing madness of the visiting area. Chloe kept her eyes fixed on the door at the far end of the corridor, trying hard not to catch the eye of any of the track-suited men who leant against walls with their hands down their pants, eyes travelling up and down her as she passed. The guard escorting her hit a button on the wall and waited.

"Smile for the camera," he said.

Chloe looked up and a red light blinked, turned green. Then a low buzz signalled that the door was unlocked. They walked out into fresh air.

"First time in a prison, is it?" the guard said. He ushered her around the corner towards another of the identical grey buildings.

"Might just be a one-off," Chloe said. "I'm covering a session for Jo. The usual creative writing teacher?"

The guard rattled his keys, choosing the correct one, as they approached a green metal door. "Mind yourself, Love. They can smell fresh meat a mile off."

He unlocked the door and pulled it open. Inside, more men in tracksuits waited. Chatting, loitering.

"Afternoon, Miss," one of them said. An older man, with neatly parted hair and thick black glasses. Chloe tried not to shudder, imagining what brought him here.

The other men swarmed in on her and the guard waved an arm, ushering them back. "Give the lady some space, eh?"

She hurried up the staircase, trying to keep in step with the guard, who hadn't told her his name, but whose legs were significantly longer than hers.

"What's he in for?" she said, keeping her voice low.

The guard laughed. "Best never to ask that, love."

He marched her to the end of the corridor. There was a window, partly covered with posters for arts competitions and other opportunities. A heavy wooden door with a thin pane of glass. He unlocked it with another of his many keys and ushered her inside.

"Chloe! So nice to meet you in person. Come in, come in." The prison librarian took her by the elbow and led her to a small office area. He flicked on the kettle. "Cheers, George." The guard grunted something in reply then disappeared back out into the corridor, letting the door bang behind him.

"William. Hi," Chloe said, taking the hand the man was offering. He was short and slight, with very piercing blue eyes. How on earth did he manage in this place? From what her friend Jo had told her, this was a Cat-B prison— meaning there were potential murderers and rapists mixed in amongst the fraudsters and the drug barons. Certainly men capable of violence. Maybe even that old man downstairs. He could be a lifer. He was probably a gang leader who sliced people up with a flick-knife, back in his heyday.

"Tea? Coffee?" William said, taking a couple of mugs from a shelf. "Are you looking forward to your session? We've got twenty signed up. They won't all come, but I put up posters last week and you've had a lot of interest." He dropped a tea bag into a mug. Waited.

"Tea would be great, thank you."

"They're always excited to get new speakers coming in. Well, for a lot of them it's the highlight of their week, this class."

Chloe smiled, glanced around at the bookshelves. "Do you mind if I—"

"Of course. Go on, go on," William said. "We're quite well-stocked here. We get a lot of donations. You'll find that most of them are into Sci-Fi or true crime, so we have a lot of those titles."

"True crime," she said, amusement in her voice. "I suppose they would be."

Chloe wandered slowly around the aisles. There was a surprisingly wide selection of books on offer. "So, what kind of…men, are they? Jo briefed me as much as she could, but—"

William came out of the small office area and followed her into the book aisles, holding out her tea. "They're a mix. Some of them are just here because they've earned the privileges to be out of their cells for the afternoon, and they'd literally do anything other than be stuck in there. So, well, some aren't too interested in what you have to say. They should all be respectful though, so if you've got any issues with any of them, just give us the nod,' he paused, "there'll be an orderly in to help supervise."

"What about their writing ability. Literacy, even. I guess that's a mix too?"

He nodded, taking a sip of his tea. "Most of them will be able to do the exercises you set them. Some will join in more than others. You'll get some noisy ones, usually. You can tell them to shut up." He smiled. "You'll get some clever ones too… and I don't just mean educated 'clever.' Just be a bit careful of how much you share with them about yourself. I'm sure I don't need to explain, but a lot of these men have spent a long time inside. They can be masters of manipulation."

Chloe raised an eyebrow over the rim of her mug. "Interesting."

A buzzer sounded, and a moment later, George the guard was back. He wedged the door open, and a stream of men begun to file into the room. Chloe waited behind the bookcases, feigning interest in the history section as they got themselves settled into chairs. A man with a different coloured sweatshirt—the orderly that William mentioned, she assumed—started to hand out pens and sheets of paper. The men chatted to each other, occasionally glancing her way.

The room grew warmer, from the heat of the bodies. Smells mingled—sweat, anticipation. George kicked away the doorstop and disappeared out of the room again, locking the door behind him. Locking her in with all of these men. All of these criminals.

Excitement fizzed through her like freshly poured champagne.

She walked to the front of the room, stood next to the whiteboard. Ready. After a brief introduction from William, she was on her own—twenty pairs of curious eyes trained on her. Taking in her plain black dress, tights, boots. Her thick blonde hair tied back in a neat ponytail. She'd kept her makeup minimal. And yet despite her demure look, she recognised the hunger in the men's eyes, and doubted that it came from their desire for learning. She turned away from them, picked up a marker pen, and wrote on the board: *How to craft the perfect story.*

***

She took them through her tried and tested formula for storytelling, and the class flew by. Her checklist remained on the whiteboard:

1. *Introduce the protagonist*

2. *Set up the mystery*

3. *Lull the reader into a false sense of security*

4. *Ramp up the tension*

5. *Throw in a curveball*

6. *Make them gasp at the end*

They'd loved it—happily discussing their favourite books and movies, applying her formula to make sense of the structure. She'd managed to keep the men engaged, while also getting through all of her prepared material, and it was great to see the enthusiasm from many of them after the practical exercises she'd set. They were desperate for homework, and, it seemed, desperate for her to return.

But she had no plans to return.

And as nice as it was to get a positive reaction from teaching, this really wasn't why she had agreed to cover this session for Jo. It was more like serendipity, in fact, that such a perfect opportunity had presented itself.

The questions started innocently enough: "so what made you want to be a teacher?", "have you been in prisons before?" then they moved on to a little more direct, a little more personal: "so how much money have you made from your book sales?", "are you married?", "have you got children?"—she batted them off like flies, smiling her way through it. Until a good-looking man in his thirties leant on the desk beside where she was packing away her worksheets into a folder.

"So where do you go drinking?"

He'd spoken to her earlier, this man. He'd been one of the more attentive ones, asking well thought out questions about the material, helping when some of the others were struggling; when some of them got distracted, and rowdy. He'd quietened them down and given her a smile that said "I've got this for you. I'm protecting you."

She'd overheard him talking to the others when they'd had a fifteen-minute break. He was getting out very soon—either tomorrow or the day after—just waiting for one last piece of paperwork to be dealt with. He had everything set up and sorted. He had his missus waiting for him, but she might just have to wait a bit longer—know what I mean?

He'd looked right at her when he said that, and she'd looked away, pretending not to notice. Not to care. She didn't want to give him, or any of them, any inkling that she was flustered. There was a lot riding on this.

"Ah, you know," she said, sliding the folder into her bag. "Here and there."

She leant across the desk to pick up a textbook that she'd brought into show around, and he leant in at the same time, his hand brushing hers. She could smell him. Warm sweat under spicy deodorant. She swallowed, feeling that fizz of excitement shooting through her again. She remembered Jo's words to her now. *"Don't get too close to them, Chloe. These men are predators. They will suck information from you, and they will use it. Don't be fooled by their charm."*

"You know the Wetherspoons in Camden, yeah? On the canal."

She nodded, once. Discreetly. She didn't want any of the others to notice, although she could feel the weight of the gaze of one of them—the older man she'd seen downstairs. She turned away, pretending she wasn't listening to the man next to her anymore. Jared, his name was. He'd told her earlier. A lot of them had told her their names, but she hadn't paid much attention to most of them. She knew from the minute she set eyes on him that Jared was the one.

"Thursday at seven," he said, under his breath. Then he moved away from the desk. "Thanks, Miss. Great class."

The door opened and George appeared inside, and everyone moved at once. They shoved and jostled their way out of the library, with a chorus of "Thanks, Miss"—several of them stopping briefly to shake her hand or say a few more words. And then they were gone.

William was at her side, grinning. "How did it all go? They seemed happy?"

Chloe smiled. "I think it went perfectly. Thanks so much for having me."

William escorted her out through the building, back around the edge of the recreation area, and out through the visitors' centre and security—then he let her go. She walked quickly to the train station, buzzing with excitement.

It had been so much easier than she'd expected.

And with Jared getting out so soon—everything was going to go much quicker than she'd ever thought possible.

***

Thursday evening came around fast. She'd spent the days since the prison teaching session getting everything prepped. Jo had asked her a couple of times for her bank details, so she could transfer the day's fee—but Chloe hadn't bothered getting back to her. If things went to plan, that three hour writing fee would be nothing but peanuts compared to what she was cooking up.

She spent two hours getting ready. No demure black dress and tights tonight. No bare face and ponytail. Nope, tonight it was a plunging leopard print number, as tight as her own skin. Her push-up bra had her practically spilling over, and she was already aroused as she ran a finger into her cleavage, dabbing on her most alluring perfume. No tights. No underwear. Very, very high heels. She threw on a cropped black biker jacket, added a final coat of shimmering red lipstick, then tapped her phone to order an Uber. She was a bit over the top for a shitty Wetherspoons in grungy Camden, but she had a plan and she had to make sure there was no doubt about it being followed through.

The taxi dropped her off on the bridge and she endured a few friendly wolf-whistles from the punks as she tottered her way along the path towards the pub. As usual, the area outside was swarming with drinkers—a mix of locals, after-workers, tourists, and the cool kids who liked to hang out in this little enclave of iniquity in north London. Glancing around at some of the girls, she wasn't that far off with her outfit after all. There was more than enough flesh on display here and she no longer stood out as much as she'd expected. But it was still enough. She flicked her hair over her shoulder, throwing a smouldering look towards a bunch of lads who looked like they'd come straight from work. They'd stared open-mouthed as she passed them by, leaving nothing but a hint of seductive perfume in her wake.

Inside, the pub was packed, and she had to jostle her way through the crowd to get to the bar. She sat on a stool and was served quickly, ordering a gin and tonic plus a shot of Sambuca that she downed in one while waiting for the barman to offer her the card machine to pay. He'd given her a slow wink before sauntering off to serve the next customer. The shot gave her the final bit of courage she needed. She was stirring her drink when she felt a hand on her elbow. Felt the heat of a body pressing in behind her. She inhaled his scent.

"Well… this is a turn up for the books." He spun her stool around to face him, slid himself between her legs.

She licked her lips. "You didn't think I'd come?"

Her mirrored her, his tongue running slowly over his teeth. "Oh, I never had any doubt about that." He spotted the empty shot glass on the bar behind her. "Another shot?"

She nodded, leaning in close to him. "You must be glad to be back out in the wild."

He picked up the shots from the bar, handed one to her, appraising her. "Have to say, love, you're a fast worker. Fancy yourself a bad boy, eh?" He tapped the shot glass against hers and they both downed the drinks.

It burned her throat, the fire emboldening her even more. "Look, I'm not here to play games. I like you." The surroundings seem to fade away as she crossed her ankles behind his back, drawing him closer into her. "I want you." She took the shot glass from his hand and laid it back on the bar, then guided his hand up her thigh, under her dress. Her skin tingled as he ran his hand further. Then he paused, raising his eyebrows.

"Well, this is a nice surprise." He ran a finger down her inner thigh, in between her legs.

She gasped. Then she uncrossed her legs, pushed him away gently. Pulled her dress down as far as it would go. The surroundings came back into focus. The smell of stale beer and body odour, the cacophony of chatter, clinking glasses, bursts of raucous laughter. Chloe slid forwards off the stool, pressed into Jared's chest. "Let's get out of here."

Things went further in the short taxi ride back to hers. By the time they arrived at her house, she was aching with desire. A cool night breeze whipped her hair around her face as she clambered out of the cab, the fresh air giving her a jolt.

Focus, Chloe.

He paid the driver then climbed out of the cab behind her. She pushed open the gate of the tiny front garden, to the pretty arched doorway of her Victorian terraced house. She paused to catch her breath and find her keys, taking extra time to root around in her bag. Calming herself down, sobering herself up. He wrapped his arms around her waist, stuck his knee up between her legs, and she had to wriggle away from him to open the door.

"Stop, get off me. Not out here," she said, twisting her shoulder trying to shrug him off. "The bloody neighbours." She tried to keep her voice low, hoping he'd get the message and back off until they got inside.

"Christ, hurry up then. I need a piss."

Chloe took a deep breath and pushed the door open. *Get a grip!* She'd got a bit carried away. She needed Jared to come home with her, and it had been fun luring him in like that. But she'd started to enjoy it a bit too much. That wasn't the plan. She had to stick to the plan.

He followed her inside, and she pointed to the door under the stairs. "Toilet's down there. Keep it down a bit, OK?"

He looked puzzled. "Is there someone else here?"

Chloe swallowed. "No. Just… thin walls. The neighbours are a nightmare." She kept her voice low, still, keeping up the pretence. The walls weren't thin at all, as it happened. And the neighbours on the left were elderly and half-deaf. The ones on the right were on holiday at their second home somewhere in Cornwall. She glanced around the hallway. The front door was tightly shut. Everything was in place.

She stood in silence, listening to the sound of Jared peeing in her downstairs toilet, and wondered, just for a moment, if she was making a terrible mistake. She kicked off her shoes, and one of the heels hit the radiator in the hallway, making a clanging sound like a gong.

A floorboard creaked upstairs.

Jared came out of the toilet. Saw her looking up the stairs. "Chlo? What's up?"

She put a finger to her lips. Whispered, "I think there's someone upstairs."

He gave her a hard stare. Hissed, "Who? What the fuck's going on?"

Chloe shook her head slightly, then turned her eyes towards the front door. At what she'd propped up in the corner. A baseball bat.

He licked his lips, still staring at her. "Who's upstairs, Chloe?"

She widened her eyes, clenched her fists, did her best impression of someone scared out of their wits—it was all meant to be an act, but she was starting to feel it. Starting to believe it. She hadn't expected it to feel so tense. She was already beginning to shake from the effects of the adrenaline coursing through her veins. "It's my ex… he's the only one with a key. He's… he's not meant to have it anymore. He's not meant to be here anymore." She peeled away the side of her dress below the scooped neckline, exposing pale skin above her left breast. Just under her clavicle, a deep purple bruise blossomed like a hideous flower. "He…" she shook her head. Felt a tear roll down her cheek. It felt real now. It was really happening. "I keep the bat by the door, just in case…"

Jared stepped forward and snatched up the bat. His face had grown dark, his heavy brows knitted. His smooth jaw set hard. "That fucker. I've got no time for arseholes who hit birds."

Another floorboard creaked upstairs, followed by the sound of footsteps.

Chloe took a deep breath. *Don't come down. Please don't come down.* Then she heard a click, and the sound of the en suite extractor fan coming on.

Jared was walking slowly up the stairs. That click again. The light being turned off. He paused on the stairs and turned back to her. "Stay here. I'll sort it."

Chloe felt sick. She waited until he was nearly at the top of the stairs, then she pulled her phone out of her handbag. Jo's message was already waiting for her.

What's happening?

Chloe messaged back quickly. *Nearly done. Come round.*

She dropped the phone back into her bag and followed Jared up the stairs. He was outside her bedroom door. He gestured at her to go back downstairs, but she shook her head. She widened her eyes again and nodded towards the closed bedroom door. Then she whispered, "If he finds you here with me, he'll kill us both."

Jared's face twisted into a sneer. "Not if I get him first." He lifted his foot, leg bent, ready to kick the door, then there was another creak of a floorboard and the door opened inward with a gentle creak. A slim man in boxer shorts with sleep-ruffled hair stood in the doorway, his face crunched in confusion.

"Chloe? What the hell are—?"

She felt a moment's hesitation, ready to shout *STOP* just as Jared's foot connected with the man's chest, sending him spinning back into the room. He fell to the ground, hitting the wooden floor hard, the air knocked out of him with a *whoomph.*

"What the fuck are you doing in here you piece of shit?" Jared was on him in a flash, dropping the baseball bat, kneeling on his chest, punching him in the face.

The man—the one she used to call "baby" and "darling" and "honeybun" until a few months earlier, when she'd found out what he'd been doing with his secretary on all those "work trips" he'd been taking—the clichéd fuck that he was—the man that was still her husband, but who had told her that *she* had to leave this beautiful home that she'd designed and decorated from a raw, rotten shell—the man tried to call out, tried to fight back, but he was weak and pathetic and he deserved every damn punch he got.

Who did he think he was to try to get rid of her? To channel his considerable wealth into airtight funds that she couldn't access? To change from using their joint solicitor and accountant, to a new one who wanted to leave Chloe with barely a pittance after all these years of being a dutiful and faithful wife?

Chloe picked up the bat.

There was a lot of heavy breathing in the room now. Jared was hunched over her husband's prone form, panting.

"Is he dead?"

Jared nodded. His head hung down over his chest. Blood and snot dripped from him. He'd taken a hit himself, it seemed. That was good. That would help. "I… went too far. I get this red mist, Chlo," Jared said. He sounded broken. "I've been out twenty-four hours. At least I got a couple of drinks and a quick fumble though, eh?" He started to turn his head towards her. "Any chance of a shag before you call the cops?"

Chloe swung the bat.

It connected with Jared's face with some force, knocking him clean off his knees. A spray of blood arced across the room, hitting the bedspread. He slumped on the floor next to her husband, a small moan escaped his lips, followed by a burble of blood and saliva and air.

"Nnnnngh," he tried.

Chloe brought the bat down on the top of his head, and the noise stopped. Shortly afterwards, there was a long, slow hiss, like a slow puncture on a bicycle. Then there was nothing. She wiped a hand across her face. Sweat and blood, and something else. Something a bit more solid, like a chunk of Jared's scalp, maybe. It was hard to see it properly in the dim light of the bedroom.

She blew out a breath, as she heard the rattle of a key in the front door. Then she tossed the bat on the floor and hurried downstairs.

"Holy shit, are you OK? You're covered in… Jesus, I don't even know what that is, Chlo. Come here. Fucking hell." Jo tossed her keys on the hall table and walked towards Chloe, pulling her into a tight hug. "Is everything OK? Did it all work out? Do you need a drink? Fuck…" She shook her head. "I sort of can't believe it."

Chloe swallowed. "There's brandy in the cupboard above the sink. Unless the fucker already rearranged the cupboards. Or got his fancy piece to do it." She pulled out a chair from the kitchen table and slumped down. Jo slid the bottle towards her, and she opened it and took a long slug.

"How did it go with Jared?"

Chloe took another mouthful of brandy, enjoying the burn. Grimaced, then sucked in air. "He was perfect, Jo. Exactly like you said. I didn't have to do a thing to lure him in at the class. He hooked on to me straight away."

"Told you, didn't I?"

"I quite liked him, you know… he was pretty sexy. In the pub tonight, and then in the taxi, I—"

Jo slammed a fist on the kitchen table. "You do know what he was in for, don't you?"

Chloe shook her head.

"He stalked and raped a fifteen-year-old girl. She was a temp at his office. Told the judge he thought she was older, and he thought she wanted it. Said it was consensual. She tried to kill herself after the trial. Luckily, she was found. A lot of therapy, and she might make it. He's a predator, Chloe. I told you to be fucking careful. I told you to—"

Chloe felt the blood drain from her face. She closed her eyes, flashing back to the pub. The feel of his hand on her thigh. The taxi. His mouth on hers. She jumped up from the chair, just made it to the sink before she was sick. Jo stood up behind her, ran a soothing hand down her back. Pulled her hair away from her face. Then when Chloe was sure she couldn't bring anything else up, Jo turned her gently around and cradled her face in her hands.

"It's done, darling. It's over." She pushed a strand of hair behind Chloe's ear. Leant forward and kissed her gently on the tip of her nose. "Let's get the difficult stuff out of the way, then we can start to look forward to the future, OK?" She wiped a tear away from Chloe's cheek. "Don't waste your tears on a rapist… nor on that cheating scumbag of a husband who was going to leave you with nothing. It's over, OK? We have rid the world of a couple of oxygen-wasters and in time, you'll forget that either of them ever existed."

Chloe nodded, pulling away. She took a glass from the draining board and filled it with water from the tap, drank it down greedily. Then she walked gingerly back to the kitchen table and sat down. She pulled her phone from her handbag. Her hand shook, as she tapped in the numbers. Jo sat down beside her, took her other hand. Squeezed. After a moment, the call was answered.

"Hello? Police, please. My name's Chloe Summers. I live at 57 Warren Avenue. My husband is dead… and I think I've just killed an intruder."

Bliss

By Joseph S. Walker

Bliss. One syllable. Start with mouth closed, the *B* percussive, the *L* a glancing touch of tongue to roof of mouth, then the soft exhalation, the lingering sibilance. Bliss. Just saying her name a tiny erotic act.

She put the duffel bag on the coffee table, casual in her nudity. Nothing like the faceless blondes of Marc's fantasies, the huge tits stuck on skinny frames he favored in his porn. Bliss was compact, athletic, her black hair always pulled back into a utilitarian ponytail. A gymnast's body. She used it with a focus and intensity that gave him the greatest pleasures of his life, coming to him with an unashamed hunger that made his own seem pathetic, inadequate.

Marc got lost for a few minutes in that phrase. *Greatest pleasures of my life.* Was that a movie? How had those words come into his head? It was hard to think straight. He worried about it, the world getting fuzzy, until Bliss walked through his line of sight again and he fought things back into focus. She was gathering clothes. Getting ready to leave.

He thought of the times he'd breathed her name as he entered her. He tried to say it now. Couldn't, of course. He willed Bliss to get closer one last time. He wanted to run his eyes over her again, slowly, from the face he'd caressed to the toes he'd kissed, storing up every detail for whatever came next.

She would have to come over to him soon.

She had to see if he was dead yet.

***

It was just two months ago he ran into her, literally. He was outside his office building, pacing the patio of shame set aside for smokers. He spun on his heel, angry at some forgotten scrap of career ladder politics, and a woman jogging too close to the edge of the sidewalk ran full bore into him.

Marc backed up, cursing. The woman cried out in surprise and spun away from him, hopping on one foot to get her balance. She was wearing red shorts and a light blue T-shirt. Before anything else about her, Marc noticed the strip of bare skin, perhaps an inch wide, between the two. Then the woman recovered her footing, looked at him and said his name in a tone of surprised pleasure.

"Mr. Davis!" She took off her mirrored shades, smiling, her eyes bright. "Oh, gosh, you probably don't remember me at all. It's Bliss? Remember Bliss and Cris?"

The way she ran it together, *Blissencris*, tugged at a memory. "You were Cris's roommate."

She slipped one arm of the glasses into the neck of her shirt, the hem pulling down a bit as she let them hang there. "You do remember! Oh my God, I've been such a bad friend. I've been meaning to text Cris forever. How is she doing?"

"She's fine," Marc said automatically. His stepdaughter was making minimum wage in a pet supply store and trying a new antidepressant every month. "She might go back to school in the fall."

"She should," Bliss said. "It was a shame she had to leave." She propped her left foot up on a bench and leaned into it, stretching her right leg out behind her. "It's so funny running into you. Do you work around here?"

"Yeah." He'd dropped his cigarette when she ran into him. He shook another one out of the pack and lit it, gesturing at the building behind them, though his eye was on her taut thigh. "Thirtieth floor. I'm an office manager."

"Nice," she said. She put her foot back on the ground and sidled a little closer to him. "Can I get a drag?"

He handed her the cigarette. She took a long inhale and savored the smoke slowly seeping out, her eyes closed. He noticed the fine sheen of sweat on her face. The line of her bra was clear under the thin cotton shirt. He barely remembered her. They'd only met a couple of times, once moving Cris into the dorms, once moving her back out near the end of the ruined semester. That was, what, six years ago? Flattering, come to think of it, that she so immediately remembered him. She opened her eyes, saw him watching.

"I know," she said. "So stupid, stopping in the middle of a jog for this poison. Talk about counterproductive, huh? I've just about managed to quit, but sometimes you've got to be naughty." She flicked ash and handed the cigarette back to him.

"I hear that," he said. "So, you must have graduated by now. What are you up to?"

She went back to the bench, stretching the other leg. "I switched around a bunch, but I ended up getting my degree in theatre. I'm giving myself a couple of years to hit auditions. I tried LA for a while, but you have to be built like a Barbie doll to get in the door out there, so I just moved here."

He resisted the urge to say there was nothing wrong with her build. "Any luck?"

She laughed. "Not so far. I've got an editing gig I do on my own time at home to pay the bills, so at least I don't have to wait tables."

"Well, that's great." Marc dropped the butt on the sidewalk and ground it out. "Nice to run into you. I'll tell Cris you said hi."

She put a hand on his arm. "Actually, Mr. Davis, I hate to let you go so quick. It's been awfully lonesome since I moved, and it's nice to see a friendly face. Would you maybe want to have lunch tomorrow? Tell me a little about living in New York?"

He could swear the place she was touching tingled.

***

Bliss was ten minutes late for lunch, just enough time for Marc to convince himself that she'd been deliberately teasing him. When she showed she was out of breath. "Oh my God, I'm so sorry. I was at this horrible cattle call to be a beggar in *Les Mis* and they just dragged everything out *forever*."

"No problem," Marc said. "I'm just happy you could make it."

"I wouldn't have missed it," Bliss said. She ran her eye down the menu. Marc ran his eye down her, noting the low-cut neckline on her silk blouse.

"Do you think you got it?"

She shrugged. "Probably not. That's okay. You spend half an hour putting on your makeup and costume so you can go onstage a few times, vamp through a couple bars of 'Do You Hear the People Sing' and look awestruck at the guy playing Valjean. It's eight times a week being part of the scenery."

The waiter came. Bliss asked for a few more minutes to decide.

"I'm sure I'd notice you," he said when they were alone again. "There can't be many beggars as good looking as you."

He was surprised by her blush. "Aren't you sweet."

"I try." He took a sip of his scotch. No reason to tell her he'd already had one while waiting for her. "So, what can I tell you about living in New York?"

She smiled and propped her chin on her hand. "Can I be honest with you, Mr. Davis?"

"Only if you call me Marc."

Her smile deepened. "I grew up in the city. I don't really need a guide."

"Oh. Then—"

"Were you surprised that I remembered you?"

"Truthfully? Yes, I was."

"Well." Bliss took a deep breath. "The thing is, you really made an impression on me when we met. You seemed really strong and confident, you know? There were all these boys my age around, seeming silly and desperate, and then there was you, just kind of calm and in charge. I used to think about it a lot."

Marc didn't remember a thing about that day except that it had been a monumental pain in the ass. "That is surprising."

"Well, I tried not to embarrass myself," Bliss said. "I don't worry about that as much now. But I still think guys my own age are mostly just boys."

His mouth felt dry. "I'm a married man, Bliss."

First time he'd said her name.

"Oh, I know," she said. "Honestly, though, I'm surprised you're still married. I know Cris's mother is older than you, and Cris said the two of you fought a lot." She put her hand on top of his. "I don't think you should have to live like that, Marc."

First time she'd said his.

He took another drink. "What are you saying?"

"I guess I'm saying this," she said. She glanced out the window, thinking for a moment, then looked him directly in the eye. "We could have lunch here, and chitchat, and act like we're just catching up. And then have lunch again, maybe next week. And eventually dinner. And maybe in a month or two, or six, end up where we both know we're heading. That's one choice."

"What's the other?"

"I have a friend who's spending six months in Europe. She gave me a key so I can check on her apartment. It's about three blocks from here." She squeezed his hand. "We could go there now."

***

He got to know the friend's apartment well in the following weeks. Bliss didn't have her own place and was couch surfing among various old classmates. The vacant apartment was tastefully decorated, but not much more personal than a hotel suite. The home of a person who didn't spend much time at home. It was easy to start thinking of it as their place. He had his own key made and as often as not, when he arrived, she would already be in bed, waiting for him, her clothes draped carefully over the back of a chair.

First came the long lunch hours. Before long, he was concocting stories about going out with the boys for a few drinks after work or staying in the city to catch a Knicks game. The excuses were flimsy, but it hardly mattered. It had been years since Janelle, Cris's mother, seemed to give much of a damn where he was spending his time.

"I married her for the money," he told Bliss late one night. He'd never said that out loud before, never confessed it so boldly, even to himself.

The open bedroom window brought in the sounds of traffic and distant sirens. The only light was a strip across the ceiling from a streetlight below. Gauzy curtains shifted lazily in the barely-there breeze.

She was lying on her back, holding his hand. The sheet came to her navel and even in the cocooning dark he could see the marks on her breasts where he'd bitten her. Marc was propped up on one arm, running the other hand idly over her. She was so young, so damn young, and it made him feel young too. He hadn't realized until Bliss that he had stopped feeling young. He wanted to stay here all night, just forget the tiresome, awkward business of getting dressed and going home and pretending. He knew he wouldn't, but it was what he wanted.

"Not for money, really," he corrected himself. "For the business. Her family's media firm was just starting to take off then, but I could tell it was going to be huge. Cris's father was an idiot to leave Janelle when he did. Another couple of years and he could have scored really big in a divorce."

"Couldn't you do that now?" she asked.

He groaned and let his head drop to the pillow, rolling to his back. "Prenup. Her parents insisted. She didn't care one way or the other, she was just tired of being a single mom. I went along with it because I thought I'd get mine with the job they'd give me. Make some connections, eventually jump ship, and take the juicy accounts with me. So, what do I get? Fucking office manager. No travel, no working with clients, just handling the cash flow and making sure everybody has paper clips."

"Do people still use paper clips?" She took her hand out of his and reached for his body.

"Not much," he said. "I bought a case of them five years ago and I've still got plenty. Why, you need some?"

"No," she said. She turned on her side so she could reach him better. "I'm sorry, baby. They don't know what they're missing by not giving you a chance."

"Damn straight." He laced his fingers behind his head and closed his eyes, focusing on what she was doing, slowly but deliberately, with her hand. "I've thought about killing her."

Her hand didn't stop. "Your wife?"

"Yeah. If I could figure a way to make it look like an accident. Trouble is, the same assholes who made the prenup did her will, too. I don't get a dime unless we've been married twenty years. Ten to go. Until then it all goes to Cris."

"What if they both die?"

He opened his eyes and turned his head. "Isn't Cris your friend?"

The light from the window was behind her now. He couldn't see her expression.

"She was," Bliss said. "But we had our share of fights, too, and I haven't talked to her for years. I was meaning to get in touch, be the bridge builder, but then you and I happened, and I got afraid I would let something slip. Have you told her about us?"

"No. I barely talk to her. She comes to the house for dinner every couple of weeks if her mother begs." Her hand was still moving, and his breathing was starting to change. "Anyway, that's no good. Cris's will funnels everything back to the family. Not a dime to the wicked stepfather."

"That probably is how she thinks of you," Bliss said. "I think she kind of hated you back when we were roommates. The way you were always calling her, making sure she got up in the morning, making sure she was doing her homework. I thought you were being a good father, but it just drove her crazy."

Marc grimaced, hoping there wasn't enough light for her to see. "That was kind of the idea. I knew what they were grooming her for. If she got her degree, I would have ended up working for her. No fucking way I was going to let that happen. I convinced Janelle she'd been too easy on her, then I put the pressure on."

"Clever boy." She began to nuzzle at his neck. "See, you can make things happen. So, what are you going to do, Marc? You must have another plan. You got Cris out of your way. I don't believe somebody with your mind is going to sit around for another ten years."

He swallowed. He'd already said things out loud that he never thought he would. He hadn't expected how good it would feel. Showing himself to her. All of himself. "I've been skimming," he whispered. "Very carefully. For a long time now. Inflated invoices, fake vendors. You don't need to know the details."

"Oh, my smart boy," she murmured.

"Nothing stays on the books for long," Marc went on. "No accounts for the IRS to stumble across. I turn it all into cash and keep it in a safety deposit box. No interest, but almost impossible to trace." He snaked his arm under her and pulled her entire body close. "I figure when I get to a million, I'll do something. I haven't decided what. Fake my death or something. Just run."

"How close are you?" she breathed in his ear.

"I'm about to hit eight hundred thousand."

Bliss made a sound in her throat, threw her leg over him, and rolled on top. "Clever boy," she said again, as she took him. "Just don't you go anywhere without me, clever boy."

He wanted to say *never*, but it was a few minutes before he could speak.

***

Two weeks later they were in the shower together. Bliss had been odd all night, affectionate but quiet, withdrawn. She broke away from a kiss and put her head against his chest. "I need to talk serious for a minute," she said.

"Oh, God," he said. "You're late."

"What?" She jerked away, slapped him not quite painfully on the arm. "No! Anyway, I thought you had a vasectomy."

"I did. I was just kidding."

She snorted and pushed open the glass door, grabbing a towel. "Sure." She walked out into the living room. Marc turned off the water and followed, watching as she ran the towel along her arms. Even after all these weeks, the sight of her without clothes made his breath catch.

"I'm sorry," he said. "You tell me what it's about. I'll listen."

She spun. He was startled that she seemed to be crying. "That's what you think. That I'm trying to trap you. That I'm another Janelle. Next you'll be thinking about killing *me*."

"Hey, no." He draped his own towel over his shoulders and held out his hands. "You and me, baby. For real."

She shook her head and paced as she kept drying herself. "I think you just like getting off."

"You know that's not true."

It took fifteen minutes for her to calm down enough to talk. She wouldn't let him get close. He sat at the tiny kitchen table watching her as she sat on the couch, looking down at her folded hands.

"You've told me some things you probably aren't proud of," she said. She paused. Marc didn't say anything. "I guess it's my turn." She took a long breath. "I didn't leave LA because I wasn't getting auditions. I left because I got caught up in something bad." She looked up at him. "Real bad."

"Okay," he said. "Whatever it is, we can deal with it."

"I needed cash," she said. "Rent, food. This guy Brandon from my acting class, he arranged for me to let some friends of his use my apartment." Her shoulders slumped. "They were dealers. They used my place to store their shit."

Marc gave a low whistle. "That sounds dangerous."

"Dangerous enough for me," she said. "Brandon was always trying to get me to do more. He said they could get me a fake passport so I could bring stuff in for them. I told him no fucking way."

"That's smart. You don't want to get mixed up in that."

"Yeah, well," she shrugged. "Not smart enough. One of his friends got shot in my parking lot. Could have just as easily been inside the apartment, and then I would have been well and truly screwed. That was it for me. I was on a flight to JFK twelve hours later."

"Oh, little girl," Marc said. He came and sat down next to her, but didn't touch her. "That was a good move."

"You can quit telling me how smart I was," Bliss said. "It was stupid of me to get anywhere near it." She turned to face him and took his hand. Her hair was still wet, plastered across her shoulders. Showering seemed to be the only time she took it out of the ponytail. "But now I'm glad I did."

"Why?"

"Hear me out. Do you promise?"

Marc nodded.

"I called Brandon. For fifty thousand apiece he can get us passports in whatever names we want."

Marc frowned and leaned back. He started to speak but she put a finger to his lips and tilted her head. He nodded and closed his mouth.

"This is a dead end, baby," Bliss said. "You have to see that. I'm not booking any parts and you go into that office every day gritting your teeth. Do you really think we can keep this up for another ten years?" She scooted closer to him. He could feel the warm humid air coming off her damp skin, smell the clean fresh scent that was more than soap. "I don't want to wait. I want to be with you every day. Is that what you want?"

"Of course." His voice sounded strange in his ears.

"We take the money you've saved," she said. "We get new passports and new names, and we go to Costa Rica. Or maybe Belize. I know a woman who went there a few years ago, runs a boating charter now." Her eyes were wide. "Do you know how far seven hundred thousand would go down there? We could have years before we have to work again. Years to just be together."

"That's a nice dream," he said.

"It doesn't have to be a dream," Bliss said. "It can be a plan. We'd have to drive to LA. We can't fly until we have our new names." She pulled herself closer, wrapped her arms around him. "I've been driving myself crazy just thinking about the drive. Imagining us in some hotel in Kansas or something. Nobody in the world knowing who we are or where we are. Just us." She kissed him.

"Just us," he said, a long time later.

***

They picked a weekend when Janelle was going out of town to her college reunion. Marc could come to the apartment straight from work on Friday, and they would finally have a whole night together, the first of many. Saturday morning, they would drive out of the city. They'd have two days before anyone noticed Marc was missing, probably another couple of days before serious looking started. By Wednesday or Thursday, they would be on a plane leaving LAX. They decided on Belize, at least to start.

He made sure the duffel bag he took to the bank at lunch was strong. Even mostly in hundreds, eight hundred thousand dollars weighed close to twenty pounds.

"See you Monday," Ashley, the front desk receptionist, said to him as he was leaving at the end of the day. He gave her a little salute. Riding down in the elevator, he thought about the fact that those were the last words anyone would ever say to Marc Davis. In a few days she'd be telling some cop that he had seemed perfectly normal. She might not even remember the duffel bag. Plenty of people brought exercise gear to work.

The last words Janelle had said to him were a reminder to empty the kitchen trash. He emptied it before he left. All over their bed.

He couldn't remember the last time he'd talked to Cris. Nor could he remember the last time he'd felt the way he felt walking down the street in the end-of-week crowds. Like he was setting his own path, not settled on rails that could take him only one place.

***

He let himself into the apartment and felt a momentary buzz of apprehension when he didn't immediately see her. Then she came around the corner from the small kitchen. She was holding a drink and wearing a gold necklace and red high heels and nothing else. She came into his arms, and he dropped the bag and kissed her, long and deep and slow.

When he started to move them toward the bedroom door, she broke away and put a hand to his chest. "Not just yet," she said. "We've got all night, Mr. Davis. And then a whole lot of nights after that." She pushed him down onto the couch and handed him the drink, a scotch and soda in a big glass with ice cubes. "Drink. I'll have dinner ready in twenty minutes."

"You're cooking?" This had never happened before.

"I am feeling domestic," she said. "Good hearty food to get your strength up, mister man." She winked. "I have a feeling you're going to need it." She headed back toward the kitchen, her backside swaying. "Let me get this in the oven, and then we can entertain ourselves for a bit."

So this was it. All the bridges burned. Marc lifted the glass in a silent toast to the duffel bag on the coffee table. He took a long drink from the glass. She'd mixed it very strong, but that was fine. There was no reason he couldn't get completely trashed tonight, since he had nowhere else to be. He drank again, thinking back over the day, looking for mistakes, trying to think the way the cops would think. He couldn't see a string for them to pull on. He'd even dropped his laptop in an alley dumpster on the way over. They wouldn't see the hours spent reading websites about living in Belize. He finished the drink, imagining it as a margarita on one of the endless golden beaches. Bliss in a bikini with less material than a handkerchief.

Or just topless. They had topless beaches, right? Sure. What tropical paradise would be complete without them?

The glass dropped from his fingers. He heard it hit the carpet. He lolled his head around and looked at his empty hand. He should lean forward and pick up the glass and put it on the table. Easy.

He couldn't do it.

"It was in the drink," Bliss's voice said from some distant world off to his left. She walked in front of him. She was still wearing the necklace, but she had taken off the heels. One of the things he loved about her. Her comfort in being nude, her willingness to let him look. She picked up the glass and put it on the table and then she straddled him and put her arms around him. He could see her doing it, but he couldn't feel the weight of her on his legs.

"You bought the ingredients at three different chemical supply stores over the last week," Bliss said. "You used your credit card. That and the suicide note you're going to leave on your phone should answer any questions."

Marc couldn't talk, but she must have seen his lips moving. She kissed his forehead. "Of course, I don't know when they'll find you. This apartment belonged to an old woman who died last year. I imagine sooner or later somebody will complain about the smell, and then there will be a hell of a mystery to solve. How did you get in here, and what happened to that young woman who showed up to clean the place out and take over grandma's lease?" She shrugged. "It doesn't really matter. They won't find any fingerprints that aren't yours. Not so much as a hair. I've had a lot of time to plan this, Marc."

All he could do now was open his eyes wide. A question.

"You're wondering why you."

He did it again.

"Do you know what I really remember about the first day we met?" she asked. She stroked his cheek. "Not you. I barely remember you. I remember Cris. She was beautiful and funny and smart, and so excited to be getting out of the house. I think I fell in love with her a little."

She tousled Marc's hair.

"And then you started," she said. "Phone calls a little earlier every day, just to be sure she was up and heading for class, and a little later every night, demanding she send pictures to prove she was doing her homework. Calling her teachers and telling them that she would slack off unless they kept an eye on her. Calling the RA to see if boys were coming around." She shook her head and straightened his tie a little. "You had the damned campus chaplain coming around to try to make her go to church. When she tried out for volleyball you called the coach and said she couldn't play and keep up her grades. I bet you had fun, thinking of all the things you could do."

He couldn't even move his eyes now.

"I watched that beautiful girl fall to pieces," Bliss said. "She started pulling her hair out. Cutting herself. She gained ten pounds in a month then lost fifteen in two weeks. She tried to get Janelle to make you stop, but I guess Janelle was still taken with you back then." She bit her lip. "Then I came back to the room that day and found her, after what she tried to do. There was so much blood. At least what I'm doing to you is supposed to be painless."

He had no way to tell her it wasn't.

She stood up. "I've stayed away from Cris. Seeing me only makes her relive that whole time. But I keep tabs on her. I've been in her apartment, seen the pills on the nightstand, read her journal. And I've planned. You know, for a long time I thought you were just an asshole. Finding out you did all that so Cris would never be your boss?" She shook her head. "Weak, Mr. Davis. Weak."

He drifted for a moment. It was getting harder to focus on what she was saying. When he became fully aware of things again, she had the duffel bag on the coffee table and was looking through it.

"The money is a bonus," she said. "I really just wanted you to know what it feels like to be afraid." She leaned forward to look at his eyes, and saw them jerk slightly downward, following her breasts. She laughed. "Lord, you made it easy. I swear you lose an IQ point for every inch of skin I show." She cupped her breasts, licked her lips. "Does it make you happy, Marc? Are you happy that my body is the last thing you're ever going to see?" She shook her head in disgust and walked off somewhere behind him, coming back with her clothes, which she put on the table next to the bag.

"It is a nice little bonus," she said. "It will give me time to make more plans. I've been thinking a lot about Cris's real father. He just vanished on her, after the divorce. I think he could have done better for her. Don't you?"

Bliss looked at the couch and closed her mouth. She was only talking to herself.

The Smoking Gunners
By Ashley Lister

Beatrix stood over the corpse, a smoking gun in her hand and a smile of almost comic regret playing on her lips. If not for the enormity of what she had done, Jim would have sworn she looked like a woman who wanted to say, "Oops!" or "fiddlesticks!" and then giggle as though the matter was of no consequence.

Instead, she glanced at Jim and murmured, "This looks bad, doesn't it?" Not waiting for his response, flexing a diplomatic smile, she said, "But I promise you now: as bad as this looks, worse things have happened." Her features turned momentarily solemn as she added, "And we both know, too often, Wilkins has been the cause of those worse things."

Jim wanted to scream.

It was rare for anything about Beatrix to look bad, but this scenario was an exception. She was a strikingly attractive brunette with her hair sculpted into a fashionable shaggy bob. Her scarlet heels accentuated her long coltish legs. The vibrant colour of her shoes complemented Beatrix's scarlet nail polish and lipstick. The black stockings, thong, suspender belt and balconette bra made her look as though she was posing for some tawdry photoshoot in a men's magazine. But, because she held a smoking gun as she stood over a still-warm corpse, he couldn't think of her as appearing desirable, sexy, or arousing. He could only concede that the scene looked bad.

"It looks bad," he groaned softly. Operating to the procedure he knew he had to follow, Jim pressed a finger against his earpiece and spoke for the microphone at his throat. "Ambulance to floor eight," he snapped. "Urgent. Also, I want a secure guard on all exits. Beatrix Geraghty must not leave the building." He glared at her and this time, looking as though he was saying it for her benefit, said, "Repeat: Beatrix Geraghty must not leave the building."

Jim glanced over his shoulder as though he expected to see subordinates rushing up to ask what was going on whilst demanding to know how he was going to explain this to his superiors. "You shot Wilkins?" Jim whispered. "Why? What happened?"

It crossed his mind that the questions were now redundant. He was standing in the open doorway of a hotel bedroom, looking in. Wilkins, facedown on the floor and bleeding out from a GSW (gun shot wound) to the head, had his trousers around his ankles and his bare arse sticking high in the air. On the hotel bed the pristine sheets were hidden beneath an open briefcase filled with used fives, tens, and twenties. And the prostitute Jim had brought in for Wilkins, a prostitute that shouldn't really have been allowed anywhere near a man who had been arrested for sex-trafficking charges, a prostitute Jim had thought he could trust, was standing over Wilkins's corpse holding a smoking gun and wearing an expression of contrition that looked as sincere as a politician's promise.

"What happened?" Jim repeated dully. He was deliberately keeping his voice low for fear of starting to scream at her. "What the hell happened?"

"It's kind of a long story," Beatrix admitted.

She flashed a disarming grin that, on any other occasion, would have made him swoon. Her teeth were white and even and her smile made him think of sultry bedroom promises. Even in the panic of this moment he could feel the heat rising in his loins and he tried to quell his arousal by thinking of his now-doomed career.

"It's probably best if I tell you what occurred whilst we're somewhere else." She gave a light shrug and pointed her gun idly at Wilkins' corpse before adding, "This place is going to be very busy soon, and neither of us will be able to say a thing that won't be used against us as evidence." Without waiting, she began to unroll the silencer from the barrel of the gun, before turning around and placing it on the bed next to the open case.

Jim didn't watch what she did with the silencer and was only vaguely aware that she was wiping down the gun, meticulously removing fingerprints. Beatrix had bent over, and Jim's gaze was riveted on the sight of her backside. Her buttocks, the lightly tanned colour of a latte macchiato, were taut and muscular. The black fabric of her thong slipped between the peachlike orbs and moulded itself to the plump shape of her labia. The shape of the lips looked swollen, and he thought he could detect a glimmer of dewy wetness on the centre of the crotch, as though this situation had brought her some arousal. The sight was sufficiently enticing to keep Jim enchanted until she stood up and turned to quizzically stare at him.

"It looks like you're drooling a little," Beatrix told him, pointing at the corner of her mouth to illustrate where she meant. "That's never a good look on a Detective Inspector. People will think you aren't able to control the situation."

Jim wiped his face with the back of his cuff and stepped into the room. "Wilkins is dead, and you shot him," he hissed in a stage whisper. "What's going on?"

Beatrix frowned. "You've said it yourself. Wilkins is dead and I shot him." Shaking her head as though dismissing the discussion, and clearly demonstrating disdain for the folly of Jim asking something to which he already knew the answer, she said, "Could you grab that briefcase for me whilst I get my coat? I'm trying not to touch anything. I don't want to leave fingerprints, do I?"

Too stunned to think of an appropriate response, Jim did as she asked. He wanted to know whose money he was holding, and how she thought she was going to walk out of a busy hotel, bustling with his fellow police officers, with guards on the door now looking out for her.

He snapped the clasps on the briefcase shut and turned to see that Beatrix had donned a man's camel-coloured trench coat, cinched tightly at the waist, and accentuating her slender figure. The idea that she was wearing only the skimpiest lingerie beneath the coat made his cheeks flush and guided his thoughts away from more pressing issues such as the death of Wilkins, the money in the briefcase, and the consequences that were now going to fall on him.

"Let's get a drink," she said, donning a pair of sunglasses and stepping past him into the hotel corridor.

Jim cast a glance at Wilkins, decided the man wasn't going anywhere, and fell into step behind Beatrix's long-legged stride. They were on the eighth floor of the hotel and, on Jim's instruction, every room on the eighth was unoccupied to help ensure the security of their key witness. There were officers securing the fire escapes and stairwells, as well as a pair in front of the lift doors.

Approaching the pair in front of the lift doors Jim recognised both men. They were broad and clearly capable, with faces as impassive and unreadable as the hotel's wall art. One of them acknowledged Jim with a terse nod. Neither of them seemed to notice Beatrix, as though their job description specifically forbade them from seeing prostitutes. Jim knew, if Beatrix had been alone, they would have stepped in to stop her from making a getaway, following his command to prevent Beatrix Geraghty from leaving the building. But, because she was accompanied by their boss, the eighth-floor guards did not intervene.

Jim considered telling them they were no longer needed, that the man they were guarding was no longer going to make a statement in court, unless he was being interrogated by a barrister with a Ouija board.

Pragmatically, he decided that bombshell would wait.

He had to hear Beatrix's story before he set events in motion for her arrest on a charge of first-degree murder. Once he had her story, he would have a better idea of how his own miserable downfall was going to be intertwined with hers.

And yet, as much as he wanted to know what had happened, he remained silent as they stepped into the lift. He said nothing as they swiftly descended and continued to say nothing when the doors opened on the mezzanine floor where the hotel's bar was located.

"Bourbon," she told him, taking the briefcase from his hand and stepping towards a seat at an empty table that overlooked the lobby below them.

The bar was busy, many of the customers wearing the red and white shirts of the Arsenal home kit: *Emirates Fly Better* emblazoned across each breast. Seeing so many of them, Jim realised he had been lucky to secure the eighth floor for Wilkins when the hotel was clearly trying to cater for crowds attending an important weekend match. It looked as though the place was filled with Gooners, most of them having a congratulatory beer or two prior to going on elsewhere for a prolonged session of celebration and debauchery. Given the excited clamour of conversation, and the general geniality amongst them, Jim figured Arsenal must have won.

"Bourbon," Beatrix repeated, as though she knew his mind had wandered. "Make it a large one."

He was going to argue and say that he wanted to hold onto the briefcase, and thought they should remain together, until he had heard everything she had to say. She'd just killed an important witness. The only reason he was allowing her the courtesy of a final drink in the lobby was because he needed to know everything so he could work out how badly his career was going to suffer once she was arrested.

However, when Beatrix slipped onto the chair the split of her trench coat opened revealing a tantalising glimpse of stocking-clad leg and a milky-white band of flesh at the top of her thigh. Trying to resist the surge of desire that thrilled inside him, Jim nodded abrupt acceptance of her order and elbowed his way to the front of the bar.

He figured it was relatively safe leaving Beatrix alone for a moment. It looked like she was the only woman in the mezzanine bar, which made her easy to spot. Even if she made a break for it and started to run, there were CCTV cameras all over the place that would let him know where she was. On top of that, his officers at the front and back doors of the hotel were familiar with her appearance and had instructions to hold her if she tried to leave the building.

"So," Jim said, handing Beatrix her bourbon and slipping into the seat facing her. "What happened?"

At first, she said nothing. She simply lifted the glass, placed it against her perfectly painted lips, and sipped at the golden liquid. After allowing herself a moment to savour the taste, her throat muscles briefly tightened. Jim could imagine the liquid sliding down her esophagus as she released a small sigh of satisfaction. When she stared at him her eyes were bright with excitement. "I promise you now," she told him. "As bad as this looks, worse things have happened. And we both know, too often, Wilkins has been the cause of those worse things."

"You said that before," he reminded her. "But you've not given me anything to support the idea."

"The media hype was big for Wilkins's arrest," she reminded him. "But it's going to be like nothing compared to what will happen now."

"What happened?" Jim asked, aware that he had posed the question several times now and was still waiting for an answer.

"Wilkins was first arrested a month ago," Beatrix told him, placing her glass on a coaster emblazoned with the hotel's name. "But you lot have known about him for years."

Jim had the good grace to blush. "There have been suspicions," he admitted. "But it's misleading to say we've known about him."

Beatrix lowered the glasses to the tip of her nose and peered over them as she studied his face. Her features wore the expression of a disappointed school mistress. "Wilkins's name was mentioned a decade ago in a report about sex trafficking."

"A lot of people were mentioned in that report," Jim reminded her. "Many of them have been proved innocent over the years. There didn't seem to be any point in destroying careers unnecessarily."

She pushed the glasses back up the bridge of her nose and shook her head disdainfully. "Have you read the report?" she asked, taking another sip from her large bourbon. "Did you notice that senior police officers made sure that Wilkins's name was redacted from every published transcript?"

"Redaction isn't unusual," Jim assured her.

"Did you know the transcripts were redacted by a mason from Wilkins's lodge?"

Jim closed his eyes and shook his head.

"Have you ever wondered how he's managed to secure so many super-injunctions?" Beatrix asked. "Don't the words 'cover up' ever cross that pedestrian little policeman mind of yours?"

Jim opened his mouth to argue each of her points, but Beatrix continued to speak before he could respond.

"Despite all the super-injunctions, one of the tabloids did an exposé on him and his links to the sex and drug trades the year after the sex-trafficking report." Whilst he couldn't see her eyes, the tilt of her head made him think that she was staring at him with venomous intensity. "Did you ever read that?"

"I read it," Jim admitted. "And I also read the retraction they printed after a court case where Wilkins received record damages." He paused to take a sip from his own bottle of beer and said, "You do know, when they print those retractions, it's usually a sign that the story was made up and should never have been published in the first place?"

Beatrix shrugged. "That's one of the reasons why retractions are printed," she admitted. "One of the other reasons retractions occur happens when someone with power and authority, and a vested interest in concealing the truth, puts pressure on the publisher." She held up a finger, stopping him from interrupting, and added, "I recall that the information supporting that retraction came from one of Wilkins's lodge colleagues who happened to work at Scotland Yard." Her smile was cold as she asked, "Do you remember that detail?"

"Is that where you're going with this?" Jim wondered. "Masonic conspiracy theories?" He laughed drily and asked, "Was Wilkins Jack the Ripper as well?"

"Call it a conspiracy theory, if you want," she allowed. "Whatever you call it, it doesn't change the fact that Wilkins belongs to the same masonic lodge as the man who produced evidence to support Wilkins's claims of innocence."

"Masonic conspiracy theories," Jim sighed. "That's why you killed him?" He took a long swig from his bottle of beer and then shook his head. The shit was going to hit the fan in a spectacular way. He felt as though the beer was helping him celebrate the end of what had, for a while, been a rewarding career.

A Gunners supporter asked if he could take the third chair from their table and Jim nodded consent. Beatrix sipped her bourbon in silence. The chatter around them echoed hollowly because of the mezzanine's funky acoustics. Some of the sounds from the lobby reached them more loudly than conversation from adjacent tables in the bar. It made for a heady experience that didn't help Jim to feel calm or ready to accept his fate. He watched a trio of paramedics run into the hotel lobby below and then disappear inside one of the lifts.

Jim figured he knew where they were going.

A crackle in his earpiece made him start with surprise. One of the officers on the main door was asking for him. Jim tore the device from his ear and throat and pushed it into his pocket. He would communicate with his team when he was ready: not before.

When Jim next turned to face Beatrix she opened her lips, as though she had been waiting for him to glance at her. "Five years ago, the FBI tried to have Wilkins extradited to the states."

"And he wasn't extradited because the case against him had no substance."

"He wasn't extradited," Beatrix contradicted, "because a lodge colleague in the home office refused to authorise the extradition."

Jim shook his head. "More masonic conspiracy theories?"

"No," she said quickly. "It's the same masonic conspiracy theory as I mentioned each time before. Wilkins has a masonic brother, or a family of masonic brothers, looking out for him."

Jim studied her without saying a word. He had a friend who said that arguing with conspiracy theorists was like playing chess with a pigeon, in that it knocks the pieces over, shits all over the board, and still struts around as though it was victorious. He groaned at the idea of his career going down the pan because of a conspiracy theory.

Beatrix fixed Jim with a challenging stare and said, "And now he's been arrested because of the Walsh sisters."

Jim couldn't argue with that. The story of the three Walsh sisters was a national tragedy. Two of them were dead. All of them had been the victims of sexual assault. And the one who hadn't died was on life support in a vegetative state.

The buzz on social media suggested that one of the Walsh sisters was a former victim of Wilkins's, and she was building an airtight case against him. But no one appeared to know which of the sisters this was. And, curiously, none of the usual newspapers had picked up on this as a story.

There was CCTV footage of Wilkins visiting the media offices where the Walsh sisters were working. There were mobile phone recordings, images, and sound of Wilkins beating the eldest Walsh sister to death whilst one of the others tried to pull him away. There was the testimony of an emergency services operator who had overheard one of the Walsh women begging Wilkins to leave her sister alone. Forensic evidence, including fingerprints, blood, and semen samples, was sufficient to ensure Walsh's conviction.

Yet it seemed, because of his connections, Wilkins wasn't going to be convicted. In return for his testimony, which would help to identify several of those who had escaped the original sex-trafficking charges, and for the information he could give incriminating the main profiteers from a drug cartel that he'd been involved with, Wilkins looked set to escape prosecution.

Jim could understand Beatrix's righteous anger but, as a police officer, he couldn't condone such a vigilante approach to justice. "Are you telling me you've just decided to take the law into your own hands and kill Wilkins because of this latest atrocity?" he asked eventually.

"Not at all," Beatrix laughed. "I decided to kill him when a group of people offered me a substantial amount of money in return for putting a bullet in Wilkins's head."

Jim studied her sullenly. "How the hell do you think you're going to get away with it?"

Instead of answering his question, Beatrix finished the last of her bourbon and then chased her tongue along her lips as she treated him to a smile. When she leant forward, he could see the enticing shape of her cleavage, forced up through her balconette bra. The flesh of her breasts looked milky, plump, and irresistible.

"You're going to get into trouble for what I've done, aren't you?"

Jim thought she was understating the severity of his problems. He would be a laughingstock. Not only would he be out of a job, but the tabloids would string him up by the balls and beat him like a piñata.

She moved closer and placed a hand on his knee. Pushing her mouth close to his ear, speaking in a sultry whisper that was barely audible over the clamour of conversation from the football supporters around them, she said, "I need to make this up to you."

She wore a perfume of honeysuckle and violets, a smell that was light and innocent in contrast to the piquant tang of the bourbon on her breath. Even more exciting was the lingering scent of her beneath those aromas: the taste of her perspiration, nervousness, and sexual excitement.

Her fingers lingered on his knee for a moment before slipping softly upwards. He could feel the weight of her caress on his thigh as her hand moved slowly higher and closer to his crotch.

"What are you doing, Beatrix?"

"I'm thanking you," she mumbled. Her fingers traced the shape of his thickening hardness through his pants. The glasses had slipped down her nose again and, this time, her eyes met his with a shine of eager need. "Do you want me to thank you?" she asked.

He hesitated for the longest moment.

What he wanted was a time machine that would take him back to earlier in the day, before he had been asked to organise the procurement of a prostitute for a protected witness who was supposed to be involved with sex trafficking, drugs, and sexual assault charges. If he'd been able to take such a trip, he would have maintained his resolve, told his boss that, despite the promise of potential promotion, he still did not think it was acceptable to expect a Detective Inspector to act as a pimp. Such a refusal would have meant that Beatrix never got invited to the hotel and that would have meant his career was not being flushed down the pan.

But Beatrix wasn't offering him a time machine. She was only offering her gratitude and Jim figured that was the best offer he was going to get this evening.

He drained the last of his beer and said, "You want to thank me?"

"Would you like that?"

He nodded. "I'd like that very much," he told her.

Laughing, Beatrix snatched his hand and dragged him out of his chair. She pulled a path easily for the pair of them through the scarlet and white shirts of the bar's customers, urging Jim to follow her to the toilets.

He wanted to refuse. He wanted to tell her that, whilst it would be nice to see her gratitude, he had never had any desire to experience sex in public toilets. Before he could form that thought into words, she had pulled him into the dimly lit room, slammed the door behind them, and then pushed him into a cubicle.

Jim had never wanted to have sex in public toilets, but Beatrix certainly showed him that his lack of imagination had been keeping him from some surprisingly pleasant experiences…

Afterward, he was sufficiently distracted that Beatrix had time to pull herself away from him and move out of the cubicle. Shaking the threat of weariness from his thoughts, he quickly stood up, fearful she would be trying to make an escape whilst he was still on the lavatory seat.

But Beatrix had made no attempt to run. He saw that she was standing on the sink that faced their cubicle and reaching above her head into a panel of the suspended ceiling. The trench coat was still on the floor of the cubicle they had used. She was wearing only her heels, stockings, thong, and bra. Jim watched as she shifted the suspended ceiling panel aside, pulled out a rucksack and dropped it on the floor.

"What the hell is that?" he asked.

She didn't reply. She made sure the ceiling tile was back in its proper place and then dropped nimbly to the floor. Opening the rucksack, she pulled out a pair of jeans, a sweatshirt, trainers, a cap and a large jacket. As Jim watched, Beatrix stripped off her stockings and heels, dropping them both into a wastebin, and pushed her way back into the cubicle they had used for sex. She closed the door behind herself.

"What are you doing?" he demanded.

"I'm saving your job," Beatrix explained. Her voice carried easily through the closed door. "The media would have a field day if they found out you were the one who hired a prostitute to visit Wilkins whilst he was in a hotel room waiting to give evidence."

Jim blushed. That worry had crossed his mind. It would likely be one of the main crosses on which he was crucified. "I'm not looking forward to that coming out," he admitted.

"That's not going to come out," she called cheerfully. "The agency that I work for will tie the original call back to a local masonic lodge. If anyone starts to investigate who ordered a hooker for Wilkins, the enquiry will throw so much shade on the Masons that Wilkins and myself will become inconsequential characters in the whole media circus."

Jim thought about this for a moment. He figured it was likely that her agency could make such a claim, and he knew that there were technologies that could change telephone information on official reports. Given the way she had been spouting masonic conspiracy theories earlier, it seemed plausible that she would happily throw lodge members under the bus. "OK," he said eventually. "That would leave me in the clear. But what about you?"

She laughed, a sound that was sufficiently innocent and charming to make him feel ready to grow hard again. "Oh! Sweetheart," she breathed. "I didn't know you cared."

Quashing his need for her, and unhappy to think she was mocking him, Jim said, "My officers know your name."

"No," she corrected. "They know the name I use with the agency."

"The agency will have to give up your address."

She laughed again. "The agency doesn't know my address."

"There's footage of you from all the CCTV in this building," he said eventually. "You're not even going to be able to make it out of the hotel."

"I think I might," she said, opening the cubicle door.

The transformation had been surprisingly efficient. She was wearing a dark red Gunners football shirt that matched those worn by most of the men in the bar. Her irresistible legs were hidden beneath a pair of shapeless jeans and her scarlet heels had been replaced by a pair of androgynous trainers. When she donned a zip-up hoodie and baseball cap she looked sufficiently androgynous to pass for the twin of any of the Gooners he had seen in the bar this evening.

"You came in here with a glamorous looking hooker," Beatrix explained. "And you're going to leave alone. The glamorous hooker has disappeared forever."

"And how are you getting out?"

"Over the next half hour, a handful of those football supporters will visit and I'll simply step out with them. The CCTV footage will show two or three Gooners coming in and three or four leaving. I doubt anyone will notice the anomaly."

"And you've done all of that for this paltry sum of money?" he asked, holding up the briefcase.

"Of course not," she laughed. "That money is for you, to compensate you for the inconvenience of having to cover up for me and maybe miss out on the next promotion available." Her grin broadened as she added, "My payment is far more substantial and sitting in an offshore tax haven, waiting for me to turn up there and start to spend it."

"This isn't right," Jim said eventually. "You should have simply left justice to take its course."

"Yeah," she agreed, pulling the brim of the baseball cap over her face. "The way justice has taken its course with all of Wilkins's other crimes." She grinned and added, "This looks bad. But I promise you now: as bad as this looks, worse things have happened." She was interrupted by four football supporters walking into the toilets and squeezing between her and Jim. He didn't see when she disappeared, or how she made it out of the room without him seeing. But he heard the words she hadn't spoken: "Too often, Wilkins has been the cause of those worse things." That unspoken sentiment made him think, on this occasion, things had probably worked out for the best.

Haunt Me

by Michael A. Gonzales

R oger "Chunky" Ellison's first memory was the odor of Big Daddy's cigar smoke as his grandfather stood over the playpen. Chunky was two years old when the towering man, his daddy's daddy, stared down at him as particles of ash fell in the crib and thick smoke twirled towards the ceiling. Twenty years later, standing in the TWA check-in line at New Orleans International Airport, Chunky was returning to his hometown of Peterson, Virginia after four years away playing football at Tulane University. Folks in Peterson started calling him Chunky from when he was the high school football champ. It pained him to think of those long-gone days that were filled with promise and possibilities. After a triumphant season and winning a scholarship to Tulane, he'd strutted out of town prideful as a rooster in a house full of hens, but was returning broke, busted, and disgusted.

His first three years in college was all about touchdowns and pussy, but senior year it all came crashing down. The massive players that smashed him as he ran for a touchdown were built like buildings with feet. That frigid day he was carried off of the football field with a few broken bones and a damaged spirit, Chunky was rushed to the hospital and, just that fast, his glory days were over. No longer was he the kind of champion Queen once sung about; he was just another sullen faced guy with a troubled mind and broken bones.

For three months, when he should've been preparing to graduate and beginning life as a running back, he stayed in hospital. His mother and father called every day, but he hadn't heard one word from Big Daddy. After the accident, it seemed as though the old man simply lost interest in him. Even when Chunky reached out to say he was returning to Peterson, he never heard back one way or the other.

***

Big Daddy used to watch Chunky practice almost every afternoon at Peterson High. From the time he was a pee-wee player to his transformation into a well-toned teenager, Big Daddy stood on the sidelines and swelled with pride as the boy got bigger, better, and tougher with each passing season. Chunky's plan was to put Peterson on the map with his skills on the field. He wanted to make his family proud, but especially Big Daddy, who funded his entire sporting life since the beginning.

A widower, Big Daddy was a handsome chestnut brown man who stood over six feet. He had muscular arms and a chest broad enough to land a helicopter on. A former college football star, his real gift was wheeling and dealing in the real estate business. A natural at negotiating contracts and transactions, over the years he built a thriving firm that owned much of the Black neighborhoods in Peterson.

Big Daddy owned many rental properties including stores, apartment buildings, and empty lots. When Chunky was a kid, he often rode shotgun with him to collect rents. When Big Daddy stepped out of his shiny Cadillac, folks greeted him as though he was the mayor. They offered him tall glasses of iced tea or short shots of moonshine. "See you got your grandson with you today. Boy gettin' big." Smiling down at Chunky, someone might ask him, "You going to be as big and handsome as Big Daddy when you grow up?" His grandfather smiled proudly and rubbed the boy's curly head.

***

After three hours on the plane, Chunky walked sluggishly through the airport. He passed kissing couples and screaming children. Clad in rumbled black jeans, a slightly wrinkled black button-down shirt and black shoes, he turned right at the end of the corridor and stepped onto the silver escalator. He saw his father James, a tall quiet man with copper colored complexion, leaning against the wall. With his thin frame and somber manner, James was haggard as an undertaker.

Seconds before he reached the luggage carousel, his father looked up and smiled. He rushed to his boy and gave Chunky a big hug. "It's good to see you, son." Minutes later, they were headed to the car. After throwing his luggage into the neatest trunk he'd ever seen, Chunky climbed into the rusty old Ford that had been in the family for years.

"Are you all right, son?"

"Who knows that I'm coming back?"

"Everybody in town knows, I suppose. Your momma's mouth ain't a refrigerator, you know. I hope you know, Chunky, nobody blames you for anything. Getting hurt was a terrible thing, but you're home now, son and we're proud of you. You remember that."

"Does Jenny know?"

"She might son…she might. You know, a lot of things changed in Peterson, people too. The girl you left behind four years ago, she a woman now."

***

In his suitcase there were plenty of pictures of Chunky standing next to his pretty ex-girl Jenny Youngblood. Often clad in fashionable 1940s-styled dresses that she bought at the Goodwill and restored to mint condition, back in high school Jenny was Olive Oyl skinny, with long legs and juicy lips. Then there was her sweet, always-wearing-Jean-Nate smell that she thought was fancy.

Jenny was an energetic, smile-bright cheerleader when she and Chunky met sophomore year. They spent hours together at school, church, and on the football field. Coming from good stock, her daddy worked for the government while her buxom mama provided the perfect home. Still, Chunky knew that Big Daddy wasn't a fan. "Don't let that girl distract you from what's important," he told him often.

Jenny too had big dreams. Sitting on the couch, she'd glance over at Chunky and suddenly start talking about living in New York City, where she'd be a fashion model. "I want to be somewhere where I can hang out at one of those chic nightclubs that I read about in *Vogue*." Jenny's words came in a rush of excitement. "I'll be dressed in furs and boas, living in a beautiful penthouse with you, my professional football player husband. And we'll have maids and dinner parties and a Christmas tree bigger than the one in Rockefeller Center."

"What's so special about New York anyway?" Chunky asked.

Sweetly, Jenny pinched his cheek. "I can't believe you. I'm not trying to be a small-town girl for the rest of my life."

"Don't let that girl distract you from what's important," he heard his grandfather's voice in his head, but that didn't stop them from becoming lovers. Jenny had been his first and he hers. That first time they drove two counties over to a motel where they wouldn't be seen.

The Lysol-smelling room at the Capri Motel was tacky as hell with a mirrored ceiling, but, as Sade sang "Haunt Me" on the radio they fumbled around with each other's clothes and private parts until they figured it out. For both of them, it was as though a beast had been released, and they snuck out to the motel every week. Room 108 became their personal haven away from the world.

Chunky left for college in August of 1984. Between starting classes and football practice, he began hanging with the big dogs on campus, pledged Kappa and began shedding his small-town skin. Still, he talked to Jenny often and still loved her. She stayed local, taking classes at Peterson Community College while hoping Chunky would propose over Christmas vacation. For months she bought every wedding magazine on the newsstand and made no secret that when her man went to the NFL, she would be on his arm with a big diamond on her finger.

Coming home for Christmas break his freshman year, he and Jenny agreed to meet at Red's Tavern. Chunky walked out of his parents' house and was surprised to see Big Daddy sitting in his Cadillac listening Dinah Washington's "This Bitter Earth." Chucky walked over to the window. "I didn't know you were coming by. I'm headed over to see Jenny."

"That's what I want to talk to you about, boy. Get in the car." Chunky knew he was too old for a beating from the old man, but he was still afraid of him. Without asking why, he got in the ride and Big Daddy sped off. "Do you know that fool girl is going around town telling people ya'll going to get married?"

Chunky laughed. "I haven't even asked her yet. I was going to ask her tonight."

"You'll do no such thing. We've worked too hard to get to where you are. You don't need to get caught up in some fool girl's spider's web. And God forbid she gets pregnant. Then what? Worry about getting into the NFL, don't worry about some small-town bitch."

"She's not a bitch. You've known Jenny and her family for years, so stop acting like she's not good enough."

"Good enough for what? In a couple of years, you'll be a very rich young man, and I plan on helping to manage you the way I've been managing you since you were a kid. You're not getting married, period." Big Daddy pulled up in front of Red's Tavern. Chucky sat for a few minutes, boiling mad but trying not to show it. He reached into his pocket, removed a small ring box, and slammed it on the dashboard.

Chunky climbed the staircase that led to the front door. Clouds of cigarette smoke billowed through the air as Al Green's "Love and Happiness" blared from the jukebox. The décor looked like it hadn't changed since Nixon was in the White House. Taking its name quite seriously, the bar was decorated in various shades of red. "Hey, Chunky," the man the joint was named after stood behind the bar with a burnt red complexion and dirty red hair. "Welcome back, kid. You still drinking milk?"

"Very funny, Red, but the drinking age is eighteen and I need something stronger than milk. Better make it a rum and coke."

Red's son Hawk stood next to him. Fernando was the boy's real name. "What up, Hawk?" The lanky boy nodded his chin forward. Back in high school, Hawk was one of those wanna-be tough guys screaming rap lyrics in the lunchroom and banging beats on the table as "White Lines" blared.

Red placed the drink on the bar and Chunky took a healthy swallow. "Here's to courage," he said, rising his glass before chugging some more. Without asking, Red refilled the glass and said, "You better slow down, kid. What you need courage for anyway?" Red smiled devilishly. "You plan on asking that pretty Jenny to marry you?"

For a second, as he thought about Big Daddy's demand, Chunky got sullen, but then he smiled as though life was wonderful. "Marry me? I ain't getting married, lest not now. Fact is I was planning on doing just the opposite." He walked across the room and sat down at the far end of the room by the black curtained window. The table was covered with a red tablecloth. Chunky sat his drink next to a black ashtray. Minutes later Jenny walked in dressed in stylish winter boots and formfitting black and red sweater dress.

Chunky could smell her perfume before Jenny got to the table and he stood. "Chunky," Jenny hugged him tightly. "I missed you so much," she whispered seductively, biting his left lobe. If she had known what was coming, she might've bit it off. All was cool for the first twenty minutes, but suddenly a ghastly shriek filled the bar and Jenny began to cry. "You bastard, you fucking bastard!" She jumped from her seat. Turning around, she picked up an empty highball glass and threw it at Chunky's head. It missed by a mile, but her intention was quite clear.

***

Exiting the freeway, his father turned down a block of boarded-up homes, liquor stores, and a greasy Chinese joint. Chunky glared angrily at the crumbling houses. He hated seeing Peterson so broken down. "You all right?" his father asked. Sadly, Chunky nodded, but his heart sank further when they drove through the block where he first learned to play football. The old field as well as the three neighboring houses had been replaced by seven connecting low-income buildings that stretched from corner to corner.

Each building was three stories with four apartments on each floor. In front dirt patches was littered with cigarette butts, candy wrappers, discarded beer bottles and whatever else was blown up from the gutters or thrown out of the windows. "Damn," James mumbled when they were stopped by a red light. "I hate getting stuck at this corner. Makes me sad, seeing these kids always out here selling that stuff."

When his daddy talked about "that stuff," he was referring to the crack business that had cropped up in Peterson since he's been gone. While most folks had thought of crack and the zooted zombies that puffed it as a big city problem, the hyped-up drug soon travelled into hick hoods down south and left more devastation than locusts.

"Didn't Big Daddy used to own this land over here? Why did he sell it?"

"For money. The same reason he does anything." Outside the car window, small children screamed as they played a few feet away from where their older brothers were gathered looking like some kind of outlaw posse. Chunky noticed a man wearing a blue tracksuit, matching Gucci framed sunglasses, gold chains, and virgin white sneakers. He looked as though he had just stepped out of a hip-hop video, but his swagger hinted at a threat of violence.

"That's one man I would like to see gone," James said, and sucked his teeth. On second look, Chunky realized he knew the dude. "That's the bastard bringing down Peterson one crack vial at a time."

"I went to school with him," Chucky said. "That's Red's son Fernando. We used to call him Hawk."

"They still called Hawk, except his nest has gotten bigger. Red barely got anything to do with that boy anymore. Had him working at the bar and the little rascal was dealing cocaine from behind it. Can you believe that?"

"The sins of the son."

"It's more than a few sins, that boy is the devil. He the one running all the stuff in Peterson, now I hear he's opening a strip club called Bottoms Up. That boy is big trouble." With Hawk's high top fade hairstyle and neatly trimmed goatee, he carried himself with arrogant authority. People on the street looked at him with an awed mixture of fear and respect. Chunky stared as he climbed into his silver 300e Mercedes.

Still, nothing prepared him for the next second seeing a striking woman dressed in the stylish vintage summer dress and purple pumps that highlighted her fine stewardess legs. The full-figured goddess had swaying hips and ice sucking lips. Flicking a long curly weave out of her pretty face, she stood next to the stylish ride and slowly removed her Chanel sunglasses. It was at that moment that Chunky realized that the woman was his old girl, Jenny Youngblood.

"Goddamnit," Chucky yelled. "Jenny is his woman?"

"They're together a lot, but I don't know their business, son. Way I see it, that isn't your business anymore either."

At that moment, Jenny turned around. She did a double take and looked directly into Chunky's eyes. Silent, but deadly, she stared Uzi bullets into his heart. Her eyes were cold while also transmitting joy for his obvious misery. Finally, after a million years, the light changed.

A mile from the shabby housing projects, James made a sharp right and pulled into the driveway of his beautiful house. The once large house where he was raised looked so small now. Taking a few deep breaths, Chunky got out of the car. Standing in the window with her freshly done hair, pearls, and a crisply ironed dress, his mother wept joyfully.

Carrie finally came outside. For a second, he stood in front of his mother, not knowing what to say. Leaning over, he kissed her lightly on the cheek. "Your hair smells like biscuits and gravy," he said. Carrie slapped him on the arm and smiled.

"That's because I've been in the kitchen slaving all day just for you." Wrapping her thin arms around Chunky's thick frame, she said, "Feels like you lost a little weight. We gonna change that."

Chunky was often amused at the façade of happiness his mother shrouded over herself when things were bad. Whenever anything rattled her cage, she put that nervous energy into cooking. Walking across the carpeted floor,

Chunky cut through the dining room next to the staircase. He saw roast beef, spinach, potatoes, pickled beets, and a boat of gravy.

Upstairs, Chunky felt like a stranger in his old room where posters of Lawrence Taylor and Vanity Six hung on the wall. He changed clothes for dinner. Walking down the stairs, he heard his parents whispering. Chunky cleared his throat loudly and walked down the rest of the steps.

With all the food on the table, as well as glasses of iced tea, they joined hands as James led the family in prayer. Afterwards, Carrie piled food on Chunky's plate as though he'd just returned from a hunger strike. "I saw Jenny today," he said looking at his mother. "She didn't seem surprised to see me. You tell her I was coming back."

"What are you talking about? Peterson is a small town and you're an important person in this place."

"I'm a loser, ma."

"I don't have any losers in my family, boy. Not a one."

"Saw her new man too. Good to see she's moved up in the world."

"Don't forget, son, you're the one that broke it off with her. Who she dates is her business." Their conversation was minimal as Chunky tore into the food, but, after his second plate, his mother asked, "So, have you thoughts about what you want to do now that you're home?"

"Not really. I got a little cash saved; thought I would find a place to live first."

"A place to live? You already have a place to live. I left your room basically the way you left it. It's a little neater, but it's still the same.

"No offence, but I'm not trying to live in my old bedroom. I'll crash there for the next few days, but by next week I want to be gone."

"We understand that, son," his father said. "If that's what you want that's what you want. But, let me tell you what we want; we want you to come and work at the store with us."

"I don't know about all that."

"What is there to know? You grew up in there, been seeing me order from the wholesalers, haggling with the delivery men. You know your way around that store as well as you know anything."

"What your father is trying to say is trying to say is, the store is a family business. We know all is this going to be a heck of an adjustment, but we family and that store is as much your business as it is ours. We can't pay you much, but it's Peterson, you don't really need much."

"Can I think about it?" he asked.

Carrie gave him the mama side-eye, and smiled. "You do that, son. You think about it, but when we open back up on Monday morning, I pray in Christ's name that you're standing next to me at that counter." Everyone sitting at that table knew that come Monday morning, Chunky would be in that store next to his family.

Before they finished eating the doorbell rang, and his parents glanced at one another and smiled. James bounced up from his chair to open the door. Though out of sight, Chunky smelled the cigar smoke before he heard his granddaddy's booming voice. Seconds later, he stood in front of Chunky and stared at him. "Can't you stand, boy, and greet your Pop-Pop right?"

Chucky laughed nervously. He got up slowly from his seat and hugged the old man tightly. Instead of returning the hug, Big Daddy patted him on the back. When Chunky finally let go, Big Daddy sat at the head of the table and glared at him. "How you been, boy?"

"Better, now that you're here. I thought you were mad at me."

Bitterly, the old man laughed. "I'm not mad, boy, just disappointed. You would think at this point I would be used to my children disappointing me."

"Dad, please, that's not necessary."

Big Daddy stared at James and screamed, "You're no help, you know. All the work and money I invested in this kid, and he still winds up weak as you. I was hoping that *punk* gene skipped a generation, but I guess not." Full of anger, Big Daddy smashed his fists on the table. "Both of you are pathetic." He rose from the chair. Without uttering another word, Big Daddy stormed out of the house. Chucky looked at his shocked parent's faces and, holding back the tears, slowly shook his head.

***

The days moved swiftly, and, before he knew it, he had been back three weeks. Chunky worked at the store and rented a studio apartment a few blocks away. From behind the store's counter, he could see pity for him in the eyes of friends who happened by the store, mostly for cigarettes and beer. Beneath the counter his father kept a loaded nine-millimeter that Chunky often thought stealing to blow a hole in his head. But suicide was more of a fantasy than an option.

Instead, he simply stood behind that counter facing old acquaintances, elders from church, and other random folks. Everyone came in the store, except Jenny. Since seeing her that first day back, he thought about her every night as he lay in his single bed and imagined her sexiness next to him. Eyes closed, he stroked himself gently, picking up speed as the imaginary Jenny snaked her up his body with the charm of a cobra.

Three days later, the snake finally slithered through the front door of the store. She looked at him and sneered. "Never thought I'd see you in this town again, unless they was throwing you a parade while you were showing off your Super Bowl ring." Dressed in a tight black dress with a white collar and bejeweled pumps, she looked like she had just stepped out of Chunky's wet dream.

"I'm sure you heard about my accident."

Jenny sucked her pretty teeth. "Don't bring that mess to me Chunky. Everybody in town knows what happened to you. Half of them laughed when they heard about, said it served you right for being so cocky."

"I was a football player; I was trained to be cocky."

"Were you also trained to be an asshole? Were you trained to treat your woman like she was nothing? I gave you my heart and my virginity, and you shit on me. Then, karma shit on you."

"Karma, huh? What happened to New York City? I thought you wanted to be a model not some crack dealer's bitch. At least I tried to get out of this town. All you did was fall into the arms of some tired drug dealer. Does he pay you well?"

The sharp slap across Chunky's face was firecracker loud. Chunky closed his eyes just as everyone in the store stared, shocked, but by the time he opened his eyes, she was gone.

***

After nightfall, Chunky laid on the small bed in the low-ceiled apartment listening to soul ballads on the radio. Staring at the ceiling, he got lost looking at a large water stain. Reaching over to the worn wooden night table, he took a sip of brandy. Suddenly, there was a knock on his door. Chunky wasn't expecting company, but he thought maybe his mama was bringing him some dinner.

Opening the door, he was shocked to see Jenny standing there wearing a mink coat, a flowered dress, and heels. She pushed past him and walked into the stuffy room. Carrying a plastic shopping bag, she put it on the table and removed a bottle of Johnnie Walker Black. "I wanted to say I was sorry. I lost my temper today. I shouldn't have slapped you."

"It's all right. Sometimes I forget how much of an asshole I've been to you. That slap reminded me." Walking over to the small sink, Jenny took two glasses from the dish rack. Chucky screwed off the top and poured a generous amount. For a long time, they were both silent. Leaning over, he kissed her tenderly and then abruptly stopped.

Dramatically, he looked her in the eyes as though searching for deeper meaning. Kissing her again, he pulled Jenny close and embraced her with all his strength. He believed that she had forgiven him, and she was ready to be his woman once again. As if they had made a request, Sade's sweet and sorrowful "Haunt Me" came on the radio. With its crying guitar, sad piano, and the singer's melancholy voice, they were transported back to their first intimate night together.

"Haunt me in my dreams if you please/your breath is with me now and always/it's like a breeze," Sade sang as Jenny and Chunky slow danced across the dusty floor. Seconds later Jenny and Chunky were on top of the bed making love. It was a sweaty and passionate night that led to a sweaty and passionate month. For the next thirty days, she was slipping between his sheets.

They talked about the past, but rarely the present. She didn't like talking about her life outside of his apartment.

"What about Hawk?" he asked her their second week together.

"What about him?"

"Hasn't he noticed that you've been slipping away?"

"Hawk just opened a strip club out on the highway. As long as I get home before him, we're cool. Why?"

"I just wanted to know."

"You trying to call me a hoe?"

"I said nothing like that."

"You don't have to say 'nothing like that,' I'm not stupid. I know what you're trying to say and I don't appreciate it."

"Can you please calm down?"

"Fuck calm down. You just watch how you talk to me. Don't treat me like a hoe." Sex was always the hottest after an argument, and that night theirs sizzled. Jenny didn't like being treated like a hoe, but between the sheets she didn't have a problem becoming one.

***

A month later, when she thought Chunky was asleep, Jenny quickly got dressed and crept out of the apartment. Her car was parked across the street. As he did every night, Chunky put his face to the window and watched as she gracefully walked to her BMW. The town was dead and the streets were deserted, but that night a car sped up, screeched to a stop, and fired shots at Jenny. "Oh, God, no," Chunky yelled and quickly dashed downstairs.

Jenny was sprawled on the ground crying. Chunky dropped down beside her. "Did they shoot you? Were you hit?" On the quiet street, Jenny's cries were loud, but thankfully she wasn't hurt. Chunky stood up, picked her up from the ground and carried her back to his apartment. She was still crying when he laid her down on the bed. Chunky went to the dresser and retrieved a pack of Newport's and lit two. He put one between Jenny's quivering lips.

"Well, at least now we know that he knows," Chunky blurted. He took a deep breath. "Now what?"

"We should runaway together," she said. Chunky, figuring she was joking, chuckled. "I'm serious."

"Yeah? And what are we going to do for money? I don't imagine either of us has much savings."

"Why you got to say it like that?"

"Because, it's true. Where you think we going to go, anyway?"

"New York City. We used to dream about going to New York, so let's go now while we're still young."

"We going to need more than dreams if we're going to survive."

"It don't have to be New York, it could Chicago or Los Angeles. I just want to live in a big city in a tall building that touches the sky. A place where there are fancy stores, nice restaurants."

"Who we going to rob to fund that fantasy?" he asked aloud. He said it as a joke, but it got serious real quick. And then, the answer came to him clearly. "I suppose we could always rip off Big Daddy."

***

Business was Big Daddy's passion over everything else. Many a Saturday evening, after taking Chunky to football practice, he drove down to the converted barn that he bought cheap years before. The paper-cluttered office was on the outskirts of town. Though most of Big Daddy's businesses were in the city, he preferred having the office located far from the prying eyes of the locals. Most had no idea where it was located. But, in his small-town way, Big Daddy was lax in terms of security: no cameras, no guard dogs.

Most of the time, Chunky just watched Big Daddy going over ledgers, reading contracts and stuffing the big cast iron floor safe with cash. Many of his renters who didn't have bank accounts paid Big Daddy in cash. In the beginning of the month there was always a lot of money in the safe. Sometimes Chunky helped Big Daddy, who had given him the combination years before. When they finished, it was Chunk's job to make sure the safe was locked.

"Any man would be a crazy to steal from me, but I'm not trying to tempt these fools either." Afterwards, he'd drive Chunky home and then headed to Red's for a few night caps. Though he didn't leave until last call, come Sunday morning Big Daddy was always the first inside the sanctuary of Grace Baptist Church. He was always refined, elegant, and sharp as a tack as he stood proudly next to his family.

***

Over the next few hours, Chucky and Jenny talked about the money and the possibilities of their future together. "We have to do this quick. By tonight, this town is not going to be safe for either one of us," he said. Chunky reasoned that the following night would be the best time to do the job. It was a rush, but they had no choice. It the first of the month and that's when the rent cash would be there.

"I'm sure there will be at least $20,000 in there."

"I'll go with you," Jenny whispered in his ear. She had a way of telling him to do things that he later thought was his own idea. "Then we'll just head straight out of town and keep on moving."

"I'll take the car out early and get what we need from the hardware store." They got in the bed, but neither slept.

That day at work, Chunky tried not to act as though anything was wrong. He eyeballed the nine-millimeter and, when he was sure his parents weren't paying attention, he slipped it in his pants pocket, which was covered by his grocer's smock. He and Jenny hadn't discussed guns, but better safe than sorry, he reasoned.

With his back to counter, he heard a strange voice behind say, "Yo, kid, get me a pack of Kools."

Chunky pulled down the cigarettes and turned around to place them on the counter. He damn near jumped out of his skin when he saw Hawk's smiling face. "Damn, Chunky, I didn't recognize you. Been home long?"

"Few weeks."

"Cool." Hawk tossed a five-dollar bill on the counter. "Let me get a pack of matches." Chunky hated that gangster smirk on Hawk's face. At the door, the bastard turned around. "I'll be seeing you around, Chunky," he said and winked.

Chunky felt as though his blood was flowing backwards, but he wasn't no punk. "Not if I see you first, Hawk…not if I see you first." When the hood walked out, Chunky's father asked, "What was that all about?"

"Nothing, Dad. Nothing."

Jenny had stayed at the apartment, but when Chunky returned, he didn't mention his encounter with Hawk. He sat down on the bed next her. Though Jenny was dressed in the same clothes, she had showered and was wearing makeup. You would've thought they were going out on a date instead of ripping off a safe. A part of him was beginning to regret planning it. Who was he to rob Big Daddy just because he was mad at the old man?

"What's that look on your face?" Jenny asked.

"I've been thinking?"

"Thinking? Thinking about what?"

"Tonight."

"It's too late to think about tonight. Better you think about tomorrow or the day after that. Tonight is already been set into motion. Tonight is spoken for." Her strength turned him on. He felt the fire in his loins, a flutter in his heart. "Get it together, because in one hour we going to be on a fantastic journey."

They headed out at eight o'clock. Chunky insisted on driving. On either side of the highway were farms, fast food spots, strip malls and private houses. At some point the neon and white light signs disappeared, and he drove by the glow of the moon. For the next twenty minutes they rode in silence until they reached Big Daddy's barn. Slowing down, Chunky pulled into the lot and cut the lights.

Jenny laughed. "You scared?"

"Of course I'm scared. You not?"

"I'm more scared of staying in that town for another day. If we go back, Hawk will still have us killed."

Chunky got out of the car carrying two knapsacks, walked over to the barn's front window and peered inside. There were bushes on either side of the door. He stuck his hand in a bush and found a rusty metal box that contained the front door key. He turned around and waved the box towards Jenny. She smiled and stepped out of the car. Chunky got the door open and they stepped inside. Jenny pulled a mini-flashlight out and they worked their way through the room.

The smell of Big Daddy's cigar smoke hung in the air. Even when he wasn't around, his presence was always there. They walked the length of the barn until they reached the main office, where the black floor safe was behind the desk. Chunky kneeled down in front and twirled the knob. "37-45-82-5," he mumbled to himself. But when he tried to open the door, it wouldn't budge.

"What would make you think the combination would still be the same."

"Fuck it, I'll be right back." Chunky walked out to the car. He opened the trunk where there was a new sledgehammer. He picked up the heavy hammer as though he was Thor and carried it back inside. When Jenny saw the hammer, she smiled. Chunky grunted as he wacked the safe door five times before the box finally bent and the door popped open.

Just as he expected, the safe was full of money. Unable to contain her excitement Jenny jumped up and started clapping. "We're not there yet, baby," Chunky said, throwing her one of the sacks. Within minutes they filled up the bags and, was back outside in seven. They tossed the bags in the back and jumped in the car.

Chunky revved the engine and put the pedal to the metal. A few miles down the highway, Chunky said, "I haven't had a workout like that in months. My body is sore as hell."

"You'll feel better when I rub you down with some of that money." They were both laughing when they saw the bright neon of the Capri Motel in the distance. It was Jenny's idea that they layover at their special place, the spot where they lost their innocence to one another in room 108.

"Baby, pull up in front of the door," Jenny said. Chunky pulled into the Capri parking lot, which was mostly empty. "I'll be right back." Chunky went to rent the room while Jenny pulled the knapsacks of money out of the car and waited by the motel door.

Walking back, Chunky felt a little swag slip into his steps. At that moment he was the happiest he'd been in years. A minute later he opened the door and stepped inside. He turned on the light and Jenny followed behind him. She tossed the knapsacks on the floor. Chunky plopped down on the bed. Jenny sat in his lap and leaned over to kiss him. She put her lips to his, but instead of smooching Jenny bit him hard as a snake.

A droplet of blood fell on the sheet.

"What the fuck," he screamed, as Jenny bounced off his lap. "What the hell is your problem?" Smiling crazy, she backed up to the wall. Behind him, Chunky heard the bathroom door open. "The party's over," a voice said. It was Hawk. "I'm through with sharing my lady with you."

Chunky looked at Jenny's smiling face. "I thought we were in love again."

"After what you did to me, you thought I could just forgive and forget?"

"But Hawk tried to kill you."

They both laughed. "If he had tried to kill me, I would be dead."

"So instead, you set me up?"

"I didn't set you up, I paid you back. Fuck you and your grandfather. I know it was him who forced you to kick me to the curb. Bastard got drunk in Red's a few nights later and bragged about everything he did to keep your weak ass away from me. He laughed and he bragged. Hawk heard it all."

"That was four years ago."

"And I've been haunted by it ever since. Now throw the car keys over here." From twenty feet away, Chunky tossed the keys and then Hawk fired at him five times; only three shots connected. Chunky fell to the floor. He was still conscious, not that they noticed. Jenny grabbed the bags and ran out the door, but the minute Hawk turned around Chunky reached for his gun and started blasting. Hawk's arms flew up as though he was trying to grab hold of the air. Evidently, gravity did its job.

Through the open door Chunky watched Jenny throw the bags of cash into her trunk. Slamming the lid, she walked towards the driver's side. Before getting in, she looked directly into Chunky's dying eyes and grinned. Putting her hand to her mouth, she threw him a kiss. Before closing his eyes permanently, the last thing Chunky smelled was Jenny Youngblood's sweet perfume.

The Night Walker
By Bernie Crosthwaite

Rachel started walking at night during the early days of the pandemic. It was extraordinarily quiet. There was no traffic at all, and without car fumes, the air tasted clean and sharp. And the sky…she had never seen the stars so clearly, or so many of them.

During the day she worked as an administrator for a pest control company. It was her job to deal with enquiry calls and emails, to organise the daily routes of the technicians, and to order supplies of chemicals. Callers were often upset, and she needed to calm them down and reassure them that the infestation of grey squirrels in their attic, the wasp nest in their garage, or the cockroaches in a restaurant kitchen could be dealt with. She prided herself on being efficient and reliable, even while working from home. She could have skived off whenever she wanted, but instead, she put in an eight-hour day with just short breaks for coffee and lunch.

Then after dinner, feeling restless and in need of exercise, Rachel stepped outside her front door and strode briskly up and down the street, head down, feeling nervous being out alone at night. Then she ventured a little further, to the next street and the next, along the rows of small-terraced houses.

She rarely saw anyone, just the occasional dog-walker or jogger, who would cross the road to avoid her, catching the infection being on everyone's mind. Gaining confidence, Rachel extended her routes as far as the park, or the new housing estate, or along the river path. And it wasn't just the pure air or the sparkling sky that she enjoyed. She liked to note the nightly habits of her near neighbours—the Simpsons in their bedroom by ten, light on, curtains closed; Noah in the box room he had turned into an artist's studio, working on his A Level art; Mrs. Singh working on her sewing machine in the front room, making beautiful dresses for her daughter who had taken up Irish dancing.

Further afield, where she didn't know anyone, Rachel was still curious about the lives of others, especially those who left their curtains open, such as the two young men curled up on the sofa watching TV, or the old gentleman grooming his cat, listening to loud classical music. Outside one house on the new estate, where the curtains were closed, she often heard raised voices, a man and a woman. She would stop and listen, but frustratingly, she could never decipher the actual words, the fierce passions muffled and distorted by brick walls. On a couple of occasions, she heard the woman cry out, as if in pain. Rachel walked on, counting her blessings that she no longer had to deal with a marriage gone sour and now lived alone.

On one of their occasional phone calls Rachel told her brother about it.

"You what? At night? Like a prostitute?"

Rachel laughed. "Martin, no one's going to pick me up. I'm too old."

"Some men have specialised tastes, you know."

"Don't worry about me. The truth is there's no one around at night. That's why it's so lovely."

"Seriously, I don't like the sound of it. There have been a couple of rapes recently, same guy we reckon, down by the canal."

Martin had worked for the police for many years. These days, he was a detective and had a dark view of human nature. He was planning an early retirement, tired of the ugly things he'd seen and the stress of the job. Rachel reassured him that she would avoid the canal path and was in no danger.

"Just be careful, OK?"

"I promise."

Her favourite route took her along Copper Beech Lane, a leafy cul-de-sac on the outskirts of town, where the detached houses were set well apart. As she walked to the end of the street, the darkness seemed deeper, the silence even more profound. Maybe it was the trees blocking the streetlights, or the dark hedges bordering the gardens, but Rachel always felt a slight sense of unease walking here. Despite her brother's warning, or maybe because of it, she found the sensation thrilling, as if she was an explorer of the unknown, experiencing a frisson of danger. It was an unusual sensation at a time when there was so little stimulation in her life, the lockdown having robbed her of almost all human interaction.

But Rachel wasn't venturing into unknown territory, quite the opposite in fact. She always stopped at the house at the end of the street. It was called

Windermere and her widowed aunt had lived here until she died a few years back. Rachel had visited her regularly, especially when she became infirm and completely housebound. Aunt Lily was actually her great aunt, and she was extremely old, nearly, but not quite, making it to her hundredth birthday.

Rachel was very fond of the house. She had occasionally wondered if her aunt would leave it to her in her will, a recognition of all the care she had given, the only one of her relatives to do so. But Aunt Lily had left everything to her estranged son, who duly turned up after his mother's death and sold the house for a vast sum.

The new owners—a young professional couple—had made a lot of changes: an extension over the garage, the front garden uprooted and replaced by gravel, new dark grey window frames instead of the old wooden ones, which Rachel had to admit, had been in a bad state. It was understandable that they wanted to update the place, but she couldn't help it—she hated the renovations.

She would stand outside the gate, contemplating the dark bulk of the house, then close her eyes and imagine it as it used to be. After a few moments she opened her eyes, before walking on with a satisfied sense of putting things right, if only in her imagination.

One night, when the moon was startlingly full and bright, Rachel was standing motionless outside Windermere, when she heard a vehicle coming down the street, very slowly. Her eyes snapped open. She realised that as it got nearer, she would be picked out by the headlights and lit up by the moon. She didn't want to be seen staring at the house, like a burglar checking out a property to rob.

In a panic she opened the gate and scuttled into the garden. She crouched down behind one of the gateposts, her ears on high alert for the approaching car or van—it was probably a supermarket drop, the young couple no doubt got their groceries online like so many people these days. She held her breath. The vehicle stopped. There was silence for a while, then to her relief, the engine started up again. She heard the grinding gears as the driver turned round and drove back up the street. Someone lost, a wrong turning, that was all.

Rachel waited until she couldn't hear the car any more before standing upright. But she didn't immediately come out of her hiding place. Instead, she turned to look at the house again. She was officially inside the property now; she had literally crossed a line. She found herself walking down the path towards the front door. She turned left, following the path round to the back of the house.

Under the stark moonlight the back garden looked ghostly. There was no lawn anymore, no borders or shrubs. Just stone slabs and decking and trimmed box trees in pots, like green lollipops stuck in compost. Rachel was appalled. The only word she could find was *desecration*.

A light snapped on upstairs, sending a blast of illumination into the garden, just missing Rachel where she stood at the corner of the house. She scuttled back along the path and out of the front gate as fast as she could. Heart pounding, she made her way home.

She slept badly that night. She lay in bed, staring at the ceiling. Images of the changes to Windermere whirled around her brain, keeping sleep at bay. At one point, deep into the early hours, Rachel remembered something. Aunt Lily had given her a back door key so that she could let herself into the house without disturbing the old lady. She still had it somewhere. Not that it would be any use now. No doubt the new owners had changed the door along with everything else. But the thought of it, that last connection to her aunt and to Windermere, gave her an odd sense of comfort. She rolled over and fell asleep.

Next morning Rachel was late to her computer. But luckily, she didn't have to field too many enquiries, stock levels were up to date, and none of the vehicles had broken down. She was drinking a second cup of mid-morning coffee when she got a text from her boss, requesting a Skype call at two o'clock that afternoon. There was something oddly formal about the tone of Madeleine's message that put her on edge.

When her boss's face appeared on the screen her expression was grim.

"Rachel, there's no easy way to say this."

"Say what?"

"The firm is struggling."

"But I've been as busy as ever."

"No, you haven't. You just think you have. Everything slows down when you work from home."

Rachel was silent. There was some truth in what Madeleine said. She worked her full eight hours, but had been stretching the jobs out within that time for some weeks now. She guessed what was coming.

"The fact is, we've decided to invest in some software that will take over a lot of your responsibilities. It will save money in the long run." Madeleine threw her hands up in exasperation. "This bloody virus! The restaurants and shops that provided most of our contracts—all closed. We're left with domestic call-outs and it's not enough, especially as most people don't want us in their homes right now." Madeleine rubbed her eyes with one hand. "I'm sorry, Rachel."

"Do you want me to work out my notice?"

"Just to the end of the week. We will pay you in full for the next month, and we'll organise a redundancy package too. It won't be huge, I'm afraid. And after that…"

"Universal credit. I know."

Rachel was about to end the call, but the sense that she had been feeble and compliant put her in a sudden rage.

"You do realise that I've worked for the firm for twenty-seven years?"

"Really? That long?" Madeleine sighed. "Like I said, we'll do the best for you we can."

Her face disappeared. The call was over, leaving Rachel feeling as though she had been punched in the stomach. She finished what work there was in double-quick time, with a kind of venom. She ate an early dinner, then the evening yawned ahead of her. She was impatient for the darkness, which was descending later and later as spring dissolved into summer. While she waited, she searched the drawer where she kept a jumble of items and found the key to Windermere. Without really knowing why, she slipped it into her coat pocket. It was like a talisman, a lucky charm. Her fingers closed over it as she walked. She found herself heading towards the leafy cul-de-sac, as if she craved the deepest silence, the most profound darkness, to match her mood.

As usual, Rachel stood and stared at the house. She told herself to go home, but her feet had other ideas. They took her through the gate and onto the path that led round to the back of the house. She ventured further than before, until she was next to the kitchen window.

A security light snapped on. Rachel froze, but no one came. She approached the back door. It was the same one, with a ribbed glass panel, but the frame was freshly painted in sage green. She reached for the key in her pocket and inserted it into the lock. It turned sweetly with just a quiet click. She pushed the door open and quickly stepped inside. She paused in the familiar hallway, which was illuminated by the outside light. She was pleased to see that the new owners had kept the lovely tiled floor, but they had painted the wood panelling slate blue and the walls pale grey. It looked utterly different. Where now? The kitchen was on the right, the dining room on the left. She chose the kitchen.

Rachel noted the shiny red cupboards, the massive fridge, the halogen hob. When the outside light clicked off, she stood for a moment in the darkness, inhaling scents of cooking—fish, garlic—and under that, something floral, roses perhaps. She switched on the torch on her phone and cast it around the room. Yes, a vase of bright yellow flowers stood on the windowsill. Other things caught her eye—a bulky food processor that must have cost a fortune, a wooden knife block, a deep square sink with weird-looking industrial taps.

Pinned to the fridge with magnets were a dozen or more postcards. She looked at these more closely. There were scenes of Venice and Barbados and the Maldives. Rich friends perhaps. Or had the couple been to these places and brought back postcards to remind them of their trips? They were too lazy, no doubt, to print off photos from their phones and put them neatly in albums. If she had ever been to Venice or Barbados that's what she would have done. Her own holidays in Scarborough or the Scottish Highlands suddenly seemed paltry and unambitious.

There was a noise upstairs. Footsteps. A door opened, then another, the sound of someone peeing a torrent, the flush of the toilet. Doors closing. Silence.

Rachel's mouth was dry. What on earth was she doing in someone else's house in the middle of the night? She waited a few agonising minutes, longing to leave, but needing to be sure that the couple upstairs were asleep. Finally, she could stand it no longer. She let herself out of the back door, locked it, and shielding her eyes from the unforgiving security light, hurried onto the lane.

She walked quickly away from Windermere, but not so fast as to look suspicious. Once the thumping in her chest eased back into a normal heartbeat, she began to giggle. Breaking and entering—wasn't that what Martin called it? Except she hadn't broken anything. Even so, surely it was a criminal act, illegal almost certainly. Or at very least, downright rude, invading someone's home while they slept. But she couldn't help it, she almost laughed aloud with a surge of unfamiliar joy. What she had done was foolish and dangerous.

And, she had to admit, it was exciting too.

***

On Monday morning, Rachel scoured the job vacancy sites, but found nothing remotely suitable. In the afternoon she emptied her small garden shed, cleaned it out, and put everything back neatly, apart from the items that needed chucking out. It was satisfying in its way, but strange to be doing a job like that on a working day. Tomorrow she would tackle the spare room. And the cupboard under the stairs needed an overhaul too. The future stretched ahead like a blank sheet of paper, however often she told herself to take one day at a time and make it count.

One evening her brother rang.

"Are you still doing that night walking thing?"

Rachel hesitated for a moment. "Occasionally," she said.

"I wish you wouldn't. There are stories going round—a woman got beaten up because she refused to go in a car with a guy, and some man went walking by the coast at night and fell fifty feet. He's lucky to be alive. So, my advice is: don't do it again, OK?"

"Noted."

"Good. Anyway, how are things with you?"

"Great, thanks."

"How's work?"

Rachel hadn't told him that she no longer had a job. "Fine."

"Right. I'd better go. Early start tomorrow—everyone on call."

"Really? I heard that crime rates had fallen during the pandemic."

"In some ways. But there's a big rise in domestics, and kids being groomed to peddle drugs is always a problem. All that, plus a couple of violent burglaries. We're pretty stretched right now. Take care, Rach."

"You too," she said, but the phone had already gone dead.

As the lockdown eased and the summer progressed, the town was busy again, with cafes, pubs and restaurants opening up. But Rachel hardly ever went out during the day—just rapid trips to the supermarket—and never at night. She sat in her tiny back garden instead with half a glass of cheap white wine. She told herself she was heeding her brother's advice, but it wasn't really that. What she had always loved about her nocturnal excursions was the freedom to go where she pleased, unnoticed, practically invisible. Now there were too many people about. Instead, she stayed home and brooded on her situation. Her life had always been small, but she had been self-sufficient, satisfied that she worked hard and that she wasn't a burden to anyone. But her search for a new job had been fruitless. Soon she would be dependent on the state for benefits, she might even have to sell her house and rent some poky flat.

She missed her night walks. It was almost a relief when, in November, another lockdown descended, and the town went into hibernation again. Late at night Rachel wandered the streets, feeling as insubstantial as a ghost and that suited her fine. She flitted along unnoticed now that the weather had turned cold and wet, and the streets were deserted. The silence and emptiness enveloped her, as comforting as old friends.

Rachel tried to resist the urge to return to Copper Beech Lane, but eventually she felt like an addict needing another fix. When she arrived at the house she slipped through the gate without hesitation. She already had the key in her hand and the back door opened smoothly once more. This time the security light didn't bother her. It could be triggered by a passing cat or fox after all. The occupants had taken no notice last time, so why would they on this occasion?

In the hallway, Rachel swapped her leather gloves for the latex ones she had brought with her. She was drawn to the kitchen once more. She switched on the light over the cooker, which cast a soft glow over the room. First, she peered into the fridge, noting the variety of fresh vegetables, the Italian cheeses, and several bottles of white wine, one of which was open. The cupboards were full of elegant white crockery, copper pans and tins of interesting foods, such as guava paste, foie gras, and hearts of palm. And what the hell was *cuitlacoche*? She'd never heard of it.

On the worktop was a large brown envelope. She flipped it open and drew out the papers inside. They were architect's plans for a kitchen diner, opening up the small kitchen and underused dining room across the hallway to create a large open space with an island for food prep and bi-fold doors leading into the back garden.

Rachel stared at the plans with dismay. Windermere was old-fashioned, it was true, but it had pleasing proportions, and this design would destroy that. It showed no respect for the fact the house was nearly a hundred years old, as Aunt Lily herself had been. More desecration, more destruction of the past. The thought hurt her as strongly as a physical pain.

A door opened upstairs. Rachel stood still, expecting to hear the flow of urine, the flush of the toilet. But instead, she heard heavy footsteps coming down the stairs. She stared around her—nowhere to hide. She switched off the hob light, hurried out of the door, across the hallway and into the dining room. Moonlight streaming through the window revealed a large table surrounded by tall chairs. She scooted around the table and squatted down behind the chair furthest from the door.

Someone barged into the kitchen. Rachel heard the rush of water from the tap, a cupboard thrown open. Then a popping sound, which mystified her, then another, and she realised that it was the sound of tablets being released from a blister pack.

Headache probably. Too many Zoom meetings, too much pressure. Even working from home was stressful. Headaches were part of her life too. *Try night walking*, she mouthed silently. She almost burst into hysterical giggling at the thought. Then she remembered she was no longer working from home. She wasn't working at all. Redundant. That thought sobered her up at once.

A grunt, the deep timbre of a man. The cupboard door banged shut, footsteps in the hall and up the stairs, then silence.

Rachel waited a few minutes, then slipped back into the kitchen. The scare had made her ridiculously hungry. She felt in need of something to eat before she set off for home. There was an open can of mackerel pâté in the fridge. Then she found crackers in a jar. She took a glass from a shelf and poured herself a good slug of white wine. She ate standing up. It was all quite delicious. When she was finished, she ran a quiet trickle of water into the sink and washed up carefully. She dried her latex gloves on a tea towel but left them on. Finally, she put everything back where it belonged.

As she turned to the back door to leave, she noticed the building plans still scattered on the worktop. She tapped the papers together and slid them back inside the envelope. It was time to go.

Rachel endured a restless night, her mind conflicted. How could she have broken into the home of strangers like that? She didn't know the couple who lived there, had never met them, though Martin had heard that they were in the legal profession. What was she thinking of? But she had done no harm, nor intended any. She looked back over the months of redundancy. Most of the time it had been empty and depressing. She realised that standing inside the kitchen of Windermere, quiet and unobserved, had been the only thing that made her feel fully alive.

It was tempting to walk as far as Copper Beech Lane every night. There was always a magnetic pull in that direction. But Rachel refused to give in to it. She took to striding into the town centre which was lit up with Christmas lights, offering a suggestion, a vague memory, of warmth and pleasure, even though the streets were empty.

Her brother rang on Christmas Day.

"Happy Christmas, Rach," he said. She could hear Martin's young granddaughter in the background, her voice raised in excitement.

"Same to you."

"Sorry we couldn't ask you over. But you know—Fiona's Mum, Stacey and Matt, and little Olivia—that made six of us in all, and that's the limit."

Rachel was fairly sure that small children didn't count, but she didn't argue. "I know. It's fine. Remember what Aunt Lily used to say? *Worse things happen at sea.*"

"Yeah, I'd forgotten that. And what about, *Better the devil you know than the devil you don't.*"

Rachel laughed. "That was one of her favourites. Not forgetting, *Never throw good money after bad.*"

"She was a dismal old stick, wasn't she?"

"I don't think that's fair. She was grumpy and demanding when she got ill, but before that…"

"She took advantage of you. You waited on her hand and foot at the end."

"Don't exaggerate. I went round most days to check on her, it's true. But she had professional caretakers too."

"All the same. She didn't leave anything to us in her will, did she, even you? It was mean."

"She didn't have all that much to leave."

"What about that big house? It must be worth a fortune now."

"I'm sure it is. The new owners have made a lot of changes. I suppose it adds even more to the value."

"Yeah? How do you know? Have you been round there?"

"No…no." Rachel cleared her throat, gaining time. "Someone told me. I haven't seen it myself."

"Yeah, well it still rankles with me." He broke off. She heard his muffled voice telling the toddler not to tear the decorations off the tree. "Sorry, I'm needed for grandad duties. Don't drink too much prosecco, OK?"

After she put the phone down, Rachel stared out of the window for a long time, thinking about what Martin had said. Did she resent the fact that her great aunt hadn't recognised her contribution, not even with a small amount of money, or a piece of jewellery?

As the afternoon light faded, her mind seemed to become clearer. Yes, she *was* hurt that Aunt Lily had regarded her kindness as not worth acknowledging. It made her think of Madeleine and the way she had been tossed aside at work. She realised that the emotion she felt was deeper than resentment, deeper than hurt. It was anger. Yes, she was furious, but it was impotent fury. There was no way to show it or express it. She knew that kind of anger was destructive. It took a while, but eventually she felt it loosen its grip enough to allow her to observe it from a distance. She must learn to let it go.

She watched the daylight dimming, cloaking the featureless street at last. That was why she liked the dark so much—it made ugly things more beautiful. Even her own ugly thoughts became more bearable as the night arrived. She had roasted a small chicken for Christmas lunch, now she cut some cold meat and made a sandwich, with cranberry sauce and stuffing. Two mince pies and a cup of tea followed, and all the time, Rachel was watching the clock. Finally, at ten thirty, she put on her warm woollen coat, hat, and gloves, and set off.

***

Something felt different. Rachel stood in the kitchen of Windermere and wondered what it was. She realised it was chillier than usual. No central heating on. So, the young couple must have gone to see family for Christmas. The restrictions had been lifted for this one day only. But the fact they had turned the heating off suggested they were breaking the rules by staying elsewhere overnight, possibly longer.

It was liberating. Rachel opened the kitchen door and peered into the hallway. The silence was so deep it felt like a solid thing. She approached the stairs and stood at the bottom, peering upwards. Using her phone torch she mounted the stairs, pausing every three or four. Still no sound, not even breathing or snoring. Gaining confidence, she climbed to the top.

The door straight ahead led to the main bedroom. Rachel turned the handle carefully. She peeped through the narrow opening. She saw the outline of the bed, neatly made up. She pushed the door wide open and switched on the light.

The room was transformed. Instead of her aunt's heavy oak furniture, the fitted wardrobes and dressing table were made of pale wood. A grey and white striped duvet covered the bed. The walls were painted a soft glowing pink. Aunt Lily had died in this room. There was no way she would recognise it now, and the thought gave Rachel a perverse pleasure.

She inspected all the other rooms, including the bathroom, no longer dingy, but sparkling with lots of white tiles and stainless steel. She retreated downstairs, eager to see the living room. The fireplace wall was covered in paper with a startling tropical pattern, the other walls painted dark teal. There were two sofas, one a deep gold, the other bright fuchsia. The only word Rachel could think of to describe it was *vivid*. She tried to imagine sitting here, watching TV, drinking chilled wine. The idea was both appealing and painful. She moved slowly around the room, examining the many photos of the couple. They were in their thirties—she was blonde, he was dark with a neat beard. They were always smiling, their heads touching.

A sound cut through the silence. A car. She stood very still, willing it to turn around and drive away, but the sound grew louder. There was a car coming down the drive at the side of the house towards the garage.

Rachel scuttled down the hallway. She slid through the door, locked it, and crouching low, ran into the back garden. She squatted down behind a conifer in a pot and prayed that she hadn't been seen.

A car door slammed.

"He shouldn't have said that." The woman's voice carried across the garden. She sounded angry.

"He didn't mean it." A man's voice this time. "Stop being so sensitive, Tara. You do not look pregnant."

"Stop it!" the woman wailed. "I'm never going to see your parents again!"

"It's just a bit of extra lockdown weight. Everyone's put on a few pounds."

"Oh God, Felix. I hate you!"

"Come on, love. Let it go. It's Christmas!"

There was more shouting. It diminished in volume then stopped abruptly. They must have gone in through the front door. Rachel stood up. She edged around the garden to avoid the security light.

Felix and Tara…She had seen photos of them, now she had their names, and heard their voices. She even knew intimate details of their relationship. It gave her an odd sense of kinship with them.

As she made her way home, Rachel realised that although what she had done was risky, she had gotten away with it. Again. Tonight, everything could have gone disastrously wrong, but she had acted quickly and escaped without being discovered. Tara and Felix had no idea she had entered their house, had done so more than once. It was a kind of victory.

The following evening Rachel left it very late, past midnight. Why not? She had nothing to get up for in the morning. She was ultra-careful as she entered the house. But there was no disturbance. She made herself a snack—parma ham from the fridge and sliced sourdough in the bread bin. She poured herself a glass of prosecco, which had gone a little flat. She ate her snack standing up, relishing every mouthful. She washed up and put everything back in the right place. She liked the fact that she knew the layout of this kitchen as well as her own. Now she was ready to go.

The tinkling sound of fractured glass startled her. Rachel twisted her head trying to locate it. It came again, from across the hall in the dining room. Then came the noise of a window scraping open. Her mind seemed to empty, and she stood paralysed for a moment. Scrambled thoughts followed. Tara and Felix—had they been out, forgotten their keys and had to force their way in?

The kitchen door opened. A tall figure stepped through. He wore a balaclava so that Rachel could see nothing but his eyes. He was carrying a baseball bat. He saw her and halted abruptly.

He raised the bat. She felt behind her for the knife block. She drew out the one in the middle, the largest.

The intruder ran at her, bat held high, exposing his broad chest. At the last moment Rachel held the knife in front of her and simply let him run onto it. The knife juddered against bone. She angled it upwards and thrust hard. It passed through soft flesh and organs. She let go of the knife. The man grunted and staggered backwards. He stood upright for a moment, very still, then his knees gave way. His body sank downwards and keeled over. The baseball bat fell from his fingers. Rachel caught it neatly to stop it clattering onto the tiled floor. The man lay on his side, curved as if he was sleeping.

Rachel waited for Felix to rush downstairs to find out what all the commotion was about. But he didn't burst through the door as she expected. She realised there had been almost no noise, just the window being broken and forced, and the low grunt from the intruder as she stabbed him.

She put the bat on the worktop, then bent down and lifted the man's right arm. She pressed his gloved fingers around the knife that was embedded in his chest. It was hasty and improvised, and she knew it was unlikely to fool anyone, but it was the best she could do.

There was blood flowing out from the body in a dark pool. Rachel left the hob light on so that she could carefully step around it and exit through the back door. She locked the door with fingers that almost refused to work. She wanted to run but her feet refused to fly. They felt like leaden weights. It took so long to reach home she could hear a lone bird begin to sing, as if complaining that it was still dark and the dawn needed to get a bloody move on.

By the time she stood outside her front door, her hands were freezing cold, and she saw that she was still wearing latex gloves. Once inside she peeled them off and dumped them in the waste bin. She didn't bother to go to bed. Surely they would come for her this time. Someone would have seen her, or a CCTV camera would have picked up her movements. All she could do was sit and wait.

She imagined Martin or one of his colleagues interrogating her. What was she going to say? Alternative versions of events churned in her mind on repeat.

No, she hadn't been to Copper Beech Lane since her aunt died. Yes, she went there frequently, but not that night.

She had never entered the house. OK, yes, once or twice, just out of curiosity.

She had seen the burglar. She hadn't seen anyone.

She hadn't killed the man. All right, she had done it, what else could she do? It was self-defence.

But no one came.

*****

The news of a man's death from stab wounds, in a house on Copper Beech Lane, made the local TV news the following lunchtime, and for several days after that, though no name was given, or the circumstances. Still Rachel waited.

She rang her brother.

"This man who got stabbed on Copper Beech Lane, it wasn't Aunt Lily's house, was it?" She laughed lightly as if to suggest it was a remote possibility.

There was silence, then Martin coughed. "I shouldn't really be talking to you about this."

"Oh my God, it was her house. That's terrible." Rachel paused, suggesting shock and disbelief. "What happened exactly?"

"It looks like a burglary gone horribly wrong."

"So it was the owner of the house that died?"

"No, not the owner."

"Oh, it was the intruder that got stabbed? So, it must have been one of the people who live there that…"

"Looks like it. Mind you, there's no forensic evidence to… Sorry, Rach, I'd better not say any more."

"Of course not, I understand. It's scary though, isn't it? A murder so close to home. And at Aunt Lily's place…it's hard to believe. It's really dreadful." She sighed heavily. "Keep me posted if you can, Martin."

"It'll all go public fairly soon. Take care, Rach."

"Sure."

Rachel pondered on what she had learnt. Inevitably, Felix or Tara were the main suspects, only the lack of forensics was a problem. But there wouldn't be any, would there? Not unless one of them had bent over the body, grasped the knife, and got their shoes and clothes covered in blood. It wouldn't have happened that way. No one in their right mind would have gone near a dead body found in their own kitchen, swimming in a pool of blood. She imagined Tara opening the door that morning, clapping her hands to her mouth, paralysed, then screaming in horror until Felix came running down the stairs. Or Felix, arriving on the scene first, and swearing loudly before backing away. He would have yelled to Tara not to go into the kitchen, then fumbled for his phone and rung the police.

The local media dropped the story when there was nothing new to report. Rachel wanted to ring her brother every day for updates but was afraid it would look suspicious. She rang him a week later, on a Thursday evening, when she hoped he'd had his usual few beers.

They chatted for a while, then, just as they were about to sign off, Rachel mentioned the burglary, apparently as an afterthought.

"By the way, any progress on the stabbing at Aunt Lily's house?"

"It's a strange one, that. Obviously, we are looking at the owner, but there's not a drop of the victim's blood on his clothes, or anywhere else in the house. And, of course, he was the one who called it in."

"Well, he would, wouldn't he?"

"True. But between you and me, Rach, this guy—the burglar—he was a known criminal with a string of convictions. If I'm honest, my heart doesn't bleed for him."

"All the same, killing is wrong. And if the owner did it … "

"Yeah, but if he is charged, he'll plead self-defence, or at worst, involuntary manslaughter. He won't get a long sentence."

"But he's not admitting to anything?"

"Far from it. He claims he's innocent, very loudly. And so does his wife."

"Do you believe them?"

"I think so. Which begs the question: who else was in the house?"

"Did he have an accomplice? Did they fall out over something?"

"There's no trace of unidentifiable DNA, just a partial fingerprint on the worktop."

Rachel's heart skipped. "So…there was someone else?"

"Yeah, but it could be the electrician, or the plumber, or the architect they hired to convert the downstairs. We're checking it out."

"There's no chance it was suicide?"

"If you were feeling suicidal, would you break into a stranger's house, grab one of their knives and kill yourself on their kitchen floor?"

"I suppose not."

"Anyway, the angle's wrong."

"The angle?"

"The postmortem shows he couldn't have thrust the knife into himself at that angle."

"Right. It's proving a tricky case then?"

"It's wearing me out, Rach. Roll on retirement."

"Yeah, absolutely. Lovely to speak to you, Martin. Let's hope this bloody pandemic is over soon, then we can meet up properly."

"Look forward to that. Bye."

Telling herself it was for self-protection, Rachel slipped a knife into her coat pocket and went out for the first time since the incident. It felt good to be stroked by the velvety darkness again, even though the January night was very cold and there was still snow on the ground from a recent fall.

She stood outside Windermere, staring at the house. Was it still a crime scene? She couldn't see any blue and white tape. The place felt empty somehow. She wasn't surprised. How could Felix and Tara bear to live there now? No doubt they had gone to stay with his parents. She had to smile at the idea. That wouldn't work out well.

Rachel was tempted to break in, but no, not this time. That would be downright stupid.

As she turned to walk away, she noticed a pole beside the gate, half masked by the trees. *For Sale.*

Felix and Tara would never return here then. They would move away, possibly to another town, start afresh somewhere else. She didn't blame them.

New people would come to live at Windermere. They would make more changes and impose their own taste. Rachel didn't like the thought. Still, she could call by, mark her territory, without leaving any trace of course. After all, she still had the key.

Walking home, Rachel thought about the burglar, how he had got what he deserved.

He had broken into a private home, prepared to steal anything of value and ready to use violence to get what he wanted. He had left the owners traumatised and defiled. She had never done that. She had treated the place and its occupants with respect. She had no regrets about ending his life.

Then she remembered the man on the new estate who beat his wife, the rapist on the canal path, the dealers who groomed young children to carry their drugs. When she went night walking no one ever noticed her. She was invisible. She fingered the knife in her pocket.

When you thought about it, it was just another form of pest control.

Belle and Donna

By Keith Brooke

When Donna got home from a morning at the estate agency where she was temping, coppers were everywhere. Panda cars were parked with two wheels up on the pavement, uniformed men knocking on doors. A black transit van was open at the back to reveal boxes of what looked like scientific equipment. Forensics? She'd seen enough episodes of *Juliet Bravo* and *The Sweeney* to be experiencing a strange sense of *déjà vu* right now, as if she'd stepped onto a movie set.

There must have been a burglary, or an incident at a neighbour's house or in the street.

She parked her Mini Clubman down the road and for a moment all was normal again. A tidy row of 1960s semis, all neat lawns and rockeries.

She locked the car and walked up the street, back onto that movie set.

They were at her house, another panda car in the drive, a uniformed constable at Donna's open front door.

She approached up the narrow concrete path that ran parallel with the drive, and just as she was about to accost the constable a man emerged and paused on the doorstep. Brown rocker hair in a quiff that wouldn't quite stay up, old-fashioned sideburns, an orange-brown polo-neck under a scuffed leather jacket.

He raised a hand, palm outwards, to stop Donna. "DC Marcus Fletcher," he said "CID. And you are?"

"Donna Currie. I live here. What's going on? Why are you in my house? Don't you need some kind of warrant or something?"

"We had reason to fear for your safety, Miss Currie. A body has been found. We thought it might be you."

Just as she'd thought she was getting over the initial shock of seeing her home turned into a police show, they kept piling it on. A body? In her house?

"Do I look dead, officer?"

DC Fletcher looked down at the ground, his face flushing. "No, you look very…" There was something about Fletcher that told her he almost never normally stumbled over his words like this.

"Alive?" she finished for him. He looked down again, and that flush didn't go away quickly.

"Anyway," he told her, straightening up with a roll of the shoulders. "That was why we forced entry. A postman looked in through a window, saw signs of a kerfuffle—"

"Kerfuffle?"

"He called us. We just knew there was a body. At that stage we didn't know the deceased was a man."

"Then clearly it wasn't me."

Donna moved quickly and was past the detective before he even seemed to notice she was making a move.

Nothing seemed to have been disturbed in the small entrance hall, but through the open glass door to the living room everything was surreal again: the room had become a crime scene. A boiler-suited man was on his hands and knees by the sofa, a uniformed man bending at the waist to look at something he was indicating; two suited men stood at the bay window, heads close in conversation. The coffee table was tipped over, its inset brown glass top crazed with cracks.

And lying in the gap between sofa and armchair, twisted awkwardly over the magazine rack, was the body of a man. Unfashionably flared jeans, a brightly tie-dyed T-shirt. Long hippie hair that had once been mousy blond but was now matted with red that had coagulated into something like jam.

"Do you recognise this man?" Fletcher asked. He'd clearly noticed how Donna couldn't help but stare at the empty shell of what used to be a human being.

How could you not stare at something like this, when it was plonked down in the middle of your own living room?

"I've never seen him before in my life, DC Fletcher."

He seemed pathetically pleased that she'd bothered to remember his name. "Do you have anywhere to stay, Miss Currie?"

"Why?" She didn't understand at first: they were standing in her house, for goodness' sake. Why would she need to stay somewhere else?

Fletcher indicated the living room with a nod of the head, a wave of one hand. It was going to take quite some time for them to process all the evidence and release the crime scene, or whatever it was they did. Donna couldn't exactly carry on around them as if nothing had happened…

She turned in the doorway, but Fletcher blocked the way so that they came to stand so close she could smell his Hai Karate aftershave and the leather of that scuffed brown jacket. She peered up at him, amused again at his evident discomfort around her.

"Sorry, but you can't just…"

"I need to get some things," she said. "From my room. Underwear, a change of clothes. Then I'll leave you to it, I promise."

Upstairs, she pulled her bedroom door closed behind her, then went across to the wardrobe and retrieved a leather shoulder bag. She opened a drawer and grabbed a handful of tanga briefs, a couple of bras, then reached up for one of the framed photos standing on top of the chest.

It was a photo from her university days, taken almost eight years ago, back in the early seventies. Everyone had big hair, bright colours, big lapels. Half a dozen of them, pulling together in a drunken group embrace for the camera.

And there, with the same long hair and muttonchop sideburns covering most of each side of his jaw, was Gav, the man who now lay awkwardly twisted across her magazine rack with the back of his skull caved in.

Why had she claimed not to know him?

It was a lie that would inevitably be found out. She'd been confused, thrown by the whole scene—the police, the aftermath of obvious violence, the body… Him… Gavin. Lying there with death in his blank eyes.

She'd had very good reason never to expect to see that face again, those eyes.

Denial had been a reflex response to that shock.

***

Fletch knew as soon as he clapped eyes on Donna Currie that she was one to watch closely. And not just because of the way she looked—the perfect blonde bob, the way she filled that dress, the way she moved as if she knew every man's eyes would be following her. Not because of the expression that fell somewhere between amusement at him and just waiting to reel him in.

Donna Currie was one to watch because Fletch could tell right away that she was being cagey, a woman with mystery and secrets, always trying to stay one step ahead and throw him.

And boy did she have him thrown! From the outset he'd been suckered by the classic tension between knowing she was a bad'un and being irresistibly drawn to her nonetheless.

He tried not to watch her as she headed upstairs to her room to pack a few things. He failed.

I need to get some things. From my room. Underwear, a change of clothes.

Said with a flutter of those blue eyes. She knew exactly what she was doing. But why? What was she trying to distract him from?

She was a skinny slip of a thing. He didn't see her as the kind of woman who would take a heavy object—an ashtray? Or a brick?—and bash a lover's brains out in her own front room. Poison, perhaps, but not this kind of violence.

She only took a couple of minutes, and then she was coming back down the stairs, a leather bag swinging from her shoulder. She smiled at him, flashed those baby blues again, and then, before he knew it, he was watching the swing of her perfect backside as she headed down the path to the street.

He reached into an inside jacket pocket for his notebook and pencil, then cursed and slapped the notebook against his thigh. Why was he so distracted?

He pushed past Turner on the door, made the pavement in six long strides, but she was gone already.

Grinning at Fletch making such a fool of himself, Turner nodded leftwards to indicate which way she'd gone.

Fletch set off at a trot, remembering his regular vow to get fit—a vow he made every time he had to break into a run on the job.

A few houses down, he was out of breath, and came to a pause next to a Mini Clubman the same shade of browny orange as his polo-neck.

"Did you forget something, DC Fletcher?"

He turned, and she was standing in the street on the other side of the Clubman, about to get in the driver's side.

Fletch straightened, then walked around the car. Leaning back so that he was half-sitting on the bonnet, he produced his notebook and waved it at her. "You said you had somewhere to stay," he said. "But I need the details. Address. Phone number."

"I have a friend with a place on Marine Parade," she told him. "I'll stay with her."

She held a hand out, and Fletch passed her the notebook, open to a clean page so she could write down the details.

She handed the notebook back, then reached for the car door. She'd been more confident back at the house; now she just seemed to want to get away.

"Anything else I should know about?" Fletch asked, still leaning against her car as he tucked the book back into the inside pocket of his jacket.

"I don't think so, officer," she said. Now she did that thing again, the tip of the head so she had to peer up at him through lashes and fringe. That thing that made his heart skip and something deep in his abdomen tighten.

They both knew the game she was playing, and Fletch certainly didn't want to be the one to put a halt to it.

But he did, nonetheless.

"You did recognise him, didn't you?"

She held the look for a moment longer, then her shoulders slumped, and written all across her face was the acceptance that she'd been found out.

Unusually sensitive for Fletch, he acknowledged that there might be all kinds of reasons a beautiful woman might lie about something like this, and only one of those reasons was that she was the one who'd stoved in the guy's head with a heavy, blunt object.

"His name is Gavin Porter. I knew him at university in the early seventies."

"An ex?"

"Very much so," she said. "I never expected to see him again. Never."

"Why?"

"Because I thought I'd killed him years ago."

***

She didn't know why she did it. Flirted with DC Fletcher, like this. There were coppers swarming all over her house, her ex-boyfriend murdered in the living room, and somehow that combination of adrenaline and shock seemed to bring out the flirt in her.

Maybe it was because it was so easy.

He'd made it obvious from the start, when he'd stopped her at her own front door, his cheeks flushing, his eyes so uncertain of where to rest that they just crawled all over her instead. All it took was a flutter of the eyes, or a rolling back of the shoulders to push her tits out, and he was all over the place.

But although she didn't know why she did it, she suspected the main reason was distraction. Not for him, but distracting *her*. From her own stupidity. From the hole she'd dug for herself almost as soon as she opened her mouth.

Why had she claimed not to know Gavin?

She'd known the lie would be found out.

Hell, DC Marcus Fletcher had seen through her straight away, even in his distracted state.

"Why?" he insisted.

"Because I thought I'd killed him years ago."

She might as well come out with it now. She had nothing to lose, after all. Because, quite clearly, she *hadn't* killed him years ago.

"You…" Fletcher was shaking his head, clearly struggling to catch up.

"I thought he was dead long ago. I was in shock, I suppose, seeing him here, like this. Denial. It couldn't possibly be him. So, I said I didn't know him. But it was. It is. It's Gavin Porter back there in my front room, and I don't have the faintest idea why he's in my house."

"You're going to have to—"

A shout, the words indistinguishable. Fletcher looked away from her, back towards the house where one of the uniformed men was gesturing at him.

"I'm going to have to take a statement from you," Fletcher said, tapping the pocket where he'd tucked his notebook. "Ask some more questions."

"You know where to find me." She was doing it again, the flirting, the eye contact, the little smile. A defence mechanism she'd never known she had.

A short time later she was at the sea front. It was an early afternoon weekday in May, and most of the parking spaces on Marine Parade were full, but she managed to find one big enough for the Mini.

She stood for a time on the pavement opposite Belle's place, peering up at the Victorian villa where her friend had a flat.

It had been inevitable, really. When you show up at university on your first day and the girl in the room next door at the halls of residence introduces herself as Isobel. Belle and Donna, known from that point on as the Poison Sisters. Fate decreed that they must become best friends.

Donna buzzed her friend, and the main door clicked. She pushed through into the lobby and went up one flight of stairs, thinking as always that this felt like a school building, or a hospital.

"What's happened?" Belle was waiting for her on the landing, rocking from foot to foot. Somehow, she knew something was wrong.

"It's Gavin," Donna said, as she climbed the stairs. "He's dead."

"Gavin *Porter*?" Belle said. "Of course he's fucking dead, darling. Has been for years."

"No. No he hasn't. But he is now."

"You'd better come in."

"I know. Because I don't have anywhere else to go."

It was only mid-afternoon, but a short time later they sat on the big sofa facing each other, knees drawn up, each clutching a large glass of Blue Nun.

"Dead, you say? Are you sure?"

"Well, half the local police force was in my house, and they seemed pretty sure," Donna said.

"But… what was he doing in your house? Did you know he was there? When did you last speak to him?"

"Of course I didn't know, Belle. He's been dead for eight years. Or at least I thought he was." She took a long sip of the wine. "He must have tracked me down," Donna mused. "Found out where I live. Broken in… I don't know."

"Gav always was a bit of a weird one. I don't know what you saw in him."

"You told me that at the time. Once or twice."

She was right, though. Probably Gav's biggest regret in life had been that he'd just missed out on the sixties, barely adolescent at the peak of Flower Power. Obsessed with eastern mysticism and too much weed, he had an intensity that occasionally hinted at great wisdom, but more often was simply strange. Belle had put him down as a pseud from the start and had never missed an opportunity to point this out to Donna.

"Are you sure you don't know why he was here?" Belle pressed.

Donna shook her head.

"You were like a magnet to him," Belle said. "He couldn't resist you."

"Clearly."

Another long sip. The Blue Nun was going very quickly.

"You okay, kiddo?" A hand on her arm, a squeeze.

Donna shrugged. "I don't know," she said. "I… It's shock, I suppose."

"Well obviously. You just saw a guy with his head smashed in, absolutely ruining your living room carpet."

"No, not that. Not *just* that." She took another sip. "But… all of it. What if I'd turned up an hour or so earlier? What if I'd walked right into the middle of it all? What if… Whoever did this: had he been lying in wait for *me*, and Gavin had shown up unexpectedly?"

Belle squeezed her arm again. "The police have got it now," she said. "They'll find whoever did this."

There was more, though. What had Gavin been doing at her house? Why had he tracked her down now, after all this time?

That was the real source of the shock, beyond the obvious. The feelings stirred up. Feelings she'd thought long lost, but which lingered even after all this time. Feelings for Gav. All the *what might have beens*, and the loss of what might possibly *be*.

"Another drink?"

"Oh yes."

***

Fletch prided himself on his self-awareness, and, in that spirit, he'd be the first to acknowledge that he'd always been a sucker for a bit of skirt. A long list of scrapes and narrow escapes, including a particularly short-lived marriage, would attest to that. But he'd usually been able to rise above it when he was on the job, at least. On the job he was a good, no-nonsense copper.

So why was he allowing his judgement to be so easily clouded over now? Why was Donna Currie getting to him, with the way she looked at him, the smile, the way she moved?

After all, it was looking increasingly open and shut.

She'd lied to him, for a start. Tried to stop him drawing a connection between her and the victim. She'd been playing him from the beginning.

But there was more than that. Real evidence starting to mount up.

They'd been interrupted when he'd chased her back to her car. When she'd just said that strange thing about believing she'd killed Gavin Porter years ago.

The shout from Constable Turner had been to alert him to the arrival of DI Waller on the scene. Fletch had a minute to bring his superior up to speed on the investigation before Fai Lee, the lead forensic scientist, led them on a tour.

"Obviously it's all preliminary at this stage, until we have lab results and finger mark analysis, but so far I'd say there's only evidence of two individuals recently on the scene, including the deceased."

"Who's the other?"

"Female, blonde. We'll need to take fingerprints for confirmation."

"Donna Currie," Fletch filled in. "She lives here. Knew the victim, although only from years ago, she claims. Thought he was dead, apparently." He didn't add that she thought she'd killed him—he still needed to get to the bottom of that strange claim.

Lee had led them through to the kitchen, and now he indicated two cups on the draining board. Each had the remains of either tea or coffee in the bottom and bore the unmistakable dusting of fingerprint powder.

"Prints?" asked Waller.

Lee nodded. "Two sets," he confirmed. "I'm confident one set will belong to our victim, and the second appears to match others we've found all over the house."

"Donna Currie," Fletch said. "She had coffee with him." He was leaning in close to examine the cups, and sure enough, one cup was smudged raspberry pink around the rim. The same shade as Donna Currie's lipstick.

"What can you tell us about the victim?"

"No ID on him," Fletch said. "But Miss Currie has identified him as Gavin Porter, an old university friend of hers. An ex."

"Get to work on his background, Fletch," Waller told him. "There must be relatives and friends somewhere. Make some calls. We need to know what he was doing here. Cause of death?"

"Blunt force trauma to the occipital bone of the skull," Lee told them, indicating the back of his own head as he did so. "We haven't found the weapon."

"Anything else about him? Intoxication? Defensive wounds?"

"The postmortem will tell us that," said Lee, clearly struggling not to get too defensive. "But there's no sign of intoxication, although he did have a small amount of cannabis on his person. He had a few scratch marks too. Not from an animal. And not fresh: these were scabbed over. From a day or two ago, I'd say."

It didn't look good for Donna Currie. She'd lied. She claimed she didn't know why Porter was in her house and yet had clearly had coffee with him.

She was the only other person who'd been in the house. And the scratches—Porter had fought someone in the last couple of days, which might have been the catalyst for his murder, and only a woman leaves scratches like that.

It didn't look good for her at all.

***

They were two bottles down and well into the third when the buzzer of Belle's flat went off partway through the evening. Other than a bag of prawn cocktail crisps, the Blue Nun was all they'd had for dinner. Sometimes it went that way, particularly where Belle and Donna were concerned.

"You've kept *this* one quiet," said Belle, as she led DC Fletcher into the living room moments later.

"He's with the police," Donna said, rising to stand uncertainly.

"I *know*. Or at least, that's what he told me. Do you have handcuffs, DC Fletcher? I know a naughty game if you do…"

He took a step back from her, as if distance might somehow protect him from her teasing. "Miss Currie," he said. "I need to ask you a few more questions."

"I bet you do, darling," said Belle. She'd closed the gap between them, so that if Fletcher retreated again, he would have his back against the wall. The Poison Sisters had always been a double act that would daunt any man.

"This is serious business," he said quietly, and that seemed to get through to her.

Belle turned to Donna. "You two should talk," she said. "Clear the air. Tell him everything, Donna. All the sordid details."

As they spoke, Fletcher's eyes had been darting about the room, taking in the painting above the fireplace—an almost abstract nude, and very explicit when your eyes adjusted—the three bottles on the coffee table, the shelves crammed with books, with more books stacked on any available surface, the dirty washing in one corner that had somehow only made it this far from Belle's bedroom.

"Outside?" he said, holding Donna's look. "Some fresh air might help."

She smiled, caught in that strange place of feeling quite tipsy and yet utterly clear-headed at the same time.

"Fresh air would be good, thank you," she said, and reached for her coat where it was hanging over the back of a chair.

A short time later they were down on the promenade, a long sweep of concrete paving with a metal rail separating them from the short drop to the beach. Out in the bay a cargo boat stacked high with containers trudged out into the North Sea.

Fletcher went to lean against the railings, his back to the bay. Donna stood facing out, the sea breeze fresh in her face.

"What did your friend mean?" he asked her. "Tell me everything. All the sordid details."

"She studied drama at uni," Donna said. "She never misses a chance to put it into practice."

Fletcher grunted what might have been a laugh. "I can't work you out," he said. "Everything about you is contradiction and confusion. Smoke and broken mirrors. You say you don't know the dead man in your front room, and you turn out to have been lovers. You say you thought he was dead, but until this morning he was clearly very much alive. You say you thought you'd killed him several years ago."

"I was in shock when I said all that."

"That excuse can only get you so far."

She wished she hadn't drunk so much. She was struggling to keep up—and even that wouldn't be enough: she had to keep *ahead*.

"We know what happened eight years ago."

She looked at him, couldn't work out if he was bluffing or not.

"We know that just after you all finished university, Gavin had some kind of crisis. Apparent suicide, although the circumstances were complicated to say the least. We know it hit you hard."

"I had a nervous breakdown. That's what they called it, to be polite. I tried to kill myself."

Fletcher looked away. Doing sensitive was clearly unfamiliar territory for him.

"Gav was… fragile. He was brilliant, but he struggled to handle the world. He kept looking for some kind of deeper meaning to things. I was entranced by that. Belle always argued that underneath the veneer of mysticism he was just plastic, like everyone else."

"A fake."

"Aren't we all? To some extent or other." She could see Fletcher didn't agree—this man who hid behind his own veneer of laddish, wideboy charm.

"Gav struggled with me and Belle. He found our friendship a bit much to handle. She liked to wind him up."

Fletcher laughed, and she wondered if he was recalling how Belle had teased him minutes before, up in her flat. "Was there anything there? Gavin and Belle? A love triangle?"

Now it was Donna's turn to laugh. "Oh, no. Belle was too intent on pricking his bubble. She hates pseuds, and in our circle, he was the prime example."

"So, what happened?"

"It was the early seventies. Gav was a hippie, into enlightenment and peace and love."

"And drugs?"

She shrugged. "We had plans to go to Nepal after we finished uni. Gav thought that was where he'd find enlightenment; I just wanted to see the mountains. Belle hated that he was taking me away, as she saw it. There was lots of arguing. I was torn… I think even then I knew Gavin's journey was taking him away from me, even as I did my best to tag along."

"Did you go?"

"No. I knew he'd just get worse when we were out there, and I didn't want to be stranded alone on the hippie trail. I told him I wasn't going. I said it was over."

"And he took it badly."

"He never did anything by halves, breakups included." His body was found two days later in a burned-out caravan. For the longest time nobody really knew what had happened. His remains were so badly burned they were beyond recognition, but nobody doubted it was him.

"You said you killed him."

"He left a suicide note. And in Gavin's charmingly forthright manner, he left no doubt about who was responsible. He blamed me. For leading him on, for choosing friendship over love. It was a nasty, poisonous piece of writing, but it was clear that it was all my fault."

"He was lashing out."

"He found his target. In the end, I think he hated me, and he felt he had nothing left. And so he killed himself."

"He didn't, though. He did what you had planned together. He went to Nepal, and then on to India. On his own. He spent the last few years there."

Donna stared at the detective, staggered at the cruelty of Gavin's actions. The vindictiveness.

"What we need to determine," said Fletcher, "is why he came back now, and sought you out. And why is he now dead?"

***

This is precisely why Fletch didn't do relationships. Why he kept things simple and didn't get involved. He liked things to be clear-cut: get out by morning at the latest, and don't look back. Otherwise, you end up with something like this: misunderstandings and jealousies, minds taken over by passions, tangled webs that messed up other relationships, lives misspent and wasted, brutal murder… It just wasn't worth the hassle.

He couldn't help thinking of that poor sod, Gavin Porter. Rings run around him by Belle and Donna—just their names should have warned him off!

He'd travelled to the other side of the world, just to get away from them. Spent years there, not so much finding himself as hiding himself away.

On one level at least Fletch understood the guy. Life with someone like Donna—or her friend Belle—must be so damned intense. And while the attraction was undeniable, no man could handle that on a day-to-day basis.

But what Porter had done was unforgivable. Even if you accepted that he hadn't actually faked his own death—that somehow that body in the burnt-out caravan was mere coincidence—he'd written that suicide note with the sole intention not only of misleading those who cared about him, but of loading the blame and guilt onto Donna.

And the body… Fletch had spoken to an officer who had worked on the case. It had seemed pretty clear-cut at the time: one of Porter's dealers owned that caravan, and the coincidence of the death and Porter's suicide note had all added up.

Had Porter seen his opportunity and written his note *after* the fire, using it as cover for his departure? Perhaps.

But there was also the more disturbing possibility that he'd had a hand in the fire. The body had been too badly damaged for a clear identification beyond a loose physical match for Porter. The jaw and skull had been too badly damaged to be of any use—perhaps by the intensity of the fire, but perhaps also due to some kind of physical assault intended to prevent dental records being used. Had Porter done that?

The coroner had recorded it as death by misadventure: perhaps suicide, or perhaps the result of violence, with the suggestion of some kind of disagreement between Porter and his dealer.

Whatever the truth of it, there seemed little doubt now that Porter had used that death as cover for his own escape. What kind of person does that?

Fletch mulled over all this on his drive back down to his flat by the old harbour, but he didn't reach any conclusions. He knew he should be concentrating on the facts of the case before him but found it hard to escape the belief that what had happened eight years ago might somehow be part of the explanation. He was damned if he could work out how, though.

The next morning, he got the call that they'd found where Porter had been staying, so instead of heading to the station Fletch drove back down to the bay.

The place was a bed and breakfast in a terraced street just back from the seafront, not far from the flat where Donna Currie was now staying with her friend. A panda car was pulled up in the street behind Fai Lee's Escort.

The front door was open and Fletch went in, following the sound of voices to a kitchen at the back where a woman he took to be the landlady sat at a big wooden table with Lever, one of the other DCs on duty today.

"This is Mrs. Cunningham," Lever told him, straightening in his seat and trying hard not to look like a schoolboy in his father's suit—a feat he never quite achieved. "Says Gavin Porter showed up here two days ago, kept himself to himself."

"Always polite," chipped in the landlady. "Which was nice, given the look of him."

Fletch nodded and smiled and refrained from pointing out that there were a lot worse things than looking like a sixties throwback. "May I?" he said, nodding back into the house.

"Upstairs, first landing," said Lever.

Fletch went back through to the hallway, then up the creaking stairs, past walls lined with fading, sepiaed photographs.

Four doors opened off the landing, one of them standing open, more voices from within. Fletch went to stand at the threshold. He saw a fair-sized bedroom, with space for a double bed, a wardrobe, an armchair by the window, and a basin and mirror in the corner. Fai Lee had the wardrobe open, a rucksack part-emptied on the floor before him.

"Guy travelled light," Lee told him.

"Obviously didn't plan to be here long."

"No, I think it's more that he didn't have much in the way of belongings. This bag is all he needs: a few clothes, a couple of books."

"No worldly possessions," said Fletch. "Apparently he travelled out to the East to find some kind of enlightenment."

"Maybe he found it."

Careful not to disturb anything, Fletch had a look around the room, easing drawers open with the tip of his pencil, squatting to peer under the bed. There was nothing other than the rucksack. If it wasn't for the small amount of cannabis found in Porter's possession, he might have been a monk.

"Hey, Fletch, you might want to take a look at this." Using a pair of tweezers, Fai held up a sheet of paper covered with closely spaced writing, before placing it on the bed for Fletch to examine.

Fletch read it quickly before using his pencil to flip it over so he could read the other side.

It was a letter, an apology, apparently written by Porter. Loaded with guilt and regret. Apologizing over the faked suicide… *I'm so sorry I misled you, my love.* Feeble excuses about being weak, and it being the only solution he had been able to see at the time. But now…

Now Porter was truly sorry. He was a different person. Stronger and wiser. He understood his place in the world and needed to make reparation for past transgressions. He'd come back to put things right.

"And how did that go for you, Gavin?" Fletch muttered, earning a strange look from Fai Lee.

***

"Hi. Belle's phone." Belle was in the bathroom, so Donna had answered her phone.

"Donna? Is that you?" Despite answering with her best telephone voice, the caller had recognized her.

"Mum? Why are you calling Belle's number?"

"Donna. How are you? We heard the news. So awful. We always knew that man was no good."

She rushed to catch up. "Mum, what are you saying?"

"Gavin Porter. How could he do such a thing? How could he put you through what he did?"

"Have you been speaking to Isobel?"

"Does it matter? He did all that, and then he came back and…"

And had himself killed in my front room? Donna didn't say this out loud, though.

"It's fine. I'm handling it. Belle shouldn't have worried you."

"She's concerned for you. And we are, too. How are you handling it, Donna?"

"I'm fine. I'm not having another breakdown." Even as she said this, though, she wondered how true it was, how close to the brink she might be, all over again. Had Belle seen warning signs?

"That man…"

"It's not Gavin's fault, Mum. This whole thing is awful, but you can't blame him."

"He lied to you, Donna. He lied to everyone. And he broke you. I can't have him doing that again."

"I'm okay, Mum." She swallowed. She was struggling not to let her mother hear the break in her voice, struggling not to cry.

"You don't really remember how you were last time, do you, Donna? You blanked a lot of it out."

It was true. Donna's memories of the time after Gavin's apparent death were littered with gaps. Whether that was due to her mental condition or the medications they ended up putting her on, she didn't know. Maybe it was simply that she didn't *want* to remember.

"I'm okay, Mum. Really I am."

Just then, Belle emerged from the bathroom, clutching a terry-towelling robe closed as she reached back with one hand to find the belt.

"I've got to go, Mum." Then, when she'd hung up, she said to her friend, "You didn't have to tell my parents. I'm fine."

"Are you, Don? I'm concerned. I can't bear the thought of you going downhill again, like you did back then."

When they hugged, Belle smelt of Pears soap.

"I'm okay."

The door buzzer sounded almost immediately, and Belle went to the window and looked down. "It's your copper friend," she said. "I think he has a thing about you."

Belle opened the door to the flat and stepped back, still clutching her robe shut with one hand. "Officer!" she said. "Back so soon. You simply can't stay away, can you?"

Yesterday, Fletcher would have been thrown by this. He'd have flushed and stumbled over his words and not known where to look. This morning, though, there was something different about him. Something harder in the look he gave Belle and then Donna as he stepped into the flat.

"Miss Currie," he said, with a nod. "I've just come from a bed and breakfast two streets away from here."

"Yes?"

"Did you know Gavin Porter was staying in town? That he'd been here two days?"

She shook her head. Gav knew where she lived. Had he known where she worked, too? Had he been spying on her?

"We found a letter among his things," Fletch went on. "An apology for all the pain he'd caused by faking his death."

"I… I never saw that letter," she said. Then she thought. "But you say it was among his things… Then obviously he never sent it, did he?"

"The paper was crumpled, as if someone had balled it up and thrown it in the bin—or back in his face when they confronted him."

Donna was shaking her head. "No," she said. "That didn't happen. Gavin never sent me a letter. I didn't see him. I didn't know he was here."

But even as she spoke, her mind was racing, stirred by the call from her mother. Last time… Last time she'd sunk to depths she'd never imagined possible. Such a dark place. So dark she'd blanked it out…

And here was this detective, standing in front of her and recounting a scene so vivid, in which she had starred and yet did not recall. She could even picture it: the look on Gavin's face as she scrunched up his pathetic letter of apology—as if that could ever make amends for the damage he had caused—and thrown it back in his face.

She could picture it so clearly that, for a moment, she wondered if it was some kind of fleeting memory.

Then DC Fletcher turned to Belle.

"That's what really puzzled me," he said. "Why did he still have the letter? Was he the one who had screwed it up? Or had he shown it to someone else?"

Belle?

Donna stared at her friend, and in that moment she knew. There was no surprise on Belle's features. Just a slight twitch at the corner of her mouth, a tightening of the jaw.

"What's he saying, Belle? What did you do?"

"You had a thing for him, didn't you?" said Fletcher. "Eight years ago. Did you give him some kind of ultimatum back then? Did you seduce him? That's what Gavin couldn't handle, isn't it? That's what he couldn't work out how to escape from. The guilt and confusion. That's why he fled. But he found what he was seeking. He found enlightenment. He made peace with the world and who he was, and he came back to confront his mistakes and make amends."

"Really?" said Belle. "Is that your tidy little explanation? Filled with eastern wisdom, Gavin comes back to make everything right again?"

"Well, what was it, then?"

For a moment, Belle held his look, then she shook her head. "This is ridiculous. You're just making things up to fill the gaps. It really is nonsense."

With that, Belle turned and went into her bedroom.

Donna pushed past Fletcher, reaching the bedroom door just as it slammed shut. She reached for the handle and felt resistance, as if Belle was holding it from the other side. Then the handle turned, and Donna stepped into the room.

"Belle?"

Belle moved away from the door and across to the window, where she stood peering out through the net curtains.

"Is it true, Belle?"

Her friend said nothing. The fact that she no longer objected said it all, though.

"Why?"

Now Belle turned. "You can forget all the enlightenment bullshit," she said. "Gav didn't see the light and make his peace with the universe. All he wanted was another chance with you, Don. Yes, he and I had a thing back then. I thought it was something meaningful, but Gav only saw it as a mistake, buried in the past with all his other mistakes. When he showed up here two days ago, he came to me, not you, and for a moment I thought it was *me* he wanted…"

"What happened?"

"He wrote that letter and actually had the nerve to show it to me, to see if I thought it would work. He didn't care about me—he just wanted me to help him work out how to approach *you*. So yes, that part's true: we fought, I screwed up the letter. So what? It was just a row. Bad timing, given what happened to him at your house."

"You did more than that, though, didn't you?" said Fletcher, moving into the room past Donna. "What was Gavin doing at Donna's house? He was hardly going to break in if he wanted to make his peace. He must have been invited there, let in… Someone planned this, because they were careful to leave very little evidence, and what evidence they did leave pointed squarely at Donna. Her coffee cup in the kitchen—a quick cup before work, I presume—and then one with Gavin's prints on it, arranged to make us believe they'd shared coffee before fighting. By that act alone, you've made it clear that this was no spontaneous act of passion. It was planned. Cold-hearted and planned."

All Donna could do was stare, as a flood of emotions flashed across her friend's face. She didn't know where to begin. Had Belle harboured this resentment all this time, along with the secret of her affair with Gavin? She remembered how Gavin had been in the lead up to their Nepal trip. So erratic and moody. It was that which had led to Donna saying she didn't want to go. And it was all Belle's fault…

"I never did answer your question when I first came here," Fletcher said to Belle. "But the answer is yes, I do have handcuffs on me. And now I'm going to use them."

Bait

By Simon Bestwick

It was late night, in a bar where you couldn't smoke anymore but where the memory of stale tobacco hung in the air like a ghost. I was nursing a double Black Bush against the evil hour of having to go out into the cold, when the door flapped open and in she came, chased by a flurry of snow and a gust of bitter wind.

She barely looked old enough to drink but the barmaid didn't bother her for details like ID; Mulligan's wasn't that sort of bar, or the kind that can afford to turn away paying customers. So, she served the girl—a pale slip of a thing, flower-pretty and flower-fragile to look at, dark-haired and white-faced—a beer, then went back to polishing glasses while the girl sat at a table and drank.

With its old worn carpets, padded bench seats and faded, flock wallpaper, Mulligan's isn't the kind of bar that pretty, innocent-looking girls like this one came into either, as a rule. While my normal tendency's to mind my own business, I found myself keeping an eye on her as I nursed my drink. Some of it might have been out of a vestigial sense of chivalry or paternal instinct, but—at least to start with—it was probably the kind of fascination that draws the eye to a car wreck as it happens.

There were three or four other customers in the bar, none of whom I knew by name and a couple of whom I knew by sight; I'd never exchanged more than a dozen words with any of them. Because—all together now—Mulligan's isn't that kind of place. You don't go there to socialise or get lucky, except maybe on the rare occasions one of the working girls from Becker's Lane comes in to warm her bones between customers. You go there to drink and either brood on—or temporarily blot out any recollection of—the circumstances that had made you the kind of person who spent their nights drinking at Mulligan's.

That, and occasionally you'd put something on the jukebox. They had a
good selection—Pink Floyd, Sisters of Mercy, Leonard Cohen—along with
the usual crowd-pleasers. Just then it was playing *Shine On You Crazy Diamond*,
all thirteen or fourteen minutes of it. That's what's known as value for money.
The song was still on the intro, where the opening G-Minor chord's giving
way to Wright's low, mournful Minimoog solo but Gilmour hasn't come into
on the guitar yet, all of which suited the mood of painless melancholy I'd been
sinking into throughout the night.

And then the prick in the corner had to spoil it all.

He didn't do anything—not there, not then—but I'd seen him in Mulligan's
a couple of times before. He wasn't big, but he was wiry, with scrubby gingery
hair and an equally scrubby ginger beard. There was an eerie stillness about
him: I'd never seen him move except to drink. The rest of the time he'd just
sit, staring blankly ahead, until it was time to get another vodka and coke
or to leave.

Except this one time; the last time there'd been a pretty woman in the
bar at the same time as him. Ginger's head had swivelled round like part of
a machine, and he'd hunched forward, staring at her. It was the only time
I'd ever seen anything resembling emotion on his face. It had looked like
hunger. When the girl had gone out—maybe because his scrutiny had started
to disturb her—Ginger'd sat in silence for a count of five, then got up and
followed her out, leaving his drink half-finished on the table. I hadn't gone
after them, and I'd purposely avoided reading the papers or looking at the
news for several days afterwards. I'd done my best to screen out the bar gossip,
which I normally liked to eavesdrop on. But I didn't want to know. I knew
enough. And while not much bothers me these days, that did.

And so, I wasn't surprised to see Ginger looking at the girl, the same way
he had the other one. Nor was I at all surprised when, after the girl finished
her beer—tapping the base of the bottle to coax the last few suds into her
mouth—got up and went out, Ginger sat still for a mental count of five before
getting up and going out too. The only surprise was the one I gave myself,
when I knocked back the last of the Black Bush and went across the bar,
pulling my parka on as I went.

***

I had no real idea what I was going to do beyond not letting history repeat itself, and I had even less of a clue once I made it out onto Cairn Street, because there was no one in sight—not the girl, and not Ginger. A car swished by, wheels churning at the slush on the tarmac and headlights trapping swirls of snow, but the only person in it was an old man with white hair and thick moustache.

I spun first one way and then the other, but all I saw was the light shining on wet empty pavement and grey slush. Cairn Street cuts a pretty straight line through downtown, linking two other main roads, and there's little or nothing branching off.

Other, I remembered then, than the side alleys that connect it to China Row, a narrow, cobbled backstreet that runs behind the buildings on this side of the road, where the various businesses put out their garbage. One of those side alleys was three or four yards ahead, and now I could see what'd happened very clearly, projected onto the screen on the back of my skull: Ginger coming out of Mulligan's, seeing the girl, and then accelerating after her with a cat's speed and silence.

I went towards the alley, converting my normal shuffle into something like a shambling trot, and I was almost there when I heard the scream.

I did the only thing I could think of and blundered down the alley onto the backstreet with a bellow. "Get off her you bastard," were, I think, my exact words. Definitely something along those lines, anyway. Something that would have immediately made clear why I was there; I know that much, because I left China Row alive.

I caught a glimpsed blur of motion darting into the shadows, but my main focus was the small thin body lying on the ground and the blood shining black around it in the reflected light pollution from the snow clouds above. "Fuck," I said, and then "Fuck," once again. I dropped into a crouch by the body, although I could already guess from its stillness and the amount of blood that there wasn't much point. Maybe I was just glad of the excuse not to try and chase Ginger and risk serious injury, even if I caught the bastard.

I genuinely thought the body was her, though—I'll blame the dim light and the influence of several Black Bushes for that—until I flipped it over and saw who it really was.

Ginger was actually still alive, if only just. His eyes were staring up at the falling snow and his lips were twitching. If I had to guess, I think he was trying to say something along the lines of *What just happened?*

A switchblade laid in the snow beside him, but there was no blood on the blade: his weapon, not hers, so I guessed I'd read his intentions correctly. There was a stab wound in his throat, but it wasn't a cut. I felt a little sick when I realised what she'd done: her knife had both a cutting edge and a sharp point, and she'd used the point to puncture his voicebox, so that after the initial scream all he'd been able to manage were the thin whistling sounds I finally registered he was making.

As for the rest of the wounds: he'd been cut up badly, and in what could only have been seconds, given the time it'd taken me to get down the alley. But I could see, too, that it hadn't been a frenzied act; madness might or might not have been involved, but a method of some kind certainly had been. One of the wounds, for instance, ran down his right arm from the shoulder to the elbow, slicing through coat, clothing, and muscle like warmed-up butter. Bone gleamed white through the red. That would've been when he'd screamed, at a guess: when she'd turned on him and turned the tables. Then the stab to the throat, silencing him. And then, the rest of the damage.

The crotch of his jeans was a sodden, ragged hole, and the source of most of the blood, although he was leaking from a couple of torso wounds too. When I looked across the alley, I could see something else lying wet and steaming in the snow. A chunk of blood-soaked denim, and something else. It was too shadowy to see it in any more detail, thankfully, but lying a few inches from it was something small and egg-shaped, and I quickly looked away.

A *very* sharp blade, indeed. She'd grabbed his groin and sliced—quickly and surely, presumably without injuring herself—then stabbed him and run. If I hadn't turned up, I suspected she'd have taken a lot more time and been considerably more inventive. What she'd done to Ginger hadn't been about self-defence, it had been punishment.

Boots clicked on the cobbles, down in the shadows she'd run into. I could hear the sound of cars up on Cairn Street, the hiss and swish of their tyres on the road, but it seemed very distant suddenly, and China Row seemed far colder and lonelier than it usually did.

She was holding two knives when she came out of the darkness. Both had long, thin, black, triangular blades. Old-style commando knives, I guessed. One glistened and dripped.

I stood up and stepped back from Ginger, who let out a last whistling breath which then rattled in his ruined throat. I hadn't realised how much noise he'd been making (relatively, at least) until he stopped and the alley was silent.

She stood there, very still. There wasn't, as far as I could see, a drop of blood on her, not counting the knife and the fingers of one preternaturally white—latex-gloved, I realised—hand. Her face was very pale, haloed by her dark hair, and utterly calm, almost like a Madonna. Dark eyes, studying me.

She cocked her head, lips pursed. I was a problem: not a threat, because she clearly knew how to deal with one of those and could have caught and finished me long before I reached the alley, but a puzzle, a conundrum. I'd come to help her, after all. And I wasn't trying to run, or screaming for help or cops (which, in my experience, are rarely the same thing). All that, I suppose, is why she hesitated; for a few seconds, she had as little idea as me what to do next.

And so I said, "Fancy a drink?"

The corner of her mouth went up; then she showed her teeth in a small laugh and nodded. "All right," she said, then motioned with her blade in the general direction of Mulligan's. "Not there, though."

"Obviously."

She moved across the alley, moved one of the bins aside and took out a rucksack, shrugging it on. "Know anywhere near the bus station?"

"Yeah."

"Lead on, then."

***

But not from too great a distance, she added without actually saying it aloud. She was no more than a couple of paces behind me when we came out onto one of the city's more populated streets, the knives out of sight but no doubt ready to be deployed at a second's notice.

"You broadminded?" I said, nodding in the direction of the Black Swan.

"Take a guess."

I guessed she was and led the way into the bar.

Once upon a time, the Swan had been the hub of the city's queer community; these days it was more of an outlier, although it still had a loyal, if aging, clientele of the drag queens who'd frequented it in its heyday. But when they'd built the new coach station—twenty years ago now, so not really so new—the Black Swan had had the good luck to be on the corner beside it, giving it a new lease of life from people just arriving or departing who wanted the permanent chill chased out of their bones.

"Get us a drink," she said. "Bottle of Beck's for me."

I did as she told me to, plus a double Jameson's for myself—the Swan sadly didn't run to Bushmills—and joined her at the out-of-the-way corner table she'd selected. I didn't sit too close; I didn't want to crowd her, having seen how swiftly and decisively she reacted to anything she interpreted as a threat. Not to mention gruesomely. I had a mental flash of the dark, clotted thing lying in the alley a few yards from Ginger, and that little egg-shaped object beside it. I took a larger sip than I usually manage of the Jameson's, and wished I'd ordered a triple.

The girl, meanwhile, had picked up her beer. She'd scooped up a couple of the paper napkins the Black Swan's staff left on their tables—they serve food within certain hours—and wrapped it round the bottle's neck. No fingerprints that way. Good at covering her tracks, this one.

"You've done this before, haven't you?" I said.

She raised an eyebrow. "Done what? Gone for a drink with a strange man in a gay bar?"

"What you did in the alley back there."

"Keep your voice down." She wasn't even looking at me while she said it, but scanning the bar; even so, and despite the lack of volume or inflection, I knew that was a threat. She spent a little longer taking in her surroundings, then returned her attention to me. "You only just realised that?"

I sighed. "Suppose I always knew it. Ginger didn't stand a chance, did he?"

"You're sorry for him now?"

I suppose a part of me was, having seen how thoroughly and brutally she'd dealt with him; besides, anyone dying like that is going to look so lost and alone in those last few seconds it's hard not to feel a glimmer of pity, whatever they've done. But I shook my head. "He got what he paid for," I said, which was just as true.

"That he did." She smiled for the first time, and there was something oddly genuine and warm about it; in that moment she just looked like a girl, barely old enough to drink legally, who'd just heard a joke she liked. "They always do."

"Right."

I hadn't meant to sound sceptical, but her smile faded. "Hey. You saw what happened. You didn't come chasing after us for *his* sake, did you?"

"No, I didn't."

"Well, then." Another swig of Beck's, and she leant back in her seat. "This is nice."

"Really?" I've heard the Swan called a lot of things over the years, but never that.

"Mm." She closed her eyes. "Actually being able to relax in someone's company—specially a man's. Don't think I've ever done that bef—"

I only moved to pick up my drink, but that was enough; her eyes snapped open, and she sat up straight, one hand in her pocket where her knife lived. After a moment she breathed out and settled back again. "Sorry," I muttered.

"Forget it." A sigh. "Force of habit, I suppose. I'm out of practice relaxing. But it's nice, all the same. Nice to be honest with someone for once."

"Yeah, I can see that wouldn't be an option."

"It's easier with women," she said. "You can tell some of the truth. Cry them a river about abuse or whatever. But even then, it tends to mean having to play the victim." When she looked at me this time, all the warmth that had seemed to accumulate between us was gone; I think I actually drew back from her a tiny bit, hunched inside my parka against the sudden chill. "And I don't like that."

Sometimes it's better to say nothing; I couldn't think of any response that wouldn't have sounded either fatuous or like clumsy, unsubtle probing. So, I waited instead; if she wanted to talk, she would.

"I never do anything," she said. "Well, you saw that yourself, back in that shithole bar."

"Hey," I said. "That shithole bar's my local."

She gave me a look that rendered words superfluous. "I just need to go in and have a drink. That's all I ever seem to need to do. Have a drink and look halfway pretty—that's all any girl needs to do in the right place, right time of night. Sometimes you don't even need that. And they come trotting after you. Just like that little creep did tonight." She smiled now; it would have been warm and welcoming if not for the context. "They think they're going to have their fun with you."

"And you disabuse them."

She nodded. "Pretty much, yeah." She looked mildly impressed that I knew a fancy word like 'disabuse.' Well, as she'd said, opportunities for this kind of conversation couldn't be common, so it must be nice to feel as though you were talking to someone with half a brain.

"It's very easy," she said. "Because they think it will be. They think it's going to play out one way, and before they know it, it's playing out the other. That's half the battle right there; by the time they even realise they're in trouble—"

"Their knackers are lying on the floor," I said.

She actually laughed out loud at that—a genuine laugh, like her smile a minute ago. "You're funny," she said, with what sounded like real … affection? No, that would be going too far. Warmth, anyway. "But yeah. I mean, not that I can't handle myself in a fight, if one of them *did* know what'd hit him. I know that because I *have*. But nine times out of ten—ninety-nine out of a hundred, really—they never get that far."

"Ninety-nine out of a hundred?" I asked. "You've done that many?"

The smile faded. "I've actually lost count," she said. "I'll go somewhere new, enjoy myself for a bit, then catch the bus or the train or whatever before anyone starts asking questions. You've just got to keep moving."

"Like a shark?" I heard myself say. "If you stop moving, you die?"

"That's a myth," she said. "About sharks. But—" Another smile. "I suppose, yeah. I kinda like that idea. And if you think about it, it's a kind of public service. Cleaning up the streets."

"How long have you been—"

"No idea. Feels like forever. Next question." There was a sudden, brittle coldness in her voice: I don't want to explore that topic, it said. Move on if you know what's good for you.

"All right," I said. "Why, then?"

She gave me a long, cold look: I guessed—and it shouldn't have been hard to—she found this question no less intrusive than the one before it. I remembered the knives and sat very still; I wanted to look around for potential escape routes if she went for me, but I was afraid to break eye contact. It was hard to gauge how long that moment lasted, but in the end, she reached for her beer, picked it up again and took a swig. "A man raped me," she said. "He raped me, and he got away with it. So, I went after him and I punished him myself, and then I ran away, so that the police couldn't get me. And since then, I've got by doing the same thing over and over again. Your friend, back in the alley there?"

"He wasn't my friend—"

"Emptied his wallet out first. That's how I do it. Revenge and money."

She finished her beer and put the empty bottle down. "No?"

"What do you mean, no?"

"Is that a neat enough explanation or not? How about this? It was my daddy. He used to molest me when I was a little girl. Died before I ever got the chance to do anything about him. So now I'm getting my own back. Again: plenty of men like that out there, and there's nowhere near enough being done about them. Which works better for you? Both are pretty clichéd, I know. The childhood trauma angle makes me more sympathetic, doesn't it?"

"I just asked why."

"You did, yes. But those were the answers you were expecting, wasn't it? I was a victim, so now I'm a monster. I told you before—I don't play the victim. I hate that. That isn't why I do this."

"So, what is?"

"Does it matter? You want an explanation. X happened, therefore Y. It isn't like that." She leant forward. "There was somebody I thought was the one I'd marry, and he dumped me. Or ghosted me after one date. You wouldn't feel so sorry for me then, would you? And you'd be a lot more scared of me."

I wasn't exactly feeling free of fear just then as it was. "Is *that* true?" I said. But she just smiled.

"Maybe," she said, "there *isn't* any explanation. Maybe I just do it because I like it."

I think—I can never be sure, of course—but I think that she didn't know, herself. Or she'd forgotten, along with how long she'd been doing it. I wondered how old she was; even under the lights in the Black Swan, which were brighter than those in Mulligan's, she looked no older than her early twenties. How many Gingers could there have been for her? Maybe she didn't get old: maybe she was a kind of Flying Dutchwoman, condemned to walk the earth eternally luring predators to their doom, like a landbound siren with a sharp knife. Too many whiskies talking, there: I shook my head.

"What?" she demanded.

"Nothing," I said. "Just… I suppose you're right. It doesn't really matter why."

"That's right," she said. "This is what I do. It's what I am."

I thought, again, of sharks: moving, killing, and moving on. Or maybe it wasn't even that. *It's what I am*, she'd said. She was a function; she was what she did. Like a machine. This little encounter was an aberration: what had happened in the alley was the norm.

"So, what happens now?" I said at last.

She shrugged. "Are you going to go to the police?"

"I don't think we'd be here if I was, would we?"

"Do you not think so?"

"It's a bit of a public place for a murder," I said.

"It wouldn't be murder. It'd be simple self-preservation on my part."

"The police wouldn't agree."

"The police." She gave a short laugh. "Yeah, well. They've never been a problem in the past." She settled back in her chair and gave me a calculating look. "You've seen how fast I work. And I didn't pick this seat by accident. We're tucked away, out of sight. And you're the one who went to the bar. How many people here do you think would remember my face?"

Under the parka, under the sweater, under the shirt, under the vest, I felt sweat run down my spine.

"You're thinking you could call out for help. And I mean, yeah, you could try. You could definitely *try*. Like I just said, you've seen how fast I am."

I licked my lips, which were very dry. I badly wanted to take a sip of my drink, but I was afraid to move. She was right. It had taken her seconds to practically dismantle Ginger. She wouldn't need anywhere near as much time for me.

"Oh, it'll be a quicker death than *he* got," she said. "You're not like him. You're just a loose end. Nothing personal. Just covering my tracks. You've got a few layers on there, but…" She shook her head. "My knives are good. Very sharp, very strong. And I know exactly where to slide it in. Straight into your heart. You wouldn't make a sound. It would look like a quick hug, if anyone even bothered glancing our way."

She settled back and added, distantly: "And then I get up and walk out, get the first coach to somewhere else. I get off, somewhere along the way, find a place with a bathroom and make a few quick changes." She tapped the rucksack beside her. "Makeup. Hair dye. A change of clothes. And then go back to wait for the next coach. Everyone's looking for a brunette in a long coat, but I'll be a blonde in leather, or a redhead in a hiking jacket by then. Or…" she shrugged. "You can take your pick. That's if anyone here's even noticed you by that point. But none of that'll matter to you, will it?"

A shark, a machine. A process repeated over and over again, and she didn't even know why. Despite everything, I almost felt sorry for her, but I didn't say that and hoped to God she couldn't see any sign of pity on my face. I was pretty sure she *would* kill me if she did.

"Will it?" she said.

"No," I said. "I suppose not."

She looked at me for a few seconds, toying with her beer bottle (still keeping that paper napkin between her fingers and the glass). I felt more sweat trickling down my spine and wondered what she expected to see in my face and what she'd do about it if she did. I tried to keep my expression blank, but in the end she smiled. "You *are* a cool one," she said. "Especially for a drunk."

I shrugged. It seemed safest.

"That, or you've just got a good poker face."

I shrugged again, for the same reason.

"I don't want to kill you," she went on, "but I'm struggling to find a good argument why I shouldn't."

"Still very public out here," I said. "Still a risk you'd be seen."

"True," she said. "But we could walk out of here, then down an alleyway. Plenty of them around the coach station. Two minutes' work before I get the coach."

"And you think I'd go with you? When staying put's my best chance?"

"I can be very persuasive."

"I bet." I reached for my whisky, very slowly. I couldn't wait any longer for another sip. "I've already said I'm not gonna go to the police."

"And why should I believe that?"

"Because he deserved it. Ginger did."

"Come on. Can't you do better than that?"

"Maybe I lost someone to a scumbag like him," I said. "How's that? Maybe that's why I'm drinking myself to death in shitholes like Mulligan's."

"I thought you said it wasn't a shithole."

"I said it was my local," I said. "Not the same thing. It's different when I call it that. So, there's one reason. Or hang on, here's another: maybe I've got a daughter I haven't seen in years and you're the right age and you remind me of her. How would that be?"

That got me an eye-roll by way of a response.

"Or how about this one?" I said. "I just don't give a shit."

She laughed. "That's a good one. *But*—" She pointed the bottle at me "—if you really didn't give a shit, you wouldn't have gone chasing after Ginger in the first place."

She had a point.

"Not looking good for you, is it?" she said.

"Suppose not," I admitted. "But what's it to you if I *did* go to them? You said yourself, they've never been a problem."

"I don't like tempting fate," she said. "Hm. What to do? What to do?" She extended a forefinger and began tick-tocking it back and forth from side to side. "Ip, dip, sky, blue, who's it? Not you." She pursed her lips and cocked her head, looking over my shoulder. I had a brief, momentary fear there was someone behind me, an accomplice, and that in a second the edge of a knife would slide across my throat.

Then she grinned. Suddenly, she was just a young girl again, and the idea of her being any harm to anybody was ridiculous. "Oh, what the hell," she said. "Go on. You can live."

"Thanks."

"You're funny. I don't get to have a proper break very often. This has been nice. Better get on, though."

She stood up, then hesitated. She rummaged in her pocket, took out a couple of high-denomination notes and dropped them on the table. "You're a lucky man," she said, then leant over and kissed my cheek. It was like ice, and I tensed up, convinced that the knife was going to slide between my ribs after all, but it didn't, and she straightened up. "Have a drink on me," she said, "lucky man."

And that was it. She turned away and walked out of the Black Swan, into the night and (presumably) towards the coach station, and I never even got her name. I don't suppose it would have been her real one, anyway, even if she still remembered what that was. No one else in the bar even looked up to see her go.

As for me, I finished the rest of the Jameson's, then went on out in search of another bar that served Black Bush. *Have a drink on me, lucky man*, she'd said. So I did.

Miss Scarlett

By Rose Biggin

T here's been another murder, *yet another murder*, and your presence is
required, again, and you know full well where you're going, no need to
RSVP to the glittering, black-edged invitation, you'll be there: Miss Scarlett
sighs and drops her cigarette to the ground, crushes the ash under the heel of
her satin shoe and looks about for the nearest exit. As usual, there isn't one.

***

As for the victim, there's only a chalk outline on the ground. A heavily-marked
absence and an instruction: solve this. The suspects will also be required to act
as detective, witness, cross-examiner, judge, jury, courtroom stenographer…
and they can trust no one, not even themselves. Place of death: huge
crumbling great sprawling ancient manor house on a stormy darkened night.
That much, at least, everyone can agree on.

***

Miss Scarlett is the first to arrive. She lets herself in: she no longer bothers
with the ritual of banging on the door and waiting a great stretch of rain-
sodden time for nobody to come and open it. The great brass doorknocker has
long since rusted into place anyway. So, Miss Scarlett pushes the heavy door
herself and steps inside, high heels tapping on the neatly tiled floor.

She calls out a greeting, simply for the pleasure of hearing her voice travel
down the empty hallway. The door slams behind her, and that echoes too.
For a moment she stands there, breathing the familiar smell of must, rotting
wood, mystery.

Miss Scarlett: a woman of secrets. A woman *for* secrets. Highly visible
and at the same time, utterly unknowable. Can you look at her directly? In
the darkened manor house hallway she blazes like a flame, a chili pepper

in red-hot satin and lipstick to match. In a red dress, always a red dress, she simply won't be imagined any other way: whether revealing or, alluringly, not revealing *yet*, Miss Scarlett is a wearer only of the most bespoke pieces. Off the shoulder but never off the peg: no, Miss Scarlett favours high fashion, skyscraper-high, designed and created and sewn up especially. Honestly, it's the only way to get dresses that fit like that. On hearing news of the murder, it's easy to imagine Miss Scarlett looking languidly over her wardrobe before doing anything else, running a hand across all those fabrics, all that red, ignoring the more dazzling items spangled with sequins or edged with fringe to eventually choose the long satin number, in which it's easier to visit the opera than explore a crumbling old mansion house in the dark. Miss Scarlett, holding her favourite red dress up against herself and looking into the mirror, sighing slightly at the divine vision reflected in the antique glass. She sighs as if asking herself: has it come to this? (And does she mean murder? Well, she might. There's no relying on Miss Scarlett, suspect number one.)

There are others, though, and Miss Scarlett knows they're coming. Soon there will be six in the house, and they all know one of them did this. For a long time, that will be all they know. Distrust will permeate the house like fog, only to be lifted when there is some degree of certainty. And so, Miss Scarlett and the others skulk through the otherwise empty house, seeking to learn the secrets of the crime that drew them here, looking to recreate the chain of events that ended with the chalk outline of the body there midway up the stairs, an X marked on the spot sparking a ghastly search for treasure.

Questions, theories, accusations, and counter-accusations: eventually the mystery will be solved. That's the only thing Miss Scarlett can know for sure.

(Although, that's just a theory: it's difficult to know what Miss Scarlett knows. What was her relationship to the deceased? One can only imagine adoration coming her way, but that's based on our own response to the sight of her in that red dress. Infatuation we may take as a given, then, but remember, that needn't lead to anything further, dangerous or otherwise. Or perhaps infatuation is being unfair, too flippant. Miss Scarlett might want to solve this mystery quickly because she also loved, deeply and truly, and she wants to know who is responsible for the death of someone who made her feel that way. None of this is incompatible with her being suspect number one, of course. Look at her, in that lipstick: no doubt she could love and kill the same person on the same night. If anyone could, it's Miss Scarlett.)

She enters the library, one of the quieter rooms in an already quiet house, the hush insulated by all the mouldering books stacked two or three volumes deep along the shelves. It's one of the warmer rooms, too: Reverend Green has gotten the fire going, and the light flickering away from the fireplace reflects golden shapes over the gilt spines of the books. There is an antique revolver on top of the drinks cabinet. Miss Scarlett knows a thing or two about firearms, enough to be drawn to it.

There's a sound behind her, something like paper rustling. A leather-bound book falls from the shelf, lands with a dull *thunk* on the floor.

"I didn't touch it," says the Reverend, a soft-spoken man it's difficult to imagine telling lies, or at least lies about books. He's backing away from the fallen book, pointing: "Look at the dust: those books haven't been moved for years. It must be the wind getting in from an open window."

Miss Scarlett goes to investigate, but before she can reach for the book, there is another soft sound behind her. She turns; the Reverend is gone.

***

This is not a house you can relax in.

Even if there wasn't a chalk outline on the floor to remind everyone of the deadly truth among them, the house is too big, too overreaching to be comfy. It's never been welcoming, even in its heyday of flung-open doors, hearty greetings, a string quartet playing in the corner as guests mill about: even in those days this house was intimidating, cold. It's exceedingly drafty: there are huge spaces between the rooms, long stretches of empty hallway, and the rooms themselves are somehow too large, containing sharply-carved furniture that towers over you from slightly too far off. The lamps are low, so shadows are always thick, and every footstep echoes, and sometimes the suit of armour's sword moves, and there is hardly any brandy left. The conservatory has not been tended for many years, and most of the glass panels are broken: the whole thing is more outside than in, these days. Ivy strains its fingers into the old hothouse and rain batters the dry stumps of the few remaining tropical plants, bending the leaves of the ferns that cower in the face of the storm. Sometimes, the headiness of being inside the mansion too long takes its toll, and somebody will declare they are going to the conservatory for fresh air: but they never stay long. An abandoned hosepipe is tied in a way that hints, shudderingly, at a knot around a neck; or the rusty secateurs show too much of their curved sharpness in the moonlight. Shards of terracotta all too easily resemble a series of blades or fragments of deadly broken glass, scattered over the gravel. Never mind the chalk outline on the floor over the stairway, the conservatory is the true memento mori in this place.

***

Miss Scarlett has someone in a headlock. They gasp for breath as she tugs them across the room, their feet scrabbling uselessly to get purchase, the Persian rug bunching up under them, aiding Miss Scarlett's efforts to get her opponent into the corner to immobilise them, somehow, quickly, any way she can. Her breath comes heavily with the strain of a sudden vicious ambush. Adrenalin makes her vision shake and everything slows down: she times the seconds through the pumping of her own heart, the sound resonating in her ears. There's blood in her mouth: it's coming from a cut on her face.

The job done, Miss Scarlett dusts her hands and locks the door behind her when she leaves.

***

Just outside the dining room, Miss Scarlett hears a conversation:

"Found anything?"

"Only this."

There's a metallic rattle, followed by the thump of something heavy. Miss Scarlett, hardly daring to breathe, inches closer to the open door.

Their voices are urgent, the words come quickly. "Well, what do you make of it?"

"On the whole, as a piece of evidence, I think it's convincing. Much more likely than strangulation."

"How so?"

"Easier, more straightfoward: these things are all over the house, you'd just have to pick one up. Much less messy."

"Having your skull bashed in with a candlestick is *less* messy, in your opinion?"

"You know what I mean. Less messy to organise beforehand: just pick it up and the job's done, right there on the spot." There's another heavy sound, as if the weapon is being demonstrated against some old furniture. "Besides: where would someone like *that* gather the nerve to plan to stab the bugger? I say, if it's the candlestick, we're talking something emotional. Snap decision, nothing premeditated. Spur of the moment. A crime of passion, if you like."

The response to this, when it finally comes, betrays some scepticism. It's easy to imagine the speaker sneering a little. "*That's* your theory?"

"Well, I…" There is a clatter, as if a candlestick has been dropped to the floor.

"Enough of this nonsense. I'm getting out of here." Footsteps approach the door and Miss Scarlett quickly ducks behind an old tapestry. As the figure stalks by she hears their further contemptuous muttering. "*Crime of passion* my foot." They practically spit the words in disgust.

Miss Scarlett understands why. Someone always ends up getting bogged down in the question of motive. They attempt to learn things that would shine light onto the relationship(s) between the victim, the suspects and the killer, answers that might begin to unlock what led to the tragedy in the first place. But Miss Scarlett knows there's no use thinking that way. It's far too late for *why*.

Miss Scarlett has known these people for years, that's the tragedy of all this. In other circumstances, they would have gotten to know each other so intimately by now. But hoping to reach any level of understanding is like coming across yet another locked room in this great dusty house. *Why* is an unknowable black hole around which the suspects all move, pulled along by its gravity but unable to reach the centre. They can never know each other that way, learn those sorts of answers. Miss Scarlett knows there's no use getting sentimental about all this: in fact, there isn't time to, and it would be dangerous to try. She cannot risk the vulnerability it would require. And so, she finds herself, like the others, surrounded only and always by potential enemies. The six of them dance around each other's uncertainties, never getting below the skin, forever bristling with distrust and double-bluffs, lying to each other and lying about lying, they are a company wracked with paranoia and suspicion and doubt.

For this reason, Miss Scarlett has taken to wearing a Glock at her upper thigh.

***

Colonel Mustard! Now there's a chap, a true man-about-the-place and no mistake and definitely one to keep an eye on: you mustn't ever trust a man who wears a pith helmet indoors. Or outdoors, for that matter: wearing a pith helmet at all might safely be considered a warning sign. We can at least hope that, when the body was discovered, he temporarily removed the pith helmet as a sign of deferential respect, but there's no way to be sure. (Assuming he was there, which we can't yet.) Even when he doesn't wear the pith helmet the faded yellow of his duds implies one. Here's a man with a past, with experiences: both endured and inflicted. This is a man who has pulled off some shady business, who has cast some insidious orders. No doubt there are many noble statues of him to be found in his hometown, and/or any towns he has made himself at home in, through the years: equally we may be sure those statues are regularly defaced with graffiti, chewing gum, a series of strategically placed traffic cones. Upright, ever upright, with his yellow clothes, military bearing, stunning moustache. What a hero.

Miss Scarlett avoids him when she can. Here he comes, there's no mistaking the regular march of his footsteps.

He stops, standing to attention as he always does. "Looking about here, are we?"

"Who's *we?* You can help me look, if you like." Miss Scarlett rises (she had been bending to examine footprints in the dust). She leans against the doorframe, winks at him.

He bristles at that. She does have the power to wrong-foot him, sometimes. They all do: the colonel underestimates everyone, so it's a hobby they all share, wrong-footing him. Except for the Reverend Green, who's far too nervous for that sort of thing.

The colonel taps his foot, looks nervously from his own foot to the markings in the dust. "I've got my eye on you," he says, sounding unsure. "Just you remember that."

Miss Scarlett could do all this in her sleep. "I will. And I bet you do."

***

You'd think, from the job description, anyone going by the moniker "Professor Plum" would be an old, jolly sort, long in the tooth and with smiling cheeks exceedingly well-red from happiness and beer, not to mention a plump mind that's exceedingly well-read from decades of thinking, debating, taking ideas out for a walk (while remaining sitting down, of course, no dedication to exercise in this one). A bushy beard and a home-knitted jumper in warm, welcoming purple, stretched over a huggable stomach. You may think all this. But no. Professor Plum clawed through the education system like a young wolf, and now looks at you with hungry eyes from the peak of the scholarly clifftop. You can barely imagine him without a tenure position: he must have gone without for a week at the most before landing the (ahem) plum job at the prestigious university. Yes, he's working on his next book; and yes, the grant came through, and oh, in the meantime, he has a few questions about *your* latest efforts...? Long in the tooth, yes, to take sharp bites with. There is a rich purplish tint to his polo-neck jumper, but the royal tone does not imply happiness or warmth along with the wealth: certainly nothing like mercy. No, this professor's purple puts you more in mind of a Roman emperor, swathed in the colour no commoner may wear on pain of death, and like a bloodthirsty voyeur at the gladiator games he casts a casual eye over your bibliography, laughs at the sight, and loosely throws out an arm to give the whole thing thumbs-down.

So much for the professor. But murder?

It seems unlikely he would need to employ a messy and attention-grabbing technique like *murder* to get anyone out of his way. Surely he has access to cleaner, smoother methods to destroy someone: ways that are quieter, more devastating, tactfully eloquent, perhaps containing passages in Latin. Far easier to imagine someone setting out to get rid of *him*, and the poor victim outlined on the mansion cobbles is only an accidental crossfire-catch, a third party striding innocently into the wrong place at the wrong time just at the moment one of his long-suffering colleagues *finally* gets their own back. Still, you never know, maybe the messy and attention-grabbing technique of murder was the best way for him to achieve his very precise and particular research aims this time around. Best keep an eye on him.

***

Sometimes Colonel Mustard and Miss Scarlett meet, quite by accident, in the ballroom. The varnish on the dancefloor has faded to dullness, and the chandelier has long since been taken down and now sits bulbously in the corner, half packed into a bag. The crystal drops that are still visible swing slightly in a barely-there breeze. Sometimes music plays, and when it does, they usually dance. They take it in turns to lead.

Miss Scarlett usually asks something like: "Do you ever imagine this place all done up, filled with happily dancing people?" (It's something she often thinks about.)

He shakes his head. "I despise social gatherings. Garish; flippant."

Miss Scarlett laughs, resists the temptation to bury her face into his shoulder. "I'm not saying you'd be *invited*. But can you imagine it going on?"

His face falls into a sadder shape. "To be honest with you, I can't."

"I know what you mean. I can't imagine life happening here. Everything's so wretched, the sadness is worn in."

"Careful, you're getting romantic."

They reach the corner of the ballroom, perform a perfectly executed turn. These moments are the closest thing to a truce between the two of them. They've had all the political arguments possible. *Let's agree to disagree*, says the colonel, and Miss Scarlett gives up, because after all, he's the only passable dance partner in the place.

Miss Scarlett sighs, feels the press of the Glock pistol beneath the satin fabric of her dress. "*My* life certainly doesn't happen here."

***

Think about it, it's never going to be Mrs. White, is it? Safe and dependable Mrs. White, the *cook* of all people, almighty provider of nourishment, creator of delicious hot things, a cheerful reminder of life in this deadly place where everything is decay and darkness, the antidote to the cold and clawing *hunger* of all that betrayal and distrust in flickering candlelight. Her name isn't even a colour, it's the soothing calmness of a fresh tablecloth, the richness of whole milk, the thick sweetness of royal icing. Mrs. White whipping past you in her starched apron to get to the stove before something boils over. The metallic clattering of pans, the soft sprinkling of sugar, the breaking of eggs, her presence brings all these sounds with her and a sense of calm with it: the sense that the most important things in life are being taken care of, somewhere. Fine dust of flour on her cheeks and hands even though she isn't actually baking anything: that's Mrs. White, no murderer, the closest she'd get to killing is running after a troublemaker with a rolling pin. When it's Mrs. White, it's a fluke.

Miss Scarlett knows this, and that's why she and Mrs. White, out of all of them, have the strongest enmity. Absolutely hate each other, these two.

You'd think Miss Scarlett would reserve her strongest feelings of anger and
resentment for Mrs. Peacock, that louche widow dripping with sapphires—
Mrs. Peacock, one might suppose, being a vision of what Miss Scarlett will
become in a few decades' time, a mutual hatred arising from the vanity of
small differences. But no, Miss Scarlett's biggest rage is reserved for Mrs.
White, the cheerful cook, and she is hated right back in return.

In one way this is easy to understand, for they embody pure opposites: one
is the bringer of the feast, chief creamer off the top of the harvest, while
the other would have you believe she never eats. One was made to host and
manage night after night of joyful communal gathering: the other remains
fiercely individual, destined for a life of clandestine meetings in darkened
alleyways even outside of this particular murder case, a life riding roughshod
over the normal schedule of a private citizen's mealtimes, a life swapping
betrayals for secrets, a life spent trading deadly knowledge for deadlier
certainties. But in another way the rivalry between them is a great shame.
They have more in common than they'd like to admit and naturally they both
wish, secretly, that they could be each other, if only for a day.

***

"Quick game, while we're here?"

The billiard room is one of the more comforting rooms in the old house.
Although admittedly this is not a house that prioritises comfort, the billiard
room is where you might at least feel you may attempt it. This is perhaps due
to its feeling, somehow, doubly antiquated: an entire space dedicated to the
pursuit of leisurely gaming feels luxurious enough these days, and this game in
particular is evocative of a slower pace of life, priorities our own age has left
behind. Kitchen, dining room: fair enough. We have those too, even if they're
smaller or combined. Even the notion of a ballroom survives in parts (we've
all danced about indoors), and if you don't have space for a conservatory, you
might manage a few plant pots. But an entire room—for *billiards*? A whole
chunk of the estate dedicated to a great heavy table and the gentle click of
smooth multi-coloured balls, glass of brandy with a dexterity challenge? We
can only dream. Thus, we gravitate to the billiard room, and wonder at the
sheer novelty of it.

Naturally Miss Scarlett often lingers in here. It's not uncommon for a game
to be played while the case ticks over through the rest of the house, not to

mention the fact that the soft baize covering of the table has seen other kinds of action. Energies grow high and intense in the presence of death, and during a mystery investigation there may pass long stretches of time when there is nothing to do. The unique combination of high feeling and deliberate idleness means it cannot be a surprise that a patch of the billiard table, where the initial triangle is made before the break-off shot, has been rubbed raw.

But, you know what they say. What happens in the billiard room…

Miss Scarlett runs a finger along the soft felt of the table. "I don't want to play," she says, noticing the blue chalk dust newly over her fingers. "Thanks for asking."

"None of us do." Mrs. Peacock, leaning heavily against the far end of the table, her tone betraying a state of utter exhaustion. "Why don't you tell me what I saw you whispering to the Reverend just now."

"Oh, don't try it." Miss Scarlett rolls her eyes. "I have nothing to say to him."

Mrs. Peacock narrows her eyes, presents an expression of absolute distrust. It gives Miss Scarlett an opportunity to examine her refined acquaintance more closely. Ever distinguished, Mrs. Peacock, even when she's clearly bone-tired… ah, her blue eyeshadow. Miss Scarlett looks down at her fingers. Same shade. Maybe *that's* why Mrs. Peacock is out of breath. The colonel was leaving this room earlier, and didn't he have a bit of a spring in his step…? Mrs. White, too, left here looking rather jolly. But then, Mrs. White always looks jolly. So maybe it's nothing sordid, and Mrs. Peacock is simply tired the same way they are all tired and has taken to retouching her makeup with the cue chalk.

***

The secret passages beckon with dark charisma. They're perfectly positioned, for one thing: one in each corner of the house, linked to the room in the opposite corner. The secret passages are built on paradox: they imply a journey of great length, given the distance they cover, but there's also, so it would seem, hardly any travel involved. Reappearance at the other end of the house is instantaneous. This structural secrecy might be one of the chief reasons for their appeal: the ongoing question of what traversing these passages actually entails, even for those who have just done it, can never be answered. The secret passages are like repelling magnets, bouncing you back if you get too close, and you've really no idea what they are.

Miss Scarlett knows. She travels through here often, picking a careful way across the treacherous terrain, treading over the gaps in the floor, the uneven wood, the slippery patches of mould. Her eyes slowly adjust to the darkness, and eventually she can pick out the brass pipes here and there (duck to get under them), a few splinters of old furniture (turn and contort to get past them), the air thick with dust and silence, everything cobweb shrouded and untouched for years. Once, to Miss Scarlett's utmost surprise, Mrs. White's old catering trolley. So *that's* how she so quickly responded to the Reverend's whispered wish for tea and buns.

A shadow moves before her, at the far end of the passage. Miss Scarlett whips the Glock from her thigh and holds it out. "Who's there?"

The shadow moves, slowly and gradually: both arms being raised. "Only a friend."

She wants to laugh. "That tells me nothing. You can't be a friend of *mine*, so are you a friend of the *killer's?*"

"I could be both. Not to mention that you could be the killer."

Miss Scarlett says nothing to that. She continues to aim the gun.

A gentle sound, like a sigh. "If you fire that down here, you'll blast through something structural." They sound weary. "You want to kick a hole in the foundations? You might bring this whole place down."

"If it makes you answer me. What are you doing down here?"

"Oh, making my way about. Searching."

"What for?"

"I don't know yet. So, I suppose I'm searching for whatever I'm searching for. And once I know that, maybe I can search for it properly." There's a particular quality to their voice: it takes Miss Scarlett a moment to place it and when she does, surprise makes her tremble, and her aim wavers. She remembers their grunting with pain as she pulled them over the Persian rug.

"How did you get out of there?"

The figure gestures broadly to the secret passage that surrounds them both. Then they take a step: Miss Scarlett's hand grips the gun tighter, but too late.

"Damn it," she says. Subtle changes in the acoustics confirm she is alone.

Miss Scarlett leans against the wall, not minding the scratches of old stone. This is always the most jarring of discoveries: that she herself can be surprised.

From above comes a high whistle, which within moments, even down here through the stone, grows in volume to a piercing shriek. It's the sound of Plum bringing the old kettle back to life to make himself a coffee, so she must be below the kitchen.

***

Pity Miss Scarlett. It's hard work, being the alluring figure of danger in the red dress all the time. Come towards me, back off, come closer, stay away—it's difficult to constantly put out such contradictory messages. She'd let the act drop if she could, but she's forgotten how, and she doesn't know who she'd be if she did. Not to mention the fact that she might be a killer: she really doesn't know herself at all.

Her entire existence is a lesson in the unknown. It's true for all of them, trapped in a house of nightmares, voyaging into the darkness that pervades these ancient rooms, groping towards an answer—*any* answer—but never able to get beneath the surface of themselves. Miss Scarlett knows she'll never be the one holding all the cards, of course, but it runs deeper than that: she knows they'll never solve the true mystery that runs through this place, the mystery of death itself, and that's the real pull, what really draws them here, regardless of the chalk outline and who's responsible for it this time, who did it and where and how—the best they can do is to leap once more into the impossible and try again, swimming against the current, straining to reach out towards the promise of an answer but knowing, deep down, that a real answer would be impossible, that you can't look the real question in the face, never mind an answer, and so here they are, *again*, spiralling ever further into the unknowable, Miss Scarlett's red dress screaming danger to herself as much as to anyone else, but—

***

But all this is yet to happen. Miss Scarlett sighs and goes back to polishing her gun.

***

The dark horizon suddenly bursts into a long line of light. Somebody is opening the box.

The Dance of Love and Hunger

by Robert Lopresti

T he first time I saw her was at a party on Treaty Street, over by the
university. K.C.'s brother was working at Hale's Ales, and he would tell us
whenever somebody ordered a keg. We knew if that much beer was flowing
near the school, we could probably crash the scene.

This was a big one. Four or five kids were living in the house, and they must
have invited everybody they knew. There were nearly fifty people, so slipping
in was no sweat.

I had a couple of beers and went looking for K.C. but he was already
talking to a redhead in a tight blue dress. I don't know how he does it.

I headed toward the dining room, hoping for something to eat. The speakers
were blasting Kings of Leon, but a guy with pink hair turned it off. "Show's
starting in the back," he yelled, and people headed outside.

I didn't know what kind of show it was, but I followed the crowd.

In the middle of the backyard someone had laid down strips of yellow tape
and made a sort of a circle, maybe ten feet across. Everybody gathered around
it and the folks in front sat on the ground.

There were two people in the circle. One was a dude with long blond
dreadlocks. He sat cross-legged on the grass, playing a tabla. The other was
the most beautiful girl I had ever seen.

She was a head and a half shorter than me, maybe five foot six. She had
black hair that went past her waist and a bright green blouse and a white skirt
that almost reached her bare feet.

Nobody in Broughton looks like that.

"This is the Song of the Gray Ghost," she said. She had an amazing smoky
voice, but she didn't sing. Instead, she raised her hands and I saw that she was

holding a violin and a bow. The drummer played a beat, and she closed her eyes and played.

I couldn't breathe. Didn't want to, because it would take energy I needed to watch and to listen.

Nobody tried to dance to the music. Nobody except her. She swayed and flowed like water down a brook. The audience just stared at her like I did, like we were all hypnotized.

She played for nearly an hour, only stopping for applause and to announce the next tune. "The Way of the Sinner." "The Fire Hymn."

I didn't know what any of the names meant, but I remember them all. They all sounded wild and amazing and strange, just like her music.

Just like her.

When she stopped, everybody was dripping sweat like it was August instead of October. The crowd went crazy, and everybody rushed up to congratulate her.

I just stood there.

"She's something, huh?" said K.C.

"Who *is* she?"

"A music student at the university, believe it or not. Calls herself Wren. Drummer is Larry somebody."

"Are they together?"

K.C. did a double take. "I'll be damned, Hugh. You hot for Wren?"

I went red. Some girls like me 'cause I'm big and strong, so it's not like I'm a virgin, but *they* find *me*. I've never been able to go after girls.

I sure as hell couldn't hit on someone like her. I wouldn't even be able to *talk* to somebody like Wren.

I got another beer and went into the basement where some guys were watching a Steve Carrell movie. By the time it was over, K.C. had left with that redhead, a philosophy major, he told me later. I walked home.

All night long fiddle music played in my skull.

***

"Get your head right," my father said. It was the morning after the party, and we were working on a deck in Graymoor. Dad called that part of town "North LA," because so many Californians had moved in.

"Houses in Washington are damned near free compared to what they pay down the coast," he had said a hundred times. "So they retire and move up here and goose everybody's taxes."

My dad is a contractor, and those Californians are most of his customers. Lately he's been doing a lot of work for a couple named Bud and Pepper.

Bud's a big guy, even older than my dad, and starting to go gray. He has curly hair and a broken nose. He looked like a movie mobster, and he used to work in Hollywood. Dad says I shouldn't ask him about his job, because it was something dull, like lighting, so Bud would rather keep it vague, pretend he was a director or something.

We worked on the deck and every few hours Bud came out to look at the view of Broughton Bay and complain that it didn't compare to what he had had in Laurel Canyon.

Then why not go back there, I wanted to say. But we needed the work.

His wife, Pepper, was younger than him, hot if you like older women. She would bring us lemonade wearing outfits that were way too skimpy for our fall weather.

That morning she was wearing a red tank top and denim shorts. "How are you today, Hugh?"

"Doing great, Pepper."

"Isn't it beautiful out?" She stretched, going up on her toes, and swinging her arms out and back.

"Beautiful," I agreed.

"You're so strong," she said. "I don't know how you work in the hot sun all day. Have a drink, Hugh."

She went back in the house, and I heard Dad behind me. "Keep it in your pants, son. We need this job."

"Not my type."

All Pepper did was make me think about that fiddler. While we sanded wood, I dreamed of ways to meet Wren. Go to the music department at the university, or another party.

Even in my head I couldn't picture myself having the nerve to talk to her.

***

That Friday I had to see my parole officer. His name was Mr. Topper and he looked like that district attorney from *Law and Order.*

I showed him the pay stubs my dad had made out for me and told him I was still living at home.

"You keeping away from the bad guys, Hugh?" he asked, looking over the top of his glasses.

That surprised me because he usually said, "bad companions."

"Excuse me?"

"I know it wasn't your idea to steal that car. I just hope you aren't hanging around with people like that anymore."

"I was the only one in the car. Ask the police."

"I did. They said the driver's seat wasn't set for a man of your size."

"Maybe that's why I hit the tree."

Mr. Topper sighed. "Whoever was with you didn't care enough to help you get away. I don't know why you care enough to protect them."

That hadn't been their fault, although the whole thing was K.C.'s idea and George was driving. I sprained my ankle in the crash, and they couldn't carry me, could they?

"You're a good man, Hugh. Keep yourself clear of bad companions."

***

George had an apartment over a restaurant downtown and we went there Sunday night to watch the Seahawks get clobbered. When the game was over, they wanted to go to a bar.

"I can't," I said. "It would violate my parole, remember?"

"Don't be such a pussy, dude."

"Ease up," said K.C. "If Hugh weren't a stand-up guy, we'd be on parole too."

"I just say you can't let it run your life. What are the odds your mother hen will wander into a bar on a Sunday night and see you?"

"I know Topper checks the bars. I'm not taking a chance on going back to jail."

We argued some more, and they decided to go without me. I felt bad about that. Worse, I was only allowed to drive for work, so I was gonna have to walk home.

I turned onto Devon Avenue around midnight and heard somebody screaming. There were three people up the block in front of the Devon Tavern. The screamer was short, standing between two tall guys.

It was Wren. She was wearing a white tunic thing, but I recognized her. I started running. The two men were almost as big as me. One of them had Wren's fiddle case in his hand and he held it way over her head while she jumped.

"Give that back, you bastard!"

"What'll you give *us*, baby?" said the bald guy. He kept her back with one big hand.

"Let's go for a ride," said the one with a buzzcut. "You can show us what it's worth to you."

There was a metal trash can on the sidewalk. It was a heavy thing, but I picked it up.

Buzzcut was closer to me, facing away. I thought about bringing the can down on his head, but I didn't want to kill anybody.

I threw it at his legs. The can bounced on the sidewalk and smacked him behind the knees. He fell backwards and screamed.

Wren and Baldy stood staring at me. "Give it to her," I said.

"Fuck off," he said.

I took a step toward him. "If I take it, I'll break your arm."

Baldy looked from me to his buddy. Buzzcut was flailing around, holding his leg and moaning.

"Don't drop it," said Wren. Her eyes were locked on the fiddle case. "Tell him you'll break his arm if he drops it."

Baldy gave up. "Screw this." He shoved the case at her chest. "You and Godzilla deserve each other."

He helped his friend up and they stumbled off.

I was alone with Wren. I knew I was blushing.

God, she was beautiful. I wanted to walk away before I said something stupid.

Then she collapsed to the sidewalk, hugging the fiddle case and weeping into her other hand.

"Hey," I said, "it's okay."

"Because of you," she said. "God, I was so *scared.*"

"It's okay," I repeated. All my words drifted away as I looked at her.

"Those bastards were—well, you know what they were trying to do." She looked up at me, wiping tears away. "You were amazing!"

"It wasn't anything," I said. "Glad I could help. You okay now?"

"Am I?" She seemed to be trying to decide. "I'm not hurt, thanks to you. Just shaking with fear. But that's nothing new. I'm *always* afraid, except when I'm performing."

She held out a hand and I helped her to her feet. Her hand was tiny and strong.

"You saved me. I'm Wren."

"I'm Hugh. I know. I mean, I know who you are." And I told her how I had seen her at the party on Treaty Street.

"God, was I lucky you were here. Let me buy you a drink."

So, I told her about being on parole, which was a stupid thing to do, but I couldn't think of anything else to talk about, and if I stopped talking, she might leave. Her eyes went wide, and I couldn't blame her. Here she was out on the street in the middle of the night with a convict.

But she just nodded. "How about a sandwich?"

There aren't many places downtown that stay open past midnight, but the gyro place did, and she bought me a platter. She had a veggie sandwich. "I don't eat meat. Have you lived here all your life?"

"Yeah. My folks met at Broughton High."

She smiled. "High school sweethearts. Are they still married?"

"Mom died of breast cancer." Like an idiot, I looked at her chest.

She didn't seem to notice. "I'm from Redmond. Daddy works for a software company. Mom left years ago."

"Another Microsoft millionaire?"

She laughed. That felt great. "I wish. No, he worked for a little firm that made educational games. They got bought out last year and he's starting a new company. What does your father do?"

I told her.

"Wow." Her eyes went wide. "That's cool. The two of you making things together. My dad says no one in this country knows how to build anything anymore."

"Well, they haven't started outsourcing deck building to India yet."

She laughed again and I could feel the blood pounding through me. I can't remember the last time a girl laughed at one of my jokes. And a girl who looked like Wren?

"I better get home," she said, when we were done.

"Should I walk with you?" I asked. "In case those idiots come back?"

"Oh, I think you scared them off, but sure. If you don't mind."

I didn't mind.

As we walked Wren talked, telling me about places she had played and hoped to play.

Wren was living in a funky house on West Hill, just below the university. She shared it with three other students.

Of course, I had a movie running in my head where she invited me in and gave me a special reward for rescuing her.

Of course it didn't happen. K.C. could have probably talked his way in. I didn't try.

"Thanks so much, Hugh. I'm glad you came along."

"Me too."

She hugged me and I was so shocked I barely hugged back. I felt like all the air had been squeezed out of me, even though her arms hadn't even reached all the way around me.

"Hey, I'm playing at another party next week. Want to come?"

***

"So, what did you do last night?" K.C. asked me on Monday. We were at a burger joint after work.

"What do you mean?" I asked. "I was with you guys."

"I mean after we split."

"Not much, I guess."

"I felt bad about leaving you, Hugh. But George really wanted a drink. You know how it is."

"It's okay."

"Saw some hot stuff there, too. We're supposed to call 'em later this week. Hey, maybe they have a friend for you."

"Don't bother."

I'm not sure why I didn't want to tell him about Wren. Maybe because if I had he would have asked me if I got any and kidded me because I hadn't.

Maybe he wouldn't even believe it had happened. Hell, I barely believed it and I was there.

***

My dad and I were almost done with the deck when Bud decided he didn't like it. "I didn't tell you to stretch it out over the hillside that way. It looks like crap."

I thought Dad was gonna blow a blood vessel. But he just stood there and if you didn't see the muscles in his throat, you would think he was as calm as the pine trees down the hill.

"I did what you asked. If you want changes—"

"I'm not paying extra for it, I'll tell you that. Anyone could see it shouldn't be so close to the goddamn blackberry bushes."

"I can show you the plans—"

"Screw the plans! I'm not paying for that trash and I'm not paying you to clean it up. *Fix* it."

"Okay," was all Dad said, and it was the first time since Mom died I heard him sound defeated. "I'll need to buy more wood."

"I'm coming with you," said Bud. "They gave you craps and scraps last time. I want to make sure I get what I pay for. Come on."

He marched off.

Dad looked around, saw me, and turned red. "What the hell are *you* looking at? Start painting the east end."

So I did. A while later Pepper came out. She was wearing denim shorts and a T-shirt that said QUEEN BEE.

"What do you do for fun, Hugh?"

"Me?" I said, like there was anyone else there. I thought of Wren. "I like music."

"Oh, me too. Do you like opera?"

"I don't know. I've never heard any."

"Bud and I go to every opening night at the opera down in Seattle. All that *passion*. Life and death. You should try—"

The phone rang. "Be right back."

I turned back to my painting. I was wondering what Wren would call her kind of music. Folk? Jazz? I'd have to ask her.

"Hugh," said Pepper, "come inside please."

I followed her. "Bud called. They're offering a discount for cash. He wants you to bring some over."

We were walking down a long hallway. She entered a room at the end, and I stopped at the door. It was the master bedroom. The king-size bed had a bright red quilt on it and most of the walls had mirrors. There was a mirror over the bed too, the first time I'd seen one of those outside of a movie.

Pepper turned around and saw me standing in the doorway. She grinned. "Don't be shy, Hugh. My husband needs cash. That's the only reason we're here."

"Okay," I said.

There was a dresser kind of thing with another big mirror on it. The top was covered with her makeup and stuff.

Pepper went there and bent over at the waist. I turned around but that didn't change the view much, because there was a mirror on that wall too.

She opened the bottom drawer and I saw a metal door inside. It was a safe. I'd never seen one of those either, not in someone's house.

Pepper touched the number pad and *beep*, the door opened.

She pulled some money out. There was still a lot left inside it. A lot.

Pepper stood up and turned around. "You can look again, Hugh. It's safe."

She held my right hand with her left as she counted the bills out. "Take those to Bud and your daddy, okay? And don't stop on the way to pick up any girls."

She walked away laughing, hips moving more than they needed to.

As I walked to the truck I was thinking about the safe. Reversing the mirror image, the numbers she typed in were 6969.

No surprise.

***

I went to the party on Saturday night and Wren was amazing again. This house was almost as expensive as Bud and Pepper's, with a two-story living room looking down on the water. Wren and the drummer played on the landing, like minstrels in a gallery.

Near the end she said: "This one is for my friend, Hugh. He's my hero, too, because he saved my violin from a gang of thieves."

She pointed at me, and people cheered. I went red.

"It's called the Dance of Love and Hunger."

It was incredible.

***

Things went on like that for a couple of months. Dad and I kept working all over Graymoor, but there was one house we couldn't seem to finish. Bud was never satisfied, always finding more for us to do.

And I kept seeing Wren, and not telling K.C. and George about her. I guess since we weren't sleeping together, they would have said there was nothing to tell.

She never invited me in, not even when I walked her home in the dark. A kiss on the cheek, that was all.

But I would rather have that from her than anything other girls might been willing to give me.

My only worry was that maybe she had some other guy, a real boyfriend. I didn't mind not getting into her room if nobody else was either. That way maybe I still had a chance.

***

Things fell apart just before Thanksgiving.

Dad and I were getting ready to go to work when the phone rang. Soon Dad was shouting. He got so red I thought he was having a coronary.

When he shut the phone, he just stood there, glaring at me and breathing hard. I figured he wanted me to say something.

"Are we going?"

"Going? Going where? Didn't you hear? Bud just fired us!"

"Fired us? Can he do that?"

"He just did." Dad sat down on a kitchen chair. "I can take him to court for what he owes me, but that means paying lawyers and being tied up in court instead of working. The bastard!"

"We've got other customers."

"That's another thing. You know those California refugees all stick together. If I take him to court, he'll badmouth me to them. *Damn* it."

I didn't say anything. I was thinking about Pepper. If I had been nicer to her, maybe this wouldn't have happened.

***

I couldn't talk to Wren about it until she got back from Redmond, where she'd spent the break. We went out for coffee on Monday afternoon, and I told her why I wasn't working. Dad was out looking for new jobs.

"God," she said. "Everybody's life is in the toilet."

"What do you mean?"

"Remember I said my dad's trying to start a new software company? The deal fell through." She shrugged. "We're gonna be living on breadcrumbs next year. I'll have to apply for scholarships and drop out till something comes through."

"Oh man, that sucks." The thought that she'd be so far away made me sick to my stomach.

"It's not fair, Hugh. Not what happened to your family, or to mine." Her hand was shaking so badly she had to put down her coffee cup. "Christ, I'm too scared to think."

"You should record a CD," I told her. "You could get rich."

She patted my hand. "Thanks, but I'm not nearly ready. Besides, it takes money to record. What we ought to do is rob a bank."

I grinned. "Like Bonnie and Clyde? Remember how *they* ended up?"

Wren nodded. "You're right. Banks are too dangerous. What we need is some private citizen with a house full of money. Hugh, what's wrong?"

***

"We can't," I said, for the tenth time.

"Why not?" She asked again.

We were walking back to her house. The street was empty, but I kept looking around as if there was a cop on every corner.

"Have you ever been in prison, Wren? I have. And I don't want a return trip."

"It won't happen, Hugh. You said they go to the premiere of every opera in Seattle, right? So that's all we have to do; wait for an opera night. Why would anyone suspect us?"

"Because the first thing the cops will ask is 'who has been in the house since you moved in?' And Bud will say 'Well, there's the guy I fired, and his son the ex-con.' "

We reached the front door and I followed her up the steps. She was frowning, which just made her look prettier. "What about your friends? Could they give us an alibi?"

An alibi. I couldn't believe we were having this conversation.

"I wouldn't ask them. Besides—" I shrugged. "They aren't so reliable."

We were in the front hall now, the first time I'd been inside. Typical student ghetto stuff. Bright amateur paintings on the walls. Junky furniture.

"Come upstairs," said Wren.

I followed, trying to look anywhere but at her ass. Her room was all white. Bright white walls and ceiling and rug. A black blanket on the bed. Two posters on the wall of women playing the violin.

"Hugh?" She was looking at me.

"Sorry. Nice place."

"Please listen. I know how we can have an alibi that doesn't depend on anyone lying for us."

She told me.

"That might work," I said.

Her eyes grew wide. "Does that mean you'll do it?"

"Yeah," I said. "I'll do it."

"Fantastic!" She grabbed my jacket and pulled me forward for a kiss. A real one.

I couldn't believe it. I tried to put my arms around her, but she was falling backwards and, even though she was only half my size, she pulled me down with her.

I stuck out my arms, so I didn't squash her flat and we landed on the black quilt together. I was amazed the bed didn't break.

About an hour later, it did.

***

As Christmas got closer Dad got more and more depressed.

The only good news came on one of my visits to the parole officer. "Congratulations, Hugh."

"Me? For what?"

Topper held out a card. "You've stayed on good behavior, so you get your regular license back, right on schedule. You can drive whenever you want, now."

"Wow." I stared at it. "At the trial it felt like it would be forever before this would happen."

"That's the thing about time, Hugh. It passes." He rubbed his forehead. "Whether you do the right thing or not. But drive on the straight and narrow, okay? And keep away from bad companions."

Finally, an opera opened in Seattle. It happened to be the same night Wren was playing for a party in the Sunny Valley neighborhood, east of Graymoor.

"It's perfect," Wren said. "The party's maybe ten minutes from their house. No one will ever know we were gone."

She played an amazing show. At one point I saw her drummer look up bewildered, like he couldn't keep up with her, couldn't understand where all this energy was coming from.

I knew.

After the congratulations that followed the second set Wren slipped out to where I was waiting with the car. It was warm for December.

I looked at her. "You still want to do this?"

"Christ, yeah."

There were at least forty people in the house, most of them drunk or stoned or both. None of them would be able to swear whether we were there or gone.

As I drove Wren took off her golden blouse. Under it was a tight black T-shirt and black pants.

I was already dressed in black. She laughed. "We look like a couple of Goths, babe."

My heart was pounding. I don't know if it was because of what we were planning to do, or because she called me "babe."

"We don't have enough piercings," I told her, and she laughed some more.

We drove into Graymoor.

"Welcome to North LA," I said, just like my dad always did. "Home of the California refugees."

We drove slowly past Bud and Pepper's house.

"Is that it?" Wren asked.

"Yup. No lights on, except the one over the door."

"How can we get in?"

"The back door doesn't lock right. It's loose. My old man told Bud to get it fixed, but he was too cheap to hire a locksmith."

I looked over at Wren. She was shaking all over, really shaking. "Look, let's forget this. We'll just go back to the party."

"Are you crazy, Hugh?" She smiled. "Let's go."

"But you're scared out of your wits."

"Always scared, babe. Except when I've got my instrument in my hand."

She leaned over and kissed me. "Park a couple of houses down, facing east."

I did. Then I reached for the door, but Wren put a hand on my arm. "Wait. Let's make sure no one is around."

So, we sat in the darkness. A few houses had lights on. A bird called. That was it.

Wren reached up and turned out the ceiling light. She opened her door and I followed.

There was a little tang from the bay, which meant the tide was low. I remember thinking it was funny how you could sense the water more when it was farther away.

We went around the house and silently climbed the stairs to the deck. They were absolutely silent, and I was proud of the job my dad had done on them, building those steps without one loose nail or squeaky board.

I gently opened the screen door and Wren pulled it back. I wondered what would happen if Bud had finally gotten the lock fixed. I'd look like an idiot.

I grabbed the doorknob and turned. It was locked. I took a deep breath and pulled it to the left, away from the jamb.

It shifted in my hands, and the door opened.

I turned to Wren. She smiled and nodded.

And then we were in.

I walked as gently as I could from the dark kitchen into the living room. I heard Wren padding behind me.

There was a pale stream of light there, beaming down from the streetlight through the picture window.

"Wow," Wren whispered. "They have beautiful stuff."

I nodded. "The bedroom is down the hall."

And Bud stepped out of the hallway, blinking at the light. He was wearing black pajama bottoms. He saw me and staggered back a step.

"What the hell? Hugh? What are you doing here?"

I wanted to ask him the same thing. He was supposed to be in Seattle.

But he hadn't seen Wren. I had to keep him looking at me so she could get away.

She was backing toward the kitchen, so I moved the other way, straight into the shaft of streetlight.

"Listen, Bud. I can explain."

"Yeah? I'd like to hear that, Hugh, because I can't think how. Is your father here, too?"

I felt panic now. If Wren got away, would they think the other person here had been my dad?

Bud tried to say something else, but he couldn't. He staggered forward a step. His eyes went wide.

Then he doubled over, and I saw the carving knife sticking out of his neck.

Wren was right behind him, eyes and mouth wide with astonishment.

"What have you done?" I whispered. "My God!"

"You can't go back to jail," she said. "I won't let you."

"Let's get out of here."

"The knife. It's got fingerprints."

Bud was on the floor, shaking. I guess it was what they call a death rattle.

I couldn't believe how deep she had stuck the knife in. I had to put my hand on Bud's shoulder to yank it out.

"Let's go," I said, but Wren wouldn't move.

She stood still, hand held out. "Gimme."

The blade was covered with blood and the handle was sticky with it. I didn't want to give it to her, but she wasn't moving, so I held the knife on my open palm. She picked it up.

I caught her arm. "Come on. *Now.*"

That's when Pepper stepped out of the hallway. She was wearing the black pajama top to matched Bud's pants.

It was like a nightmare, endlessly repeating.

I grabbed both of Pepper's shoulders. I had no plan. Just didn't want her to see her husband dead.

"Don't go in there, Pepper. You have to—"

She pulled away, backing straight toward Wren.

"Don't!" I yelled.

Pepper fell on the floor beside her husband.

"What the hell is *wrong* with you?" I said. Shrieked, I guess.

Wren looked at the bloody knife in her hand. Then she looked at me and her eyes were wide with love and hunger.

She smiled and gestured with the knife. Her hand wasn't shaking anymore. "Come on, babe. There's probably more next door."

Blindsided

By Eric Brown

I stopped dictating a letter on my laptop's voice recognition program, turned my head and listened.

I hadn't been mistaken. There was someone downstairs. I heard footsteps on the linoleum in the laundry room and cursed Mrs. Jones. She came twice a week to do the washing, and invariably left the window open.

The sound was faint, muffled by the intervening rooms—but my hearing has always been acute, to compensate for my lifelong blindness.

Maria, my secretary, arrived every day at one o'clock. She'd unlock the front door with her own key and call my name. It was now just after twelve, so I couldn't rely on her arriving any time soon and saving the day.

When Charles, my lover of two years, had left three months ago—or rather, when I kicked him out after learning of his serial unfaithfulness—Maria had suggested she move in for a while, but I insisted I was fine and could look after myself.

I wished, now, that I'd accepted her offer.

Sam, my dog, would be no help. He was the most peaceable mutt in the world—a *guide* dog, not a *guard* dog. He'd be fast asleep in his basket in the dining room, and nothing short of an earthquake would rouse him.

The intruder moved from the laundry room, and I heard the lounge door opening.

My first impulse was to call 999. But the landline phone was downstairs in the hall, and my mobile in the lounge. I didn't like to be disturbed while I was working.

I tried to marshal my breathing and think clearly.

The intruder was a burglar, at best.

And at worst?

He left the lounge, crossed the hall, and moved towards the stairs. He climbed. The third step creaked.

I turned my swivel chair and stood up, facing the door. What could a small woman—I was five foot one in stockinged-feet and weighed in at eight stone nothing—do against a burglar, presumably a man?

I reached across the desk and found my treasured Crime Writers' Best First Novel award, an oval bronze paperweight that could do a skull a lot of damage.

If only I could hit the bastard's head with any accuracy.

There was nowhere in the room where I might hide, so I stood my ground and concealed the paperweight behind my back.

I kept my study door fully opened, as with all the doors in the house. Why create extra obstacles when moving from room to room? As soon as the burglar came to the top of the stairs, he would see me standing here.

I heard his cautious footsteps as he approached the landing, and then I heard his breathing. I guessed he was young: he wore Cool Water aftershave, all the rage with fashion-conscious twenty-somethings these days.

The footsteps stopped.

I sensed him watching me as his breathing became more rapid. The Cool Water was overlaid with something else. He was sweating, now, as his quarry came into view.

When my third novel became a bestseller and was made into a TV mini-series, I endured a flurry of visitors. They had the public's prurient interest in celebrities, especially one so young, pretty, and so *tragically* handicapped. They said they wanted me to sign copies of my books, but really they just wanted to ogle.

I almost asked this visitor if he would like an autograph or a selfie, but stopped myself.

I heard him take a step towards me. I tensed in preparation, ready with the paperweight.

He said, softly, "I love your novels," in a voice like hot cocoa with extra cream.

A satisfied reader, then?

Like hell.

"That's good to know," I said, attempting to keep the tremor from my voice. "You've read all five?"

"All of them, three times." His voice told me more: educated, from the south, intelligent, and sensitive.

Was he a psychopath, I wondered? An educated, sensitive psychopath?

"So… which one is your favourite?"

If I could keep him talking until one o'clock, when Maria arrived…

He was closer now. I could tell that by the intensification of mingled sweat and aftershave. This time I hadn't heard his footsteps as he approached.

Which meant that he had *crept*.

He said, "I like *The Boy Who Cried* best of all."

The first book in my Dangerous Women trilogy, about a female private eye as strong-willed as she was streetwise… Charles had once hurt me by saying it was wish fulfilment on my part.

Then I realised what the intruder had said: *The 'Boy' Who Cried.*

The actual title was *The 'Man' Who Cried.*

That was significant, for some reason beyond me just then.

"I could give you a signed first edition," I said.

"I don't want a signed copy, Emma."

The way he said my name evoked an intimacy I found sickening.

"Then"… I swallowed… "what do you want?"

"You," he said.

A breath, almost a whisper: *You…*

I was really scared now.

His sweat glands were in overdrive, spiced with testosterone. I sensed him before me, tall and looming—his voice came from about a metre away. I would swing the paperweight when I judged he'd moved a little closer.

"You're coming with me."

I tried not to panic. "Where to?"

"Away from here."

Then it came to me. *Click.* The mental connection.

Those emails…

"You're 'Dan,' right?"

That surprised him. He even took a backwards step. "How the…?"

I get fan mail. Emails by the dozen. I have a program that renders them audible. Last week I received an email from someone calling himself Dan. He said his favourite novel by anyone, ever, was *The Boy Who Cried.*

I replied with a form email expressing my thanks, then forgot about it. So what if a devoted reader couldn't even get the title right?

A day later I received another email from Dan, sent from his iPhone. What had inspired the novel? Was the character of Kenny based on a real person? And why had I portrayed him so negatively?

This time I made the effort to reply in person.

A mortgage had inspired the story, I joked. Kenny was *not* based on a real person. And I was negative towards him because he was a murderous psychopath.

The following day, another email. Kenny was his favourite of all my characters, Dan wrote—but he'd heard a rumour online, in chat forums, that I was planning to kill him off in my next book, due out next month. Could I confirm this?

How the hell had that become public knowledge? I *had* killed Kenny in the sequel, *The Woman Who Won*. But only my editor, a few alpha readers, and the publicity people at my publishers were aware of the fact.

I replied to Dan that I never revealed the contents of forthcoming novels and hoped that I'd hear nothing more from him.

Fat chance.

He'd emailed an hour later with a simple two-word message: I'm disappointed.

And I'd deleted the email and blocked him, instantly.

***

"How the hell do you know who I am?"

"A guess," I said. "You called the novel *The 'Boy' Who Cried*, as you did in your emails. The actual title is *The 'Man' Who Cried*."

That calmed him. His breathing became even.

"You're coming with me. Now."

Something occurred to me. I'd left the voice recognition program running on my laptop, and it would have picked up our dialogue and transcribed it to the screen—or rather my side of the dialogue, as it wouldn't have recognised Dan's voice. When Maria discovered that I was missing, and saw that the laptop was still running…

I said, "Is Dan your real name, or is that a tag? I'd like to know who I'm talking to."

"Dan's all you need to know."

"So, Dan, where are you taking me?"

"That doesn't matter," he said. "We need to talk."

"We can talk here."

"Where we're going, we won't be interrupted."

"What do you want to talk about?"

"You. Me. Life."

"Okay… so how long will it take to get to wherever we're going?"

He didn't reply, and his silence was ominous. Then he said, "Shit!"

I heard him move to the desk and rattle the keyboard as he deleted whatever was on the screen and shut down the program.

"Very clever," he said. "But not clever enough. Now move to the door."

I tried not to give in to despair.

"Wait," I said. "I need something."

"I said move to the door—"

"My medication. I need to take my medication."

He thought about it for all of two seconds. "Where is it?"

"On the desk, beside the laptop."

I heard him pick up the cardboard box.

"Levothyroxine," he read. "What's it for?"

"What the hell has that got to do with you?" I snapped.

A year ago, I was diagnosed with an underactive thyroid, which had led to depression, muscle cramps, weight gain, and other unpleasant symptoms. I took three pills a day and was back to my normal self.

I reached out with my left hand, and he passed me the box.

Before he had time to object, I backed towards the sofa and sat down, my right hand still behind me. I let go of the paperweight and opened the box.

"I need some water."

"You can swallow them dry, Emma, or not at all."

"I've got to take them with water," I said. "The bathroom's next door, and my mug's on the desk. If you don't get me the water," I went on, "you'll have to drag me from the house kicking and screaming."

He hesitated, then relented. I heard him take the mug from the desk, then move to the door. He took the precaution of closing it behind him: I heard it click shut.

***

We'd been travelling for about twenty minutes when the van slowed and stopped. I braced myself.

Would Maria have arrived at the cottage yet, and found the door unlocked, Sam all alone, and the medication on the sofa?

The cab door opened, then the sliding side door. A warm breeze caressed me as I sat there, trembling. I listened, but heard nothing that might have indicated our location. Birdsong, the engine of a distant tractor. Nothing more.

I expected him to pull me from the flatbed and drag me to his lair.

But he just stood there, a miasma of body odour and aftershave.

"You're going to phone your publisher," he said, "and speak to your editor."

"O…kay," I said. "But why, exactly?"

"Tell her you want to see the proofs. You want to rewrite something."

"Too late for that, Dan. The book's already gone to press. It's out next month—"

"You're lying."

"Okay, so we'll talk to Carrie and see what she says."

I have a Braille mobile with keys a little larger than the norm, and a program that verbalises the names as I scroll through the list of stored contacts.

"Set the phone to speaker," he said. "Then tell her you want the proofs. That's all. Nothing more. You want the proofs because you've spotted an error that needs fixing—"

"It doesn't work like that—"

"Do it!"

He passed me the phone. I activated it with shaking fingers, found Carrie and pressed call. It came to me, as I waited, that perhaps the police would be able to trace the phone—if all else failed.

"Emma, darling! How lovely. How's things?"

"Carrie, hi. Look, this is awkward…" My mouth was dry. I wanted to scream that I'd been taken by a madman.

I felt his sudden grip on my upper arm.

"No probs, darling. How can I help?"

"The proofs of *The Woman Who Won*… Any chance I can have another quick run through?"

Carrie sounded terribly disappointed. "Oh, Emma, babe… No can do. Book's already down at Clays. Nothing important, I hope? We can always correct it in the trade paperback."

Dan snatched the phone from my hand and cut the call. "Shit!"

He dropped the mobile and ground it underfoot. So much for the police being able to trace it, now.

I said, "You want me to rewrite the novel so that Kenny lives."

He took a few deep breathes. "He doesn't deserve to die…"

For Chrissake, Dan *identified* with the maniac!

"Okay," I said, placatory. "Very well. Listen. I can fix it. The second book of the trilogy is out next month. And yes, Kenny dies—but I'm still plotting the third book. I can bring Kenny back from the dead. If Conan Doyle can do it with Sherlock, so can I. Thing is, I can't bring back Kenny if you don't let me go."

I wasn't expecting the blow, and when it came it was both painful and shocking. A quick backhander across the face with plenty of muscle behind it.

I screamed and rolled into a protective ball, expecting more.

He slid the door shut, moved to the cab, revved the engine and sped off.

I sat up and took deep breaths, calming myself.

***

The van came to a halt perhaps an hour later and Dan climbed from the cab.

The door slid open, and he grabbed my upper arm. He dragged me out and it was all I could do to land on my feet. I felt the sunlight on my face and heard birdsong. The scent of jasmine was heavy in the air. There was no traffic noise at all. We were still in the country.

He hurried me away from the van, gravel crunching underfoot. Through a swing gate and down a path. I could tell he was enraged from his breathing, from the force of his grip on my arm.

I expected him to open a front door. Instead, we turned right, presumably along the front of the house, then left and left again, around the building. We stopped and he unlocked the back door.

Cool, still air after the spring sunlight, and the scent of beeswax and mildew. The placed smelled *old*. A cat had pissed on the carpet at some point.

He marched me along a short corridor, turned right, and opened a door. He thrust me forward and closed the door behind me. I heard a key turn in the lock. I could sense he was not in the room.

In surroundings I knew intimately and where nothing changed spatially, I was a like a kid in a playground. On *terra incognita*, I was not so confident. There might be all manner of obstacles lying in ambush, waiting to trip me.

I moved cautiously around the room, hands outstretched and questing. The room was small, eight feet by eight, and unfurnished. Empty, in fact. No windows. The perfect cell.

I moved to the wall opposite the door, slid down it and sat on my haunches, waiting.

My only hope now lay with Maria.

If Dan tried anything, I'd fight. I'd attack him. I swore I'd do him an injury he'd never forget.

***

Fifteen minutes later the door opened, then closed. He didn't lock it.

I caught the reek of his body odour and aftershave.

"We can talk about Kenny—I can bring him back in the third book," I said. "Do you want me to do that?"

"You didn't know, did you?"

"Didn't know?" I shook my head, confused.

"When you replied to my email, you told me that Kenny wasn't based on anyone. But you were wrong."

I swallowed. "What makes you think—?"

"Charles told me."

That stunned me. It was a few seconds before I could gather my thoughts and respond. "You know Charles?"

He ignored the stupid question. Of course he knew Charles.

"*The Boy Who Cried…*" he said. "When you were writing about Kenny. Charles said you got him wrong."

Charles had studied psychology at university, graduated with a first and gone into banking (as you do). But he'd retained an interest in psychology that came in useful when he dissected the characterisation in my first drafts.

"He said you'd got Kenny's childhood all wrong, his motivations. What he'd experienced as a child wouldn't have made him act as he did in the book. He needed to have suffered *more*."

"He was right," I said. "What Charles said certainly helped—"

"He told you *exactly* what Kenny had gone through to make him like he was." He paused. I could imagine his smile as he asked, "Do you know why that is, Emma?"

Heart pounding, I said, "Go on."

"Because he *knew*," he said.

"Do you mean that… that Charles had suffered, just as Kenny had?"

That might explain a few things, I thought. His selfishness, his serial affairs…

He laughed, without humour. "Not Charles," he said. "*Me*."

"You?" I said. "You told Charles all about your—?"

"I didn't need to *tell* him," he said. "He knows."

"He knows?" I shook my head. "How does he—?"

"Charles," he said, "is my father."

***

My thoughts reeled.

Charles had said nothing about having a son.

"No," I said, doing the arithmetic. "How old are you? Twenty-five?"

"Twenty-eight," he said.

"Then, no… That's impossible. Charles is *forty*, so—"

He just laughed at that.

"What?"

"He lied to you, Emma."

"No…"

"He's fifty-two," he said. "But then you couldn't *see* his wrinkles, could you, his greying hair?"

I swallowed, feeling sick. So Charles had lied about his age, as well as about all the women he'd seen while professing his undying love for me.

"Okay," I said. "So…" I drew my legs up against my chest and slipped my arms around my shins, hugging myself protectively. "So… why all this? Why kidnap me—?"

"When I read about Kenny's childhood," he said, "it all came flooding back. I relived it all over again. The pain, the suffering, the *neglect*…"

"I'm sorry," I stammered. "I'm sorry if he treated you—"

He interrupted with a shout. "My father didn't neglect me, you fool! My father was perfect. *Perfect!* It was the bitch he was married to. My mother… Some mother she was! A drunken slut."

"He was *married?*" I said.

"Another thing he didn't tell you?" he sneered. "He was married to a shallow, sadistic alcoholic. When I was five, she left him for another man and she took me with her. Can you imagine what my life was like, after that? I'd had a loving father, and now my own mother treated me like… like an *animal.*"

He wept, and his pain filled the room like a rank smell.

"I'm sorry," I murmured.

"Save your sympathy!" he cried. "You've no idea… Is it any wonder I was jailed?"

I echoed the word. "What… what did you…?"

His breathing was coming in uneven, ragged spasms, now. "When I was twenty, I met someone. Shelly. She was beautiful, loving. She told me she *loved* me. And then… and then I found out she was just like my mother… *just* like her."

I swallowed, at a loss to respond.

"I found out she was seeing other men. So I…"

I hung my head, hugging myself. I didn't want to know.

"I made her confess, and then, when she told me the truth, that she didn't love me and never had, I strangled her." He paused. "Or tried to."

The silence in the small room pulsed.

"I did six years," he went on, "and when I got out, my father took me in. We talked about Shelly and what she'd done. He said she was typical. Like all women. Like my mother, like *you*—"

"Me?" I said, incredulous. "*Me?*"

"Oh, he told me," he said. "He told me all about you. How, after all the help he'd given you with the book, after he'd helped you make Kenny a real, believable person, you thanked him by having affairs—"

"He lied!" I screamed. "I was never unfaithful to him! It was Charles—*he* cheated on *me.* He had affairs. Multiple affairs. He lied to me…"

"My father would never lie, Emma. He told me all about you—your need, to compensate for your blindness, your craving for affirmation from other men."

"The bastard!" I shouted, sobbing. "The cheating, lying *bastard!*"

I could sense him staring at me, delighting in my distress.

Little by little I calmed myself, then faced him defiantly.

Into the silence that followed, like a stone falling into a millpond, he said, "It was never really about Kenny, you know?"

"What?"

"I never really thought you'd be able to bring him back to life," he said. "But that doesn't really matter. I have you, now, and I'm going to do what I should have done to my mother, and to Shelly."

I pushed myself up the wall until I was standing upright, facing him.

I could hear his breathing across the room, smell his supercharged sweat.

I said, "Hurting me won't—"

He came at me and punched me in the face. I reeled, fell over and scrambled quickly to my feet. I lashed out, missing him.

He hit me again, and while I was on the floor, on my back, he straddled me and gripped my throat and squeezed.

I knew, then, with consciousness ebbing away—I knew, with an icy clarity, exactly what I should do.

I reached up and found his eyes. I plunged my thumbs into his eye sockets, digging deep with all the strength I possessed. I felt the squelch, heard his piercing cry as something liquid squirted across the back of my right hand.

He wailed in pain like a slaughtered animal.

I bucked, threw him off, and scrambled across the room. I found the door and hauled it open. I turned towards the back of the house and ran along the corridor, careering into something and stumbling. I came to the back door with a surge of relief and found the handle.

The door was locked.

I cried in desperation, yanking futilely at the handle.

Then I stopped, taking deep breaths, and told myself to *think*. He was blind in one eye, maybe two. At any rate, even the least damaged eye would be seeing nothing for a while.

We were, for the time being, equal.

I *could* attempt to locate the front door, but then it might be locked, and Dan might hear me in the process of trying to escape.

I had to conceal myself somewhere, lie low and out of the way until he left the house to seek help.

On fleeing down the corridor, I had hit something. Banisters.

I retraced my steps, hearing his cries in the small room as he barged about in search of the door. I came to the banisters, felt my way along them. My hand found what I was seeking, a small wooden handle.

A door, under the stairs. A small cupboard. Taking care to make not the slightest sound, I eased open the door and ducked inside.

I turned and pulled the door shut carefully behind me with a feeling of supreme relief. I crouched in the warm, fusty-smelling confines. I took slow, even breaths, calming myself. I was safe, for the time being. I could assess the situation, make plans.

He exploded into the corridor like an enraged bull, startling me. His cries were terrifying in their pain and rage. I expected him to know exactly where I was, haul open the door and complete what I had interrupted.

Instead, he went reeling off along the corridor and into another room, searching for me with murder in his heart.

I pressed my hands to my face and listened.

He was in a room at the front of the house, tearing it apart in his rage. I heard furniture topple, glass shatter. I heard his cries, his exclamations of hurt both physical and mental.

Could he see? Was his right eye still functioning? If so, it was only a matter of time before he found my hiding place.

Then, a strange, sudden silence settled upon the house.

I heard his slow footsteps in the corridor, mere feet away. My heart pounded. I was convinced that he knew just where I was cowering. He was in the corridor, facing the door under the stairs, smiling to himself as he reached out...

I heard something, then, and almost wept with relief: the distant sound of a police siren.

The ululating wail increased as the squad car sped towards the house and pulled up with a screech of brakes.

I heard voices, shouts, and Dan's enraged cry as he stumbled towards the back door.

I heard voices outside, then the percussive blows of a battering ram as it broke down the front door. The clatter of multiple footsteps in the hall and voices calling my name.

Then I heard an officer's incredulous, "Jesus Christ," and envisaged him staring at Dan and the gouged mess of his eyes.

I heard Dan trying to open the back door, followed by an officer saying, "Stay right where you are and put your hands up..."

I pushed open the door and ducked out into the corridor.

I heard a woman's indrawn breath, then inhaled Maria's perfume. I was aware of the sudden silence and imagined the officers staring at me.

"Emma!" Maria cried, and I stumbled towards the sound of her voice and fell into her arms.

***

The police insisted I go to the hospital for a check-up. I was interviewed for an hour by a kindly policewoman, then allowed to leave when I'd agreed to see a counselor the following week.

Maria drove me home. "That was a brilliant idea, Emma."

"I just hoped you'd see the blister cards, then make the connection."

"It was blindingly obvious—sorry!—as soon as I entered the study and saw the cards lined up on the sofa." She hesitated. "You didn't take *all* the pills, did you?" she asked, concerned.

"Of course not," I said. "Just three. I slipped the others into the pocket of my jeans, just in case."

At home, I led the way upstairs to my study. I heard Sam follow us into the room.

I sat on the sofa and reached out, found the first card, then the second.

Five of them in all, the missing pills spelling out a cryptic clue, in Braille.

"As soon as I read it," Maria said, "I accessed your account and found 'Dan's' emails. Then I rang the police and explained the situation, and their tech people traced the owner of the iPhone that'd sent the emails."

"I couldn't remember his full address," I said. "I only hoped you'd be able to work out what I meant."

My fingers traced the message I'd left on the blister cards. ⠙⠁⠝⠁⠞

danat…

"Tea, Emma?" she asked.

"Please."

At the hospital, I'd asked after Dan. Word was that he would recover the sight in his right eye, in time.

I sat back and wondered how I felt about that. Then I thought about what Charles had once said: that my writing about a strong woman was nothing more than wish fulfilment…

I smiled to myself as Sam trotted over and placed his muzzle in my lap.

She Told Me About You
By Ali Seay

He smokes after sex. Always. He says it brings him joy but I think he does it because it looks cool. Because he's seen the men in the movies do it.

I sit and watch him blow the smoke toward the ceiling. I laugh softly.

"What's so funny?" Chris asks, watching me.

He loves to be the center of attention.

"My sister used to do that," I say, noncommittally.

"Smoke after fucking you?" he asks with a smile. He thinks he's funny.

"Blow smoke at the ceiling," I say, letting his ignorant remark go. It's one of many. A drop in the bucket, really.

"Used to?"

He's not as dense as he looks.

"Yeah. She's dead."

A flash of humanity that he was trained to have. Some poor parent told him what to say when someone mentioned a dead loved one. The same way they told him to say "Bless you" when someone sneezed or "Thank you" when someone gave you something. It's a reflex.

"I'm sorry," he says.

I smile.

"Thank you."

I give him a moment to ask about her. He doesn't. Of course he doesn't.

I go on anyway. Compelled to. Even when I am the one to broach the subject of my sister's death, I have to talk about her. Even if I don't want to. Even if I feel like a broken record. Because my sister, Simone, had once been alive and vibrant and her death was a fucking travesty, and she fucking deserves to be remembered.

I take a deep breath to calm the rant in the center of my brain and smile. "She committed suicide about a year ago."

He grunts, "Awful," is all he says.

He catches me looking at him and turns on his side. His cock is flaccid, his belly a wee bit too big, his eyes unkind, but he's still holding on—just barely—to his pretty boy looks. He knows it and he's going to hang on as long as he can. Hence the gym trips and Keto and all that shit.

The realization that he is supposed to say something here slowly dawns on his face and he mutters, "What happened?"

I play it off. Swallow all my words except, "She got out of a bad relationship. He was…unkind. She thought herself better off dead than alive."

He tsks. It is a ridiculous sound coming from him. The man who cares about nothing but himself.

"Sorry, babe," he says and returns to blowing smoke at the ceiling.

Wow. What a man.

***

It's the anniversary of Simone's death and we have a date.

I primp in front of the mirror. I have on her yellow dress to remember her. It's a vintage tea party dress. I go the extra mile. Hair done for the fifties, buckled low spectator pumps, bright red lipstick, a hat pin in my collar as a stick pin.

It's all vintage. It's all Simone's. And it's all I have to remember her by. Her things. Her laugh is gone, her smile is gone, her company when I am sad, her advice when I am lost.

She's gone. And she deserves to be here.

The doorbell rings and I flounce over. I open the door doing my best dutiful girlfriend happy to see her man routine.

"Babe," he says, stepping inside.

"Where are we going?" I ask, fluffing my hair.

He grabs me and yanks me to him. It's supposed to be a manly move, but it's just a ham-handed grabby moment.

Per usual.

"You look like a snack. I thought maybe we could stay in, and I could eat you."

I push back from him. "You said we were going out to eat."

"But you look so—"

"We're going out," I say.

He looks angry at first. Then amused. Then put out. "If I'm not enough for you—"

I smile. "You are. But I dressed up."

"And I can undo that," he says with a predatory leer.

He thinks he's charming. He thinks he's irresistible.

We've been dating for a while, and I haven't seen every horrid facet of his personality. So, I push him again.

"Well, I'm all dressed. You can stay here and wait for me if you want. But I'm going out."

I reach for my purse and my keys. He stills my hand. Can't be outdone by a woman. God forbid.

"Sweetheart, I was only kidding. I'm ready to go. I have the perfect place to eat."

"Wonderful. It's a hard day for me. I'd like to take my mind off it."

A worried look drifts across his face. Oh no! Emotions! Listening? Being a good human even if it's just for pretend.

"Why is it a hard day?"

"It's the anniversary of my sister's death."

I literally watch him swallow a sigh.

If he isn't supportive, he might not get laid.

Can't have that happen now can we.

I take his arm and lead him toward the door. "I think talking would do me good."

"Of course."

***

Simone there on the steps crying. I go to her. I take her thin hand. Thinner than before.

"Where have you been? Where did you go?"

She looks at me, big blue eyes wet with tears. She's never been a crier. She's always been the peppy one.

"Oh, Sarah. I've missed you."

"Then why haven't you called? Texted? Anything?" I hold both her cold hands in mine and then break the connection to sit on my concrete front step next to my sister.

"I don't have a phone anymore."

I frown. Confused. Her number still rings through when I try. My texts still say delivered.

"I don't understand," is the only thing I can think to say.

"Chris said I can't be trusted with it."

This is not the first thing Chris has done that makes alarm bells go off inside me, but this is the one that makes my blood boil in my veins.

"And why is that?"

In the past, anger doesn't do anything but drive her closer to this asshole. So, I opt for staying calm.

"I spend too much time on it. Time we could be together. And I look up too much stuff. And I'm too chatty..."

She rattles it all off, a woman brain washed into thinking there is something wrong with her.

"Can I help?"

"I'm fine. I just missed you, so I came."

I grab her hand again. Desperate this time. "You can live here. We can figure it out. I'll drive you. Just get your stuff and come here and you and I will figure out what—"

She smiles through her tears, cuts me off. "It's fine. I'm fine. I was just feeling weak. I love Chris and he loves me. He only wants what's best for me."

I try to say nothing. I fail. "He wants you separated from your family. From me! He wants to control you. He's a bad man, Simone. He's a bad man and I'm scared for you."

She shakes her head as if I am simple. My sister. Staring at me. My almost mirror image—we are fraternal not identical—except I am not crying, and I do not look too thin. Where's that twin thing that everyone talks about that will allow me to magically make her choose me?

There isn't one.

"I have to go, Sissy. I'll see you soon. I love you."

She hugs me, her long hair in my face. Her thin body shaking against mine.

She goes off to him. That man. That bad man who is going to be the death of her, I think, off the cuff.

Only, eventually he was.

***

I'll give it to him. He listens to me talk. Never once has he made the connection between the woman I speak of as my sister and his former lover. He pretends to listen and uh-huhs when necessary. All while eating his sirloin steak and loaded baked potato. Multi-tasking at its finest.

He's never once noticed or remarked that I look like or remind him of someone he'd known.

Chris is the poster boy for narcissism.

He doesn't think twice about not listening as he drives me back to my place intending to fuck me.

I mean, I have fucked Chris often. Every mission has its requirements. Some harder than others. We're creeping up on six months together. Which is around the time he started to manipulate her. What does he think he's going to do to me? I wonder.

I make sure my dress rides a bit high on my thigh, so my tan skin is visible. I make sure I wiggle with that provocative motion that always seems to transfix him. I make sure he wants me very badly. I do all of this so that when I say, "Wine?" he'll agree without any real thought.

I open the red, and make sure he's transfixed by the baseball scores on TV before tipping the crushed-up Valiums into the drink. More than any one person should ever have.

Simone had an entire bottle left when she jumped. It would be a shame to waste them.

I give him his glass and he drinks it, almost as an afterthought while muttering about the game. I let him mutter. And I let him stay distracted. That's the way I want him.

I sit back, smooth my dress, and watch the drugs hit him like a slow-moving eighteen-wheeler. He shakes his head a lot, like a dog with ear mites. He sits back—sits forward—hangs his head, and then sits back again.

"Sim—Sarah?"

I laugh. He almost said her name. Somewhere in that lizard brain of his is the connection.

"Yes, Chris?"

"I don't feel very well."

"Maybe you should lie down."

"Maybe."

His voice is slow and deep, his movements disjointed. I'm very prepared for vomit due to mixing Valium with booze, but it's a risk I'm willing to take.

I lead him to the bed. Lie him down. Mumble sweet nothings. And then when he's out. I get my handcuffs.

***

I'm patient. I stir my tea and wait. After some time, he starts screaming.

"God damn it, Sarah, this isn't funny! Why have you done this?"

I take my time walking in. I go nice and slow. When I enter the bedroom, he freezes. Something on my face is telling him that things are different.

"Let me up," he says. But it's almost a question. That lilt at the end.

"No."

He frowns briefly, opens his mouth, closes it, then starts bucking like a tethered animal.

I let him exhaust himself.

"Why are you doing this?"

I blow the steam off my tea and walk closer to the bed. Each ankle is tethered to a bedpost with ropes. Good rough ropes that will abrade and hurt.

Each wrist is cuffed to the bedposts of the headboard.

"She told me about you," I say.

He looks at me. Desperate now. There is fear there. And it is sweet. Sweeter than anything I've ever experienced.

"Who?" he finally asks. I can tell he doesn't want to.

The fact that he has to ask who and doesn't automatically know makes me wonder how many women. How many like my sister?

I sit on the edge of the bed to really let him study me. He's paying attention now. Look how much it takes for that to happen.

"Simone. My sister."

"Simone?"

I wait.

"Simone...oh, Simone. I haven't seen her since—"

I push my fingers to his lips and smile. "You haven't seen her since you killed her."

His eyes fly wide. Wider than I thought eyes could go, to be honest. I know what he's going to say, but I let him say it anyway.

I move my finger away.

"I've never killed anyone!"

"I knew you'd say that," I say. Then I smack his face. Really hard. Because I have a moment where I literally cannot control myself. My rage and my sadness are too big to wrangle. Too strong to tame.

He stares at me dumbstruck. Has no one ever hit this dumb fuck before? I'm going to go with no.

"I haven't," he blurts and instantly flinches.

Well, he's a fast learner.

***

"Tell me why you're crying."

"He makes me do things," Simone says.

My stomach bottoms out. That cold water feeling running through my system. Dread.

"What kind of things?"

She shrugs and wipes her eyes. Tries to blow it off. I can read her face. I've said too much. I never should have told her. I've made a terrible mistake.

I grab her wrist before she can move too far from me. "Tell me, Simone."

"It's nothing. Stupid things really."

"Like?"

I want to push my fingers into her mouth, down her throat, snag the words, and drag them out.

Instead, I breathe and try to be patient as I wait.

She turns to me and clasps me. Her want of spilling the beans to her sister overrides her worry of oversharing.

"He makes me suck his toes!"

I almost laugh. Almost. Thank God, I don't. Because without a breath, she goes on.

"And he keeps his feet dirty. On purpose. He knows—he knows it makes me ill. Literally. He knows, and he does it anyway. And when he's had enough of that and we... when we have sex, he's not gentle, Sissy. He's rough with me. It turns him on and then it winds him up."

Rage.

It is white hot and sudden. I know of humiliation for sexual gratification, but both parties are supposed to be on board. Consenting.

My sister has literally turned shades of green telling me this tale. She is not a willing party.

"Leave him," I say. "Please, leave him. Come here. Stay with me."

She shakes her head.

"He loves me."

"How can he love you if he makes you do things that sicken you and then gets off on it! How is that love?"

She offers me her apologetic shrug. The one trait of hers I've never had. "Everyone has their thing. Everyone has a flaw."

"Simone—"

She gathers her bag, heads toward the door. "I'm sorry. I never should have said anything. It's really not that bad, Sissy. Don't worry."

I am worried.

Her hair is kind of dirty, her skin kind of pale. Dark circles ring her eyes, and her dress hangs on her. She's lost weight. More weight.

She's depressed.

I've watched her go down that rabbit hole once.

The hospital stays, the therapy, the medication, the help, and the hope. I've seen her come back from it. But now I'm seeing it return for her.

Unfinished business.

Thanks to him.

***

He's shut his eyes to try and block me out, so I throw my tea on him. Not as hot as when we started but hot enough to make him thrash around and bellow like some kind of air horn.

"Shut up or I'll put a sock in your mouth."

He shuts up.

I must look serious.

I go over and unlock the cuff on his right wrist. His dominant hand.

Then I untie his left foot.

He watches me the same way you'd watch a dog that has already bitten you. Good.

"Which ones?" I ask, staring at him.

"Which? Which ones…what?" He's terrified to ask me a question and yet he must because he doesn't understand.

Confused. Scared. On red alert.

Just like Simone was for so many months.

"Which toes did you make her suck? Unwashed, nails long, walking through mud. And you'd make her suck those toes and then you'd fuck her. Rough. The way you like it."

He opens his mouth and I hold up a hand. He grows silent.

"I know how you like it, Chris. So, don't try to convince me otherwise. I went all the way for my dead sister."

I extract the cigar cutter from my pocket. I've felt its lovely solid weight there all night and now that it's in my hand I feel a little giddy.

I click it a few times so he can see it and his whole body starts to
buck in panic.

I wait for him to exhaust himself.

"Which ones?"

"I don't—"

"You don't know? Really?"

I go to the foot of the bed and look at his feet. Not great but not awful. But
then again, that was his thing with her. She told me he'd start days beforehand.
Showering but not washing his feet. Walking around barefoot, inside and out.
She could always tell, and it always set her on edge days ahead.

Why had she stayed? I can't answer that. But I can make some of this right.
A little tiny bit. An eye for an eye. A toe for a toe.

I put the cutter to his big toe. It won't fit. Too fat. But I wink at him.

"I can always do that one with a knife if I need to."

He squeaks. Literally sounding like a stuffed toy you'd give a dog.

I put the second toe through the cutter, press it, let him feel the steel.

"What are you going to do?"

"Answer my fucking question. Which toes did you make her suck?"

"Any!" he blurts. "I didn't have—I mean, it's not like I had
fucking favorites."

I sigh. "Okay, I can see that. So, let me ask you this, which ones would you
like to cut off in penance for what you did?"

"None!"

"Oh," I say and then smile at him. "I'm sorry, that's not an option. See, I'd
like my sister to be alive, and yet—she's dead. Because of you."

"I didn't—"

"You fucked with her and fucked with her until her depression came back
with a vengeance and she jumped off the goddamn roof!" I squeezed the cigar
cutter in my rage and the very tip of his second toe comes off.

Of course, he starts to scream.

I shake my head, shove a sock in his mouth. "Look at what you
made me do."

He used to say that to her. When she got upset and he had to double down.
If she got upset about having to suck his toes, then he made her crawl around
like a dog. Sleep on the floor. Eat off the floor.

I want to cut off all his toes. And his fingers. And his fucking tongue.

Instead, I go into the bathroom and wait while my curling iron heats up.

He's making muted noise in there. Let him.

I take the hot iron in and without ceremony press it to the raw bleeding tip of his toe.

His body bows from the pain. Arching up as he howls through the black sock in his mouth.

"The solution is as painful as the problem sometimes," I say.

He looks at me, eyes rolling wildly. He's over the top now.

"Pick one," I say.

His eyebrows go up.

I hover over him and say, "I'm going to take this sock out. If you scream, I'm taking the cutter to your groin. Got it?"

He nods over and over again.

"Good." I pull the soaking wet sock out and repeat myself. "Pick one."

"One what?"

"A toe."

"For what?"

I put the cutter in his freed hand. "To cut off, of course."

"What?" he bleats. Very loudly. I move toward him with the sock, and he says, "Sorry! Sorry!"

"I want you to cut off a toe. Penance. You deserve to suffer the way you made her suffer. I think you should remember who's on top here."

I nod to his foot. "Pick."

"I can't!" he screams.

I shove the sock in his mouth and lean over so we're nearly nose to nose. "Pick a fucking toe or I will take my time cutting them *all* off."

He thrashes, and I watch.

Finally, he nods.

I take the sock out.

"Baby toe."

"Okay then. Go for it."

He has the cutter, and his hand is free, his opposite leg is free. And he has to get to it.

"I need to sit up."

I laugh. "Hardly. I've seen you do your yoga poses. For your gut and your posture and your vanity. Go on and cut it off."

He makes a big production of it, but of course he does. He has to cut off his own toe.

He gets his left leg up and his right arm down and his toe in the hole and he starts to shake.

"I can't."

I shrug. "That's fine. If you can't do one, I can do all ten."

The color drains from his face and miraculously, after a slight hesitation, he presses. Then he presses harder. He's sweating and he's crying, and he's gagging and then *plop!* off comes that baby toe. Right onto the bedspread.

He turns his head, throws up, and then passes out.

I press the curling iron to the toe stump, and it has just enough heat left in it to slow the blood flow to a sticky ooze.

"That'll do for a moment," I say.

***

"I don't want to leave him."

I pass her a glass of wine and she takes one sip and sets it down.

"Simone—"

"Sarah, please. I'm a grown woman. He's just a complicated man who has some troubles."

"That he takes out on you. Without care."

"Oh, he cares," Simone says. "He's always very sorry."

They always are. Very sorry. Until they do it again. I've heard the tales of battered and abused women my whole life. I never thought my sister would be one. He doesn't hit her. At least, not normally. But what he does between her ears. The things he does to her mind. I can't even comprehend.

"You don't like the wine?"

"I just need to watch my weight."

I feel the look of surprise on my face. "Simone, you're a rail."

"No. I'm getting a little belly." She pats the nonexistent stomach through her vintage sundress. Her clavicles stand out sharply, her cheekbones could cut paper.

"How about a soda?"

"That's worse. I'll just have water."

Water. She'll just have water.

***

"I'm starving," he says.

"Here." I put a straw in a bottle of water and let him sip it.

He complains again. "I'm *hungry*. I need food."

"I don't think so. You're getting a little chunky," I say and poke his stomach. He actually could stand to lose a pound or two.

It infuriates him to hear it said.

"Whether or not that's true, I've been here for a long time—"

"Only a few hours," I say, looking pointedly at my watch.

"Please?"

"No. I think you're too big."

I grab his right hand and put it back in the cuff. Even though he kicks, I manage to get his left leg back in the ropes.

Then I free his left hand and right foot. He gets the idea.

"No—"

"Oh, yes."

"You can't make me."

"You're right. I can't. But it still stands, what I said earlier, cut off a few or I cut off all of them."

I don't have the willingness to go back and forth with him.

"This one," I say, and tap his pinky toe.

"No."

I grab for the cutter. "Okay, I'll take that then."

"Okay, okay, okay! Bitch!" Spit flies from his mouth as he screams.

Bitch?

I cut the tip of his second toe off with the cutters.

He screams, and I stare at him. He remembers the sock and shuts up.

"You starved my sister. You humiliated her, used her, shook her mental health like a maraca because you could. And then, when you had her all molded and melded and mutilated, you left her."

"It wasn't working out."

I laugh. "You want me to think that, but I know from her stories, from the things she told me, you got off on it. On controlling and manipulating and hurting her."

I press my fingernail into the raw end of his toe and watch him struggle not to scream.

I shove the cutter at him and nod. "Do it. Or I will fucking take them all."

He bends his body, shaking, bleeding, sweating, seething. He bends, and he cuts. He's losing his strength, so it takes for-fucking-ever but finally he gets it through.

He gags, spits, faints.

I put the toe with the other toe, and I don't worry about the curling iron this time. I just use a lighter.

He wakes up screaming.

He calms.

He bargains and he pleads.

Then he tells me again that he's hungry.

"Here," I say, and I push the toes into his mouth, cover his mouth with my hand, and snarl, "Swallow. Or I'll cut out your goddamn tongue."

He swallows.

***

"You have to eat, I can practically see through you."

She's sobbing now. Her whole body shaking. Every part of her grieving. And she hasn't told me why.

"Please, Simone. How about a coffee? Or just a soda or—"

She gags. "Please stop. Please. I can't."

"What is wrong? You have to tell me."

She's got her head in my lap and she's sobbing.

"He's left me. And I can't sleep. I can't eat. I can't…I don't know what to do."

Relief. So sweet and powerful it stuns me. I am so fucking relieved. So grateful to whatever is out there—God, gods, universe, chaos—that he's gone.

"We'll get through this," I say.

She can get seen by a therapist. She can talk it out. Get back on medication maybe. Rebuild. I'll help her. He's gone, and she will be okay.

"Come and stay with me," I say.

I am even more relieved when she says yes.

We get her stuff. Get her set up in the guest room.

She looks bad, sounds bad, sleeps poorly, won't eat, won't talk—but she's here. With me. She's away from him. And she's safe.

Right?

***

He's been tied to the bed for five hours and I'm tired.

"Now what? What are you going to fucking do?"

"How many?" I ask.

He blanches. Then he plays dumb. "How many what?"

"How many have there been? Women that you broke?"

He's who he is, so he doesn't catch himself before a coy smile curls his lips. He realizes his mistake almost immediately and wipes the expression from his face. But it's already too late.

Minus two toes (well, is he? They're well on their way to his stomach) and bloody he's still an entitled asshole.

"I enjoy women who enjoy humiliation and control."

I sit on the side of the bed close. I'm not afraid of him. He's tied. And the anger that is in me makes me strong. The knife in my pocket even stronger.

"See, the problem with that," I say, "is it implies consent."

He shrugs as utterly at cocky as you'd expect. "She could have left at any time."

"And she could have," I sigh, on the verge of tears. "I never understand that. But my sister…she struggled. You knew that though. That's why you picked her."

I had found him. Flirted. Made it clear that I was a bit on the kinky side. I did it all to get close to him. To buy myself this time. This moment.

Before me was a string of Simones. Women who wanted love, to be appreciated, to please. Women who coveted a relationship even if it meant a sacrifice.

He shakes his head.

"Predator," I say.

"Your opinion," he says.

I laugh. And then I laugh some more. I draw the knife from my dress pocket and pop the button on his pants. His eyes grow bigger and rounder.

I tug his zipper down and fish around inside his boxer for his incredibly flaccid cock. He is far, far down the road from aroused at the moment.

"You have a choice," I say.

"What's that?" he's moving. Flexing. Panicking.

It's delicious.

I tap the head of his cock with the knife point. You've never seen a man freeze so fast.

"I don't think you're going to like either one, I fear. But this is the grave you've dug yourself." I laugh softly. "So to speak."

His eyes are wild like a spooked horse. It warms my heart to see it.

"You can get up and we can walk you to the roof of this building and you can jump—"

He opens his mouth to cut me off and I put the blade of the knife against his lower lip. He shuts up.

"Just like my sister did," I go on. "*Or*, I can cut off your weapon of choice here and you can be a eunuch. You'll never abuse another woman again, at least not with that inchworm. Never get your rocks off by terrorizing and humiliating her. By starving her and feeding poison into her brain. You'll just walk around useless and harmless."

It's a tough decision for him, I can see. His life or his penis.

I don't tell him this but he's not walking out with either.

If he jumps of his own accord I am pretty much in the clear once they find the compressed mess of human meat he'll be. I don't think two severed toes will be conspicuous in a mass of obliterated goo.

If he fights me, I'll kill him.

Going to jail for taking out this piece of human waste would be an honor.

***

She assures me it's fine. I should go to work. She was doing better. Feeling better. She is going to take a walk today.

The cops are out front. The neighborhood is out front. And there, in the street, is the broken body of my sister.

Her pink nightgown tangled around her mangled limbs. Her dark hair, the color of mine, of very dark chocolate, is a bloody smear. She doesn't look like herself. She doesn't look like anything recognizable.

She is gone forever, and I am being led to the ambulance. The noises I hear hurt my ears. The noises I hear like sirens and agony.

The noises I hear are me.

***

He walks funny with his mangled toes. He shuffles and he's talking nonstop. Assuring me that this is a mistake. That it can all be fixed. Etc. and so forth and so on.

I have the knife pointed at the small of his back. I might miss but I'll do my best to mangle his spine if he fucks with me.

I don't care anymore.

I pray that all my elderly neighbors who are deaf, or borderline deaf, continue to sit in their apartments with their TVs blaring game shows. The few people in the building who are my age, are on the upper floors. I rarely see them.

We get in the service elevator that rarely moves. The maintenance crew are almost nonexistent now due to layoffs.

We go up and up until the elevator dings, telling us we have arrived at the roof.

"Fun fact," I say, as I push back the cage. "They never did put any safety measures into action after Simone. I guess they chalked it up to a crazy woman needing to get things over with. So, bonus for me, now it will just be a crazy man who is so grief stricken by his girlfriend's suicide he takes his own life."

I've almost always met him at his place. He's rarely been here. That was by design.

"I did nothing wrong," he says. "She could have left at any time."

"Indeed."

We walk out to the edge. The roof is old and tarpaper curls in places. It's flatter than it should be, and it probably leaks into the space above the top floor apartments. But the drop to the street below is exquisite and there's nothing more than a two-foot-tall wall along the edges. Just enough to count as a warning, I guess.

I push him with the toe of my shoe.

"I can make it right."

"You can't."

He walks to the edge and stares down. He backpedals, and I push the knife to his back. He freezes, sniveling.

"I can't."

"You have to."

Anger snakes across his face. "She was weak and easy, and I couldn't have done anything to her if she hadn't rolled over and fucking let me. Like a beaten dog."

I sigh.

I push the knife against his side. Just hard enough to scare him. "Imaging this is your cock, big man."

He shakes his head. "This is unfair. This isn't right. You can't do this to me!"

"You know," I say, smiling. "You can leave at any time."

He makes a very soft "oof" sound when I push him with my foot. He tips over the edge like a man amidst a fit of modern dance.

All arms and legs pinwheeling. He drops like a stone, and I get to stand there in the absence of sound. Not long. But long enough.

The I hear him hit with a thud. There's the sounds of screams and car horns and squealing tires.

It is music to my ears.

Balm to my blistered soul.

The Cliff

By Alvaro Zinos-Amaro

It all happened very fast: Riley's prowling coyote of insomnia after the six-mile run that evening, her watching herself from the corner of the room, as though outside her own body, write a text to Vivika while fully cognizant of the fact that it was a terrible idea, the iron girder that became her spine after she hit send, Vivika's instantaneous response, the metal beam in Riley's body liquefying into viscous ecstasy right after. The detonation of buzzing alerts on Riley's phone as they texted back and forth faster and faster, bantering just like they had three years ago before it all went to shit, was so quick and urgent that they turned the device into a vibrator. Then Riley sent the most important message of all, and it went unanswered, and there she was, hyper-alert at two in the morning, the marauding coyote of sleeplessness nipping at the heels of her mind with renewed ferocity. She scanned her phone constantly to make sure she didn't miss Vivika's response, but there was nothing there, nothing, nothing, nothing, until with otherworldly calm Riley reinstalled the app she'd sworn on her unborn children she'd never again use, so at least there was *something*, and an hour and twenty-seven minutes later she staggered forward to the door of her studio apartment, clutching her Muna "I would give my life just to hold your hand" tee tight against her chest as she confirmed the crypto-charge on her phone and watched the guy slip the envelope under the door, feeling lighter merely by holding the package in her clammy hands. Her skin blushed with maroon shadows as she entered a bathroom that had never looked so simultaneously innocent and accusatory, her pulse first steady as she transferred the powder to a micro-scale and then seemingly ribboned out of existence as she finally, finally receded into that unearthly womb, the fentanyl ushering her into a perfect and irresistible amniotic dream.

Fuck, how she'd missed it.

Riley woke up in her bed at noon the following day and unspooled herself from a semi-fetal position. Her skin tingled with alertness and every breath tasted like fresh mountain air. She smiled, checked in the bathroom to see how much was left, smiled again, more fully, like a falcon extending its wings, brushed her teeth, showered, and under the jet of hot water she remembered Vivika, fuck, Vivika, and without stopping to dry herself she hopped out and bolted to the bedroom, droplets sliding down her body like candle wax as time slowed, and she grabbed the phone and saw the message.

Two Saturdays from today, our usual spot at Enrique's, 9 p.m.

There it was. The answer. She read it several times. She started typing a response, faltered under the burn of her magnifying-glass excitement, dismissed all the other alerts that had agglomerated throughout the day, re-read Vivika's message while imagining her bright face in the restaurant's penumbra, took a deep breath and returned to the bathroom.

After three years, Riley thought, it was finally going to happen. They were going to have a face-to-face conversation and see the past reflected in each other's eyes. She sat on the toilet and peed and remembered the warmth of Vivika's lips, their oaken cherry taste, the way she used to run her two short-nailed fingers and the other three stiletto-nailed ones through Riley's scalp in a petite circular motion, a small whirlpool of teasing affection, remembered how Vivika would push Riley's head down and instruct her to snake up her legs with miniature explosions of kisses, her doe eyes fixed down icily on Riley's face at all times, unwavering, until Riley reached Vivika's innermost thighs, remembered lingering there and tracing out maps of desire in saliva just how Vivika had taught her, until Vivika finally gave her permission, with a slight lean of the head, to tongue her clit, remembered how even when she'd come Vivika never smiled, but merely nodded afterward. Remembering all this Riley cried. First, she cried a lot, then a lot more.

Though Riley now lived alone, she felt an instinctual urge to protect the just-acquired stash and moved it from the bathroom to a recess in her bedroom closet. I should go for a run, she thought, telling herself it was about stretching her legs and clearing her mind, but aware, even as she articulated those thoughts, that they were lies designed to carpet over the splotchy reality of earning. Earning was a concept she'd struggled to let go of during her center detox. Two weeks into her course of methadone infusions, she'd simply replaced the idea of earning one type of high with another. It's about letting go of future-oriented rewards, Riley remembered her counselor saying, as she put on her sneakers, more snug today than in weeks. It's about being in the moment.

She told herself she was in the moment during the run several times, emulating what she thought the behavior of such a person might be, observing the dripping sap of a nearby oak suffering from a bug infestation, glancing up at a pale sky that stretched like an inverted marble bridge riven with porcelain clouds, breathing with deliberateness, looking at nothing, being no one. All artifice. Each step that interspersed greater physical distance between her body and the white powder felt like a self-betrayal. That doesn't seem right, she thought, as she pretended to study the russet silhouette of the nearby hill from the corner park bridge. She wanted to take a silly picture of overgrown ferns, but to get to the camera app she again had to dismiss alerts that had accrued over the last hour, including messages of increasing seriousness from Marcus.

Oh, Marcus.

Against her will, her thumb opened the message string. Each downward glance of her eyes carved out slivers of hollowness deep inside.

It's weird for you to go quiet like this, Marcus had written at 8:42 a.m.

Just checking in, 10:18 a.m.

Sure everything's okay?, 11:39 a.m.

We're always here for you, 12:12 p.m. PS: Ignore this if everything is fine!, 12:15 p.m.

Hey sis, wad up?, 1:19 p.m.

A little concerned now, 3:17 p.m.

Whatever's happening, I love you, and you need to know you're not alone, 4:22 p.m.

As Riley threaded down familiar streets, the phone seemed to feel heavier in her pocket, making her pace languorous.

I can't do this, she thought, but she wasn't sure what the "this" meant, one thing or its exact opposite, and the matter was left unresolved all the way to the threshold of her front door, by which time her phone was flashing with a call from Marcus, and one thing she *was* able to do was ignore it.

Peeling her shoes off inside, her toes aching, another alert: Just tried calling you. You need to check in with the group, 5:29 p.m.

Ah, she thought. There it is.

The yoke.

In her kitchen she rummaged through the fridge and found chicken tikka masala leftovers, definitely past their beauty pageant days, but she needed something of substance to help avoid the cramps she'd be facing soon, and creamy foods and cheese always helped. It's funny that I remember that, she thought. The brain, she told herself, stores what it needs.

After eating and tossing the greasy container into the trash, she paced in the kitchen, made a half-hearted pass at the dishes. Just a short while longer and she would have earned it.

She re-read Vivika's message again, three, four, five times, in the end repeating each word out loud, as if she was memorizing the ingredients of an elixir, counting the days backward from the future rendezvous to this moment, a balloon of already-overcome time contracting back to its original singularity:

Two Saturdays from today, our usual spot at Enrique's, 9 p.m.

Magic then. The phone vibrated while she held it in her hand. A new message from Vivika.

Don't be shy.

I've summoned her, Riley thought. It used to happen all the time in the old days, one of them would think of the other, or of someone else entirely while with one another, and that person would manifest on their phones, a message out of the blue, a random but deliberate streak of probability skittering through the universe, hitching a ride on some ineffable transport from consciousness to action. We could do that, Riley thought. We can do that.

She replied, *Our magic.*

Then she stared at the phone.

Silence. Blankness.

Five minutes.

Another call from Marcus, no doubt trying to tighten that noose.

Good for you, Riley thought, deleting the voicemail unheard, thinking, I'm not going back.

Ten minutes.

She was cold but on the verge of sweating.

Thirty minutes.

The dirt-grey background of her message thread with Vivika burned into her retinas.

Forty minutes.

Now, she thought, shaking, and she stood up. Now I've earned it.

***

By the Saturday of their date, Riley, now using every day three times a
day, sometimes more, having given up on her physical running because her
body couldn't keep up with her mind, felt like she'd traveled thousands of
miles into unknown territory, venturing into the hinterlands of her own
consciousness, so far beyond the mechanisms of ordinary regulation and
accounting, that to report back to herself on the findings would require a new
imaginary language.

She planned to arrive at Enrique's thirty minutes early, but Riley knew
Vivika would probably be late—in the old days she'd be an hour or more late,
never bothering to explain why—and, hovering near her front door, perched
on a world of possibilities, Riley felt a crushing weight land and stomp on her
ribcage, and she fell to her knees, heaving. She breathed and breathed and
thought, I just need a bit more. She cut it with extreme finesse. Even angels,
which Vivika and she might have been in a previous life, she thought, don't
kiss this gracefully.

She came to an hour later with the cold of her bathroom floor tiles numbing
her face, her eyeballs aching and her sinuses dry.

Fuck, she thought, but there was no message from Vivika, as there would
surely have been once upon a time, demanding to know where she was, so
at least that could be a good sign, but then again, it might be a very, very
bad sign. She washed her face. Her bladder begged for release, but as she sat
on the toilet, nothing happened save for tormenting pressure. Fuck you, she
thought to her bladder, and decided to change her now-crumpled dress.

Ten minutes later she was on the freeway on-ramp when in her left mirror
she noticed a cluster of looming elms in a pocket of shadows right beyond
the road, their branches seeming to reach forward in an aggressive overhang.
Fucking safety hazard, she thought, and lowered the windows, feeling suffocated,
but the night air had a vicious bite, making her eyes sting, so she raised the
windows again, and started humming Jennifer Lopez's "Waiting for Tonight,"
a song that she and Vivika had danced to on their first date. The melody
had lost whatever pasty charm it had once evoked, now merely a mechanical
residue of tasteless phrases piled atop meaningless notes.

In Enrique's cramped parking lot Riley checked her lipstick and realized
with dread that she had forgot to apply any. She spotted charcoal lines under

her eyes and was absorbed by their study for a full minute. These are the rings, she thought, with which I wed my future. Before she exited her grey Honda Fit, she triple-checked the small bag inside the stitched-on flap within her purse. No matter what happens with Vivika, she reassured herself, I'll be partying tonight.

Here we go.

As she entered the joint, one of the servers gave her a knowing look, perhaps remembering that she'd been a regular years ago, or mistaking her for someone else, and Riley wanted to smile in return, but the gesture wouldn't come, so she merely walked past, heading directly towards their old table.

And there, her pouting lips harshly framed by a thin band of ashen light spilling in from the neon sign of the convenience store across the street, sat Vivika, wearing her sequined silver Milan top with the boned bodice, the one she knew Riley couldn't resist.

Riley saw Vivika study her as she approached, and there passed fleetingly in Vivika's large eyes something more profound than recognition but only a distant cousin to joy. By the time Riley had closed the distance, the emotion, whatever it was, had departed like a startled owl, and only the darkness of Vivika's eyes, which somehow secluded them from the very world they observed, remained. Vivika's eyes, Riley thought, are the place where hopes go to roost and end up falling into deathly slumber.

Riley stood before their table. Vivika made no move to rise and greet her, settling instead more forcefully into her lean. She said nothing.

"It's good to see you," Riley said, sitting with shaky legs.

Vivika looked at her briefly and, as though bored, surveyed the rest of the restaurant, rotating her head slowly back and forth. "They lie," she said, "when they say everything changes."

Riley grabbed her menu. "Share an appetizer?"

"You should know me better than that," Vivika said. "I'm not the sharing kind."

It all came back to Riley then, the fastidious rules that Vivika had made her abide by whenever they were in public, how Riley's short-lived resistance to this totalitarian reign had given way to one of the greatest secret pleasures she'd ever known, almost as thoroughly enclosing as the white powder, the thrill of utter subjugation by this gorgeous woman.

When the waiter arrived, Riley ordered a Tecate and a chili lime baked tilapia. She ordered the whole fish, which was ridiculous, but her mind concocted the fantasy that they would be here for hours, or that perhaps some of Vivika's friends would join them later, that it would become a party. "And a quesadilla on the side," Riley added, embarrassment upon embarrassment, drowning in the awareness of her own clownish inadequacy, as if a whole tilapia wasn't enough. Vivika asked for a second Mezcalita de Piña after chewing on the grilled pineapple of her first and downing the jalapeño in one swift swallow. No entrees for her. The waiter nodded with a thin repressed smile and left.

Riley didn't speak, and something resinous and similar to time, but lacking its comforting ebb and flow, encased them in a shell.

Her first attempt at small talk landed Riley in the back alley of Vivika's unconcealed boredom; the second prompted a sarcastic rejoinder about a long ago evening that spiked Riley in between the ribs. Out of instinct she reached for her phone. Marcus had texted her twice more. There was a missed call from the detox center counselor. They're so cute, Riley thought. They have to hold on the illusion of helping others because it's the only way they have to help themselves.

When the food arrived, she set the tilapia aside and took a listless bite from her quesadilla.

"That fish died for you," Vivika said. She waved her arms, as though parting an ocean. "The least you can do is honor it by biting off its head."

Riley's mind recoiled at the suggestion with intellectual acid reflux, but her body betrayed her real response, tingling at the violence of the image.

Vivika ran a hand through her jet-black hair and took a sip from her drink. "You look consumed," she said. "Not in a good way."

"Which would be how?" Riley asked.

"Remember Guadalajara," Vivika said. "That's the idea."

For a whole week they had spent the daytime having sex in a small hotel room without hot water, emerging each evening to eat and get drunk before starting again the next day. The last two days they'd stayed up through the night, snorting coke and popping ecstasy, giggling and crying and laughing, and at one point Vivika had become completely still and told Riley that she was the most perfect creature she'd ever known—that was what she said, not the hottest woman, not the most fun girlfriend, not the most dependable buddy, but the *most perfect creature*—and the absoluteness of that declaration, spoken with devastating sadness, had made Riley's chest burn and her toes freeze.

Riley took another desultory chomp from the now-soggy quesadilla. "You're the queen of planting ideas," she said.

"I'm a queen, period," Vivika said. But her eyes perked up, a tunnel of black sparkle rising within their hard duskiness. "Play your cards right and you can be my consort."

Riley wanted the game to continue, wanted Vivika to keep picking at her and then kissing the scabs, because each time she did, she felt pricked by life itself. But a submerged presence within her rose up, a combination of fear and exhaustion and something she didn't dare name, and it shoved her into confrontational irritation. "My cards?" Riley said. She pushed the plates away in disgust. The tilapia regarded her with offensive monotony. Everything in this restaurant was suddenly repugnant. "Tell me about them."

"Show me your phone."

"Why?"

Vivika didn't answer. In an automatic way the silence unlocked Riley, who in turn unlocked the phone's screen. Feeling a welcome slickness between her legs, she slid the device across to Vivika.

Vivika scrolled, clicked, swiped, and sighed. "Baby," she said. Her head fell back a fraction. "I hope the thought of us being back together didn't send you down this hole." She smiled, pure and ravishing.

Riley took a deep breath. It seemed to come from far away, and to end up farther away still. "What do you want from me?"

Vivika pushed Riley's phone back towards her. "One thing," Vivika said. "Do this one thing for me, and I'll take you to places that'll make our eight years together seem like the line leading up to the ride."

"What do you want from me?" Riley asked again.

"I want you to be free," Vivika said. "Free from all this bullshit. From the conventional expectations of your new so-called friends. You're not like them. These people don't want to help you. They want to control you, which is admirable enough, I suppose. But they don't know *how* you need to be controlled."

"And you do."

"You know I know."

"Marcus is—"

"From this moment on, they don't have names anymore," Vivika said, and it sounded plausible and absolute, like a newly unveiled law of physics that fit perfectly with all previously established laws. "They're gone. Write a quick post to the group saying goodbye. Delete your profile, then block their numbers and give me your phone."

Riley squirmed. "When did you notice that—"

"The moment you walked in," Vivika said, brushing one of her legs up against her. The graze of her skin's heat sent a fever dagger through Riley's body. She let out a soft moan.

Vivika withdrew her leg and set her hands, palm down, on the table, with such an intensity of presence that she seemed to be fixing the table to the earth, and the earth itself to its warping passage through space and time. Vivika's gaze coiled around the past and future, pythoning Riley's right-now.

Riley finished her beer and ordered another.

Vivika stared at her, right before her, yet beyond reach.

The beer came. As she took a gulp from the bottle, Riley adjusted her legs, her panties clinging to her pussy in a way she'd missed for three years.

She closed her eyes, expecting to be flooded with memories of her time together with Vivika. Instead, she saw herself in a park. She and Marcus were walking on a breezy June day and they stopped for frozen yogurt. "Look! They got pineapple, your favorite," he said. His smile widened, expanding from an expression of one's own joy to a celebration of another's. "I'm so proud of you." He was proud because she'd completed her detox. Because I made promises, Riley thought, that I knew I couldn't keep, but which I'd convinced myself were worth lying about.

I'm sorry, my friend.

A cramp on her right side crumbled the park and Marcus' face and the sunshine of that day.

Vivika's eyes gaped. She'd become a hawk, coolly riding a thermal without batting an eyelash.

"I need..." Riley said. None of the things she needed could be named, so she did what came best to her instead. "I need a minute to think it over. I'm going to use the lady's room, and when I come back, you'll have your answer."

Vivika didn't react. No nod, no confirmation, no approval, or disdain. She merely was, and by being the immensity of her control deafened the surroundings.

In the bathroom, Riley thought she smelled seaweed, or maybe conifers. There was a chill in the air. They were fifty miles from the ocean but that night-time smell was here, in her lungs. She studied her face in the mirror, her hand already partway into her purse.

Did she *ever* love me? she wondered.

Her hand unzipped the pocket, extracted the bag, and placed it on the sink. She was completely unworried about anyone coming in and seeing her. She was alone and invisible, wrapped in a protective gauze of inevitability and desire. She took off her heels. The dirty floor tiles felt refreshing to her soles, strangely porous and malleable, like sand in the immediate wake of a gentle, rolling wave.

I'm finally in the moment, she thought, and laughed because the moment was a fucking nightmare.

Her mirror face looked at her. Did she ever love me? they asked themselves, this time in unison. Did we ever love ourselves? With her fingernail she scooped out the powder, eyeballing it quickly, with certainty, and she opened her mouth wide, inserted her finger inside her mouth without touching her lips, turned her finger so that the powder fell atop her tongue, and walked back to the table where Vivika waited for her in her poised sleekness.

Riley placed her hand on Vivika's exposed shoulder and leaned down, lowering her mouth to a hair's width from Vivika's. Their lips pressed together. Riley's tongue roamed around freely in Vivika's mouth, swirled like an eddy, bold and free. They kissed like never before, and the world fell away from Riley.

She pulled her tongue out gently, resting her mouth on Vivika's for a heartbeat, tasting the warmth of her breath before retreating completely. "For old times' sake," she said.

Then she ran her own tongue against her gums, feeling everything gone.

Back in her chair, in deft strokes she said goodbye to her support group, deleted her profile, blocked her friends, and passed the phone to Vivika.

Just in time. The cosmos trembled at the periphery of her perception, and she felt her soul about to be pulled up through her own being by a vortex of unimputable contentment.

Vivika studied her phone for a moment, as though it were an alien artifact that had materialized on their restaurant table from some distant world.

She laughed.

Riley heard the little staccato bursts as though through an echo chamber.

"My part of the bargain's done," Vivika said. Her eyes were becoming more readable with each syllable, revealing true vacancy behind her pretense of studied emptiness. But something else was leaking into those eyes. A shot of light like silver ink. "You've never been dominated like this before," Vivika said. "You've never felt what you're feeling right now." The words were underwritten by conviction, but they lacked reality. Vivika's face was becoming slack. Her mouth opened partway and didn't close again.

"How could you think," she continued, but Riley could see it clearly now, the effort to form each word, the brutal work required to control her muscles and keep herself in character. "How couuuuld you think that I would want to geeet back togetherrrr with someone…" She paused, confused. "Sooo weeeaaak. Where'sh challenge in thaaat?" Vivika's face paled, first into ivory and then into the kind of chalk used to outline a corpse.

Seeing the fantastic blanching of Vivika's pallor reminded Riley of the white spume of tumbling surf, and she gave in to her own surge now. Her soul was right at the ceiling of her, about to break free. "We just shared six milligrams of fentanyl, sweetheart," Riley said, "and I made sure you got the brunt. Two's lethal. You finally got me all to yourself…"

Vivika's breath shallowed.

"You wouldn't darrrr," she said. "You're shcared—"

Her eyes closed and she slumped back in her chair.

It was like turning off a great camera that had fed Riley's world with reality instead of capturing its pre-existing essence. Ontologies reversed themselves, and a great hulking engine of captivity imploded in plumes of stereoscopic starlight.

The fringe of neon light from across the street bruised Vivika's dead face with purple.

I am myself now, Riley thought.

With the tolerance she'd built up over the last two weeks, she might make it. Or not.

But even if I die, she thought, I've survived.

As the world receded, euphoric calm took her by the hand and held her gentle. Somewhere far beyond the confines of the restaurant, evergreen leaves rustled on a tall yew tree whose reddish-brown boughs had over the years curled into the shape of an apology.

The Rise and Fall of Melody Lines, Esq.

By Rhys Hughes

S he wore men's clothes, but there was no way you would mistake her for a man, not even if you were so drunk when you entered the club that you couldn't remember what you were yourself. It was to fit in with the other musicians, of course, so that the band presented themselves as a whole to the crowd of dancers on the concrete floor.

She shaved her head too, wore no hat, and didn't stray anywhere near the weak spotlights, but it was clear from the instant I set eyes on her that she was special, dangerous, and fated to be my downfall. She played the saxophone in a way slightly different from what I was used to hearing in this place, bleaker and odder than the rhythms of the drums demanded, but her hard notes never distorted the beauty of the songs. They unfolded languidly, warmly embracing the audience.

I supposed she was a lover of free jazz who had ended up in a soukous combo with its more controlled structures out of necessity, but that wasn't quite right. She loved this music too, as did I, with authentic passion. For months I had been coming here to listen and marvel. The club was turned into a pile of rubble one night by bulldozers and you won't find it on that corner of Kenyatta Avenue and Muindi Mbingu Street anymore. Too bad. The owner forgot to pay his taxes and I forgot to extract my soul from the mess until it was too late. But that's my life.

When the show was over, the dancers cleared the floor, and the musicians packed up their equipment. Because a saxophone is easier to put away in a case than any of the other instruments, she was at the bar first, and I was there too, right beside her. Her clothes were expensive, just like those of a Kinshasa *sapeur*, and I spoke to her in French first. These soukous bands are mostly filled with refugees but no, she wasn't Congolese at all. When she replied in English I somehow forgot to wonder at her accent. Already I understood that I was doomed, and it felt right. I laughed and she didn't even blink. Then I bought her a bottle of beer.

You know how it is when you meet a new person who is on the same frequency as yourself. There is no awkwardness and time itself seems to undergo a transformation. The custom that we must know an individual for a certain number of days or weeks before we feel entirely comfortable with them becomes meaningless. I felt I had known Melody all my life, a dreadful cliché, yes, exasperating—so allow me to modify it. I felt that had I been born female and lived the same experiences she had, whatever they were, I too would be like her, exactly the same.

This was an illusion, but I believed it at the time. I regarded it as some sort of obvious truth that she was my extruded soul reversed in a magical mirror, and that it would be a crime if we didn't become close friends, at the very least. But *that* wasn't the crime. I didn't find out until much later that the mirror was shattered from the start. The shards are working their way towards my heart even as I write this. But I don't want to sound like a washed-up poet, so I'll refrain from more of that kind of talk. The night lapped itself to death around us, as we stood at that bar, and I don't recall most of what I said to her, but I know it was about music. Always rhythm and harmony and tone colour. And Melody Lines.

It was the perfect name for her, perhaps a stage name or maybe a real one, but I didn't ask for details. I said, "Look, I'm a maths teacher in the suburbs and my name is Johnny Sum. It's not so strange. Perhaps names urge us to be what they want from an early age."

"That's right, Johnny."

And she caressed my cheek with an elegant hand as she said it and in my head I yelled. It is curious, looking back, that none of the other band members came up to say hello, that none of the dancers came to say some drunken word of introduction or appreciation. But I was too enraptured to notice anything amiss. And then I asked her where she was staying, not in a predatory way, and she told me of a hotel in River Road, and that's how I knew the band was touring, that they weren't based in my city, that she might be gone tomorrow forever, and I wept.

She laughed at this. Too dramatic, of course, far too presumptuous, a really ridiculous little scene. But there was no mockery in her mirth. Then she told me that they were heading down to Mombasa in a week but that her mornings in the meantime were free. She had to rehearse in the long afternoons—the band was constantly changing its playlist—and she wanted to experiment anyway. I accepted the mornings.

And I also knew that I would be sitting on the train to Mombasa when the week was done, the six-hour express to the ocean, and that if I didn't get a grip on myself, I would doubtlessly pursue her over the continent from any shore to any highland and through any desert. Then I glanced around and saw we were the only customers left and I offered to escort her back because River Road can be perilous at night.

"Meet me for breakfast," she said when we reached her hotel, and at that instant I didn't need to kiss her for my soul to inflate inside my body. Back I walked and how I returned home I can't say. I was worn out and slept a dreamless night, dreamless in visual terms I mean. It seemed I was floating in a sea of music, that notes were bubbling beneath me like foam, and I was struggling to remain upright.

I rose very early and made my way towards her hotel. The dawn is my familiar friend, not because I am in the habit of getting up before sunrise but for the simple fact I often don't leave the clubs until they close, which is when there's no more night left to dance away. I had no idea what time Melody had breakfast, and I couldn't bear the idea of being late for her. In the end I had to hang around in the lobby for an hour before she appeared, coming down the stairs like a descending glissando. I laughed at the idea. She shared my mirth when I told her what I was thinking, but behind that smile was some sort of cryptic sadness.

We drank tea with our meal and talked mostly about music. I declared my belief that she was a free jazz musician at heart, but she reached out to touch my arm and said, "In my head, not my heart, Johnny. I love strange harmonies but that's not the point."

"Tell me," I answered.

"Resolution. That's what truly matters."

"Did we talk about this last night? My mind was whirling. I know that I was happy but nothing else."

"Be careful now, Mr. Johnny Sum. Yes, we spoke a little on the topic. You know what some kinds of music really are, don't you? Time travel, yes, it's a fact. But only certain styles."

"I'm rather lost now."

She had finished eating and smiled at me, but it was obvious she was preparing herself for an inner struggle. What she wanted to explain was complex and she was wondering if it was worth the effort. It was essential that I crease my brow and adopt a studious manner. I wanted her to think I was intelligent enough for her.

She took a deep breath as if preparing to blow a sax solo and said with her eyes closed and her hands clenched:

"I do like the wilder kinds of sonic adventure, yes, but they won't get me far in this world. Maybe half a century ago there was more interest in experimental music, I don't know. I joined the soukous band because it's popular music, and I really enjoy it, and the boys in the band tolerate my games with abstraction because I win."

I nodded my head in acknowledgement. Yes, she won. There wasn't any sourness in the combination of the catchy dance tunes and her forays into microtonal weirdness. She added a touch of the uneasy and uncanny, but it all kept resolving itself wonderfully.

"Johnny," she added, relaxing her fists, reaching out to touch my arm and opening her eyes. "I'm not joking when I say it's time travel. That's not a metaphor. But I don't travel anywhere. I remain here in the present and reach back into the past to change it."

I couldn't think of a riposte to this, partly because I wasn't sure what she was talking about and partly because she was distracting me. Melody Lines, with her foot touching my leg under the table, having removed her shoe, fluttering her eyelashes, winning again. But I know about music. It is my hobby, my passion, perhaps even the entire meaning of my life. To put such a truth so bluntly makes me seem a tragic figure, all of a sudden, and I realised I was seeking another meaning, a better reason for being in the world. I told myself to be very careful.

"Imagine a sequence of notes, all horrible, almost painful to the ears. I could play you such a series right now if I had my instrument with me but there's no need. Just imagine," she urged.

"Very well. What next?"

"Johnny, the agitation and discomfort are real. But then another note is played, a note that provides a resolution to the sequence, that *fixes* the series, makes it right, turns it from an ugly thing into something beautiful. The melody line no longer seems discordant because the discords have all been resolved, transformed, purified."

"Yes, jazz often does that. I understand you perfectly."

"But what has actually happened?"

I shrugged. "The listener made an assumption that was wrong. He had to experience the full passage of music to know what it really was. When he hears it a second time, he will enjoy it."

"No, Johnny. The listener's assumption wasn't incorrect. The notes he heard really *were* horrible. That was no illusion. But the final note altered the past. Do you see? The vibrations of that special note reached back and manipulated a past event. Time travel!"

"Like one of those particles that flow against time?"

"Tachyons. Jazz notes, yes."

She slumped as if exhausted and I hoped my laughter was kind. "That is one way of looking at it. An original way. But it hardly matters. It's an academic discussion of music, that's all."

She shook her head. "It matters. It matters a great deal."

I was struck by her serious tone.

Before I could question her further, the waiter came to take our plates and glasses and I took the opportunity to pay the bill. I wanted to suggest a walk to Melody where we could continue the conversation in the open air. I took my wallet out of my pocket.

And then something very strange happened.

The wallet was in my hand one moment then I blinked and it was gone, but I had felt nothing. It had vanished, popped like a soap bubble, and my hand was extended now as if I was making an obscure gesture. I muttered something, tried to collect my senses.

"It disappeared. My wallet just melted away."

Melody smiled tolerantly and exchanged a glance with the waiter, but he was impassive, perhaps getting ready to deal with trouble. She touched my arm again and said, "There was never anything in your hand. You put it in your pocket, and it came out empty."

"That simply can't be."

She wagged a finger. "I know all the tricks of men." She reached into her handbag and extracted enough notes to pay for both of us. I was very embarrassed.

All I could offer was: "My wallet must have been stolen earlier."

"Probably on the way here."

"You do believe me, don't you? I would never have expected you to pay for me. I'm not like that."

"I believe you, Johnny Sum. Stop worrying."

"Shall we go for a walk?"

"I have too many things to do this morning. Then it's practice for me in the afternoon and the show at night."

"I messed up," I said.

She shook her head and her smile flashed. "Not at all. Meet me again tomorrow. You are a nice guy."

And she touched me on the nose with a finger.

I left the hotel feeling both elated and appalled. The disappearance of the wallet made no sense. It was nightmarish. But the elegance of the girl, her intelligence and curves, mitigated the disaster. Yet my shame diluted my joy. I was confused and giddy.

Then a notion struck me that I did my best to resist.

But it had a terrible logic to it.

Melody Lines, the musician with shaved head and men's clothes, was a pickpocket, a thief of a particular kind, a virtuoso. She had snatched my wallet when I was least expecting it, when it was in my hand. I know that expert thieves can do such a thing. Nairobi is full of ingenious criminals. I read a lot of detective stories when I was younger and I don't think that any of those fictional sleuths would stand much of a chance in this city, a place where many thieves return home after a successful robbery to find that their apartments have been burgled.

But the vibrancy of the place compensates for much. Let's not get into that. I wanted to know more about Melody, her past activities, and I had a friend who could help me. He worked in a library and had access to most of the national and local newspapers that had been printed in the past ten years. He is just as enthusiastic about unsolved crime cases as I am about music. So, I decided to pay him a visit.

I did exactly that, explained what I wanted, and he was glad to oblige me. For the remainder of the day, I thought about Melody's curious ideas on music. If I hear music I don't like, but later something makes me like it, surely this means I have changed my mind about its worth? And I have changed my mind in the *present*. But she appeared to be saying that the change wasn't subjective, in my mind, but external. That the music really had become something else because the present had adjusted the *past*. I was bemused by the concept, and I wondered if it could be broadened to include aspects of life outside of music.

It can, of course, and we are all aware of the fact.

Let's suppose I am playing a game of cards and I am dealt three cards that have no value, the king, jack and ten of hearts. They are no better to me than random symbols and there's no harmony between them because the rules of this game regard them simply as examples of bad luck. Then the dealer gives me the queen of hearts. Suddenly everything has changed and a beautiful chord has been constructed.

A run of four cards of the same suit means I win the hand, take the pot, and depart the game a richer man. Was Melody that queen of hearts in the hand of my fate? She had dealt me a blow, certainly, and she had resolved it too. I am a teacher of mathematics. I can quote many examples of sums and equations that are meaningless until some extra factor is added. That extra factor, no matter how small, smooths the entirety, it reaches across the rest and sweeps away the randomness.

But music isn't quite the same thing as completing an equation. Music is *made* from time. So that one extra note that makes everything right has altered the past, yes. Can such a thing be said of situations and people too? What might become of us if our own pasts are open to manipulation and revision? That girl had propelled me into speculations that ached my brain, and yet I ached to see her once again.

I went to enjoy her show that night, of course, and I noticed a curious fact that had escaped my attention during the previous gig. The band weren't actually so sweet playing as individuals. They made mistakes of timing, tone, and volume, but she was there to steer the evolving songs in an uplifting direction by adding the right note, the extra factor that turned a sour equation into a spectacular formula.

She came to me at the bar when it was over, we chatted, I walked her back to her hotel. I tried for a kiss when we said goodnight, but she was quick to turn her head aside and my lips grazed the stubble of her skull. I laughed, pretending it was a joke, but she put her finger on my mouth to silence me and said, "Johnny, not yet."

"Melody, I desire you."

"You don't know enough about me."

"I am a fast learner."

And I was tempted to tell her that I had a friend who was already in the process of investigating her possible past. That would have been one of the most ruinous decisions of my life, I decided, but later I knew that in fact it might have saved me. She promised to meet me for breakfast. I swallowed my impatience and nodded.

Breakfast passed together, without a repeat of the wallet incident, and then we went for a walk. I could tell she planned to give herself to me in a highly controlled manner, like an unfolding piece of music, but I worried that soon she would slip out of my grasp, that she would be on the train to Mombasa before anything serious could be established. She said nothing about time travel and to prompt her back in that direction I said casually enough, as we strolled through the park:

"Love is a strange thing. We split up with someone and we think our world has ended. It's a total disaster. Time passes and we meet someone new, and we are happier with them than we were with the old partner. At that moment we are grateful for the painful split. It led us to the situation we now find ourselves in. The split was necessary suffering, and we know that the pain was worth enduring, and the memory of the pain is a lesson that we can digest with gratitude."

"No, Johnny," she warned me.

I turned to face her, and I held her around the waist.

"You disagree?" I asked.

"There was no suffering at all in the split. Don't you see? The meeting with the new person is like the sounding of the special musical note I told you about, the one that resolves the disharmonies. It cancels out the pain, yes, but cancels it out in past time. To say it no longer hurts is incorrect. I maintain that it goes deeper than that."

"I am waiting, dear."

"The past pain *never* existed."

"But things that happened can't change their nature. They can only be redefined, evaluated in a different way."

"The special note is far more powerful than you think. It can and does change the past. The past isn't fixed in space, it isn't a block of something hard, but exists at the mercy of the present. It is malleable, soft, and, when we are alive, we can sculpt it, smooth it, discard it. Most of us are unaware of this. Only in music does the truth become tangible. That's how I came to understand the reality of time."

My grin betrayed my glee for I had tricked her back into talking about time travel. She laughed along. Then our idyll was destroyed. A man who was walking near us abruptly fell over. He didn't seem drunk. I turned to stare, but found my legs talking me closer. I bent down to help him up. I saw that his nose was bleeding heavily.

"I was punched," he said.

"There was no one near you," I argued.

"An assailant punched me in the face! It was a blur, and I couldn't do anything to avoid the fist."

He thanked me and wiped his nose with a handkerchief and walked on with snorting noises. I returned to Melody just in time to see her wiping a stain from her knuckles. I frowned. That stain had looked like blood, but I couldn't imagine how she had managed to cut her hand. Then I saw that her skin was unbroken, just bruised.

As if she had punched someone. How absurd!

I was unable to speak.

She took my arm and said, "I have to go and rehearse soon. I hope I will see you at the club tonight?"

I nodded dumbly. We made a circuit of the park and I returned her to her hotel and once again she declined a kiss. I wandered the city streets. I am a teacher, but my school had closed for a short time while repairs were being made, so I had my days free.

If Melody had struck that random stranger, how did she manage to do it without me noticing? We had been standing side by side and there were several metres between us and the man. A crime had been committed and I felt she was responsible, but I couldn't be sure, and I didn't even know if being sure would spoil my feelings for her.

I now accepted that a person in the present could alter the past in such a way that the past event was objectively changed, but how did the insight apply to what had happened with my wallet and the passing stranger? The riddle was beyond my intellect.

The show in the night was another triumph for her and once again we walked back to her hotel, and she refused to kiss me. But she was warmer than before, allowed me to hold her closer. I was making progress. But as I walked away from River Road, I found a man sitting on the pavement. It is an area where it's best not to engage with people, but I could see that he was wounded. And he was muttering:

"She stabbed me! In the stomach! For no reason!"

"Did you get a good look at her?"

He blinked up at my voice, studied my face, frowned, and then twisted his mouth in a snarl of rage. "With you!"

"What do you mean?"

"She was with you! You are her accomplice!"

"I really don't know—"

"Police! Help!" he began shouting.

The police rarely venture along River Road, but I thought it best to run through the shadows and make myself scarce. I was trembling with shock when I reached home, and I drank quarter of a bottle of rum before falling into bed. I wanted to shut off my mind.

Breakfast the following morning with Melody was just as tremendous as on the previous two occasions, but more terrible. It wasn't a case of an absconded wallet or a sucker punch now, but a burning shop and the sort of chaos one associates with small wars. She was nowhere near the store when it happened, but her hair smelled of smoke and paraffin long before the fumes could have reached her.

The spice shop burned with little detonations, as if the jars of turmeric were exploding, which is probably what was really happening. I kept my thoughts to myself. We parted and I went to visit Mwangi in his library. I caught him eating his lunch over a large encyclopaedia and he greeted my appearance with delight.

"I was planning on contacting you later today," he said.

"You found out something?"

He nodded. "Oh yes. It wasn't difficult. There are many references to a girl named Melody Lines in the news. I have only delved back six years so far. I am sure more will turn up."

"She didn't even bother changing her name!"

"Why should she? She wasn't accused of anything and never arrested. But she was a witness every time."

"A bystander? Always in the vicinity of trouble."

"Just so. It's very odd."

It was clear to me at that moment that she was a threat to my life. Her criminal past came as no surprise, but the fact that she had found a way of committing crimes without seeming to be involved was very disturbing. I am a sceptic when it comes to the supernatural. At the same time, I know that chaos is chaos, death is death. Her kiss might be poisonous. Maybe I was her plaything, a toy to be enjoyed and destroyed. Yet my heart cared for her and overruled my reason.

I thanked Mwangi and promised one day to do him a favour in return and then I left the library and considered my options. I had none. I knew where I would be that evening and the following morning, and I was right and satisfied to be right. She played on stage, I walked her home, I tried a kiss and this time almost succeeded.

And we had breakfast and went out and a crime happened right next to us. Because this is Nairobi, witnessing one crime a day isn't anything out of the ordinary, and yet I knew she was responsible, that she was an ingenious villain, a mastermind with hips that excited my libido and told my conscience to go to hell. And it did.

A shooting, a fatal traffic accident, a bank raid…

Her last day in the city arrived. The show was extra special with one of those encores that are like a simultaneous orgasm for both performers and listeners. The musicians and dancers were satisfied, exhausted, and I walked Melody to her hotel without much hope. She had conditioned me. But to my surprise she invited me into her room and that's where I went. She closed the door and faced me boldly.

"Johnny Sum, let me tell you something strange."

I waited for her confession.

It came, but not of the kind I had anticipated.

"I have feelings for you."

My eyebrows went up. She was sincere, I was sure of that, and there was no point trying to tell her that it couldn't be true, that we hadn't been acquainted long enough, because I felt the same way, had felt like that for many days, and the velocity of love isn't an issue. I believed her. She had started to fall in love. Then I asked:

"Will you give yourself to me tonight?"

She stepped into my arms, and I removed her jacket and flung it into a corner. Then I began unbuttoning her shirt. She grabbed my wrists, stared into my eyes, and spoke slowly:

"Listen, Johnny. I am not a woman."

I retreated a few steps and cried, "You are a man?"

"Not even that," she replied.

"I fail to understand."

"The special note I told you about can make all the wrong notes right. Just one note. I wanted to be that note. Playing it wasn't enough. I wished with my all my strength to turn into it."

"What are you saying?"

"The mistakes we make in our lives are wrong notes too. Our crimes are wrong notes. The right note can fix them, Johnny, change them in the past. All the crimes I committed and will commit are wrong notes, a long series of discords. But the note I am turns them into good notes. It means my life is unaffected by evil. After you hear the special note, you can't tell that the previous notes were ever wrong. I am the special note. Anything I do is right because I change the past."

Her hands continued with the unbuttoning of her shirt. But it wasn't a shirt that came off her body. It was the flesh beneath the shirt. She kicked off her trousers. Then she raised her hands to her head and pulled and that came off too. She was truly naked now.

She was a note, a musical note. With a stalk for a body and black orb for a head. It was crazy. It was terrifying.

She was an eighth note, a quaver, with a tail, an inverted quaver. Her stem glided over the carpet of the room and her movement filled my ears with sighs. It would have been so easy to fall back on the bed, to embrace her as she settled down on me like a whisper. But I screamed. I ran out of the room, I cascaded down the stairs, my limbs jerking in all directions. It was too much for me. I had panicked.

I spent the rest of the night in a delirium, wandering the streets, trying to walk myself into oblivion. How can any girl transform herself into a giant musical note through the sheer effort of her will? It was ludicrous and appalling. I alternated between weeping, laughing, and singing. It was the first time I had seen a woman's soul.

She left for Mombasa the following day and I slowly sobered up. And then it occurred to me that she might really be the love of my life, that to let her get away was a mistake. But would she want to see me again? She had exposed herself to me, shown me the truth of her power, made herself vulnerable, and I had reacted in the worst way. Surely, she would dismiss all my future protestations of love?

Yes, she would regard me with contempt.

Unless I took drastic action.

She loved me, that was undeniable, and though she might now want to distance herself from me, if I was in a dire situation, I felt sure she would come to my rescue. She was able to erase from existence her own crimes, all her wrong notes, by virtue of the fact she had turned herself into the special note that resolves all discords. Could she perform the alchemy for another person? For me, for example?

There was a way to find out.

I withdrew most of my savings from the bank, bought a suit worthy of a Kinshasa *sapeur*. Then I went to visit a friend who was not Mwangi and obtained something else at an inflated price. I bought a ticket for the next express train to Mombasa. And I waited at the station and hummed a tune, but the tune consisted of one note only.

We rise up and we fall down, but when music rises and falls it travels laterally too. Melody had risen in my affections, fallen in my estimation, but now I wanted to be with her forever. I would take the chance. Before the train had pulled very far out of Nairobi, I pulled out the gun and took hostages. I had become a hijacker.

News would reach Mombasa long before I did.

The police would be waiting.

Would she be waiting too? Six hours the journey took. Enough time for her to know about it and be ready for me. Then she would work her magic and cancel out my responsibility.

I would become a witness rather than the perpetrator.

We would run off together.

And so I stood with my gun to the driver's head as the landscape rose and fell, gently, like a melody line.

Kane's Alibi

By Bev Vincent

I've awakened with worse hangovers. Once or twice, maybe. My body ached all over—my head worst of all. I'd neglected to close the curtains the night before, and the light streaming into the hotel room seemed like punishment for my overindulgence. I squeezed my eyes shut and tried to remember the previous evening.

After the first details re-emerged, I held my breath to see if I could hear anything to indicate the presence of another person. I eased my hand across the other side of the bed. It encountered nothing but rumpled sheets. I opened one eyelid a fraction of an inch. Flinched. After several seconds, I managed to open it halfway and convinced the other to play along, too. An oversized pillow came into view. Nothing else.

Pain pierced my brain when I turned my head to squint at the nightstand clock. Blurry LEDs informed me it was 9:17. I propped myself up on my elbows, staved off a wave of nausea, and surveyed the rest of the room. The bathroom door was ajar. I held my breath again. When I didn't hear anything, I decided I was alone.

I dropped my head back onto the pillow and took stock. My probing fingers encountered a scratch on my left shoulder. I grabbed the other pillow and sniffed. Lavender. Yes, someone else had definitely been here.

Sudden panic came over me. Clambering out of bed, I scanned the floor on unsteady feet until I located my pants under the desk. Certain of what I'd find—or rather what I *wouldn't*—I pulled my wallet from the rear pocket. To my relief, my cash and credit cards were untouched. I released pent-up breath, dropped everything, and lumbered to the bathroom. I urinated forever, flushed, and glanced in the mirror. My eyes were bloodshot, my hair a fright wig.

After swilling a glass of water, I decided I could probably manage some toast, maybe even a poached egg. I called room service, donned a robe, and cracked open the door to retrieve the newspaper from the hall. The food, when it arrived, settled my stomach, and the coffee helped ease my pounding head, but I still didn't remember much after leaving the lobby bar in the company of a gorgeous young woman the previous evening.

***

For three days, I'd been sitting through lectures on paranormal phenomena and spectral metaphysics. Most of the conference attendees looked ordinary enough, yet they spent their spare time traipsing through abandoned houses hoping to capture evidence of otherworldly apparitions.

Ghosts.

I was in Sacramento keeping an eye on Edgar Witherspoon, a balding fifty-three-year-old man with a PhD in physics. Yesterday, he'd delivered a talk to nearly two hundred attendees. After a moderately interesting presentation—if you're into that sort of thing—he fielded questions until five. When he finished, a group of acolytes surrounded him at the lectern. I trailed him and his entourage to the hotel restaurant and picked a two-person booth in the bar section where I could keep an eye on him.

Witherspoon's wife had hired Kane Investigations to follow him to California to make sure he didn't stray. Why she didn't just go with him, I didn't know, but the money was good and the work easy. So far, he was behaving himself. He'd had ample opportunity to look for apparitions beneath the sheets with comely young women, but he'd retired to his room alone each evening.

I couldn't hear what the group was discussing, but they were probably trying to outdo each other with accounts of electronic voice phenomena, spectral photography, and the parapsychology of the earthbound dead. My attention drifted to a baseball game on one of the big screens over the bar. The Padres were ahead of the Astros by two runs in the bottom of the sixth. I was nearing the bottom of my second martini when someone dropped into the empty seat across from me.

"Is this taken?" a female voice asked.

I instantly lost all interest in the Astros. My visitor was dressed in a formfitting tan top under an unbuttoned long-sleeved white shirt. Her nose turned up at the tip, giving her a soft, vulnerable appearance. The thin arches of her eyebrows peaked near the outer edges of her eyes. Late twenties, I estimated. Thirty, tops. In the dim light, I couldn't tell if her long loose curls were black or dark brown. "No," I said. "I'm Benjamin."

A hint of lavender wafted across the table when she extended her hand for a firm, lingering handshake. Her pouty lips parted in what might have been a smile. "I know," she said. "I read your nametag."

My hand sprang to my shirt pocket. Then I remembered removing the tag before entering the bar.

"Earlier, I meant. During the keynote," she said. "I was sitting behind you."

"I'm sorry I didn't see you." Emboldened by alcohol, I continued. "Though I wouldn't have heard much of the lecture if I had."

"You looked skeptical." She wrinkled her nose. "I was curious, but I'm not convinced." The edges of her mouth twitched.

My heart raced. "Can I buy you a drink?" I glanced around for a waiter.

She nodded at my empty glass. "A martini, if you're having another."

***

I refilled my coffee mug. The third martini had been ill advised. The fourth, gulped down when my new friend suggested we order room service, was definitely a mistake. That was where my memory grew fuzzy. If she'd provided her name, I didn't recall it. Had we ever gotten around to eating? There were no dishes in the room nor was there a tray in the hall when I picked up the newspaper.

Teasing snapshots flitted through my mind. Her naked body sprawled beneath me. Her soft, moist lips brushing against mine. Feline purring and warm breath in my ear. Her head arching back in response to my touch. Running my hands through her curls. Vague memories of how she had smelled and tasted—of lavender, desire and sweat.

After I passed out, she had escaped like a thief in the night. If I ran into her today, would she pretend she didn't know me? I wasn't up on the etiquette of conference affairs. Had she also been cheating on someone? I pushed away a twinge of guilt. What was done was done. No point in beating myself up over a fleeting indiscretion. The hangover was punishment enough—for now.

After a shower, I shaved, dressed, and dragged a comb through my wet hair. By all rights, I should have been lurking near Witherspoon's room to find out if he had spent the night alone, but from what I'd seen so far, I was pretty sure he wasn't up to anything. The irony didn't escape me. Still, I had a job to do. I would catch up with Witherspoon at the morning session.

The lobby seemed unusually crowded. People huddled in groups, deep in animated conversation. I recognized the bartender from the night before, standing next to a tall man wearing a dark suit and a scowl. The bartender pointed at me.

Before the man pulled out his gold badge, I made him as a cop. He approached and said, "I'm Detective Tyler. Can I talk with you?"

My skin grew clammy, and my chest tightened. "Is it Marina? Has she—?"

"In here." Tyler guided me toward a vacant meeting room.

Even with a throbbing head, I knew Tyler wasn't here because something had happened to my girlfriend. He would have come to my room instead of needing someone to point me out in the lobby.

"Could I see some identification, please?" Tyler asked.

I fumbled through my wallet until I found my private investigator license.

"Benjamin Kane," Tyler read, holding the ID up for comparison.

"My hair was longer back then," I said.

Tyler wandered to the other side of the room and made a call, reading off the information from my license. When he returned, he pulled a photograph from his coat pocket. "Do you know her?"

She was even more beautiful than I remembered. "We met in the bar last night. I didn't get her name."

Tyler wrote something on a small pad. "When was that?"

I recognized the scene: the interview that was the prelude to an interrogation. If the police were questioning me, she was dead, missing, or had filed a complaint. "During the Astros-Padres game. Sixth or seventh inning. Is she saying I did something?" I asked. "Do I need a lawyer?"

"She's not saying anything." The detective frowned. "Why would you need a lawyer?"

"What's this about?"

Tyler still had my license in his hand. "Are you in town on a case?"

I was usually protective of my clients' rights, but I had nothing to gain by being coy. "A jealous wife asked me to keep tabs on her husband at the conference."

"Ghost hunters." Tyler shook his head. "So, you met this woman in the bar last night."

"She came to my booth. We had a couple of drinks." I decided to keep my card close to my chest until I found out what Tyler knew.

"When did you last see her?"

"I had quite a bit to drink. Lost track of the time."

"What about her?" Tyler waved the photograph. "Did she drink a lot, too?"

"A couple of martinis with me. I don't know if she had anything before that."

"And after you left the bar?"

I shrugged. "Are you going to tell me what's going on?"

"You haven't been outside yet."

"So?"

"If you had, you would have seen the activity around the corner. Police, ambulance, medical examiner."

"She's dead?"

"I think we should move this discussion downtown. I don't need to cuff you, do I?"

I shook my head. The detective ushered me through the lobby. Once outside, he summoned a uniformed officer, who gave me a quick, professional pat down before opening the back door of a police cruiser.

As we passed the Sacramento Executive Airport on the way to police headquarters, I wondered how much I would tell my girlfriend Marina when I got back to Houston. Assuming I ever did. If the cops could pin this on me, they might. Clear a case, save some shoe leather, make headlines.

After I was fingerprinted—to "exclude me as a suspect"—Tyler took me to an interrogation room and left me alone. I knew the ploy. Did it myself back when I was on the job. Familiarity didn't help. The air was stuffy and dank with stale cigarette smoke, sweat and lies. No doubt someone was observing from the other side of the mirrored window, which made me fidgety. I resisted the temptation to stick out my tongue.

A technician came in to swab for DNA. I wasn't under arrest, yet, but refusing to cooperate would only make me look guilty. They were probably tearing my hotel room apart at this very moment. They would find ample evidence of the victim's presence.

I wished Tyler would start his interrogation so I could find out what kind of trouble I was in. I didn't even know how the woman had died. I felt bad about it, but anything that happened to her after she left my room had nothing to do with me. At the first sign Tyler seemed to be trying to hang the killing on me, I planned to lawyer up.

An hour later, the interrogation room door flew open and Tyler stormed in. His brow was furrowed. In one hand he clutched a photograph and in the other a cigarette pack, as if he couldn't wait to have a smoke. He tossed the cigarettes on the table and leaned on the back of a chair across from me.

"Guess this is your lucky day." His right eye twitched.

"What's that mean?"

"Someone cashed in your get-out-of-jail-free card."

I shook my head and shrugged.

The detective slid the photograph across the table. "Know her?"

It was a different pose. Harsher, as if taken in poor lighting with a long lens. She was still gorgeous. "Like I said, I didn't get her name."

"You didn't say what you did after you left the bar, either."

I looked away. "We went up to my room."

"Uh-huh," Tyler said. "You're sure you went with *her*?" He pointed at the photograph.

I blinked. "That's about the only thing I *am* sure of."

"And you were with her all night?"

"Until she left. I'm not sure exactly when that was."

"Six a.m., she says."

"She says? But I thought—"

"When are you returning to Houston?"

"Tomorrow afternoon. On the same flight as my client's husband."

"I'll be in touch before then."

I frowned. Was this a trick? If so, I'd never seen this tactic before.

A uniformed officer escorted me downstairs to the lobby. When I saw a woman standing by herself, checking her phone, my jaw dropped. She looked up. Her cultivated eyebrows gave her a permanent expression of mild surprise. Her hairstyle seemed subtly different from when I'd last seen her. I couldn't stop staring, worried she'd vanish if I looked away.

She beckoned me with a gesture I couldn't resist. I crossed the lobby to join her. "I don't underst—"

"Not here," she said. "Come with me." She headed out the front door without waiting to see if I was following. She went straight to a silver Audi TT convertible parked in a handicapped spot. The vanity plates said MRTRNO. Cops entering the building studiously ignored it.

"I thought you were…they…"

"Get in. I'll explain. I promise."

She operated the stick like a NASCAR driver and navigated the streets like she was being pursued.

"Where are we going?"

She gave me one of her enigmatic half-smiles. "How about a drink?"

"That's what got me in trouble in the first place," I said.

She returned her attention to the busy streets. The gaps in traffic into which she jammed the car didn't seem large enough to accommodate it. Several times she was rewarded with honks or rude gestures. I clung to the strap over the door.

Eventually we arrived at her destination. The sign over the door identified the establishment as deVere's Irish pub. It wasn't the kind of place that offered valet parking, but she left the keys in the ignition after pulling in next to a fire hydrant. I did my best to keep up with her after she got out. A greeter held the door open for us, and our receptionist ogled her when he led us to a booth in a dark corner, but she didn't seem to notice. She waved at the bartender. A minute later he arrived with two large mugs of Guinness and a bowl of cheese puffs.

"I love these things," she said, grabbing a fistful.

A hazy memory traversed my mind: kissing each newly exposed patch of skin as I peeled off her clothing. We were clinging to each other and giggling with the heady euphoria of people who've drunk too much and were embarking on something illicit. I had a hard time picturing her giggling now. "I don't even know your name."

"Sarah."

"Sarah," I repeated. "I have a hundred questions, but I don't know where to begin."

"What did the police tell you?"

"They showed me your picture. Said you were found dead outside the hotel."

"That wasn't my picture."

I hid my confusion behind a gulp of stout. Its dark bitterness was cool and refreshing.

"That was my sister. Sherry."

"I'm sorry," I said, although she didn't seem particularly upset. This new information raised an obvious question. "So, um, which one of you did I spend last night with?"

The corner of her mouth rose a quarter of an inch. "Me, silly. I've got the marks to prove it."

I recalled the scratch on my shoulder. "Me, too, but I don't remember much after we went upstairs."

"What *do* you remember?" Her eyes grew dark and intense.

I felt like I was facing the interrogation I'd been spared at police headquarters. "Did we eat? I'm not sure. You, uh—" I reached across the table and brushed orange crumbs from the corner of her mouth. "I remember some of…what we did. But after that, I guess I passed out."

"I think I wore you out." Her already elevated eyebrows rose further. "We dozed for a while, until I got a call. I tried not to wake you when I left."

"Who called?" I was curious to see whether she would answer.

"Sherry. I was supposed to go dancing with her last night, but I got… diverted."

"You came to the bar looking for me?"

Sarah grabbed another handful of cheese puffs. "I thought you looked interesting." Her tented eyebrows arched, and her eyes twinkled.

I looked away from her intense stare. "You were telling me about your sister."

"She called around eleven o'clock. She was pissed that I stood her up."

"So, you went to meet her."

"She said she'd wait for me on the corner, but she wasn't there when I got downstairs. I figured she was paying me back, so I went home." She shrugged as if it happened all the time.

The waiter arrived with new glasses of Guinness. "Mr. Giacomin conveys his regrets for your loss."

"Thanks, Eddie," Sarah said without looking at him.

"They know you around here," I said after the waiter retreated.

She shrugged.

"You told the cops you were with me until six."

"I didn't want to get you involved."

"So you lied."

"They'll know what time she called from her phone records. I said she was checking up on me and I told her I was fine. Having too good a time to leave." Her smile didn't touch her eyes. "What did you tell them?"

"That I had no idea when you left. But someone might have seen you. You stand out."

"No one noticed," she said.

"How can you be so sure?"

Sarah shook her head as if it was of no consequence. "The less you know the more convincing you'll be when the police interrogate you."

"Interrogate me. Again? Haven't they cleared me already?" Then I stopped. I'd been released because of her statement. As long as I said I was with her, I was in the clear—but so was she. Dispute her claim and the cops might start looking at me again.

She tapped the tip of one index finger with the other. "You never heard the phone call, so you don't know what time it was." Then she tapped her middle finger. "We fucked, slept for a couple of hours, fucked some more and then you went to sleep again. You don't know when I left, but it was long after eleven o'clock. Could it have been as late as 6 a.m.? Sure. Stick to that simple story and you'll be fine. It's mostly true."

"What happens now?"

Sarah checked her phone. Though I'd finished my second beer, she hadn't touched hers. "I have things to take care of. I'll drop you off at the hotel and meet you for dinner later." She was in complete control—had been from the moment I first laid eyes on her.

Which had been when, exactly?

"What happened to your sister?"

"We'll talk tonight. I'll know more then."

She stopped in front of my hotel without taking the car out of gear. The moment I closed the passenger door, she released the clutch and tore off down the street. I watched her change lanes three times before she vanished from sight, wondering if I'd ever see her again.

I'd been worried that my room would be inaccessible as a possible crime scene, but there was no tape across the door and my electronic key opened the lock. The room wasn't just clean—it was immaculate. The carpets had been steamed; the bathroom scoured. My clothing had been laundered and neatly hung in the closet.

A body discovered behind a posh hotel gets attention, especially when the victim is beautiful. More so when she's connected. I watched news reports on three local channels. As the details unfolded, I understood why everyone was so deferential around Sarah—even the cops.

To my relief, my name wasn't mentioned. I was already formulating the story I'd tell Marina if she heard about the murder: Everyone in the hotel had been questioned by the police. Routine. Yeah, it was a bother, but that poor woman. With a little practice, I might pull the lie off as smoothly as the ones that had emerged from Sarah's pouty lips.

I snapped off the television and sat on the edge of the bed, debating whether to call Marina. Instead, I took a long hot shower, which—coupled with the strenuous night and the taxing morning—made me drowsy. After hanging the Do Not Disturb sign on the doorknob, I collapsed facedown on the bed. When I closed my eyes, my head filled with a stream of images, none of which felt like memories.

The phone woke me sometime later. The room was dark. It took a while to reorient myself. My arms were numb from sleeping on my stomach. Before I could get them to work, the phone fell silent. It rang again a few minutes later. "Meet me out front at eight," Sarah said and hung up without waiting for a response. I glanced at the clock. It was seven fifteen. I'd slept the entire afternoon.

I'd brought semi-formal attire in case I had to attend a banquet while following my client's husband. I hoped that would be appropriate for wherever she was taking me. Still, I felt severely under-dressed when I saw Sarah, who had on a sleek black sheath of a dress that plunged at the neck and was slit up the side almost to her thigh. The thin, supple material exposed more than it concealed. It had probably cost a small fortune. Diamonds gleamed in her ears. This was Sarah in her natural state, I thought. The casual clothes she'd been wearing earlier were some kind of disguise.

I inhaled a cloud of jasmine when she leaned over to peck me on the cheek. Then she released the clutch and accelerated, pressing me back in the seat. I grappled with the seatbelt as she weaved from lane to lane and careened around corners. When the car squealed to a stop in front of a restaurant ten minutes later, I felt like I'd been holding my breath the whole time.

She tossed the keys at the valet without waiting for a claim stub and mounted the steps as if late for an appointment. The slit in her dress revealed enticing flashes of thigh. I scrambled to keep up while admiring the view.

The maître d' didn't ask for her name, nor did we have to wait to be seated. Several groups lingering in the lobby shot poisonous looks in our direction when we were ushered past them to a secluded window booth.

"I'm impressed," I said.

"By?"

"Everything. The restaurant. The car and the way you handle it. How everyone reacts to you." I paused. "By that dress most of all. You look stunning."

Sarah rewarded me with a slight smile and tipped her head to acknowledge the compliment. "I assume you watched the news."

"You didn't tell me you were a celebrity. 'Daughter of reputed crime lord Victor Martorano.' "

"They always say that."

"You aren't denying it."

Sarah studied her menu, an obvious delaying tactic.

"I don't mean to be indelicate, but this thing with your sister. Was it a mob hit? Part of a gang war?"

She snorted. "Don't be melodramatic."

"Why you were there? At the conference?"

"I suppose you think I'm a gun-toting gangster who makes people offers they can't refuse. That I don't have interests outside the family business."

"You aren't toting anything in that dress," I said.

She ignored the comment. "My father is a high-profile businessman—he's not Tony Soprano. This is Sacramento. For every transaction that happens in the light of day, five or six more take place in the dark. It's just how it's always been done."

" 'Crime lord' sounds ominous."

"It sells newspapers. Not everyone likes the way he does business."

The waiter hovered discretely near the table. When she nodded him over, Sarah ordered rare steaks for both of us and a bottle of wine that cost more than I cleared some weeks. When the sommelier arrived, he focused on Sarah as if I wasn't there, filling my glass almost as an afterthought. The full-bodied Valpolicella activated every taste bud in my mouth.

"Have you heard from the police since this morning?" she asked.

I shook my head.

"They'll want you to make a formal statement, but you aren't a viable suspect anymore."

"You don't seem terribly broken up about your sister."

She spent a few seconds rolling wine around in her mouth, then placed her glass on the table. "We weren't close. She didn't approve of the business."

"What happened to her?"

"You're better off not knowing anything. You're less likely to get into trouble that way."

"With the cops, you mean?"

"Them, too." She didn't blink. "Someone will be arrested for her murder in a few days, and that will be the end of it. He'll confess and spare us a trial. He might even die in a police shootout." She paused as if considering the sound of that.

A chill ran down my spine. Somehow, I'd become involved in a scheme of which I'd only glimpsed the tiniest corner. There were wheels within wheels and, if I wasn't careful, they would roll over me.

A voice interrupted my thoughts. "You two are chummy."

I looked up at Detective Tyler.

The maître d' stood behind him, abject terror etched on his face. "I'm sorry, Ms. Martorano. I told him he couldn't—"

"It's all right, Carlo," she said with a dismissive wave. "Can I offer you a glass of wine, Detective? Or are you not staying?"

"I have a few questions for Mr. Kane. Won't take but a couple of minutes."

"I'll go powder my nose. Let me say goodbye now, because you'll be gone before I return."

I looked from Sarah to Tyler and back to Sarah again. She reminded me of a lioness establishing her territory, daring others to challenge her. Showing up on her turf was a power play on Tyler's part, but a perfunctory one, I thought.

"A pleasure as always," Tyler said in a tone that belied his words.

Sarah slid out of her seat and strode to the back of the restaurant. Tyler and I watched in respectful silence until she vanished.

"Impressive." Tyler said. He redirected his gaze at me. "How does someone like you get a piece of that? No offense intended, but really?"

Tyler was only saying aloud what I'd been wondering myself. I shrugged.

"She approached you at the bar."

I nodded.

"I don't get it." Tyler raised his eyebrows. "She could have any guy she wants. Amazing." He leaned in closer. "I gotta know. What was she like in bed? A cold bitch or a wildcat?"

"I wish I remembered," I said, which was true. "I was pretty drunk."

"So you said. Did you hear her phone ring?"

I shook my head. Stick with the truth as much as possible, I thought.

"Earlier you seemed surprised to hear she stayed until six."

"I was upset. You had me thinking the woman I spent the night with was dead."

"It couldn't have been, say, 11 p.m. when she left?"

I plucked an imaginary speck of lint from the tablecloth and shook my head. "She was still there at three or three-thirty. I remember that much. We, uh, well…" I let my voice trail off. My words didn't sound convincing even to me.

"Look, we're not after you." Tyler glanced toward the back of the restaurant. "You may be in danger. Come to the station tomorrow at ten to make a statement." He pushed a business card across the table and got to his feet. "Call me anytime if you think of something that may have slipped your mind."

I tucked the card in my pocket, certain I would never find a reason to use it. I had no interest in getting involved in whatever scheme was playing out here. Tomorrow, I'd be on my way back to Houston, leaving this mess behind.

"Here comes your girlfriend. Gotta run." He paused. "Be careful. She bites. And not in the good way." He performed a mock salute. "Oh, by the way. Sherry Martorano registered for the ghost hunter conference, not Sarah." He looked at me for a long second. "People have a hard time telling them apart. *Had* a hard time. Guess that's not an issue anymore." He turned and headed toward the front of the restaurant before Sarah reached the table.

"That slimy creep. 'A cold bitch or a hellcat?' The nerve."

"You heard all that?"

She shrugged and leaned forward. With her elbows on the table, the front of her dress scooped open. Every cubic inch of air rushed from my lungs. I tried to figure out the meaning of what I'd just learned but the tantalizing view made it hard to think. Tyler implied I might be in danger. That they were really after Sarah. Was she responsible for her sister's death? And if Sherry was registered for the conference, who had I spent the night with? A picture began to form in my mind, but before it had fully developed, Sarah reached across the table, took my hand, and laced her fingers through mine.

"I'm not hungry anymore. Let's go back to your room. I promise you won't forget a minute of it this time."

"Tyler said I should be careful. That you bite."

"Only if you want me to," she said. She didn't wink.

I reviewed my options. Taking her to the hotel would seal my contract with the devil. However, if I said no, she'd think I was considering cooperating with the police. Could I risk that? If she was willing to eliminate her sister, I didn't stand much chance. Or was that simply self-serving justification?

I looked into those cold eyes and still wanted her.

Tomorrow I'd return to my normal, mundane life, and no one would be the wiser. I drained my wine glass and squeezed her hand. She slid out of the booth and looped her arm through mine. Heat radiated from every inch of her body that touched me. Every head in the restaurant turned when she walked by.

Her car was waiting when we reached the entrance. Ten minutes later, we were alone in the elevator on the way up to my room. As soon as the doors closed, she was all over me. Thoughts of police investigations and questions about what this lovely, lethal creature might have been doing in the wee hours of the night before flew from my mind. I was being used, but there were worse fates than what lie ahead.

Over the next several hours, I learned the answer to Tyler's question. She was both cold *and* a wildcat. She knew all the right moves to elicit a response, but even when she came I felt like she was a hundred miles away. Closing deals. Doing business.

When I awoke in the morning—exhausted, spent, and bearing several more marks I'd have to hide from Marina until they faded—she was gone. The only other evidence she'd ever existed was the ghostly hint of jasmine she left behind on the bedsheets.

I checked out of the hotel and made my statement at police headquarters. Tyler didn't try to convince me to change my testimony. My hand barely shook when I signed the statement, averring that my words were God's honest truth. Tyler took the document and left without saying another word.

I was at the airport by two. Witherspoon was already at the gate when I got there, but I no longer cared about him. That investigation was closed, too. A few hours later, the wheels of our plane touched down in Houston. On the way to the office, I phoned in my report to our client and told her to expect a bill in the mail.

I hardly ever thought about Sarah Martorano again.

What I Don't Understand Is the Music

By Ana Teresa Pereira

1: DYLAN

Everything fell silent when she entered a place. I realized that the first time I saw her. The band was playing *April Showers* and people were dancing. She was coming toward me with a vague smile, and everything fell silent. I could almost hear the sound of her high heels, like I would later when I followed her in the street at two o'clock in the morning.

Her dress was blue. All the other girls wore black dresses, but hers was blue. When I asked about that, she just said "I am blonde; it had to be blue." That was Jamie. She would tell you the most absurd things, her hazel eyes very serious, and you would believe her. How could you not?

She was slim. The first word that came to mind was lithe. Her hair was golden-blonde, not bobbed like most girls wore it, but reaching her shoulders and slightly waved. She had a beauty mark near her eyebrow, that seemed fake to me. It was. Small pearl earrings. No other jewels. When she was near me, I could feel her perfume, like a hundred different flowers. She asked, "Do you dance?" and I put my hand on her narrow waist and took her to one of the stages the silver lights were creating around us.

"Aren't you forgetting something?" I gave her the blue ticket, she gave me half of it back, but even the idea that I had paid to dance with her didn't break the spell. And then I heard the notes of *April Showers* again. "So, if it's raining have no regrets, because it's not raining rain, you know, it's raining violets."

The place was not fancy, even though its name, *Dance Academy*, created that illusion. I had never been there before but had passed it many times. It was not far from home and sometimes, when I couldn't write, I would go for a walk in that direction. There were a few bars and a cinema nearby, and a newspaper stand, where I bought the latest pulp magazine, with the same eagerness as when I was a little boy. You may well read Faulkner and Hemingway, it's those short stories you want to go home with, when you are an aspiring twenty-five-year-old writer. There was a guy named Woolrich I was particularly fond of—I liked his grim universe, and the fact that he only wrote about lonely people. I'd checked some of the films based on his stories. Not all of them were good; only a very young and fey actress could play his "girl." I think I was starting to write like him; Justin would remind me of the old clichés, show don't tell, avoid repetitions, avoid adjectives, but I didn't pay much attention.

Justin was like an older brother to me. He had left our hometown when I was just a kid, he had written a novel, but, when we met again, he worked in a newspaper and didn't write fiction anymore. I thought his novel was damn good, but he wouldn't hear about that. He was a tall guy, around thirty. Girls seemed to like him, that is, until they saw me; I wondered why he didn't resent that. I think I would.

We went out for a beer once in a while. It was one of those nights that he suggested the *Dance Academy*. "I don't want to meet girls like that," I said.

He said: "There are some nice girls there. They are just making a living. They don't write, they dance." We had already taken a few beers and that had seemed funny. "If you can't write you dance."

"If you can't dance you write."

You could hear the music from the sidewalk. *April Showers*. The guy at the entrance sold us a few blue tickets and we got in. And then I saw Jamie walking toward me and in the silence, I forgot everything else.

She smelt good and she felt good. I suppose they have rules in those places, you're not supposed to hold a girl too tight, but I wouldn't anyway. I wanted to look at her. Her skin like a petal of an unofficial rose, her big hazel eyes, her mouth that the lipstick made plump. The bones of her shoulders, her small breasts—I don't think she was wearing a bra—her waist, her slim long legs, the black sandals.

In some movies, the girl doesn't say a word during the first half hour, and it seemed to me that was happening now. After the "Aren't you forgetting something?" she didn't say a word. I asked if she was tired, and she denied with a movement of her chin; I asked if she wanted to have a drink when the song was over and she made the same gesture. And suddenly I was at the bar with Justin, and she had disappeared.

"You like her, don't you? He asked.

"Don't you?"

"She is not my type. Too skinny."

"She definitely is my type."

"Some guys pay to take them outside, you know? She may not be back."

I went home without seeing her again. My room was freezing. It was a nice room. I had found it when I arrived in town and had managed to keep paying the rent. It was in a basement. It had a little kitchen and a little bathroom, and a glass door that opened to a courtyard that nobody else used; there was grass and some shy flowers, and a small tree that was blooming for the first time since I had arrived. I often thought that if I had a girl we could manage in that place.

And I had finally found my girl.

***

I liked to teach her words. The gloaming: we were walking in the park and suddenly a strange light surrounded us. I had heard about it. A good lighting for her.

The first nights, I only bought one or two tickets at the Club. I'd spot her easily. There were other blondes, real and fake, but only one in a blue dress. Only one who knew a blonde has to wear blue. I think she had three dresses, like in a fairy tale: the first I had seen, a greenish one, like sea water, and the third, of a darker blue, closer to her eyes and that made her seem taller. I had never noticed those things in a girl—it was as if every part of her needed attention. The attention to small things, that was not a new principle for me, but when it came to girls it was more like nice breasts, nice legs, soft skin. With Jamie, I wanted to know her by heart. Some people call it love.

She was actually a good dancer when she got less defensive, less rigid. She told me she didn't care much for music, which was strange. She was a sucker for paintings, but I don't think she saw much difference between those in the galleries and those sold on the street. She was mad about movies; she seemed to have seen hundreds of them, knew every actor, was in love with a few, men and women alike.

So, I danced once or twice with her and we talked a little; then I had a beer and went out, but didn't go far. I lit a cigarette and waited at the dark entrance of a shop. I don't know why—she was often the last one to go out, with a checkered coat that made her look even younger. I wondered how old she was, not more than nineteen, twenty. Her high heels seemed somehow inappropriate, even though she walked easily with them. The men that waited for the girls every night were usually gone when she left. I followed her along the street, listening to the sound of her heels, making an effort not to whistle slowly, as I usually did when I walked alone. But that would be too creepy. I followed her to a shabby building and two minutes later saw a light on a window of the second floor; sometimes I glimpsed her shadow. I liked to imagine she was having a cup of chocolate, taking her clothes off, washing her stockings, reading a cinema magazine or one of those dime store romances girls are crazy about.

Then one night I waited for her near the door of the Club. She didn't seem surprised. We went to a bar, and everyone fell silent. I swear, I was not imagining that. There were a few men at the counter and at the tables, a few girls, and, I think, some song on in the background. Maybe the song continued, I don't know, but not the sound of voices. I talked to Justin about that, and he asked: "Have you seen her face?" Of course I had seen her face. "I'm afraid you are too keen on the details and haven't noticed the most important. She has the face of an angel."

Jamie and I sat near the window, and we talked. She had come to New York because she wanted to be an actress. She had studied acting for a while, made the usual photos, gone to auditions. When she ran out of money, she got a job as a waitress. One day someone told her about the *Dance Academy*, and they hired her. A few months later she stopped going to auditions. "I just didn't care anymore."

I thought for a moment how much she resembled Justin. Those were his words, "I don't care anymore." I feared the moment that came to me. But that seemed very remote. Even though I wasn't writing much lately because I couldn't think of anything but her, when I did the stories came easily. It seemed that when I walked at night, whistling, things were coming towards me, taking a shape, even moving me. They moved me like Jamie moved me, the bones of her shoulders, her small breasts.

It became a habit. I worked until midnight, then I put on my trench coat and walked to the Academy. I stopped for a while on the sidewalk, listening to the songs. "Treat my Baby Good," "Have You Any Castles, Baby?" They played the same ones every night, in the same order. I was beginning to understand why Jamie didn't like music. The first girls came out, in pairs, and the men approached them like birds of prey. And finally, she came out alone, in her checkered coat and her high heels, her lipstick a bit smeared, as if she had been kissed, and we walked by the river until we were freezing.

And then one day I asked her to marry me. I hadn't planned that, you don't marry a girl you've known for less than three weeks, even if she has the face of an angel. But she said yes, and the next Saturday I borrowed Justin's car, and we drove to a sinister place in the suburbs where a sinister man made us husband and wife. We kissed clumsily in the car, and I noticed the man and his wife were staring at us from the porch, a version of American Gothic. That night, in my bed, with the rain falling outside the glass door, I made love with my girl. I woke up a few times and held her closer and she kissed my arm, as if to tranquilize me, "I am here," and I fell asleep again.

Those were the happiest days of my life.

***

Tonight, when I left the paper, I walked to the Club. I didn't intend to; I was just wandering. Perhaps walking alone, with my hands in the pockets of my trench coat, whistling slowly, things will come to me. Stories, characters, scenes, images. They do, but something in me refuses to put them down.

I don't really believe in discipline. Sometimes a deadline helps, you start writing in the evening, and you write all night, and you finish at dawn. Then you go out and have a coffee, and buy a newspaper, and wonder if there is a word for that light.

Only now I don't have that freedom. I have to be in the paper at a certain hour, and cover events, from parties to murders, and write something I don't really care about. And when my work is done, I go home. After wandering for a while.

I was in front of the Club and, ironically, the band was playing *April Showers*. For a moment I dreamt of going inside, and looking for a girl in a blue dress, with her hair loose, too much lipstick and too much perfume, and a beauty mark near the left eyebrow. For a moment I thought that was the girl I loved, and she was lost forever. It took me a minute or two to remember the girl was at home, perhaps already asleep, she went to sleep early. There would be something in the kitchen for me to eat, but she was a lousy cook. It amused me in the beginning, her efforts in the kitchen, the day she tried to make biscuits, the cherry pie. We would laugh and end up eating something at the twenty-four-hour bar, on the other side of the street. And we would walk by the river and look at the stars. It seems that there were always stars in those first months.

She was as beautiful with her face washed as she was with the makeup, perhaps even more beautiful, more like an angel. But there was something, since those first days, that I didn't understand. She seemed disappointed. Not with us, she was not only my girl but my lover, and she longed for sex as much as I did. It was other things. The fact that I had taken a job to make ends meet. She liked the apartment, she liked my books, and the painting I had once bought for a bargain in an antique shop. She didn't care for the records, but she didn't mind my listening to them, she even sunbathed in the yard. But she went rigid when one day I mentioned my dream of buying a little house in my hometown, with a real garden, where our kids could play. And the day I found that beautiful necklace in an antique shop, the pearls slightly green, she seemed for a while to believe they were real.

She had thrown away her blue dresses and had bought a few new ones. But she didn't like it when I reminded her that she hadn't married a rich man. She seemed to lose interest in clothes and wore simple pants and shirts that gave her a lovely boyish look.

I don't know which one of us had the idea of the life insurance. Perhaps it was I: from time to time I thought that if something happened to me—my work could be dangerous, as the new guy in the paper they sent me to cover the nasty stories in some nasty places—she might go back to the Club, to be watched and touched by other men.

And yet that night my steps took me back to the Club. The guy at the entrance recognized me and winked at me.

"She doesn't work here anymore. But there are plenty of nice girls."

"What happened to her?" I asked.

"I heard some jerk married her."

"She was very pretty," I said.

He gave me a malicious smile. "They are all the same, you know."

No angel face for that guy, I guessed.

But somehow, I felt better. She was waiting for me, in my bed, with one of those dime store romances, perhaps already asleep. If she was awake, she would tell me the story of a film she had seen that day. In the beginning we used to go to the cinema on Saturday night, and if I could afford some cheap seats, we would see a play. But lately she went to the cinema every afternoon. I used to leave her some money when I went to work. She looked at me and there was something like resentment in her beautiful face—without makeup her lips were thinner, but her eyes were still the biggest and most beautiful I had ever seen. "I know, baby, you get bored. When I earn more money we'll spend the weekend out of town, go to the beach." And she fell in my arms as if she was hiding from something.

Did I still love her? Yes, she was my wife, my lover, one day she would be the mother of my kids.

But my girl, I had lost her somewhere in the Club or in the empty streets when I followed her at night, my girl with her big hazel eyes, her blue dress, her beauty mark near the eyebrow, her plump lips. My girl who didn't care for music but was a good dancer.

I was near home when I had the feeling that I was being followed.

2: JAMIE

Everything fell silent when he entered a place. Jamie had noticed that the first night, when she walked toward him. Maybe it was his good looks. Justin had told her girls fell for him at first sight, but she wasn't expecting that. He has tall, slim, with black hair and green eyes. He resembled a French actor she had seen once in a movie. He could have been in movies, but the idea seemed never to have come to his mind. He was passionate about his writing. A love of words, a love of stories and of images. An attention to things, to simple things. He mentioned writers she had heard of in high school but had not managed to read. Not that she didn't like books. Covers, first sentences, last sentences, illustrations. Photos on the back covers. The first time she went to his apartment, she was moved by the books. There were many, and even though the room was very clean, the books had a film of dust, they didn't seem to be on the shelves in any order, they were just there. She loved the room, its high ceiling painted in white, the glass door, the empty yard, a small tree still blooming. He told her it was almost dead when he rented the place, but he watered it every morning, and it felt like a miracle when a little stem appeared on a dry twig. That was Dylan. He would say and do the most absurd things as if they were natural. They spent long evenings in bed, him reading a book, her reading a cinema magazine or a dime novel, or one of those publications that told the story of a movie, sometimes a movie she had seen, the cover in strong colors, the stills inside black and white, a photo of one of the actors on the back.

The first night, she didn't have any plans. Justin had told her the guy had some money, he must, living in that apartment, and only writing short stories for pulp magazines. Those stories, they were so much like him, a little absurd, a little improbable, with an intermittent beauty undermining the violence and the mysteries. It rained inside the theatres in his stories…

When she danced with him, no matter how determined she was to keep a distance, she would find herself really dancing, not just going through the moves. He felt so good. She even wished he would grab her closer, to feel his body, his smell. He smelt nice. Something herbal. A light cologne maybe. Just dancing. With no plans, no resentment, no acting. Just dancing with a man. Maybe that was what people called love.

But it wasn't love she was after. She was the kid that would steal money to go to the movies. She was never happier than when she was sitting on a front row of a cinema, with the lights still on, waiting for the magic to happen. She stole movie magazines from the stands, and sat in a quiet place, learning by heart the faces of the actors, the clothes of the actresses, and their kisses. She had left home at seventeen, taking her stepmother's economies with her, to afford acting lessons, dancing lessons. The money didn't last long, and in a few months she was working as a waitress and still going to auditions. When she finally looked for a job at the *Academy*, the manager wasn't enthusiastic (too skinny) but Doyle, the owner, could see farther. "Make her wear something different. Another color, a simple model, less make up. This girl has the face of an angel. Guys don't just want to grab a nice body; they want to dream. She will make them dream of something they have lost or will never have." He looked her in the eyes: "Baby, you are the stuff that dreams are made of." And he was right. Some guys would prefer her, even though most of the other girls were still young and pretty. They often paid to take her outside, they seemed happy to be with her in some cheap joint, have a beer, talk a little. Sometimes a kiss. The tips were good.

She had noticed Justin the first time he went there. He was not handsome, but thin and ironic, he didn't pay much attention to her while they were dancing. Not a good dancer, either. But the day he asked her to have a beer after she left, Jamie said yes. And they ended up in her room, the shabby room that she hated, with that horrible painting and that horrible vase in a niche that seemed like a bad joke, and she felt like smashing every night when she got home.

Neither lovers nor friends, they liked each other's company. They often met in a quiet bar near the river. Jamie was so tired of everything that when he mentioned the young writer from his hometown who had some money, she was almost interested. She no longer expected to get a part in a movie. As for marrying a rich man or, better still, a film producer, the idea just made her laugh.

Now, she only dreamt of not having to dance. Not listening to the same songs, in the same order, until she was almost crazy. She hated the music more than she hated the men. They would disappear at two in the morning, but the music would be on her mind while she walked home and ate something and went to bed. It would be there in the morning, when she woke up, when she showered and wore a pair of pants and a coat and had coffee at a bar, a plain skinny girl with no makeup and her hair pushed back, that men hardly looked at. She could get rid of the men, and their hands, and their smell, but the music would never leave her until one day she grew insane. "Maybe you've got a few dragons you want me to kill, baby." She sure didn't have any castles.

***

Jamie was not the kind of girl that dreamt of getting married in a white church, with a long white dress and orange flowers in her hair. Still, the place looked so sinister, and the reverend or whatever he was, looked even worse. His wife, who was the witness, seemed almost friendly, but she smelled of boiled vegetables. Jamie looked at the man at her side, and for a moment an unexpected wave of happiness took hold of her. "At least I'm marrying the handsomest man I've ever seen." And at least that night, at eight o'clock, she wouldn't have to enter that damn place and go to the dressing room to leave her coat and put on more lipstick and the beauty mark she had seen on an actress once. She hadn't made any friends during the long months she had worked there. The other girls resented her blue dress and the fact that she was Doyle's protégée. She loved her blue flowery dresses when she was a teenager, but the ones she wore at the Club never seemed to be hers. Something she borrowed for a while. And as for Doyle, even though he never went too far (oh, he was a happily married man), only a few kisses, she dreaded those nights when he stayed longer and expected her to keep him company.

No, that night she would sleep with a man that didn't make her sick, in a nice apartment, and even if it was raining outside, she would feel safe. She didn't mind the apartment being so small, perhaps later she could convince him to rent a bigger place. Somewhere nice, where the smell of cooking and the noise of children didn't bother her all the time, like in her last room. With what joy she had put her things in two bags and looked for the last time at the painting and the vase. For a moment she thought seriously about smashing them. It was strange, but they had hurt her more than the shabbiness of the bed clothes, or the dirty walls on the other side of the window.

Jamie had never been afraid when he followed her in the still of the night. She liked to glimpse the light of the cigarette at the shop entrance. He never did anything to dissimulate his stalking; if she turned back, he probably wouldn't hide. They both knew. They both agreed. She entered her building and after washing her hair, she washed it nearly every night, because somehow *their* smell seemed to stay in it, she would approach the window and feel reassured by the tall figure in a trench coat on the other side of the street.

When she told Justin, he didn't smile. "He is a weirdo. I always knew that." She asked if he was jealous. He looked her in the eyes. "Baby, you're like something in a dream. The girl you glimpse in a train station once and you know it is the one for you. But you don't go after her."

At first, she still believed Dylan had money. It was when he told her he was getting a job at Justin's paper that she realized he didn't. Some money from his parents, that allowed him to write for a year or two, but he had to do something else to support them. For Justin, that was a big joke. "You shouldn't marry a guy you've known for three weeks, baby." Then he became serious. "I really thought he had some money. And he has. But not enough for a girl who wants nice dresses and pearls. You can't win them all, baby."

She left the bar near the river and went to do some shopping. She wanted to make cookies for Dylan and her to eat that evening. A cup of chocolate and vanilla cookies. It was Sunday, and he left his work earlier. Perhaps he was already home, listening to his records and waiting for her. He was. He didn't hear her coming in. He was changing a record. She could see his back, the black pants, and a white T-shirt he wore under his shirt. The bones in his shoulders were slightly visible, as

if he was a skinny young boy. She approached him silently like a cat, and like a cat
he felt her and didn't look back, just said, "Baby."

"I'll make dinner."

"Oh no," he said. "At least let me help you."

"No. And I'm making some cookies."

The dinner was not bad, fish and rice, not burnt, not too salty, but the cookies
were inedible. Too hard, even to eat with the chocolate. They both laughed,
and the following evening he arrived with a bag of fresh cookies he had bought
somewhere, orange flavored, with words written on them: Love, Sunshine, Heart.
Have a heart, baby.

Those were the happiest days of her life.

One day Justin said, as if he was thinking of something else: "You can still get
some money out of this, baby. Have you ever heard of life insurance?"

She didn't answer. She got up from the stool and fetched her checkered old coat.
It was surprisingly cold for September.

"I'm going to the movies," she said.

She went out of the bar. It was beginning to rain, and she fastened her coat. She
really needed a new one. It was a movie with Louis Jourdan. And that night, she
would tell it to Dylan.

***

Now that she had time for herself, all the time she wanted, she dreamt of going to
auditions again. After all, twenty-five was not too old. Twenty-six, really. She wore
the nice dresses she had bought after the marriage, and her old coat. Oh, that
damn coat. It had been all right last winter, she had forgotten it during the summer
and now it looked too shabby. Summer had not been long that year. It wasn't
autumn yet, but the days were grey, and it rained very often.

Dylan always left her some money on the bedside table; that was not the
shopping money, it was meant for the movies. Jamie went to the movies every
afternoon, but now when the movie was over, she didn't feel like leaving, and
watched it again. She had given up her cooking experiments, just something
very simple because they needed to eat. Sometimes he bought a bottle of cheap
wine, but she was already in bed when he arrived, and it didn't feel much like
a celebration.

Money, always money. They had made the insurance, if one of them died
the other one at least would have plenty of money. If he died, she would be

able to buy dresses, a new coat, perhaps some jewels. She did like jewels. Her small earrings were real pearls, and she would love to have a pearl necklace. She remembered the day he had arrived home so happy with the small box and the lovely necklace and how happy she was until she realized it was fake. She wouldn't wear fake pearls, as she wouldn't put plastic flowers in a vase. She loved when he bought her flowers, small bunches of violets, just a few violets surrounded by big fresh leaves.

That afternoon, she met Justin at their usual place. It was raining, it was always raining, and she felt like screaming.

"I want to be an actress. Nothing else has meaning."

"You're still pretty. But it won't last. You won't always have that angel face. You won't always be…lithe? He and his fucking words."

"I like his words."

"You just have to get rid of him."

"You're joking."

"Not really. In my job I get to know all kinds of people. It would be easily done." It was like a bad dream. He could be persuasive.

"You wouldn't have to do anything, baby. Just collect the money."

It went on like that, every time they met.

The night he knocked at the door after midnight, she was half asleep and didn't understand at first. "It's done, baby. You're a lovely widow, now."

"I don't believe you."

"You better do. There will be heat in the morning."

"How?"

"Your husband was killed by a burglar, dear. A clean job. You can have a new start."

No, he wasn't kidding. For a moment she was the little girl that ran away from home to go to the movies. She would be punished afterwards, but it didn't really matter. She was the very young girl entering an audition room with a modest dress and a cheap perfume, feeling the eyes of men on her body, reading some lines whose meaning she didn't understand. It was a sad adventure, but still an adventure.

Justin was sitting on the bed, looking at her. She knew that expression. As if everything was a joke. But this wasn't a joke.

"Why did you do it?"

"I owed you one, baby. I half convinced you to marry that jerk."

"You didn't do it for me."

They stared at each other. Then he gave in.

"I hated the guy. He had something I'll never have. Don't kid yourself, baby. Not you. You're a dime a dozen."

She suddenly understood.

"His talent."

"His passion, baby. I remember him showing me his stories when he was a kid. And they were good. Then I left our town, and I spent a year writing a novel. It was bad, and I accepted it."

"And then he came here."

"Yes… In his stories, it rains inside the theatres, you know."

"I know."

"He was distracted for a while after he met you. But that wouldn't last. He was already falling out of love with you. One of these days he would get rid of you and write a novel. And even if it was bad, he would go on and on."

"He wouldn't lose his passion."

"Not easily."

He got up.

"It's better if I am not seen around here tonight. I'll come tomorrow, to comfort you."

"Don't."

"Baby, you know I'll always be near you."

She heard him closing the door. For a moment, the sound of a whistle. She had never heard him whistle before.

***

He was there, changing a record. His tall figure leaning forward, his shoulder bones visible under his T-shirt. That image that moved her so much.

And suddenly she was aware of something she had tried to escape for the last months.

Jamie got up from the bed where she had been sitting for what seemed a couple of hours, and realized she was trembling. It was summer and she was trembling.

She loved him. Perhaps more than he had loved her. Because he could stop loving her. But she wouldn't.

And, out of nowhere, the wave of happiness took hold of her. It was the first time in her life she was in love.

Null and Void

By Claude Lalumière

A Vernon Tevis Problem

S andra had been hoping it would be a loud party. She could have danced herself to exhaustion, made herself seen, and then collapsed. She wouldn't have had to engage in any conversations, grin her way through polite platitudes, suffer unwelcome intrusions into her well-being (or lack thereof), or try so hard not to appear like she might burst into tears at any moment.

But no. This is a laid-back, beer-and-pot, sit-on-the-floor-and-chat affair. At this moment, she's part of a pentagon on Rico's bedroom floor comprised, besides herself, of a plump, fortyish transgender (wearing a skirt that's much too short, sporting breasts at least as big as his/her head, and still undecided about the fate of his/her balls and prick), and a threesome of shockingly young-looking bone-thin punk lesbians who appear to be triplets. On the bed, Rico's new clearly just-out-of-the-closet boyfriend (Sandra can't remember his name—Rico changes boyfriends more often than he brushes his immaculate pearly whites) is playing a kissing game involving a deck of cards. His play pals, two slick wolves showing off their depilated bare chests, keep sticking their hands down his shorts. When those two laugh, it's too scary for Sandra, too much like the kind of behaviour she's had put up with constantly for the last three years, and she has to look away and ignore them; she doesn't have the strength to deal with this now—besides, no one else seems to be worried about the new boy.

The triplets may look thirteen, but they sound at least forty. All three of them speak in the same slow smoky voice, often finishing each other's sentences. They can't express any ideas or opinions without quoting French theorists, Scandinavian porn stars, American S&M feminist fetishists, European filmmakers, or British punk lyrics. Are they really sisters? They've stripped off their tops, showing off all six of the pierced nipples on their boyish breasts. Occasionally one of them slips her studded tongue in another's mouth, careful not to smudge black lipstick. Their thirty fingers entwine in ceaseless slow motion, like nests of doped-up snakes.

Sandra has given her short-term memory the night off. She can't bring herself to care about who any of these people are or what they might have to say. She nods and grunts short retorts as required but instantly forgets everything. She thinks the triplets are trying to convince her to pierce her own nipples. Did they say (in some permutation or other), "You look unhappy, sad like a character in a Lars Von Trier film. You need to get in touch with your body's full potential and turn it into a shrine of post-pain pleasure, like Vadjina Pryxxxy explains in *The 1001 Orifices*. Camille-Suzanne Duras writes that pain is a learned social construct that helps authority control the masses by selectively coding as unpleasant a set or sets of bodily sensations, thus limiting existence to authority-sanctioned behaviours"? Yes, she's reasonably sure they said exactly this.

Sandra thinks, *If I tore those rings from your nipples, would the pain be a social construct?* The notion of wanting to inflict physical harm on anyone fills her with self-disgust, especially as she almost instantly realizes that's just the kind of thing he would have threatened.

How can I get him out of my head?

She had told Rico she didn't want a party. She was miserable, and she didn't want to meet anyone. She appreciated that he let her bunk here until she got herself together. Was it that much to ask to let her wallow for a few weeks? It had only been a handful of days. "It'll be like old times," he said. "You need to get back in touch with who you are. Forget the life. Forget him. Forget all that crap he told you about yourself. Forget what he did to you. You're alive. Enjoy it." With the mischievous twinkle that must have seduced hundreds of men by now (and broken as many female hearts), he added, "Cheer up, girl. Maybe you'll meet somebody."

She frowned back at him, disgusted at everything. But, in the end, she agreed.

Sandra feels a hand on her shoulder. "Are you alright?" says a woman about Sandra's age, her smile tinged with concern. Sandra is still sitting in the same spot, but the triplets and the transgender are nowhere to be seen. "You've been sitting here by yourself for a while." The woman sits down next to Sandra, holding out a handkerchief. "Here." Sandra is speechless and bewildered. *Who is she? Why the concern? Why the handkerchief? How long did I zone out?* Then she feels the moistness around her eyes and the sting of tears on her cheeks. *Oh no. I've been sitting here crying. Like a freak. So much for not drawing attention to myself. I should never have let Rico talk me into this.*

"You don't remember me, do you?"

Drying her tears, Sandra looks at the woman. She has long straight blond hair, simply parted at the middle, one side lightly tucked behind her ear. She wears no makeup or jewellery, except for loose purple plastic bracelets and a thin gold anklet. She has strong, smooth shoulders. Her lips are thin. Her mouth is wide and seems to fall naturally into a relaxed smile. Her sea-blue eyes hint at both curiosity and intelligence. She's barefoot and in cut-off jeans that show off her strong legs. She isn't wearing a bra, and her heavy breasts tug on her purple tank top.

Vivid images wash over Sandra: of her tongue and mouth savouring the woman's toes; of the woman's laughter mingling carelessly with her own; of the woman biting tenderly on her nipple, of herself gasping in pleasure—

Again, a hand on her shoulder. "Sandra?" Once more the woman pulls Sandra back from her fugue.

Sandra laughs nervously. "I'm sorry. I'm…" She trails off and blushes, embarrassed by the strength of the fantasy. She stares at the floor.

"Don't worry about it." Both of them pause in awkward silence. Then the woman says, "You really don't remember me, do you?"

"No, I … Do we know—?"

"Introduction to Logic? Anthropology of the Body? Methods of Cultural Analysis?"

"I…" Sandra hesitates. *School! That was at least a lifetime ago. But still…* "No, sorry. Are you sure we've met? I mean, I think I'd remember you…" Sandra blushes again, but resists averting her gaze.

"I'm Athena Saratsiotis. Thena." She grins, tipping her head forward. "And stop apologizing so much." Thena briefly touches Sandra's hand.

Sandra repeats the name—initially without the slightest flicker of recognition, but then her mind forms an associated image: a girl, thin and frail, big breasts, expensive clothes, snotty and/or shy, ugly perm, makeup so thick you could scrape it off with a knife. Sandra repeats the name again and mutters, "No. You? Can't be…"

Athena laughs in mock embarrassment. "Yep. That stuck-up Barbie doll, that was me."

"Weren't you engaged or something? I mean, are you marr— I mean—"

Thena cuts her off, laughing even harder. "Ha! Nick Nimikos! My father so wanted me to marry into that family. He practically arranged the whole thing. My mom, my dad, Nick—who had such a crush on me but who was so shy for such a wealthy boy—none of them noticed my silence, my reticence. I made it to the altar, but when the priest turned to me, I started laughing. I laughed so hard everything stopped. I looked at everyone, and then suddenly I was laughing and crying at the same time. Everyone was so shocked. I gave poor Nick an apologetic glance and … I ran away before anyone knew what was happening. Or rather what wasn't."

Somehow, without Sandra noticing the how or the when, Sandra's left hand and Thena's right hand have joined. Their fingers tentatively rub against each other, engaging in a conversation of their own.

"My father was furious. He disowned me. Cut off my money. I'd saved some, but not much. I'd never worked a day in my life. It was rough for a few years. But I like my life now. Fuck him, y'know?"

"But," Sandra asks, "what are you doing here? Are you a friend of Rico's?"

"Yeah. We met when I was working at a clothing boutique on Queen West. Rico was my favourite customer. Always so sharply dressed. Always nice and flirty. And so gorgeous. I was pretty naive. I completely fell for him. Rico saw it. One day, he asked me out for lunch. I thought I was gonna melt into the floor. Anyway, once we sat down, he put on a grim look and said something like, 'I'm flattered, I really am. And you're very charming and beautiful, but unless you've got a cock hidden under that skirt, forget it.' I was about to get up and run away, but Rico grabbed my arm and sat me down. He turned on the charm and just like that turned out to be the friend I'd been looking for without knowing it."

Sandra's fingers squeeze. Thena's squeeze back. Neither of them looks at their hands.

"It was a few months after I'd skipped out on the wedding. I had no idea what to do with myself. I'd go home after work and cry at the empty apartment. My old 'friends' had all been too weirded out by my behaviour at the wedding and had dropped out of my life. Good riddance. As for my family, I didn't exist anymore. I'd done most of a BA, but without Daddy to foot the

bills I couldn't afford to finish it. Rico … Rico turned my life around. He
introduced me to new people, new places, helped me find myself."

"That sounds like Rico. He was the boy next door when I was growing up. I
fantasized about marrying him." They both laugh nervously, their fingers now
engaged in an intricate dance. "He taught me to keep secrets from grownups.
Protected me. What a small world, that the two of you would meet, too."
Their fingers continue their dance, with more assurance and perhaps even the
occasional hint of abandon.

"Yeah. When he invited me to the party, he mentioned you. He flipped out
when I said I knew you from school. You won't believe this, but I used to be
jealous of you."

"What? Why?"

"Daddy's rich. He let me go to school to get me out of the way until he
could marry me off. He didn't care what courses I took, or if I graduated—
and he certainly didn't believe I'd ever be anything other than a housewife and
mother to his grandchildren. And you… I dreamed—literally: I had dreams
about you. About being like you, about being you. Free to be who you wanted,
what you wanted. Who was that girl you used to go out with? Cassie?"

Sandra frowns, remembering. That had ended with too much drama.

Thena continues, "I used to be jealous of her, too. I would never have told
anyone or even admitted it to myself, but in my dreams you kissed me."

Sandra, surprising even herself, starts crying again. She takes her hand back
and covers her face.

"Oh, damn, Sandra, I'm so sorry. I didn't mean to upset you. I've got such a
big mouth."

Sandra looks up, her face wet and hot. "Yes, you do. And it's so beautiful."
She touches Thena's lips, her fingers trembling and moist from tears. The two
women recoil from each other, briefly, without a word. Then, looking into her
eyes, Sandra firmly grips Thena's bare arms and—

Rico bursts into the bedroom, shouting: "Sandra! Sandra!"

Sandra is shocked by the look of sheer panic on Rico's face. She notices
that the music has stopped. The apartment, overstuffed with partyers, is
ominously silent.

Sandra says, "What's wrong?" Rico never gets flustered. Yet, here he is, his
mouth gaping open, unable to answer that simple question, exuding none of
his customary cool composure.

Suddenly, Sandra knows. What else could it be? They sent some muscle after her. She still owes on her contract. "Someone's here for me, right? Holyjesusfuckingchrist."

Sandra gets up and, furious, walks toward the front door. Thena and Rico flank her, but they radiate anxiety and fright, which is no help.

There he is in the doorway, built like a refrigerator, looking like the thug he is, his eyes ice-cold and merciless. They sent the biggest gun after her. Vernon Tevis. From headquarters in Montreal, all the way here to Toronto. A lot of the girls crush big time on this guy. But she doesn't see it. Plus, he pings her gaydar big time, although there's nothing obvious about it in his comportment.

"Sandra… I finally found you. Let's talk."

"What the fuck are you doing here? Didn't I make it clear enough that I wanted out?"

Vernon strides in, takes her by the wrist, and leads her to the kitchen, which, like the rest of the party, was overpacked only a few minutes ago but is now empty of anyone else. Clearly some people have fled the scene entirely, but others watch what's going on from as far as they can manage in the close space.

Gesturing toward Rico and Thena, who followed them, Tevis asks, "Do you trust these two?"

Without hesitation, Sandra nods. Her fists are so tightly clenched, she feels her fingernails dig into her palms. "What do you want here? There are tons of other girls. And there are always more. So what if I still owe on my contract? It's not like it's a legal contract. You won't miss me. What are you gonna do? Hurt me? What will that accomplish? Go away."

In a soft yet firm voice, Tevis explains: "Sandra. You've got this all wrong. I want to thank you. It's a good thing you sent that note to the boss."

"What…?"

"Listen, we were already thinking about looking into Dumont's operation. Your letter motivated us to act quickly. I wish someone had spoken up before. Attrition is a normal part of the business, but he was losing too many girls too quickly, and it was getting worse. He was a childhood friend of the boss's, so maybe we cut that abusive fucktard too much slack for too long. But that's over. He's over."

There it is again: that cold, merciless stare. He killed Dumont. Sandra is sure of it. Is she a loose end now?

"Anyway, there's always a place for you. Name whatever gig you want, and it's yours. We owe you. But I get it if you're done. Or if you need a break. The offer will stay open. Not forever, but long enough. You know where to find us. Don't worry about your contract. Consider it null and void."

"Any gig? What if I don't want to be in the lineup? What if I join management? Say, I want to take over from Dumont. Make sure the girls are treated right."

Tevis ponders for a few beats. "I can sell that to the boss. Yes. Let's drink to it. Is there any bourbon here, or do I have to put up with that shitty beer?" He points at the empties on the counter.

Rico rummages through the top shelf next to the fridge and comes up with a bottle of something amber.

Tevis nods. "That's good enough."

She notices that look on Rico's face. Without another word he and Tevis disappear together. So… her gaydar was right about Vernon Tevis.

"You were a prostitute?"

Oh shit. Thena. She didn't know anything about Sandra being in the life. This was not how Sandra would have wanted Thena to learn about all that. "Yeah…" Damn it. Things were looking so promising with Thena. Easy come, easy go.

"But you're going to run a whorehouse now?"

"Not exactly. This is an outcall operation. We go anywhere in the Capital region. I'll have to move back to Ottawa."

"Wow."

Wow? She's not freaking out. Maybe this'll work out after all. Sandra is hungry for this. For a fling. Maybe more. With her. With Thena.

"Wow," Thena says again. She hesitates, carefully choosing her next words. "Can I … Can I work for you? I've fantasized about doing this, but I was always scared, too. Not really knowing how to get started or who to trust."

Just like that, Thena becomes nothing more than a piece of meat to her. Sure, Sandra will fuck her. Once. To audition her. Because that's what a good manager does.

The Obsidian Knife

By O'Neil De Noux

Damn car wouldn't start. Melanie Green turned the key again and the starter clicked but no ignition. The hood slammed shut and Slim's beady eyes glared at her from across the hood as if it were her fault. Hell, he's the one who stole a car with engine trouble.

Slim said, "Now who the hell is this?"

Was that a light behind them?

Melanie turned to look as Slim came around the car, pulling out his pistol as he passed. "Get out. You're a stranded motorist."

Again.

Melanie climbed out and Slim huffed as he hurried into the darkness on the other side of the car. The man was anything but slim, a big man at six foot five, heavy around the middle with long, black hair, and Melanie wondered why the hell she was still with Slim.

A pair of distant headlights closed in, and she stood behind the car and hiked up her denim minidress almost to her panties. Standing five foot nine, Melanie was willowy, with long sandy hair and large blue eyes that had dark circles around them. She'd tried her best to cover the circles with the makeup she had left. Only a couple drugs stores open, all in Metairie. She was hurting and maybe they'd score coke tonight or pot at least to cut the edge.

It still wasn't cold, although it was winter. In New Orleans, you never knew what the weather would be like. Almost six months after Katrina and the long, sizzling summer had barely let up.

Melanie glanced nervously at the hulking shells of buildings to her left. Slim was there in the blackness. To her right stood the high wall of the New Orleans Yacht Harbor. They'd been past this area a couple times during daylight hours since the hurricane. Nearly all the sailboats had been destroyed, most still piled in heaps. A lone light bulb was on at the harbor. Still no streetlights. The moon was out, however, and clear skies drew starlight like distant beams from the black sky. Most intersections were four-way stops now, with stop signs nailed to sawhorses. The approaching car hit its brights and eased to a stop behind her. Melanie raised her hand to wave, knowing the dress would rise even higher.

"You OK?" It was man's voice from the car.

The car was a blue SUV and the man climbing out was in a uniform. National guardsman in camouflage clothes. He stepped into his headlights and smiled at her.

"My engine killed," she said, changing her expression from one of distraught to a shaky smile.

The man paused between the cars, easing to his right to let his headlights bathe her. Young, he was about Melanie's age, twenty or twenty-one. The flashes came a millisecond before the explosions and the man collapsed. Slim rushed out of the darkness with his pistol in hand and Melanie leaned on the rear of their car. Damn, Slim could have hit her.

Slim kicked the guardsman before going through the man's pockets, pulling out a wallet, finding cash and tossing the rest away.

"What you lookin' at?" Slim told her as he rolled the man over to get at his front pockets. "Get in his car. You're drivin'."

The engine was still running, and Melanie had to move the seat forward. Slim jumped in, slammed the door and said, "Go. Go. Go." He shoved the money into his pockets. Melanie hit the accelerator, nearly ran over the guardsman, and cut hard, the SUV skidding as it sped away.

***

A half minute after the SUV pulled away, Joe Herd came out of the shadows and crept up to the guardsman. Joe put his backpack down and dropped his overcoat on it. Too warm for the coat. Joe had been living on the streets for ten years before Katrina, had sheltered from the storm in one of those stone bathrooms in Audubon Park, had remained there through the flood as the water never made it to the park. He'd finally been run out of the shelter by the cops a week ago and had been meandering his way from near the river up to the lake, checking out the devastated neighborhoods along the way, living off cans of food the water hadn't destroyed in the flood. He'd been watching the man and the woman in the abandoned car, saw the big man move his way and couldn't believe it when the man shot the soldier.

Joe went down on his haunches next to the body, pressed two fingers against the soldier's carotid. Checked again but nothing. Joe sat heavily and closed his eyes, trying to keep his mind from recalling the rice paddies and jungle of Nam, where he'd been an army medic thirty-something years ago. He blinked open his eyes and checked out the guardsman's rank. Staff sergeant with MP patches on his sleeves. He saw the man's pockets turned inside out.

There was a pouch on the man's belt and Joe realized it was playing music. He hesitantly unsnapped it, found a cell phone. Damn, how does this thing work? The song was B.B. King's *The Thrill is Gone*. It vibrated as well and Joe pushed a green button and heard a voice say, "Hello?"

***

Slim slapped the dashboard. "Stop. You're headed the wrong way." He pointed at the black lake on their left. Pontchartrain. Melanie was lost.

"Turn around. Turn around."

She made a three-point turn around.

"Take the next left. Get away from the lake."

She clipped the edge of a sawhorse and sent a stop sign tumbling as the SUV turned off the drive running along the lakefront.

"Slow down," Slim said. "You're gonna hit something big."

***

John Raven Beau was aboard his houseboat *Sad Lisa* at its mooring in the Yacht Harbor when the shots echoed. It took him less than two minutes to climb into a pair of black tactical pants, put on his off-duty canvas gun belt, jump off his houseboat and race down the dock to the black Cadillac Escalade friends lent to him right after Katrina before they sailed to Hyannis Port. He was in all-black now, including a T-shirt and Reeboks, his special-made nine-millimeter Glock G37, given to him by ATF right after the storm, sat in its Kydex carbon-fiber holster on his right hip next to his gold NOPD star-and-crescent detective's badge, cuffs in its holster on his left hip, knife in its canted sheath at the small of his back. No use taking his police radio. Damn thing still didn't work.

He tooled out of the Yacht Harbor and paused. A sound turned his attention to the right as someone shouted. Down the street a man stood waving both arms over his head. Beau turned and the Escalade's headlights picked up the guardsman lying at the edge of the street as he pulled up. He watched the standing man as he climbed out, drawing the Glock with his right hand. He ignored the twinge in his left arm where a bullet from a gang member's AK-47 nearly killed him right after Halloween.

The man looked at his gun belt. "You're police?"

"Put your hands on my hood."

"Huh?"

"I'm patting you down." Beau, standing six foot two, was a good six inches taller than the man. His straight nose beneath a prominent brow gave the detective a hawk-like, fierce appearance. Longish dark brown hair added to his resemblance of his plains warrior ancestors. John Raven Beau was half-Sioux, half-Cajun. The persistent five o'clock shadow came from his father's side of the family, as did his sense of humor. From his mother's side, the Oglala clan of the Lakota Nation, he'd inherited his ferocity, patience, and lethal nature.

"Assume the position."

The man placed the palms of both hands against the Escalade and moved his legs apart, said, "Seen this enough times on TV."

The man was at least sixty, dirty, damp and smelled of mildew and body odor but had no weapon. Just a cell phone. Beau re-holstered his Glock.

"He's dead," the man said when Beau was finished. "I was an army medic."

Beau checked out the guardsman. No pulse. The body was still warm, three bullet holes in his back, an 'MP' armband on both arms.

"What's your name?"

"Joe Herd. Originally from Michigan. Been in the city eleven years."

"This cell works?" Beau punched in 911. He was surprised the police dispatcher answered immediately. Few cells seemed to work. He told her who he was and where he was and she cut in, telling him units were already heading to him.

"You need Emtees, correct?"

"We're going to need homicide and the corpse Hummer."

Beau closed the cell and Joe Herd said, "I seen who did it. Big man with long black hair and a small lady with light colored hair. She worn a short blue dress. She looked like a stranded motorist to the guardsman. They left that car." He pointed to an old Toyota. "Couldn't get it started. Took this man's car. A blue SUV and went that way." He pointed beyond the Yacht Harbor. Beau had him go over the story again, slower.

The first vehicle to arrive was a Humvee with red crosses on its sides. Two national guard medics jumped out and ran to the body. An MP buck sergeant came out of the back seat and moved straight to Beau, introduced himself as Sgt. Elston, said they were Indiana guardsmen. The second vehicle was another Humvee with two national guard MPs and Beau's immediate supervisor, Detective Sergeant Jodie Kintyre.

She'd recently cut her blond page boy shorter than normal and wore a black T-shirt with gray lettering—POLICE. She wore black tactical pants and canvas boots, her badge clipped to her belt next to her Glock 26 in its Kydex holster. She stepped up with hands opened.

"You're supposed to be recuperating."

"Heard gunshots."

She got close, focused those wide-set hazel eyes on his and lowered her voice, "You OK?"

"Yeah." He stretched out his left arm. "All healed now. I should be back at work."

Jodie moved around him as the medics stepped away from the dead guardsman. She let out a long sigh, went down on her haunches next to the body. Beau stood next to her now.

"Staff Sergeant Michael Montesteri," Jodie said. "Connecticut National Guard."

"You knew him?"

"He worked a couple cases with me after the storm."

"He was ambushed by a man and a woman posing as a stranded motorist. Couldn't get their car started. It's probably stolen. They drove off in your staff sergeant's blue SUV."

***

Melanie swerved, pumped the brakes and the car at the intersection blew its horn as they barely missed each other.

"Jesus. You gotta *stop* at some of the stop signs." Slim put his gun down and grabbed the steering wheel with is left hand. "You hear me?"

He let go before they reached the next intersection, and she came to a complete stop, watched a car stop at the same time to her left and she let it go through. What she didn't expect was a car coming the other way running that stop sign. She was already moving and gunned it to get out of the way, but the car slammed into the rear quarter panel and spun the SUV around.

The airbags deployed and Melanie was wearing her seatbelt. Slim was not and his head smashed through the side window. She realized this as the airbags deflated and there was blood on Slim's forehead. She got out, stumbled away from the car.

Cars exploded in movies, didn't they? Caught fire? The car that struck her was smoking, or was that radiator steam? The other driver, a man in a suit climbed out of the car with a cell phone and made a call right away.

She went around for Slim and met him near the sidewalk. He already had a green cloth pressed against his head. Must have gotten it in the SUV. Slim blinked at her, and she said, "You OK?"

He grunted.

"Son of a bitch ran right through the stop sign." Slim reached for his pistol, tucked in the front of his jeans, wavered a moment and sat down heavily. She reached for the rag and pressed it against his head as he slowly lay back.

***

The corpse Hummer, one of the army Humvees which collected bodies since the hurricane, arrived and guardsmen came out with a black body bag. Jodie held them up until the Army CID arrived. The feds were kind enough to send Criminal Investigation Division agents from Fort Polk to process crime scenes, along with FBI lab techs, who took the day shift.

Jodie's radio worked and Beau saw it was a different model, probably a new issue. He'd been on sick leave for three months and the feds were issuing new equipment to first responders all the time. She gave headquarters the BOLO on the SUV and two occupants. A minute later, headquarters repeated the 'Be On The Lookout' bulletin, adding Sgt. Montesteri's SUV probably had a Connecticut license plate number.

"So you'll be back next week," Jodie said.

Beau shrugged. "If the doctor releases me."

A beep tone came on Jodie's radio followed by headquarters announcing, "Signal 20-I. Robert E. Lee and Canal Boulevard." An accident with injury.

Beau felt a tingle on the back of his neck, looked eastward. Too far to see, of course. He reached out his hand and Jodie passed him her radio. A detective didn't believe in coincidences.

"3124—headquarters. Any script on the vehicles in the 20-I?"

"BMW four door and a Saturn VUE."

"Color of vehicles?"

"Unknown. Cell call faded."

Beau handed the radio back to Jodie and backpedaled away. "A VUE's an SUV."

"Where are you going?"

Beau pointed to Joe Herd leaning against the Humvee that brought Jodie and said, "Don't let him get away. I'll be right back."

***

Slim sat up with a jerk and Melanie fell back and sat.

"You." The other driver shouted as he came forward. "You didn't have your headlights on. Those are your running lights." He came closer, illuminated by his headlights now. "I'm with the DA's office and you just totaled my new 330i."

Melanie sat with her legs splayed, catching the man's attention.

Slim got up on all fours, stood, raised his right hand and fired three times into the man's chest. The man coughed as he fell straight back and didn't move. Melanie crawled to the lamp post and pulled herself up. She spit out the fluid which came up her throat, wiped her mouth with her arm.

Slim rifled the man's pockets, came up with a wallet and opened it in the light from the headlight. "Damn. We hit it this time." He pulled out a wad of money.

Melanie shielded her eyes from the bright headlamps, heard another car approaching fast.

***

John Raven Beau knew Canal Boulevard was right up ahead and saw lights in the blackness. He hit the Escalade's high beams as he slowed. Two cars, a black BMW and a blue SUV in the center of the wide intersection. A figure stepped into the lights, a woman with light hair and a micro-minidress.

Beau stopped, turning the Escalade away from the woman and climbed out carefully.

The woman stood crying, turned to a body lying on the pavement behind her. "My husband's hurt. Hurry. He's having trouble breathing." She went down on her knees next to the body bending over to show the rear of her white panties.

Beau stood against his car, lowering his profile by ducking below the roof. He slowly stepped around the Escalade, the other way, keeping to the darkness, Glock in his right hand. The woman lost sight of him, sat back, and looked around for him. Beau's neck tingled and he lowered himself as flashes came from his right and he dove facedown, bullets passing so close he felt their heat. He returned fire, four controlled shots, rolled to his left, his foot striking the rear tire of the Escalade. He slid part way beneath the big Cadillac.

A quick movement in the blackness drew his eyes and he heard running feet now. Beau crawled out, went back around the Escalade, and caught a flash of a big man with long hair racing across the neutral ground and out of the car lights toward the abandoned houses on the lake side of the boulevard. The woman stood now, hands on her hips.

Beau bolted away from the cars, across the neutral ground and into his own darkness, turning right when he figured he was across the street, slowed and felt grass underfoot. Running footsteps sounded straight ahead. He stayed on the grass and hoped he wouldn't trip over debris. The further from the cars he got, he realized the night wasn't as black anymore. He glanced up at the moon and starlit sky.

He spotted the large man running hard ahead before the man veered left and disappeared between two houses. Beau ducked between two houses. The front yards were wide here and so were the back yards, most fenced in. He took a knee behind a page fence and watched the yards, spotting a service lane behind the fences, which divided the backyard fences of the houses beyond. He stood and his injured left arm throbbed. Ignoring it, Beau eased to the service lane and waited. His prey did not cross the lane. He had to be between the houses or in one.

These houses had flooded, had remained under water for weeks. Some had been gutted in anticipation of renovation but most still held belongings with people afraid of the mold. The big man had darted between a blond brick home and a two-story red brick house. The moonlight seemed to get brighter by the moment as Beau's eyes adjusted to it.

The bastard could have doubled back, could be racing down Robert E. Lee, but Beau didn't think so. He waited patiently. Hunting people wasn't too different from hunting coons, possums, and nutria as he had done as a boy in the swamp where he was raised, just off Vermilion Bay. Beau used a .22 rifle back then. To save bullets, which cost money, Beau's daddy taught him how to trap, snare, hunt with a spear and hunting knife. Beau didn't know his parents were dirt-poor until the kids at school told him, taunted him, calling him *swamp rat*. Hell, he thought he lived in a boy's paradise, life one big adventure, the great Cajun floating prairie his playground, the deep swamp, dark, dangerous, and mysterious.

Beau's Oglala grandfather in North Dakota taught the boy how to create a Lakota hunting knife of obsidian with a bone handle. Sharpened on one side only, the fire-hardened volcanic glass blade honed to a razor-sharp edge that could slice through the toughest buffalo hide. The elderly man explained Lakota was their tribe's true name. Their enemies called them Sioux. Beau preferred Sioux. It sounded fiercer.

A movement down the right of way drew Beau's focus as the big man backed into the opening beyond a wooden fence. He stopped and bent over, pointing his pistol between the houses, expecting Beau to follow him directly. He did not see Beau, who crept closer, keeping his right eye closed as he moved along the fence line toward his prey. Beau closed the distance, got within twenty-five yards, ideal distance for a marksman with a handgun. He went down on one knee, opened his right eye, which took a few seconds to acclimate from total darkness to the moonlight and aimed the Glock at the man in the standard, two-handed police grip.

Beau heard his grandfather's raspy voice in his mind—"I will tell you something now, John Raven Beau. Tuck this next to your heart, little one. Your secret Lakota name is … Sharp Eyes. Tell no white man this name, not even your father. And don't let the white man say your name, because the more it is spoken, the more your strength is taken from you."

The big man stood, and Beau fired twice, his shots catching the man in the leg, spinning him down hard. The man returned fire, shooting wildly and Beau flattened himself lest the bastard get lucky. The big man hobbled away and was behind a wooden fence now. Beau backed away and went up the other side of the fence and alongside the one-story blond brick house to its front corner and waited.

The sound of breaking glass came from the far side of the house. Beau eased up on the front porch and moved to the front door, which was missing. He waited, listening, heard a scraping in the house and a grunt. Beau moved away from the door, keeping between the first window and the front door, pressing himself against the brick wall. Some of the windowpanes were broken in the front windows.

The man grunted again, and Beau called out to him. "Police. Throw out your gun and come out."

The man fired three shots, striking the door frame.

Beau waited for the echo to subside before he said, "Burns doesn't it? You losing a lot of blood, or what?"

"Fuck you."

Beau moved to the corner of the building just as the window he'd been near blew out with five more shots. He waited. The seconds ticked slowly, and the scent of gunpowder wafted through the shattered window. A small animal darted from the bushes near the street. A black cat raced past Beau. A good omen.

This was what the Sioux called *the battle calm*, the ability of a plains warrior to control his emotions, to control his breathing, even his heart rate, to focus all senses, wipe fear from his breast. It was a rise in adrenaline that tightened the throat and brought a higher level of awareness where Beau could hear better, smell better, see better. It smoothed out the rough spots and made one feel superior, with a controlled anger. It was an instant high, so good it could be frightening. His grandfather called it *the twilight of chaos between life and death*. One must use this in order to survive. This was how Beau's ancestors, Crazy Horse and his brother Little Hawk, felt at the Little Bighorn.

More scraping sounds came from the house and Beau concentrated on the noise, following the movement as the big man hobbled through the house, knocking over furniture, shoving something out of his way. Beau moved along, set up at the rear corner of the building and waited. He'd peeked in a broken window and knew he was outside the kitchen now.

What was that click?

He recognized it the second time. The big man as racking the chamber of his pistol. Was he reloading? Or was he out of ammunition? Beau still had twelve semi-jacketed hollow point rounds in his expertly pre-sighted Glock with its light-absorbing, non-reflective mottled, gray-black camouflaged finish. He also carried two magazines on his gun belt, each with seventeen rounds.

He waited. A wounded animal grew weaker with each heartbeat. There was more scraping around, then after a few minutes, silence. No. It was not silent. Beau heard the man's labored breathing. Finally, a cough and the man called out, "I'm out of ammo. I surrender."

Beau waited.

"You hear me, you bastard. I give up. You're a cop. Take me to a hospital."

"Throw your gun out the back door."

A half minute passed, and the gun sailed out, tumbling on the small porch and into the grass.

"Now come out with your hands up."

"I can't. My leg's numb."

"I can wait. You can bleed to death."

Beau waited. *The battle calm* invigorated him. More scraping now and Beau sensed the big man moving, heard a bump.

"I'm in the doorway. Come get me."

Yeah. Right. Beau eased away from the house to the bushes alongside and crept behind them into the backyard. The moonlight seemed even brighter and there stood the big man, leaning in the doorway, right hand up on the frame, the left hand limp at his side. Beau aimed at the center of the man's chest. He was about twenty yards away.

"Raise both hands."

The left hand rose slowly. Beau came around the bushes. The man was at least six foot five and outweighed Beau by a good fifty pounds, mostly flab. He had removed his shirt and had it wrapped around his thigh.

"I got two holes in my leg, you bastard."

Both bullets hit. Good. Beau kept the Glock trained on the man as he slid his left hand to his handcuff pouch and said, "Turn around. I'm cuffing you."

"Call an ambulance."

"With what? I don't have a radio or cell. You got a cell on you?"

The big man coughed again, looked around.

"You can just stand there and bleed."

The man turned slowly and the way he put weight on his injured leg told Beau the bullets hadn't struck a bone. Muscle only. If he'd hit an artery the man wouldn't have the strength to move around.

"Put your arms behind you."

The hands were empty. Beau stepped up, pressed the barrel of the Glock against the base of the man's head.

"This is a hair-trigger. Don't move."

ATF had trained NOPD officers, including Beau, the fine technique of using one hand to handcuff a prisoner and Beau snapped the cuff on the man's right hand. As he pulled the cuff to the left hand the man made his move, grabbing at the Glock, slamming his weight against Beau, twisted and both men went down. Beau rolled away, slid the Glock back into its locking holster and slipped the obsidian knife from its sheath. The man lunged for Beau who quickly moved aside, grabbed the long hair, and pressed his knife against the big man's throat. The razor edge cut a slice of flesh and the man croaked and froze.

"That's my hunting knife. Freeze or I'll slice your throat, you pig."

"I'm bleeding."

"Worse when I cut your jugular vein."

The big man went limp. Beau knelt on the man's back, pressed the obsidian knife against the man's throat.

"Don't move or you'll cut your own throat." Beau cuffed both hands behind the man's back, stood and said, "Get up, fat ass."

"I can't."

"Sit up."

The man rolled and sat up and Beau helped him stand, keeping the knife in front of the grimacing face while he patted the man down, came up with cigarettes and a lighter. He threw both away. He put the bundles of money back in the man's front pockets, found a biker's large leather wallet in the man's back pocket, which included an Oklahoma driver's license.

"Lawrence S. Slim? The 'S' sure doesn't stand for sharpshooter." The license had expired in 2003.

Beau guided his prisoner out the back way and picked up the man's semi-automatic. A Ruger nine-millimeter. They went around the house, the big man limping. Beau's injured arm ached but he steeled himself to drive away the pain, lest he show weakness to the enemy. With the adrenaline subsiding the pain caused his arm to throb.

"You ain't much of a sharpshooter either," Slim said. "You only clipped me in the leg."

"You stood. What made you stand?"

Slim tried to smile but it didn't work, his face grimacing again in pain. "I'm part Shoshone Indian. I got instincts."

Beau smiled to himself. Shoshone. Enemies of the Sioux. Shoshone, a tribe driven from the Dakotas by the mighty Lakota and their cousins the Cheyenne. Shoshones fought alongside the white eyes, the US cavalry, against the Sioux and Cheyenne at the Battle of the Rosebud, a prelude to the Little Bighorn.

"I can't walk far."

"I'm not carrying you. Until we get back to the cars, there's no way to call for an ambulance."

It was smoother moving along the sidewalk now. Slim limped badly.

"I can't make it."

"Then I'll handcuff you to a pole and hope I can make it back before you bleed to death."

The big man was leaving bloody footprints now. They hurried, the pain in Beau's arm getting worse, but he wouldn't flinch. Ahead he spotted a new set of headlights and as they grew closer, saw the Humvee ambulance parked between the BMW and VUE. Sgt. Elston spotted them approaching and pulled out his .45 automatic.

"In coming," Beau said. "Police. Detective Beau."

Elston waited until they were well into the headlights before re-holstering his weapon.

Two medics stood with the blonde woman a blanket thrown over the body in the street. Her denim minidress had risen, slim legs looking extra white in the lights. Beau passed his prisoner to the medics and told them when they emptied his pockets, put everything in an evidence pouch.

"We'll need to take off his handcuffs."

"They stay on. Work on his leg and leave his hands alone." He turned to Elston and asked if he had handcuffs.

"Sure." The sergeant pulled out a pair of OD green cuffs.

Beau took them over to the woman and told her to turn around. Her chin sank as she turned around and gave him her hands. He cuffed them quickly and asked if she had any weapon on her.

"No."

He used the back of his hand to tap against her to make sure she didn't have a knife or Saturday night special anywhere near her waist where her hands could reach.

"Excuse me, detective," Elston said. "Her husband's dead and you're handcuffing her?"

"Husband?"

Elston pointed to the body in the street.

Beau shook his head, said to the woman, "You wanna tell him, or do I?"

She let out a long breath.

"She played you, man. She was bait." Beau nodded toward Slim, now lying on a gurney as the medics worked on his leg. "Flagged you down, just like she did the MP sergeant so he could be ambushed by the man your medics wants to take my cuffs off."

He could see Elston had fallen for the woman's story.

"My throat." Slim's mouth quivered. "That coon-ass bastard cut my throat. How bad is it?"

Coon-ass—a racial epithet for a Cajun. People kept telling Beau he had a Cajun accent. He didn't see it. He brought the woman close, pulled out his ID folder and read them their rights from a Miranda Warning card he kept in his folder. When he finished, he leaned over Slim and said, "I'm not just a coon-ass. I'm your living nightmare."

"Fuck you!"

Beau looked into the woman's eyes. They were bright and blue, rather pretty.

"My mother's Oglala Sioux," he said. "We kill Shoshone and white men." He reached over and brushed hair from the woman's eyes. "And here in Louisiana, we execute murderers. Men and women alike."

The woman's voice came sharp. "I didn't shoot no one."

He looked down, realized her tight dress had risen and the headlights picked up the front of her panties.

Bait. A man would stop for her, drawn in like a fly to a spider's web.

And as they waited for the corpse Hummer and Det. Sgt. Jodie Kintyre, and whomever else she would bring along, John Raven Beau's heart rate slowly returned to normal. He looked at the hurricane litter around them, couple upturned vehicles next to the street, a doorless refrigerator, a twisted shopping cart, paper and trash littering the yards. This was New Orleans AK—after Katrina.

Earlier that evening on the radio, reporters had been questioning if the city would ever come back. Most didn't think so. If it came back, it would never be the same.

Well, Beau thought, we'll see about that.

About the Editor

MAXIM JAKUBOWSKI is a London-based former publisher, editor, writer, and translator. He has compiled over one hundred anthologies in a variety of genres, many of which have garnered awards. He is a past winner of the Karel and Anthony awards, and in 2019 was given the prestigious Red Herrings award by the Crime Writers' Association for his contribution to the genre. He broadcasts regularly on radio and TV, reviews for diverse newspapers and magazines, and has been a judge for several literary awards. He is the author of twenty novels, including *The Louisiana Republic* (2018), his latest *The Piper's Dance* (2021), and a series of *Sunday Times* bestselling novels under a pseudonym. He has also published five collections of his own short stories. He is currently Chair of the Crime Writers' Association.

www.maximjakubowski.co.uk

About the Authors

SIMON BESTWICK lives on the Wirral and dreams of moving to Wales. He is the author of six novels, four full-length short story collections and has been four times shortlisted for the British Fantasy Award. He is married to long-suffering fellow author Cate Gardner, and still hasn't kicked his addictions to Pepsi Max, semicolons, or Irn Bru Xtra. His fiction has appeared in *Crimewave, Black Static, The Best Horror Of The Year*, and many other venues, but this is his first sale to a professional crime anthology. He keeps a blog at simon-bestwick. blogspot.com, but he'd prefer a dog.

ROSE BIGGIN is a writer and theatre artist based in London. Her short fiction has been published in anthologies by Jurassic London, Abaddon Books, NewCon Press, and Egaeus Press. She is the author of *Immersive Theatre & Audience Experience* (Palgrave) and Shakespearean novel *Wild Time* (Surface Press).

KEITH BROOKE is the author of fourteen novels, seven collections, and more than a hundred short stories; his most recent novel *alt.human* (published in the US as *Harmony*) was shortlisted for the Philip K Dick Award and his story "War 3.01" was shortlisted for the Seiun Award. Writing teen fiction as Nick Gifford, he has been described by the *Sunday Express* as "The king of children's horror." You can find out more about Keith and his work at www. keithbrooke.co.uk

Born in Haworth, West Yorkshire, ERIC BROWN has lived in Australia, India, and Greece. He has won the British Science Fiction Award twice for his short stories, and his novel *Helix Wars* was shortlisted for the 2012 Philip K. Dick award. He's published over seventy books and his latest novel is the ninth in the Langham and Dupré series, set in the 1950s, *Murder Most Vile*. He lives near Dunbar in Scotland, and his website is at: ericbrown.co.uk

BERNIE CROSTHWAITE is a novelist, playwright, and short story writer. The three crime novels in the Ravenbridge Trilogy, *If It Bleeds*, *Body Language*, and *The Hemp House*, feature Jude Baxendale, a press photographer with a keen eye and a strong sense of justice. Her plays have been performed from London to Largs, and on BBC Radio. Her short stories have also been broadcast on national radio. *The Golden Hour* was shortlisted for the CWA Short Story Dagger Award. Bernie has worked as a newspaper reporter, a tour guide, and a teacher of English and creative writing. She lives and works in North Yorkshire. www.berniecrosthwaite.co.uk

O'NEIL DE NOUX writes novels and short stories with forty-three books published, over 400 short story sales and a screenplay produced in 2000. Much of De Noux's writing is character-driven crime fiction, although he has written in many disciplines including historical fiction, children's fiction, mainstream fiction, mystery, science fiction, suspense, fantasy, horror, western, literary, religious, romance, erotica, and humor.

Mr. De Noux is a retired police officer, a former homicide detective. His writing has garnered a number of awards including the Shamus Award twice, the Derringer Award, and Police Book of the Year (awarded by PoliceWriters. com). Two of his stories have been featured in the *Best American Mystery Stories* annual anthology (2003 and 2013). He is a past vice-president of the Private Eye Writers of America. For additional O'Neil De Noux material, go to: www. oneildenoux.com

Harlem native MICHAEL A. GONZALES is a cultural critic, short story scribe, and essayist who has written for *The Paris Review*, *The Village Voice*, *Wax Poetics*, *The Wire UK*, *Longreads*, *Maggot Brain*, and *Pitchfork*. His fiction has appeared in *Dead-End Jobs: A Hit Man Anthology* edited by Andrew J. Rausch, *Black Pulp* edited by Gary Phillips, *Crime Factory*, *Brown Sugar 2: Great One Night Stands* edited by Carol Taylor, *Needle: A Magazine of Noir* edited by Steve Weddle, and *Bronx Biannual* edited by Miles Marshall Lewis. He is the coauthor of *Bring the Noise: A Guide to Rap Music and Hip-Hop Culture* (1991), and throughout the 1990s he covered rap and soul for *The Source*, *Vibe*, *RapPages*, *Spin*, *Tower's Pulse*, *Raygun*, *Creem*, and *Request*. Currently, Gonzales writes true crime features for *CrimeReads*, the music column *Slept on Soul* for Soulhead.

com, and *The Blacklist*, a book column covering out-of-print Black authors for Catapult. He lives in Baltimore.

SJI (Susi) HOLLIDAY is a writer of dark fiction. She is the UK bestselling author of the creepy and claustrophobic Banktoun trilogy (*Black Wood, Willow Walk*, and *The Damselfly*), the festive serial killer thriller *The Deaths of December*, the supernatural mystery *The Lingering*, a psychological thriller set on the Trans-Siberian Express (*Violet*), and a horror novella *(Mr. Sandman)*. Her latest two novels are techno-thrillers: *The Last Resort* and *Substitute*. By day, she works in clinical research. Follow Susi on Twitter @SJIHolliday or visit her website sjiholliday.com.

RHYS HUGHES was born in Wales but has lived in many countries in Europe and Africa. He graduated as an engineer but currently works as a tutor of mathematics. In his spare time, he keeps writing. He is nearing the end of a thirty-year project to write exactly one thousand linked short stories. He has also written plays, poems, articles, and puzzles for a variety of international publications, and his work has been translated into ten languages.

CLAUDE LALUMIÈRE (claudepages.info) is the author of more than 100 stories. His books include *Objects of Worship* (2009) and *Venera Dreams: A Weird Entertainment*, which was a selection of the Great Books Marquee at Word on the Street Toronto 2017. Originally from Montreal, he now lives in Ottawa.

ASHLEY LISTER is a prolific writer of fiction across a broad range of genres, having written more than fifty full-length titles and over a hundred short stories. Aside from regularly blogging about writing, Ashley also teaches creative writing in the North West of England. He has recently completed a PhD in creative writing where he looked at the relationship between plot and genre in short fiction.

ROBERT LOPRESTI is a retired librarian who lives in the Pacific Northwest. His seventy-plus short stories have won the Derringer and Black Orchid Novella Awards, been shortlisted for an Anthony, and been reprinted in Best American Mystery Stories. His latest novel, *Greenfellas*, is a comic caper about the Mafia trying to save the environment. He is the current president of the Short Mystery Fiction Society.

ANNA TERESA PEREIRA is a Portuguese writer and translator. She is the author of more than twenty novels, novellas, and short story collections. A reader of Henry James, Ray Bradbury, John Dickson Carr, and Cornell Woolrich, she likes to think of her stories as "abstract crime fiction." Her last novel, *Karen*, won the Brazilian Oceanos Award (best book in Portuguese language published in 2016). She lives in Funchal.

For the last fifteen-plus years, ALI SEAY has written professionally under a pen name. Now she's shaken off her disguise to write as herself in the genre she loves the most. Ali lives in Baltimore with her family. Her greatest desire is to own a vintage Airstream and hit the road. Her serial killer novella *Go Down Hard* was released in 2020 by Grindhouse Press. For more information visit aliseay.com or find her on Twitter @AliSeay11 or Instagram @ introvert_fitness

LAVIE TIDHAR is the author of *Osama*, *The Violent Century*, *A Man Lies Dreaming*, *Central Station*, *Unholy Land*, and *By Force Alone*. His latest novels are *The Hood* and *The Escapement*. His awards include the World Fantasy Award, the British Fantasy Award, the John W. Campbell Award, the Neukom Prize, and the Jerwood Fiction Uncovered Prize.

BEV VINCENT is the author of over 100 short stories, including appearances in *Alfred Hitchcock's* and *Ellery Queen's Mystery Magazines*, *Black Cat Mystery Magazine*, *Cemetery Dance*, and two MWA anthologies. His books include *The Road to the Dark Tower* and *The Stephen King Illustrated Companion*. In 2018, he co-edited the anthology *Flight or Fright* with Stephen King. His work has been published in eighteen languages and has been nominated for the Edgar, the Stoker (twice), the Ignotus, and the ITW Thriller Awards. He lives in Texas, where he is working on a novel. Learn more at bevvincent.com.

JOSEPH S.WALKER lives in Indiana and teaches college literature and composition courses. His short fiction has appeared in *Alfred Hitchcock's Mystery Magazine*, *Ellery Queen's Mystery Magazine*, *Mystery Weekly*, *Tough*, and a number of other magazines and anthologies. He has been a finalist for the Edgar Award and the Derringer Award, and has won the Bill Crider Prize for Short Fiction and the Al Blanchard Award. Follow him on Twitter @JSWalkerAuthor and visit his website at jsw47408.wixsite.com/website.

ALVARO ZINOS-AMARO is a Hugo and Locus finalist with some fifty stories published in professional magazines, such as *Analog, Lightspeed, Beneath Ceaseless Skies, Galaxy's Edge, Nature, Lackington's,* and numerous anthologies, like *The Year's Best Science Fiction & Fantasy, Cyber World, This Way to the End Times, The Unquiet Dreamer, It Came from the Multiplex,* and *Nox Pareidolia.* His work has also appeared in the anthologies *The Mammoth Book of Jack the Ripper Stories* and *The Mammoth Book of the Adventures of Professor Moriarty,* edited by Maxim Jakubowski.

Mango Publishing, established in 2014, publishes an eclectic list of books by diverse authors—both new and established voices—on topics ranging from business, personal growth, women's empowerment, LGBTQ studies, health, and spirituality to history, popular culture, time management, decluttering, lifestyle, mental wellness, aging, and sustainable living. We were recently named 2019 *and* 2020's #1 fastest-growing independent publisher by *Publishers Weekly.* Our success is driven by our main goal, which is to publish high-quality books that will entertain readers as well as make a positive difference in their lives.

Our readers are our most important resource; we value your input, suggestions, and ideas. We'd love to hear from you—after all, we are publishing books for you!

Please stay in touch with us and follow us at:

Facebook: Mango Publishing
Twitter: @MangoPublishing
Instagram: @MangoPublishing
LinkedIn: Mango Publishing
Pinterest: Mango Publishing
Newsletter: mangopublishinggroup.com/newsletter

Join us on Mango's journey to reinvent publishing, one book at a time.